MW00699197

THE

LABBITT

HALSEY

PROTOCOL

Also by Andrew Ryan

The Law of Physics

THE

LABBITT

HALSEY

PROTOCOL

ANDREW RYAN

GADFLY

LEESBURG, VIRGINIA

Published by Gadfly, LLC
Leesburg, Virginia

Copyright © 2011 by Andrew Martin Ryan
All rights reserved. No part of this book may be reproduced, scanned,
or distributed in any printed or electronic form without permission.
Please do not participate in or encourage piracy of copyrighted materials in violation of the author's rights. Purchase only authorized editions.

2011

Printed in the United States of America

10 9 8 7 6 5 4 3 2 1

Print ISBN: 978-0-9802088-0-1
e-book ISBN: 978-0-9802088-2-5
Kindle ISBN: 978-0-9802088-7-0

Library of Congress Control Number: 2011923616

∞The paper used in this publication meets the minimum requirements of the American National Standard for Information Sciences—
Permanence of Paper for Printed Library Materials, ANSI Z39.48-1992.

To Jill

THE

LABBITT

HALSEY

PROTOCOL

Chapter
1

It had been three days since Ann Franklin last checked on her son, Jeremy, but that was not indicative of negligent parenting. Several times that week—indeed, nearly every time she walked down that hallway—she'd stood outside his bedroom, silently, ear to the door, and listened for him clearing his throat, milling around, shuffling in his chair. Enough to prove that he was still breathing. After which she tip-toed away, careful not to let him know she'd been there, though part of her suspected he always sensed her presence. She imagined him sitting in the dark, cringing, waiting impatiently for her to leave him in peace.

That absurd ritual had become routine over the past two and a half years. And, strong as the urge was to look him in the eye, the time between checks had gradually increased—daily at first, then every other day. By now she barely saw him twice a week. The shock would have been unendurable had he quietly packed his bags and left home, never to be heard from again. On the other hand, it was arguably much more painful for Ann to have her heart torn out in little pieces over the agonizingly slow progress of their ever-deepening estrangement. It had taken her most of that day to summon the strength to reach out and turn her son's door knob. And even as she did so she couldn't form a clear rationale for her decision.

There was an unmade bed against the wall and a smattering of neglected, dust-covered toys. A red, Mercedes gullwing was parked on the dresser alongside a half-finished Navy destroyer, still dry-docked on a piece of yellowed newspaper, a bottle of desiccated battleship gray Testers paint and several uninstalled gun batteries sitting next to it. It triggered a memory, unimaginably distant now, of the time they'd sat down together to build it. At least that's how she chose to interpret the image. Though, having seen the boat sitting there a hundred times over, she couldn't disentangle her actual memories of that relatively happy time from her subsequent reflections thereon, and was plagued by the sense that her grief was artificial and derivative.

None of it had sneaked up on her, of course. She'd known, or should have known, for more than a decade that things would deteriorate to this point. And with so much advance warning, it was all but impossible to exhibit her maternal emotions realistically. Instead, they came out contrived, plagiaristic, and inextricably bound up with her incessant ruminations on them. Understandable as that might have been, she couldn't shake her conviction that it made her a terrible mother, forcing her to manufacture feelings that should have issued forth naturally.

Protruding from under the bed was the tail fin of a gas-powered remote control Beechcraft, one propeller missing, still awaiting its maiden flight. A big wicker basket holding a tangled orgy of stuffed creatures sat on the floor at the foot of the bed. Ernie and Bert looked up from the scrum with ossified expressions of overstated jubilance, mocking the hopelessly dreary environs in which they were trapped, forever unloved. Their faces had grayed with dust and looked old and tired. But most of the room was piled with books. The shelves along one entire wall were packed to the ceiling, and the floor was covered with tall stacks, save a narrow canyon that led to her son.

Jeremy Franklin was planted in the far corner of the room on a purple bean bag chair, exactly as he had been for the better part of the last three years. The circles under his eyes looked darker than usual, but Ann allowed herself to believe they were merely artifacts of the feeble light leaking in through his bedroom windows. A large volume was pressed up against his knees—Ann couldn't make out the title—and he was flipping through it with alarming speed, turning the pages every ten seconds or so. She knew he wasn't skimming it. He was reading every word. Next to him on the floor was a half-empty, family-size bottle of chewable antacid tablets. She stood there and looked at him for more than a minute before speaking.

"Sweetie?" she said in a ridiculously chirpy voice.

He didn't acknowledge her and continued reading.

"Can I get you anything?" Chirp, chirp.

Finally, he sighed and closed his eyes, resigned to the intrusion. He turned to face her, making no effort to mask his annoyance, and squinted uncomfortably into the bright, incandescent glow from the hall that framed his mother in the doorway. Ann felt the weight of his gaze.

"Is there anything…" she started, "I just wanted to make sure…"

Jeremy let his head drop and then shook it from side to side as if to say, *not this again*. "I can't help you right now," he said, impatiently. "I wish I could. I really do."

"Watcha reading?" Ann said, pretending she hadn't heard him.

Jeremy raised his eyebrows. "What am I…" he repeated. "What on earth are you talking about?"

"Just making conversation," she mumbled, looking away, unable to maintain eye contact.

"Conver—huh?" he shot back. "Oh, for crying out loud!"

He slammed the book closed and threw it down on the floor.

"Fine!" he said, crossing his arms and looking right at her. "What would you like to talk about?"

Through the years, Jeremy had become increasingly less amenable to his mother's need to monitor his well-being, though he was rarely confrontational. Even then, as she stood there, she detected a hint of… what was it—pity—in his voice.

If she persevered, she knew his demeanor would eventually soften. She was still his mother, after all, and, distant as he'd become, there remained a kernel of affection buried somewhere deep in the recesses of that brain of his. *Had to be.*

"I… I miss you," she said, her lips twitching.

He looked at her, expressionless, and then said flatly, "Hang in there, Ann. It won't be long now."

A wave of terror swept over her. "Oh, God, baby! That's not what I meant at all! Do whatever you need to do. Take as long as you like. Don't worry about me." She was shaking all over, gasping for air. She took a tentative half-step in his direction, but then froze.

Year after excruciating year, watching helplessly. Erratic emotions, then weeks of poisonous reflection, followed by yet another explosion of fear. Everything had become so manifold, nuanced, so laced with significance that the standard emotional categories no longer applied. Her wires were all stripped down to the bare metal and wound up like a ball of yarn.

He squinted at her again. "You're rambling, Ann. How could I possibly fail to take as long as I like? What else would I do? And why do you think my concern, or lack thereof, for you would have any bearing on it?"

She paused briefly and furrowed her brow in concentration, trying to understand him, searching for hidden meanings. "Of course," she started, forcing a meek smile. "Of course it has nothing to do with me. I just wanted you to know… just needed you to know that I'm here for you."

"Here for me?" he said, doubtfully. "And where, exactly, do you suppose *here* is?"

"Where," she puzzled. "I… I guess all I'm saying is that I love you. I don't want you to forget that."

He didn't respond, instead giving her a long, anticipatory stare. She quickly crumbled under the pressure and started looking nervously around the room for another topic.

"Good book?" she asked, lamely falling back on the subject with which she had opened.

He glanced at the book and then back at his mother. She thought she saw the edge of his mouth curl into the hint of a smile, which she returned warmly but with far too much enthusiasm, chasing his away. *What an idiot!* Still, the softening she pined for was at hand.

"Despite appearances, I'm not completely indifferent to your suffering," he said.

"Then why does this have to be so hard?"

"Because it *is* hard," he answered.

Ann worked her way over to his bed, trying to be inconspicuous and not give the impression that she was settling in. He wasn't buying it, but didn't raise any objections.

"Isn't there anything I can do for you?" she asked.

"Yes. You can accept your fate with dignity, just as I have."

At that, her throat tightened into a knot, but she managed to say in a raspy voice, "My fate?"

Again, irritation pinched his brow.

"I just want to help," she mumbled, pathetically.

"Great! Fine!" he said, impatience returning. "Then go find your own answers and leave me alone to find mine."

With that, Jeremy picked up his book, snorted, and began reading again, leaving no doubt that it was time for his mother to go away. She sat on the edge of his bed, head down, looking at her hands. At least three minutes passed before she stood up.

"Please close the door on your way out," he said, not looking up from the page.

Ann slumped down the stairs, a defeated look on her face. It hadn't been any worse than usual. But neither had it been any better. She tried to console herself with the little victories. At least he was still alive and sufficiently animated to tear into her. At least she wouldn't have to go back in there for another three or four days.

She trudged through the den and out onto the patio,

not acknowledging her father as she walked to the edge of the bricks and gazed up at the crescent moon. Venus and the brightest stars were already visible in the early evening sky. The humid May air languidly enveloped her with the budding aromas of spring and she breathed them in deeply, as if trying to fortify her resolve with the purity of nature and grandeur of the heavens. Still with her back to her father, apparently addressing the moon, she said:

"I can't put this off any longer."

She heard her father shuffle his newspaper, but got no response.

"He's my son," she continued, "the only reason I get up in the morning. I've been kidding myself that this was ever a choice."

She turned to face her father, not allowing him to merely listen.

"Saying it with conviction doesn't change anything, Annie," Dr. Franklin said. "But, as I've said at least a hundred times already, you don't need my permission. This is your decision. You're the one who has to live with the consequences."

Henry Franklin was a retired philosophy professor and an insufferably reasonable man. After the sudden death of his wife he had dutifully come there to live so that he and his daughter might console one another. They were both making the best of it, but it was awkward. Ann had left home when she was young, and they'd only seen each other on holidays and a few other rare occasions since. They hadn't yet developed an adult relationship, and their behavior was an uncomfortable mix of their defunct daddy-daughter memories and the stilted gestures of perfect strangers.

"*I* have to live…" she said, bitterly. "And what about *you*? What do *you* have to live with? Or have you already escaped into the role of innocent bystander?"

"If I thought there were the dimmest hope, I'd cheerfully take up arms with you, stand shoulder to shoulder and storm the castle, come what may," he said.

The presence of her father over the previous two weeks was beginning to fray her already-raw nerves. Ann Franklin was goal-oriented. She liked straight lines and right angles: A to B to C and then on to the next challenge. She'd been that way her whole life. When she'd discovered in her first business course at UVA that her temperament was perfectly suited to project management, she never questioned it. Shades of gray. Subplots. Nuance. That sort of superfluous debris was for people with no real ambition or too much time on their hands. People like her father.

"That's just perfect!" she said. "How about this then? When it happens, I'll leave the whole mess to you. How would you like that? Who knows? Maybe you really can stop a hurricane with sanctimony."

She stood in the twilight, nostrils flared, breathing fire. Clouds of mayflies and moths swarmed around the floodlights, casting their flickering shadows on the patio. The crickets and tree frogs sang their courtship songs into the fading light. She gave him a hard look, turned her back on him, and resumed her lunar survey.

Dr. Franklin and Ann's mother, Gladys, had saved for years and were planning to sell their house and spend their retirement cruising the United States in a deluxe motor home. As the time drew near, Ann had heard more and more about it. They were almost giddy. During Ann's last Christmas visit, they proudly showed off their research: prospective destinations, maps with scenic routes highlighted, RV brochures, printed Web pages with campsite reviews, and a mountain of books on every national and state park from Key West to Anchorage. That spring was to have been Dr. Franklin's last semester teaching.

She didn't know how to express it, but Ann was frightened for him. Her parents had always struck her as one of those couples that once the first died, the other would find one foot already in the grave. Over the past forty years they'd become mutually indispensable, each an essential component of the other's existence. Since his arrival, he looked to Ann like a ghost. His habits still reflected Gladys' presence and he often appeared disoriented when an action he'd begun wasn't finished for him as it had been a thousand times before. Correlatively, he seemed unable to initiate much on his own, as half of the required formula was no longer there. Only in her absence was he becoming aware of how little of his comfortable routine, his life, was left to him. Without Gladys, his behavior defaulted to a simple, stoic dignity. But anyone who knew him couldn't help sensing that he wore his wife's death like a pall.

"Did you talk to him just now?" Dr. Franklin asked.

"If you can call it that," she said, turning back to face him.

"I know it doesn't help, but this isn't your fault."

"You're right, it doesn't help."

"Funny you should liken this storm to a hurricane. Quite true. And you're also right that I can't stop it with sanctimony," he said. "But I wonder that you think it can be stopped at all."

"Sometimes, sitting at my desk, the guilt is so suffocating I can hardly breathe," she said. "I did this to him. I can't just walk away."

"Darryl did this to all of us. I've often wondered if he died just to spite you."

Ann was thirty-five and her son was fifteen. Her husband, Darryl, was killed by a drunk driver while she was still pregnant with Jeremy, just ten months after their wedding. Darryl was twelve years older than Ann, and it had been his idea to visit Labbitt Halsey Genomics once they'd decided to have a child. He was adamant about it, despite inklings in the press at the time that the company's protocol, X-chromosome Embryogenetic Neuroenhancement (XEN), might not be the unqualified triumph that everyone believed.

Ann still cursed his memory, not only because he wasn't around to answer for his crime against their son, but also for taking advantage of her youth and inexperience. He was utterly oblivious to the fact that while he had already enjoyed his youth to the fullest and was eager to settle down, Ann was still essentially a kid with a whole lifetime ahead of her. She never in a million years would have agreed to get pregnant at the tender age of nineteen had he not pressured her into it. And then, despite her misgivings, he convinced her that it was their duty as parents to give their child every advantage, and the latest breakthroughs in genetic engineering certainly qualified. It made her shake with anger every time she recalled the way he bathed her in guilt, manipulated her. And now, in retrospect, she considered his actions little short of evil.

"I should have known better. You tried to warn me, and I spat it right back in your face."

"You were young and in love," Dr. Franklin said.

"I was young…"

Her eyes glazed over with lamentation as she traveled back down the path that had led her there. Her friends had also warned her about Darryl, but she knew that secretly they were jealous as hell. A grown man, with a house, a car, a great job, in love with me! How cool was that! She still recalled with sickening clarity that stupid, starry-eyed kid, looking back at her from the mirror in her dorm room, completely smitten. *How could I have ever been so naïve?* Sure, her girlfriends were jealous, but their admonitions still rang in her ears, compensating for whatever they may have lacked in sincerity with grim, inescapable truth. She shook her head and pulled herself out of her trance, her resolve hardening again as she paced around the patio.

Though it didn't happen to all Xen at the same age, at fifteen, Jeremy was fast approaching his moment of reckoning. At least that's how Ann interpreted his "it won't be long now" comment. He must have sensed that it was right around the corner. She glanced up at his window. He had turned on the light and would continue reading until he lost consciousness, well past midnight. A look of desperation bordering on anger crossed her face.

"Why do they do that? It doesn't make any damned sense!"

"You're too close to see it," he said. "The Xen are a warning from the gods."

"Am I supposed to find comfort in that?"

"No, but you need to be prepared for the fool's errand you're about to undertake. Whipping yourself into a frenzy is a poor substitute for a good plan, or even for a bad one."

"Brave words from the armchair general!" she mocked. "You sound like a politician."

Ann pulled a pack of Marlboros out of her pocket and lit one defiantly, inhaling deeply and blowing the smoke out with great fanfare. Her father didn't approve of her smoking, and she didn't usually light up in his presence, but right then she felt no need to placate him. In the weeks since burying her mother, Ann had, casually at first, presented her plan for making contact with the Xen. Dr. Franklin's response was predictably negative, but it soon became clear that her efforts to solicit his advice were actually meant to soften him up to a course of action she'd never had any intention of abandoning.

It was common for Xen parents to set off on one wild goose chase or another in the months and years leading up to their children's *buzz*. It may have even been the norm. The statistics still suggested strongly that there was no correlation between a parent's actions and the survival rate of his Xen child. But there were countless impassioned testimonials from parents whose children survived and desperate to believe they had some control, a cult of superstition emerged on the Internet and morning television talk shows.

To Dr. Franklin, rational as he was, they might as well have been discussing the latest miracle weight loss program or a paranormal means of contacting the dead. Every variety of snake oil, incantation, astrological alignment, and herbal supplement had its advocates and detractors. Ann had too much of her father in her to take them seriously, but she did keep one eye open in the unlikely event that something struck her as remotely plausible. In fact, it was almost universally accepted that sunlight was palliative, so she arranged for Jeremy's bedroom to have large windows that faced due south.

"Maybe you're right and I'm nuts, but I'm going to do this and I need to know something."

"Yes?"

"Are you going to stand by me, or am I on my own?"

"You and Jeremy are the only family I have left. It hurts that you even have to ask."

"Thank you." And she stalked away into the house.

She went straight for the refrigerator, poured herself a full glass of chardonnay and downed half of it in one slug. After refilling the glass she took another healthy swallow and then braced herself with both hands against the granite countertop. The expensive polished stone was cool and smooth under her fingers as she rubbed her hands along it, admiring it, proudly recalling the sacrifices and hard work that had earned her such luxuries.

It drove her mad that her father so easily and condescendingly dismissed it all as so much "stuff"—nothing more than a distraction from the *true* goal of life. He acted as if her high-level position at Steady State Technologies, Inc. had fallen out of the sky right into her lap. Nothing could be further from the truth. She had clawed her way up there, contemptuous of any glass ceilings, raising a Xen child while earning her MBA, tending bar nights and weekends, getting her ass grabbed by drunken fraternity brothers and mopping puke out of the bathrooms. Naive? Her father was a brilliant man, to be sure, but he didn't know her as well as he thought he did. She wasn't the same dumb little girl who'd married Darryl in a frenzy of adolescent romanticism.

A minute or so later, Dr. Franklin came inside and made his way to the bar to refresh his brandy snifter.

"Give it to me straight, Dad," she said. "Why don't you think I can do this?"

He finished filling his glass, meticulously recapped the bottle, and put it back behind the bar, dragging it out and making her wait for his answer. She hated it when he did that, as if

his words were so profound they merited an introductory moment of silence and afterwards a twenty-one gun salute.

"A wise man at least knows his destination before setting off on a perilous journey."

"I want to help my son."

"I won't argue with you; that's a noble motive. But if
you show up at the gates of hell and say, 'I want to help my
son,' you'll only be handing the devil the key to your heart."

"After all I've done, I owe the devil that much at least."

He smiled at her retort and ran his finger thoughtfully along the rim of his snifter. They stood in silence for several minutes, contemplating, spinning scenarios of the next few
weeks or months or however long it might take Ann to satisfy
herself that she'd done everything in her power to untie the
Gordian knot.

"I'm certain you're making a huge mistake, possibly one
from which you'll never recover. But I also know I can't change
your mind. You're too much like your old man. You have to
learn everything the hard way. But promise me something."

He wasn't pontificating anymore, and the uncharacter-
istic sincerity in his voice was disconcerting.

"I'll try."

"Whatever happens, don't lose yourself. I want my little
girl back the way I remember her."

"Will you settle for the grown woman she is now?"

"It's a deal."

Chapter
2

Ann had a professional persona she'd honed through the years for use only at work. It had become second nature to her, but even so, she prepared herself in advance for particularly important meetings, much as an actress prepares to go on stage, psyching herself up, getting into character. In her office, she was breathing deeply, yoga style, checking her game face in the mirror and trying out a few expressions: indignation, enthusiastic agreement, deep concentration. After one last adjustment to her make-up she stood up resolutely, straightened her skirt, and pulled on her suit jacket. *Perfect.*

In the large conference room down the hall from her office, Ann's underlings were busily laying out Danishes, coffee, and melon slices, focusing the LCD projector, cuing up the PowerPoint presentation, and arranging copies of SST's proposal to the Defense Logistics Agency around the jade and mahogany table. A gaggle of colonels, majors, chief warrant officers, and GS-16s from Fort Belvoir were milling around the room, talking seriously and drinking coffee. They were assembled to hear Ann's best case for selecting Steady State Technologies, Inc. for a $300 million overhaul of the military's Materiel Requisition System. SST was on the short list with Northrop Grumman and the incumbent, Lockheed Martin, the two eight-hundred pound gorillas of defense contracting. But the DLA had shown great interest in SST's unique proposal. It was considered a "must win" for SST and it would guarantee Ann stardom and possibly a promotion to vice president if she could bring it home.

"Good morning, ladies and gentlemen," Ann began, confidently. "Welcome to Steady State Technologies' Tysons Corner facility, the future systems integration site of the DLA's Joint Materiel Requisition and Engineering Validation System. At SST, we are confident that our partnership with the DLA will yield a JOMREV system that will lower the cost of a four hundred dollar hammer to well under three hundred bucks." The audience chuckled appropriately.

SST was considered small by defense contracting standards, with 4,500 full-time employees and annual revenue of $500 million. Ann had been with the company for three years. And though she was a rising star in the firm, with four impressive contracts already in her portfolio, she'd burned up most of her credits over the previous six months in pursuit of the DLA contract. The business development process itself had cost the company nearly $3 million, not an unreasonable budget considering the potential payoff, but only Ann it seemed, was confident that SST could pull it off. That the process had come as far as it had was a credit to Ann's tenacity alone. A win and she'd be instantly vindicated. A loss and she'd be unemployed.

"The SST strategy," Ann continued, "has been developed to fully support the incremental approach of DLA's JOMREV program. Our proposal combines a demonstrated methodology that provides results while simplifying the overall implementation. Our team structure leverages the proper mix of DLA and JOMREV resources, Steady State team members, subcontractor expertise, and other subject matter specialists. We propose a phased implementation to mitigate risk."

The project would be enormously complex, and many inside SST were secretly praying Ann would lose, if only to shield the company from a Pentagon lawsuit when JOMREV blew up in her face. A four hundred dollar hammer may be irksome to John Q. Taxpayer, but to fully understand that number requires an odyssey through the Byzantine requisition process that besets the military.

The DLA oversees all defense requisitions, but each of the three main branches (Army, Navy, and Air Force) supports several of its own engineering activities to assess and validate each and every valve and bolt on every conceivable piece of equipment in its inventory. If a motor pool sergeant in Kansas needs a replacement brake pad for a five-ton truck, he sends his request to the DLA. The DLA, in turn, is charged with determining if any of the engineers who oversee that particular truck have identified changes to that particular part; a change might be an upgrade requested by troops in the field, an improvement made by the manufacturer, or possibly the part has been discontinued and a different part is being used, but an adapter is required to make it fit. The permutations are virtually infinite, and that's why the engineers exist in the first place.

Much of the information shuffled between the DLA and those dozen or so engineering activities still take place on handwritten forms and over the phone, not through Web applications, central databases, or even e-mail. There is also considerable overlap and redundancy; two or more different engineering activities might be responsible for the same part, but arrive at different recommendations. Multiply that level of inefficiency by fifty million replacement parts, and the project's complexity and political ramifications begin to come into focus. There are thousands of bureaucrats and military officers with varying degrees of influence whose livelihoods depend on the existing system, and who are loathe to see it streamlined.

"We are excited about the great potential of this DLA project to create a seamless, integrated JOMREV. The SST team believes that serving clients and driving their success is what drives ours. Our collective success on this project is a straightforward proposition of team dedication, focus, and experience, backed by a solid corporate commitment to the DLA. Thank you. Now I'll open the floor to questions."

Ann knew exactly where to look for the first raised hand. "Yes, Mr. Sicherman."

The body language of everyone else in attendance

equaled a collective, "Ugh, here we go again."

"I've been over this at least a dozen times, so I'm hoping you can help me make sense of these staffing numbers."

"I'll certainly try," Ann said.

"Tell me, where will Steady State locate enough developers with security clearances in time for the project kick off? Because it looks to me like you're about forty-five warm bodies short."

"That's a fair question, and one to which we've devoted considerable resources. It's not unusual at the start of major projects to be in need of specialized personnel, and that's why SST has put together one of the best recruitment centers in the industry. We have hundreds of resumes on file from the best and brightest around the country, many of whom have already been extended contingent offers and been vetted by the FBI."

Technically, Ann was telling the truth, though she knew better than anyone that HR would have its hands full meeting the aggressive schedule. But that wasn't her department. Ann had a rock star attitude toward consulting. The rest of the company existed to handle the minutia and lift the few gems like her onto their shoulders. After all, she was the one who had made inroads at the DLA. She was the one who pushed the proposal through in spite of the naysayers. And she was the one standing in front of the customer, fielding difficult questions. There wasn't anyone from legal or accounting or contracting standing beside her. It was an unqualified coup, and if the rest of the company couldn't rise to the occasion, she could just as easily render her services for one of its competitors.

"I understand all of that, Ms. Franklin, but I'd feel better if I could see those resumes myself," he continued. "Would that be possible?"

"With all due respect, and as your own evaluators have agreed, SST has met all of the requirements of the RFP, and we are content to let the representative samples we've provided stand on their own."

GS-16, Irving Sicherman, was a forty-something, balding, diminutive man who preferred a sneak attack to a frontal assault. He could recite the Federal Acquisition Regulations by heart, was intimately acquainted with the function and development history of every major military supply system, and knew the ranks and responsibilities of all personnel who had even a tangential point of contact with his sphere of influence. He was uniformly despised, but through his own brand of Machiavellian misdirection, also uniformly feared. His customary tactic was to sit back at first and allow things to veer off course. Then, just as his colleagues were beginning to feel confident in their approach, he'd type up a bloodless indictment of the whole project, citing an avalanche of evidence from his mountain of administrivia. If successful—and he usually was—he would establish himself as, if not the leader, at least the Oracle of the Scrolls, a sacred and terrifying figure in the presence of whom lesser bureaucrats quaked in timorous awe.

But on the current project, Irving Sicherman had yet to get his footing. The JOMREV contracting officer was Colonel Simon Oxford, a battle-tested keyboard warrior in his own right. And though Sicherman had launched a few tentative salvos, Oxford had proven to be a formidable opponent. Under normal circumstances, Sicherman would have been man enough, though just barely, to scurry back down his mouse hole and live to fight another day. But this project was different. JOMREV threatened to rewrite the entire pecking order, and he had some very specific ideas about where he belonged on it. He was becoming desperate and, rational or not, Ann Franklin was at the eye of his fury.

"Very well," he grumbled. "Then I'll guess we'll just have to trust you."

With Sicherman retired, the others tossed Ann a few softballs that she knocked squarely out of the park, sometimes to approving nods, other times to appreciative laughter. Queen Ann—as she was referred to in hushed tones around SST—was holding court. At one point, she stole a glance at her impotent nemesis and smirked to herself as he slouched in his chair, steam rising off of his pasty white scalp. Sicherman wasn't the first, and certainly wouldn't be the last victim of her reign of terror. But there was nothing to feel guilty about. It was neither her desire, nor her responsibility, to accommodate the glaring character flaws of others, and particularly not of those actively opposing her. Career functionaries like Sicherman should learn their place, carve out a comfortable little niche, and learn to make a feast of the few scraps of meat still stuck to the carcass. It wasn't personal. That was the natural order of things. Survival of the fittest.

After the meeting, as the DLA representatives were filing out and exchanging pleasantries, Major Calvin Monroe leaned close to Ann and whispered in her ear. She caught a whiff of his familiar cologne.

"I miss you."

Ann smiled imperceptibly as a hot wave of adrenalin shot through her body. She deftly resisted the urge to look around to see if anyone noticed, and continued seeing her guests out the door.

Ann always ate breakfast and dinner, but had long since abandoned the habit of eating lunch. Her hectic schedule too often saw her brown bag rot away in the refrigerator while she ran between client sites and staff meetings. Instead, she stole a few minutes each day for an apple or banana, and when she had time, spent her lunch break in the company's state of the art fitness center. And that's where she went immediately following the DLA presentation. Ten minutes of stretching. Twenty laps in the pool. Ten minutes of cool-down. Shower. Make-up. And then back to the office. It was the closest thing she had in her life to a religious ritual. It left her energized, empowered, and made her skin glow with adolescent vigor. She was also grateful for its ability to punctuate her day with something completely unrelated to work, transforming it from a grinding, ten hour marathon into two manageable five hour sprints.

Later that afternoon, Ann called her team together to

discuss the meeting.

"Kim, tell me about HR," Ann said. "Sicherman is still breathing down my neck. I don't know how much longer I can put him off."

"Well, Ann, as I've mentioned several times before," Kim began in her snotty, judgmental voice, "HR can only justify the expense of hiring additional recruiters after the DLA has signed a contract."

Kim McEwen had, just the week before, celebrated her fortieth birthday right there in that very meeting room. It had been a typically sober corporate affair, complete with a soggy, mumbled rendition of *Happy Birthday* and an inedible, cardboard sheet cake from Food World, all under the blanched glare of a dozen 1,500-watt fluorescent tubes. Attendance was optional-mandatory and everyone stayed just long enough to choke down a rectangle of cake, force a smile, and issue a perfunctory wish of wellness. But even in that brief span, all present were struck by Kim's absurdly effusive response, as if the ridiculous event actually meant something. Rumors immediately took flight that SST's token acknowledgment of her fourth decade on planet Earth was the extent of Kim McEwen's merriment that day.

"We've been over this, Kim." Ann said. "If they don't ramp up now, we're never going to get a signed contract."

"That may be, but I don't have the authority to make Mr. Miller change his policies. Perhaps if you gave him a call..."

Though she'd boasted of two completed semesters at a junior college somewhere in Pennsylvania, Kim McEwen never graduated and had been with SST for more than twelve years, far longer than the degreed and upwardly mobile who bounced from firm to firm like hookers with attention deficit disorder. Changing firms was the best way to ensure rapid increases in salary without waiting on the programmatic raises that came only after waiting around like a dupe for some arbitrary period of time. But that strategy only worked when fortified by a resume heavy in accredited schools and impressive post-graduate acronyms. For the rest, those who were openly disparaged as "unbillable infrastructure," the only hope was to become indispensable to someone important and slog it out.

"Fine," Ann said, "I'll take care of it. What else do you have on your plate?"

"I'm still working with the developers to finish up the graphics for the final oral presentation," Kim answered.

"I thought you said you were almost finished. I expected that to be done last week."

"We were nearly finished, but then Larry changed some of the database architecture and we had to redo half of the slides."

"I didn't approve any changes," Ann said. "Look, I'll talk to Larry, but next time you have an issue that impacts the schedule, I need to know about it immediately. Is that clear?"

"On many occasions you've told us not to bother you with every little detail," Kim responded. "Has that policy changed?"

"Just let me know when the slides are done. Is that asking too much?"

"I can give you a daily progress report if you like."

"No, Kim. I want to know when it's finished."

Cliff especially bristled at Kim's impudence.

"Don't give it a second thought, Ann," he said. "I'll babysit them."

"And give Larry a call too, will you?" Ann said. "Remind him who's in charge of this operation. Any future changes to the architecture will go through me."

Kim's pride did a summersault in her throat and her faced flushed with resentment.

"Will do," Cliff said.

In the first few years of her tenure at the firm, Kim McEwen had hoped to exploit a little-known and rarely-used college tuition benefit buried deep in the fine print of SST's employee handbook. So confident was she that it would happen, she even went as far as purchasing the introductory coursework from the George Mason University bookstore to get a jump on her inaugural semester. Her first supervisor, one David Norloff, seemed willing to indulge her. But no sooner had Kim completed the onerous application process than he moved on to greener pastures and was replaced by a firestorm of a woman, Kelly Barnstead, whose sweeping ambitions left no room for Kim What's-Her-Name's quaint little fantasies.

With that setback, Kim attempted to circumvent her boss and work directly through HR, but was told the benefit applied only to employees whose supervisors regarded them as critical resources in need of specific training. So, once again, she bided her time. Her third supervisor made it perfectly clear that he needed her on the job more than in class and, in any case, he already had enough superstars on his staff. And her fourth was a mealy-mouthed fellow who nodded politely when she brought it up, but then seemed to forget all about it as soon as she walked out of his office. By then, four years had passed and the flimsy picket fence separating her from her future had, bit by bit, grown into an imposing stone fortress. Self-doubts began to corrode her optimism. Fate gradually supplanted her sense of control. But even so, over the eight years that followed, she never gave up on herself, at least not explicitly. That would have represented too crushing a defeat. Still, her cherished dreams had done little more during that intervening span than sharpen her tongue and gnaw away at her character.

Despite her failure to become a billable consultant, Kim McEwen had worked her way up to director of proposal development which, though impressive sounding, still only netted her seventy-five grand a year. She and her team of proposal specialists were assigned on a temporary basis to large efforts such as Ann's JOMREV bid. Technically, therefore, Kim was not Ann's subordinate, instead reporting directly to the vice president of marketing, Doug Axford, an affable, rotund fellow with a sparkle in his eye and a full Santa Claus beard. He had an easy smile and glad hand for everyone he met, but was savvy enough to flank himself with caustic little trolls like Kim McEwen to do his dirty work and protect his sunny reputation. He aggressively returned the favor and everyone grudgingly accepted that Kim was untouchable—at least for now. But rumor had it that Axford was on the verge of retiring, perhaps as early as next week, to spend more time at his beach house on the Outer Banks of North Carolina.

In addition to Kim and her proposal team, Ann had assigned her two top lieutenants, senior managers Cliff Enright and Andrea Gates and their support staffs to the JOMREV bid. Cliff and Andrea were both in their late twenties, extremely intelligent, and had followed Ann to SST from their previous employer. They were fiercely loyal and each would have happily taken a bullet for Ann, whom they largely credited with their meteoric rise in the consulting world.

"Andrea," Ann continued, shooting Kim a quick, furtive glance, "how'd your recon mission go? Anything new?"

The DLA had set up a massive documentation library at its Ft. Belvoir headquarters and Andrea was tasked with driving down there twice a week to monitor its contents for any relevant new information. Typically, Andrea would have assigned it to one of her consultants, but for JOMREV Ann had asked her to do it personally.

"Yeah," Andrea responded, "they finally caved in and provided the detailed STAT code you've been requesting for the last three weeks."

"Thank God! Get it out to Larry so he can start on that interface."

"Already done."

"And find out if he needs a temp," Ann continued. "I don't want him trying to be a hero and missing his deadlines again."

"I'll send him someone whether he thinks he needs it or not."

"Good idea. Let me know if he gives you any grief and keep me posted on his progress. We can't afford a repeat of the New Jersey eGov fiasco."

"I'm on it," Andrea said.

"Anything else?"

They all exchanged sideways glances.

"Great," Ann said, standing up and slapping the table, "go make some money."

On her way back to her office, Ann's boss caught her in the hall.

"Hey, hey, how'd the big DLA meeting go?"

"Great, Jerry, I think they're finally all on board."

"Listen, I hate to bother you with this." Whenever Jerry Gooding wanted something he started with that weak, preemptive apology. It immediately set Ann on edge. "I got another call from Harold Grant over at the SEC. He still isn't happy with their new search capability."

"How many different ways do I have to explain this?" Ann started. "They got exactly what they paid for. If Harry isn't happy, Harry can sign the change order that's been sitting on his desk for the last three weeks. I'm not going to commit two full-time developers for the next month unless he's willing to pony up the cash."

"Well... yes... of course. I completely agree. But maybe you could talk to him again, see if you can't work something out."

Jerry was in his fifties, a software developer by trade, blissfully ignorant of the principles of leadership, who had finally risen, as they say, to his level of incompetence. He had a love-hate relationship with Ann. On the one hand, she was principally responsible for keeping his department in the black. But on the other, she scared him half to death with her wild ambitions. For her part, Ann tolerated him, despite believing he was weak and myopic, only so long as he didn't stand in her way.

"Sure, Jerry, I'll talk to him. But do me a favor, next time he calls, forward him directly to me."

"Will do," he said. "And keep me posted on the DLA."

At quarter after seven that evening Ann was standing in the eleventh floor elevator lobby with her heavy laptop bag over her shoulder, her mind caught between the DLA and her family. As she impatiently pushed the down button again, Kim sidled up next to her. *Terrific!* Ann did not relish situations that were not clearly either professional or social. She didn't have a practiced persona ready at hand for them, and she wouldn't have expended one on Kim even if she did.

"Working late?" Ann asked, indifferently.

"I know you don't like me," Kim said. "But that's okay. I know who I am."

"I wouldn't say I don't like you, Kim. Sometimes I think we just aren't on the same page."

"Not like you and Major Monroe?"

Ann's heart jumped into her throat and the lobby briefly went sideways.

"What on earth is that supposed to mean?" Ann tried to force out the words with conviction, but instead they stumbled over one another, clipped and uncertain. *Shut up, Ann! You're giving yourself away!*

"Don't worry, your secret is safe with me," she said, a malignant smile creasing her lips. "I'm not one to start trouble, and I know how important this is to you."

Just then, the elevator door opened and Kim got in.

"Have a good night, Ann," she said, and was gone.

Ann stood there, frozen, for more than three minutes before she remembered she had to push the button again to summon the elevator.

Chapter 3

Three adolescent gorillas ventured down to the glass partition that separated them from the visitors. Jeremy gazed in at them, though they seemed more interested in him than he was in them. Ann pushed the button on a yellow information box.

Gorillas have two separate species, the western and eastern gorilla. Unfortunately, both species of gorilla are considered critically endangered. Groups or gatherings of gorillas are called harems, which normally contain between five and thirty-five members. A typical harem includes a silverback, one or two subdominant males, several mature females, and their young. Old males are called silverbacks because the hair on their back turns gray...

Jeremy stared at the wise little box as if it were the main attraction, oblivious to his surroundings. A herd of raucous school children made its way around the exhibit, jockeying for position and forcing Jeremy off to one side, away from the window. So small and frail, he appeared younger than his fifteen years. Ann rushed over to him and took him by the hand.

"Fascinating, don't you think?" Ann said. "They almost look human."

Jeremy surveyed the writhing mass of screaming kids.

"Debatable," he said.

"Very funny, Mr. Wisenheimer," Ann said, smiling, squeezing his hand. "But for your information, you're too young to play the curmudgeon. I looked it up online. You need jowls and a cigar."

"I'm not the curmudgeon. I'm the adorable prodigy who grates on everyone's nerves."

"Ah. Well, in that case…"

It was bliss. Absolute bliss. That morning, Ann had found the will to storm Jeremy's room, park herself on his bed, cross her arms, and sustain her obstinacy long enough to pry him free of his books. Where it came from she hadn't a clue, but there was no question of letting it go to waste. He'd given her his usual sour reception, but realized soon enough that, dead or alive, he was going to the zoo. Queen Ann was on the warpath and not to be trifled with. But in truth, he hadn't required nearly as much cajoling as she'd feared. Cooped up in his cave for more than a solid month, he must have already been well-primed for a weekend furlough. And when she started rifling through his drawers in search of an outfit, he went limp like a kitten in its mother's jaws and let her do her thing.

They walked slowly in the general direction of the giraffe exhibit, Ann's favorite. A male peacock, one of the innumerable exotic birds, wings clipped, allowed to wander freely through the park, made an impressive show of plumage six feet from Jeremy. A hundred shimmering eyes reflected the afternoon sun. Jeremy met his mother's gaze with a weak smile and her heart melted. It was a magical place.

Of the precious few memories of her son that Ann still recalled with great fondness, at least half of them were formed at the zoo. For some strange reason, it was the only place that appealed to both of them—the single point of contact between two otherwise alien universes. And on that day, even the gods were on board, the sun shining brilliantly while a gentle wind taught the young spring leaves how to dance. Ann would have gratefully sold her soul to stop time and make it last forever.

The giraffes were clustered at one end of their pen near a zoo employee who was selling carrots. Small children were on the shoulders of parents, laughing hysterically, and shoving the treats into the giant creatures' hungry mouths.

"Wanna get some carrots?" Ann asked.

"It's up to you," he said. "But don't ask me to put you on my shoulders."

"Was that a joke?" she mocked. "A crack in the philosopher's stone?"

He smiled slightly.

"Oh my God! Let me get my camera," she said, fumbling through her purse. By the time she was ready to shoot his smile was gone, but she took the picture anyway.

Ann bought a bunch of carrots and the two of them wandered away from the crowd toward a calf that wasn't having much luck competing with the adult giraffes for the attention of the crazed children. Jeremy held up a carrot and looked into the creature's eyes. It was a long, soulful look, as if he were able to read its mind. It extended its head over the wall and allowed Jeremy to stroke it between the eyes, which he did with great tenderness, muttering something near its ear. Ann snapped a picture, but somehow the scene left her cold, eager to move on to another exhibit, one with a bigger wall. *Am I really jealous of a giraffe?* She tried to shrug off the ridiculous sensation, but was glad when he ran out of carrots.

"Can I ask you something?"

He turned to face her, but didn't respond.

"All of those books you read. What are you looking for?"

"I'm not looking for anything."

"Then why do you do it? They obviously don't make you happy."

"It's not about happiness," he said.

"Then what?"

He twisted up his face at her but then, sensing she wouldn't be easily discouraged, looked off into the far corner of the giraffe enclosure, his brow furrowed in thought. After a lengthy silence he finally spoke.

"It's like a glitch," he said. "That's the best way for you to think about it."

"A glitch? What kind of glitch? Can't it be fixed? Please don't push me away if there's anything I can do to help."

"No, it can't be fixed."

He was suddenly lost in space, his eyes mechanically following the giant heads of the giraffes as they rose to chew and then returned to the kids for another mouthful. Ann found herself doing the same, and they stood there, heads bobbing, watching the beasts together.

"Eighteen feet tall and they have to stoop for their food," he muttered. "It's an insult, don't you think?"

"You're going to ruin this for me."

"Let's look at something else."

The two of them meandered aimlessly through the park as the sun lazily weaved its way between the big puffy marshmallow clouds. It was getting hot and the animals were becoming lethargic, lying in the shade, shooing bugs with their ears and tails. A rhino snorted loudly and jerked its head to remove a bird from its face. The lions were sprawled out, fast asleep, their huge paws hanging off of the concrete cliffs that extended up to the chain link net that surrounded them. A group of obese cheetahs gnawed at their food pellets.

After an hour or so of profuse sweating, Ann and Jeremy ducked into the air conditioned insect exhibit to escape the heat. It was dark and the halls curved around like the tunnels of a termite mound. The glass displays were recessed into the walls and glowed with eerie phosphorescence.

"Like a moth to the flame." He hadn't spoken in more than half an hour.

"I'm sorry, sweetie, did you say something?"

"Have you ever wondered why moths fly endlessly around a light bulb, even though it disrupts their reproductive cycle and eventually kills them?"

"No, I guess I've always taken it for granted."

"They do it because they evolved over the eons to navigate using the moon and stars. Artificial lights are new and their genes haven't kept up. So they fly in circles around the light until they die of exhaustion."

"That's so sad."

"It's like their capricious little six-legged god suddenly pulled the rug out from under them."

Ann shook her head in awe. "Where do you get this stuff? Is there anything you don't know?"

"Probably."

"See, that's what I don't understand," she said. "If I were you I'd be curing cancer or building rockets to Mars. Our children were supposed make all of mankind's dreams come true. Can't you tell me why that didn't happen?"

"Cancer?" he said, quizzically. "If you can't find a Xen who cares about himself, how likely are you to find one who cares about you?"

When Jeremy said *you*, he wasn't addressing Ann so much as mankind collectively. The Xen had adopted the patronizing convention of referring to normal humans as if they were a quaint little Darwinian sideshow, out in the hominid hinterlands, somewhere between Australopithecus and Neanderthal. The characterization stung but was hard to dispute. Hadn't Labbitt Halsey Genomics come into existence for the sole purpose of creating a superior species of human? That the company was initially festooned with roses, aglow in the fantasies of a million bleating parents, hadn't been nearly enough to overturn the law of unintended consequences.

"Don't you even care about me?" Ann asked, timidly.

He shot her a devious grin. "I care more about you than anyone else on earth."

"Only because you don't care about anyone," Ann said. "Isn't that right?"

"You said it, Ann. Not me."

Something inside her died whenever he called her *Ann* instead of *Mom*. He'd started doing that as soon as he realized she had a name, which was also about the time he realized how different he was. From then on, Ann had been nothing more to him than a cardboard cutout that changed his sheets, kept him fed, and occasionally dragged him away from his books to go watch animals from other continents run around in little concrete boxes. He'd tried to communicate with her at first, but soon after discovered that, though she possessed the rudiments of speech, her brain cavity was evidently packed with nothing but goose down and saw dust. Still, he was content to let her scurry about unmolested, just so long as she didn't interrupt him too often. At least that was how Ann saw it.

"Fine, so you don't care about us," Ann said. "Why not just do it for the money?"

"How much have you got on you?"

"You know what I mean," Ann said, unable to suppress a smile.

Maybe Jeremy wouldn't cure cancer, but on many occasions Ann had thought, quick as he was with his goofy retorts, he might have a bright future as a stand-up comedian. If only he weren't so dour. But that was all stupid fantasy. Her smile turned bitter and faded as she let her mind fill with thoughts of his impending buzz, the insatiable monster that would soon devour whatever crumbs remained of her optimism.

"Do you blame me for what's happening to you?" she asked.

"No, you aren't responsible for your actions."

"What's that supposed to mean?"

"You don't know enough about either yourself or the world to predict the consequences of the things you do."

"Charming," she said, "just charming."

"You'd prefer the blame?"

"I'm holding out for curtain number three," she said.

"Buy me a hot dog."

As they left the insect exhibit, Jeremy stopped to put his dark glasses on. His eyes were terribly sensitive to light and Ann suspected, considering how closely he held his books to his face, that he needed prescription lenses and was most likely ruining his vision. But he had repeatedly spurned her pleas to see an optometrist so, as with most other things concerning his welfare, she finally gave up in a flurry of desperation and guilt.

Ann bought hog dogs, fries, and sodas from a vendor,

and then joined Jeremy on a shaded bench. It overlooked an exhibit that featured a concrete mixer, a wheelbarrow, two shovels, and a sign indicating that the zoo staff was terribly sorry, but the wolverine was temporarily unavailable.

"Maybe his agent ferreted out a better deal for him," she said.

"Only if he could weasel his way out of this zoo contract."

She smiled broadly and for a moment thought he might have reciprocated.

It was mid-afternoon, both the temperature and humidity creeping into the eighties, and Jeremy appeared to be wilting. *So thin!* It had occurred to Ann before that passersby might peg her as a bad mother, even abusive, and she found herself looking into their eyes as they walked by, alert to any signs of contempt. The innocent days of his childhood seemed like an eternity ago.

Jeremy was five when Ann had first thought to bring him to the zoo, and before they'd been there ten minutes she couldn't imagine why she hadn't done it sooner. His excitement was so sincere that Ann knew right away the zoo would be their oasis. He ran between the exhibits, jumping up and down, pointing wildly at the creatures. "This is an ibex! It's native to the high mountains of Asia, Siberia, and Europe, and can still be found in abundance in Kazakhstan..." "This is an African Anteater! It has no teeth and lives entirely on ants, termites, and beetle larvae..." It was the first opportunity he'd ever had to apply his copious knowledge to the real world – a revelation for him. Ann spent most of their visit wiping away her tears of joy and, to that day, the residue of that wonderful afternoon still lingered in both of their hearts.

"I'm not ready to let you go," Ann whispered.

"I wish it were up to you."

"Can you blame me for trying?"

"We've already discussed this," he said. "I can't blame you for anything."

"Will you help me?"

"No."

They sat in silence for several minutes, chewing distractedly on the last of their French fries, watching a harried, young mother struggle to corral her three unruly toddlers, one of which was climbing a fence and seemed intent on sacrificing himself to the polar bear. The woman yanked him down midway through his ascent and scolded him. She was on the verge of tears.

It brought to mind an amateur video Ann had seen years ago on the evening news, of a German tourist who, in an act of breathtaking stupidity, had climbed over the outer fence, right up to the bars of a polar bear enclosure. In one second flat, the bear clamped onto the woman's leg like a vice, and surely would have dismembered her and pulled her through the bars in pieces, had an agile bystander not jumped to her aid in the nick of time. The image had stuck in Ann's mind ever since, partly because it was so disturbing, but also because she couldn't imagine how the woman's family could have explained to strangers how their wife and mother had died such a remarkably idiotic death. *Mauled by a polar bear in the wilds of Kansas City.* Shame and grief should never be forced to compete like that.

"Pretty clever of you," Jeremy said, "bringing me here to make your big announcement. I probably ought to feel manipulated."

"Does it really make any difference?"

"I suppose not," he said. "But do me a favor. Keep in mind why you're doing it."

"And why am I doing it?" Ann asked.

"All I'm saying is it would be easy for you to convince yourself that this escapade of yours is somehow for my benefit."

"Is there another way to look at it?"

Jeremy gave her a long searching look, clearly mulling over something in his mind. He took a deep breath and sighed.

"You know better than anyone," he started, "how little experience I have with people. So little, in fact, that I have great difficulty gauging what they're able to comprehend. It's always struck me as entirely random. Sometimes you get it, while other times I get nothing but a blank stare. Still, with you dangling over the edge the way you are, I have no choice but to give you the benefit of the doubt."

"How heartwarming," she said, sarcastically.

"I assume," he continued, ignoring her, "you imagine there's something you might learn about the buzz that will help me survive it. Is that about right?"

"In a nutshell… yeah, I guess so. Pretty naïve, huh?"

"Very, but that's not the point," he said. "Clear your mind for a minute. I want to tell you a fable."

"Consider it clear."

"You're on the bank of a raging river and you see a man clinging to a log out in the middle. Get it?"

She gave him a little smirk.

"Now, suppose you jump in to save him and drown in the process, but the guy on the log manages to survive anyway."

"Okay…"

"There are two possibilities. If he waved to you for help, then he is complicit in your death and will be forced to live with it for the rest of his days. But if he tried to wave you off and you ignored him, then you have no one to blame but yourself. Does that make sense?"

Ann knitted her brow. "I don't see how it's his fault either way. It's my choice to jump in."

"Not so," he said. "By jumping in against his wishes, you denied him the right to exhibit the same degree of heroism toward you that you showed toward him. In effect, you disregarded his very essence as a person. Altruism is a two-way street."

"But…"

"Just think for a second, Ann. What if I died trying to

save you? Wouldn't you agonize over it for years to come? Castigate yourself for getting into that situation in the first place? Wonder if you did enough to dissuade me from jumping?"

"I…"

"Shhh," he said, putting his finger to her lips. "Don't talk. Think."

Ann struggled with the idea for several minutes, working her mouth as if talking it over with herself. Jeremy waited patiently, watching the wheels turn in her head. Finally, the lights went on and she turned to face him.

"Are you waving me off?" she whispered.

"Yes."

"But it's not the same," she insisted. "You're my son. You're my responsibility."

"No, Ann, I'm not. Not anymore. And you owe it to me to honor my wishes on this matter. If you jump in, you're on your own."

As his words sank in they began to weigh heavily on her, undermining the nobility of her quest, blurring the clarity of her motives, and even casting the whole enterprise in an unflattering, selfish light. But then she suddenly saw it from a different angle. She was so absorbed with Jeremy's puzzle that she hadn't seen what it really meant. He was warning her! And that meant he cared about her, deeply enough even to cast her as his equal for the purposes of his ethics lesson! A warm blanket fell over her and filled her with a hope she hadn't felt in years. *You're on your own.* His words echoed in her mind. *I've always been on my own. So be it! I'll jump just the same.*

Jeremy gave her a curious look as a mischievous grin worked its way across her mouth.

"I love you, Jeremy," she said, "and I respect what you've told me."

"But you're going to jump anyway, aren't you?"

"I agree with everything you said. And in some cold abstract world I'm sure it would make perfect sense. But I'm your mother, and no amount of logic is going to change that."

"I figured as much. But you can't blame me for trying."

"Blame you?" she said, a warm smile on her face. "I may never be able to thank you enough. It means everything to me."

"Hmm. Well, since we're being so respectful of one another, let me ask you one last question."

"Of course."

"It may be months before you understand how important this is, so I want you to take some time to think about it."

"Okay…"

"Are you willing to risk your life for this?"

He asked the question with complete sincerity, not in his usual tone of academic detachment, and that alone gave Ann pause. Her instinct was to answer in the affirmative, but seeing as how she was being asked to reflect on it, she couldn't help wondering if in fact she might somehow be putting her life in jeopardy. That thought, in turn, filled her with guilt, and she chastised herself for calculating the odds that harm might come to her as her son's life hung in the balance.

"Do you really think it will come to that?"

"If it didn't, how could you possibly understand?"

Chapter 4

Ann was early, as she was for every appointment whether personal or professional, and was waiting for Calvin at Sam & Harry's, one of the many posh eateries in Tysons Corner. Only recently had she acknowledged her growing fortune and felt comfortable spending a modest percentage of her disposable income on entertainment and luxuries other than her house. Her many years of relative poverty had chastened her to the lure of conspicuous consumption. She saved every receipt and was a rapturous devotee of Quicken, with which she tracked all of her expenditures and investments in subatomic detail.

She had no intention of telling Calvin about Kim's suspicion of their affair. In the first place, it would spook him and jeopardize the entire DLA bid. Second, Kim hadn't mentioned it since the evening by the elevators. And finally, as long as they were careful, she and Calvin could reasonably deny the whole thing. In any case, succumbing to blackmail was an option too galling to even entertain and so, regardless of the consequences, she refused to alter her behavior.

Calvin was on time and made his way back to the table where Ann was drinking her second glass of chardonnay and pecking away on her Blackberry. He was athletic, moved gracefully, and had a sincere-looking smile—the sort coveted by salesmen—for everyone he met. The twentieth year of his undistinguished Army career would end only six months hence, and he was counting the days until his pension kicked in, after which he could begin his second career in consulting and start making some real money. In fact, it was his enthusiasm in that arena that had brought the two of them together during the initial stages of the DLA bid. At first their meetings were innocent enough, though still illicit given their glaring conflict of interest. But soon their mutual ambitions surfaced and everything became clear. They both felt the JOMREV project would almost certainly collapse under its own weight, so it didn't make any difference which contractor won. If everything worked according to plan, SST would make millions before the military threw in the towel, and no one would be the wiser.

"Good evening, my beautiful angel," he said as he removed his dress blue army jacket and sat down.

"I'll be with you in just a second," she said, making a few final pecks on her Blackberry.

They never talked out loud about their conspiracy. It was so simple there wasn't any point. At the critical moment four months ago they had communicated their intentions subliminally over the course of a long, innuendo-laden conversation about their respective hopes and dreams. As they looked into one another's eyes, the plot was hatched spontaneously, and had forever afterwards been buttressed with nothing more than sly winks and nods. Much of that was due to the fact that neither of them wanted to be reminded of what they were actually doing. But it was also because they both firmly believed they weren't criminals, just two intelligent people who recognized that some bureaucratic constraints were not as significant as others. No one was being hurt, lest Lockheed or Northrop be considered, and they had more than enough weight to tip the scales in their own favor: whole squadrons of lobbyists, former and highly connected military officers on their payrolls, enough R&D money to buy a small country. If anything, Ann and Calvin were merely leveling the playing field.

"I missed you," he said. "Putting me off last weekend has created a time bomb."

"Mmm, I think I have the detonator," she said, playfully. They both smiled.

Whatever their original motive for getting together, they both agreed the sex was fantastic. Ann attributed it partly to the risk they were taking and all the sneaking around, but that wasn't the whole story. Certain human bodies seem to be fashioned specifically for one another, apart from any other attraction their occupants might feel. They fit together perfectly, move in unison, and perform a spontaneous ballet that requires no practice or preparation. It was that ballet that quelled the occasional pang of conscience for both of them over the course of their association.

"There's something I need to discuss with you," he said.

"Oh?"

"The selection committee is set to make its decision early next month."

"That's great news. Do you know which way they're leaning?"

"You know which way, but that's not what I want to talk about."

Ann hadn't given much thought to what would happen to their relationship once the selection committee had made its choice, effectively bringing their nefarious plot to a successful conclusion. And she certainly hadn't considered the possibility that Calvin might have his own ideas.

"What then?"

"I realize we have an arrangement, or whatever you call it," he started, his voice suddenly thick with significance. "And trust me, this is as much a surprise to me as anyone."

"Wait a minute, Calvin."

"Please, let me finish."

He took a deep breath and looked her dead in the eyes. Ann was petrified, barely able to speak, but she couldn't let him continue.

"No, Calvin, stop right there. I'm begging you."

"But…"

"No, I… there's too much going on in my life right now."

Too much going on? How lame could I possibly be? Though terrified, in that moment Ann realized she was not entirely opposed to a proposal from Calvin, and the last thing she wanted was to put him off permanently. But the fact was she felt ambushed. In her highly compartmentalized mind, Calvin was work-related. It would take time for her brain to file the appropriate papers, get the transfer orders approved by her heart, and eventually bring Calvin on as a full-time member of her personal life.

"Too much going on, she says!" He smoothly returned to his pocket something he had been slowly raising to table level. A ring? *God, that was close!* "I'll let you off the hook this time, but you better say something nice, and fast. My self-esteem is a fragile, delicate thing."

What a nightmare. Her intention had been to tell him all about Jeremy and solicit his advice. But that would now seem like nothing more than a maneuver to spurn his affections.

"I promise, Calvin, it's not you at all," she said, haltingly. "You remember my son, Jeremy?"

"Of course."

"Well, there's something you don't know."

"What's that?"

"This isn't easy for me," she said. "You know, I'm not the most trusting person in the world."

"But you have a wonderful gift of understatement."

"Thanks." She was visibly struggling for the right words, and that alone softened her in Calvin's eyes, lending her a vulnerability that was new and welcome to him.

"Whatever it is," he soothed, "you can tell me."

Finally, she couldn't stand it anymore and whispered, "He's Xen."

Calvin's eyes nearly popped out of his head. His mouth opened as if to form words, but instead his lips only twitched and wiggled in a vain attempt. He moved his hand farther from his pocket, giving Ann the impression that he may have wanted to give his proposal another shot, but now had no such intention. Her heart sank, filling her with doubts about letting him in. At last he managed to speak.

"But he's only thirteen, isn't he? How on earth…?"

"He's fifteen."

Calvin shook his head in disbelief and repeated, "Holy crap!" over and over as if each repetition released a tiny bit more of the shock he was trying to purge from his system. It had been well-documented through the years that the parents of Xen fared little better than their children. Marriages collapsed. Life savings were squandered on futile quests for a cure. Suicides and domestic violence were common.

But worse than all of that was the painful, agonizing wait for adolescence. Some compared it to the anguish experienced by parents of missing children; their hearts consumed by the infinitesimal and corrosive hope that they will one day get a phone call their minds know will never come. Psychologists counsel them, as time passes and the probability of a happy ending becomes vanishingly small, to let their children go and get on with their lives. But in reality there is no easy path to salvation for such condemned souls. To give up on ever finding a missing child guarantees a lifetime of guilt. Whereas the alternative—hanging on despite the irrefutable statistics—crushes them into dust with a hopeless hope that leads inexorably to mental disintegration. Calvin knew as well as anyone, Xen parents were damaged goods.

Ann sat with her head down, watching as Calvin fiddled with his silverware, inserting his knife in between the tines of his fork. Her instinct was to release him from any obligation he felt and assure him that his understanding and sympathy were not required and would, in any case, be well above and beyond the call of duty. But then he spoke.

"Why didn't you tell me before?"

"Like you said, we have an arrangement. It didn't seem relevant."

"Fifteen, huh?" he said with resignation.

"You may not believe it, but I was about to tell you the

whole story."

"How are you holding up?"

"Who says I am?"

He smiled grimly and she did the same. Their relationship, the one they'd managed for so long to keep entirely professional and recreational, had become intimate so abruptly they both seemed to be dining with complete strangers. It was that awkward pivotal moment in which one either embraces the modified terms and leaps forward, or else fumbles around for the right words to make a graceful exit. Neither knew what the other was thinking, so they looked searchingly into one another's eyes and waited for a sign. Calvin broke down first.

"I've often wondered what it would be like," he said. "Being Xen, I mean."

"Any conclusions?"

"I read Meredith's book. But I'm sure you know a lot more about it than I do."

"I wish I could say that."

Their conversation turned to the relatively safe topic of Xen history, and though it may have been ostensibly painful for Ann, their tone became soothingly clinical and it proved to be a welcome diversion from Calvin's truncated proposal. They soon became animated, freely exchanging impressions and ideas, and she was encouraged by his interest in the subject. Other than the newspapers and an occasional documentary, Dr. Eugene Meredith's work would have formed the basis of any educated layman's background knowledge of the Xen.

Meredith was the clinical neuropsychologist whom, fifteen years ago, when there was still a widespread belief that something substantive could be done, Congress had tapped to research the Xen and report his team's findings directly to the committee formed to look into it. At first, Meredith was given great latitude to do his work, if only because no one had the slightest idea what they were looking for. But as the project dragged on, the committee came under tremendous political pressure to find a solution, and that pressure naturally got dumped onto Meredith and his team.

After three years, marked by increasingly unwelcome scrutiny, Meredith resigned from the project in disgust and issued a scathing criticism of the committee, outlining its grievous efforts to subvert the scientific process and force him to sign off on any plausible-sounding theory he could invent to mollify the public. The fallout cost several of the members their jobs during the next election cycle and the committee was eventually disbanded. Soon afterwards, Meredith published his book, *Dizzying Heights*, and became the foremost expert on the Xen, appearing on countless television and radio news programs over the following months. His findings, to say the least, were unsettling.

His book had the condescending tone of a Monday morning quarterback who hadn't been the least bit responsible for his team's beating. And he gave the unmistakable impression that he'd seen the whole thing coming. But that minor stylistic flaw notwithstanding, the questions he raised were essentially apropos. He pointed out, much to everyone's surprise, that Asmund Labbitt and Nigel Halsey, the company's cofounders and discoverers of the protocol, had never fully understood the neurological changes their technique wrought. The company had engineered a gene, based on their study of natural geniuses, and they postulated, not unreasonably it turned out, that splicing that gene into a normal human embryo would confer greater intelligence on its recipient. In fact, they discovered that as many as five copies of the gene could be inserted before reaching a point of diminishing returns. But Labbitt Halsey had never, despite the expenditure of substantial resources, been able to describe the precise cellular or biochemical mechanisms at work.

In the field of genetics, finding a statistical correlation between a gene and trait is difficult enough and typically cause for celebration in its own right. But determining exactly *how* a gene causes a trait is vastly more complex and, at least in most cases, such as agriculture, not considered vitally important. As long as the resulting product does what it's supposed to do and isn't an imminent health hazard, who really cares how it works? He could be justly accused of playing on the ignorance of the general public, but Meredith presented these revelations, throwing around phrases like "playing God" and "all powerful dollar," as if Labbitt Halsey Genomics had committed a crime analogous to that of Dr. Frankenstein. Perhaps he was right in some respects, and the firm certainly paid dearly in the courts. But a more objective analysis might just as easily have concluded that Labbitt Halsey Genomics was nothing more sinister than the latest example of man's reach exceeding his grasp.

But Meredith spent less time on the genetic complexities than he did on what he considered to be Labbitt Halsey's greatest oversight, namely, its paltry understanding of intelligence itself. In *Dizzying Heights* he identified two main types of intelligence: logical, which is the sort evaluated by most IQ tests and manifests itself as skill in math and science, and; analogical, a less quantifiable variety, that Meredith sometimes called "big idea" intelligence, that would have been especially high in history's greatest theoretical thinkers, such as Aristotle, Newton, DaVinci, and their ilk. All of Labbitt Halsey Genomics' records indicated an exclusive focus on logical intelligence, and indeed, the Xen typically scored somewhere around 150 on standard IQ tests, far above average, but not absurdly so.

Of course, since Labbitt Halsey was completely unaware of it, there were no records at all of the Xen's analogical IQ, so Meredith devised an ingenious test to measure it. What he found rattled him so thoroughly that he repeated the experiment three times, then changed it completely and tried it three more times before he allowed himself to believe the results. Every last one of the Xen he tested had an analogical IQ that was so far off the charts it couldn't even be evaluated. In short, he was unable, despite digging through many of mankind's most inscrutable intellectual endowments, to present the Xen with a single concept that they couldn't immediately comprehend and use flexibly in novel situations.

On the basis of interviews he conducted with Xen, both before and after the event, Meredith cobbled together a thumbnail sketch of the *buzz* that, though not unanimously accepted, at least provided a basis for further research. The Xen, apparently, are possessed by an insatiable need to unify all of human knowledge – along with anything they develop themselves – into a single coherent principle of reality. This drive is so powerful that it ultimately overwhelms all others and undermines the individual personalities onto which it was grafted. Unfortunately, as all Xen discover, the myriad concepts that constitute the totality of human knowledge are, in a manner that perhaps only the Xen will ever understand, incompatible with one another. As the buzz approaches, these many threads of thought begin conflicting with one another, as if actively fighting for dominance in the Xen mind. In the end, they undergo a radical, quasi-physiological transformation from discrete lines of reasoning into indistinguishable but innumerable adversaries. The unappeasable need to unify and the impossibility of that unification results in a devastating existential paradox. At this point, all volitional thought ceases and these warring ideas manifest themselves as so many angry bees or locusts, relentlessly swarming through the mind and lending their cacophonous racket (buzz) to the name of the phenomenon.

Meredith estimated that the Xen possessed an intelligence that would only occur naturally in about one person in ten million. But even at that low rate there should be hundreds of such people alive at any given point in history, and yet only a handful ever emerge as renowned benefactors of mankind. He posed the obvious questions: What happened to all the others? Would a comprehensive survey, assuming one were possible, reveal that most of these great minds were, like the Xen, crushed under the weight of their own genius? Is history littered with quiet little tragedies that will never be told? Meredith didn't, and obviously couldn't, answer these questions, but his clear implication was that Labbitt Halsey Genomics, and indeed everyone involved right down to the overzealous parents, hadn't given nearly enough thought to what they were doing, and were guilty in varying degrees of hubris.

Ann had read *Dizzying Heights* several times, but the book ended right where she wanted it to begin, with a clear description of the Xen themselves. Meredith had done an admirable job chronicling the entire scandal from the genesis of Labbitt Halsey Genomics, through the questionable FDA approval process, and finally the congressionally-funded research project he led. But whenever he seemed about to give some insight into the Xen mind itself, his writing suddenly became exasperatingly metaphorical and introspective, as if he really didn't understand them any better than anyone else.

Of the few other books on the Xen, one dealt exclusively with genetic engineering, another focused on the religious implications, and the others were ponderous tomes of incomprehensible scholarly philosophizing that took root only in the rarified academic soil where they were planted. In the years since that initial flurry of activity, a consensus had formed that the story of the Xen, like so many other stories in history, would depend on the passage of time for its objectivity. Only after the whole sordid mess played itself out, the argument went, could anyone gain a disinterested perspective. True, perhaps, but cold comfort to the living.

"It doesn't bother you talking about this?" Calvin asked.

"I can no longer afford to be bothered by it."

They'd put the waiter off twice during their long conversation, but as they saw him returning for the third time they hastily picked up their menus and made their selections. Ann ordered the chicken Caesar salad, Calvin, the sixteen ounce New York strip steak, rare, garlic potatoes, and a side of asparagus spears. Ann usually picked up the check, and always in places as pricey as Sam & Harry's. Like the rest of their plot, they hadn't discussed it. But there was the unspoken assumption that these meals were tantamount to business expenses; Calvin swayed the committee, Ann paid for entertainment. On his Army salary, they'd be ordering out for pizza if Calvin were obliged to pay. They made small talk about the absurdly over-priced bottles on the wine list until their food arrived.

"I took Jeremy to the zoo last Saturday. He said something I can't get out of my head."

"Yeah?"

"He asked if I was willing to risk my life to understand him."

"What did you tell him?"

"I had no idea what to say. It caught me completely off guard," she said. "I tried to ask him about it later, but he was back in his books and wouldn't talk to me."

Ann had a far-away look in her eyes and sat motionless with a piece of chicken stuck to her fork, halfway between her plate and her mouth.

Calvin gave her a curious stare. "If I didn't know better, I'd say you had something in mind."

"I'm not going to sit by and watch him die."

"Yeah? I was under the impression there was nothing you could do about it. It's always the same. Half of them commit..." he stumbled past the offending word, but then quickly recovered. "Well, you know. And there's no way to predict which ones. Did I miss something?"

"No, you didn't miss anything," she said.

"Then I'm lost. Have you gotten through to him somehow? Because if you have, you really ought to tell somebody. You could save a lot of lives."

"No, nothing like that."

He looked at her sympathetically, but completely befuddled.

"Okay, I give up. What are you talking about?"

"I don't care what I have to do. I'm going to get him past the buzz."

His confusion turned to skepticism, but he did his best to conceal it. She assumed he must genuinely love her, but she couldn't predict how long he'd be willing to endure her crusade.

"I hate to be the voice of despair, but you realize there's no evidence anyone has ever been able to do that."

"I know."

He hesitated, but then put his trademark, positive spin on it. "But you're right, of course. He's your son. What do you have to lose? Might as well give it a shot, right? What's your plan?"

"I have the address of a Xen bar. As good a place to start as any."

"Maybe..." he said.

"Not convinced?" she said. "What a shock."

"Don't take this the wrong way," he said, "but do you have any idea what you're going to do when you get there?"

"Honestly," she admitted, "I don't even know what I don't know. If I'm lucky, I'll come out of there with some good questions. It's a first step. I don't have any illusions."

"Hmm," he intoned. "Other than Jeremy, have you ever talked to a Xen before?"

"No."

"Well, I have," he said, "and let me tell you, it was the weirdest damned thing I've ever experienced in my life. One conversation in particular rattled around in my head for months. I never could figure out exactly what we were talking about."

"I don't understand. How did that happen?"

"Top secret..." he started, but then reconsidered. "Hell, it was years ago and it didn't pan out anyway, so I guess it wouldn't hurt to tell you about it."

He told her about a military intelligence initiative, abandoned more than a decade earlier that sought to use Xen to help track terrorists. Among their many talents, the Xen were capable of learning new languages with incredible speed. Though they never put the skill to any useful purpose, in the presence of "normals" they often spoke to one another in oddball languages like Inuktitut or Altaic, possibly just to be obnoxious. But, coincidentally, language experts have always been in extremely short supply at the intelligence agencies. Combing through the endless electronic intercepts for relevant terrorist communications was the principal bottleneck in the whole process. It seemed like a no-brainer, if only the military could figure out some way to get the Xen to take it seriously. Calvin had been involved in the candidate screening process, and in that capacity had interviewed dozens of Xen.

"You have to remember, back then we were dealing with basically a bunch of kids, eighteen, nineteen years old. Seeing them all lined up on the bench outside my office, they looked like delinquents waiting to be disciplined by the principal—anything but a cadre of prospective intelligence agents."

Calvin chuckled and seemed for a moment to get lost in the memory.

"Anyhow, there was this one guy in particular. Usually they didn't talk much. They were shy, I guess, and I had to really work at first to open them up. But this guy talked my ears off right from the start. I could hardly get a word in edgewise. I still don't know what the heck he did, but by the end of the interview I had the sickening feeling that my job was a joke, the terrorist threat was a matter of complete indifference, and everything that mattered to me was a total waste of time. I remember it was a Friday, because right after that I went out and got drunk and spent the rest of the weekend feeling sorry for myself."

"What on earth did he say?" Ann asked with great interest.

"That's just it. I have no idea. We recorded all the interviews and I listened to it over and over. Nothing. If you listen to the words, there was no reason for me to get the feeling I got. I've never been able to figure it out."

"So, did you hire him?"

Calvin laughed out loud and just barely got his napkin over his mouth in time to intercept a chunk of garlic potato. After a few more healthy spasms, he finally regained his composure.

"No, they cancelled the program before we hired any-one," he said, smiling. "Listen, I don't claim to understand the Xen on the basis of a dozen or so interviews, but I know enough not to take them lightly. Whatever you do, be careful."

"You sound like my father."

"Your father is a very wise man."

Chapter
5

Fester's was once a biker bar and a stray, leather-clad Harley enthusiast could still be found there on occasion. But for the most part the Xen had claimed the place as their own. Ann got the name and address from one of the parents' Internet support groups she trolled, but to which she rarely contributed anything personal. Finding them was never going to be a problem; the Xen made no overt effort to hide themselves, though they were usually left alone in places that were widely known to be theirs. If familiarity can ever be said to breed contempt, it could be said emphatically of the Xen. The earnest desire to wring one's hands over those poor lost souls was much easier to do in the abstract, at a safe distance. Much as giving money to the homeless through an intermediary is more comfortable than handing a ten spot to some particular vagrant—one openly hostile to charity, clearly deranged, or likely to blow it on liquor or crack. Looking the Xen in the eye, meeting that contemptuous gaze, tended to undermine all such benevolent condescension, and most people jealously protected their ignorance.

Ann arrived just after nine and found herself a quiet corner from which to survey the scene and form a plan.

Everything in the bar, from the tables and booths to the partitions and the bar itself, was spray painted flat charcoal gray, almost black, and looked as if it had been constructed in the owner's garage out of plywood and two-by-fours. No frills. Nothing fancy. Only the deep red vinyl cushion covers on the seats and bar stools offered the eye any contrast at all. The walls were also painted gray but featured a bewildering array of yellowing book and magazine pages, liquor bottle labels, movie posters, sheet music, photos of various and gloomy faces, foreign money, and any number of other disjointed fragments of life, affixed with glue, tape and thumb tacks, but with no discernible rhyme or reason. Taken together, with so many corners and edges peeling up, the collage lent the walls a fuzzy texture.

The music was loud enough to muffle conversations at a distance, but not so loud that Ann couldn't hear herself think. They were playing Barber's *Adagio*, over and over and over. There was an arrangement for strings, then a choral version, then one for pipe organ. There seemed to be no end to the variations. The dismal notes were grimly appropriate, but it still struck Ann as an odd choice for a bar. As she sat and listened she found herself yearning for some rock-n-roll, anything to liven up the place.

She'd gone to Fester's explicitly for research purposes, but that didn't make it any less awkward sitting alone in the corner of a bar, people-watching, conducting her reconnaissance. It recalled her first few painful weeks at UVA, before she'd made any friends or met Darryl. During that time, stubbornly resolved not to take root as a perennial wallflower, she attended a series of freshman mixers sponsored by her dormitory. As beautiful as she was it was hard to account for her insecurities, and her dorm mates would have accurately reported languishing in the shadows far longer than she. But Ann had always subconsciously oversold her travails. It cast her successes in a brighter, more heroic light and gave her a more visceral sense of her power. Still, forty-five minutes and two nervously gulped glasses of chardonnay had slipped by already, and she was getting the queasy feeling that people were looking askance at her. *What on earth did I think I was going to do here?*

With her glass empty once again, the waitress returned for the third time. The girl was in her early twenties and wore black shorts, clunky, knee-high, patent leather boots, and a white tank top full of rips and holes over a black satin bra. Only a thorough exam could have determined how many times she'd been pierced and tattooed.

"You okay, honey?" she asked, her speech somewhat garbled by a silver barbell stuck through her tongue.

"Fine, thanks," Ann said.

The girl studied Ann for a few seconds. "Not that you asked or anything but, FYI, no one's going to talk to you if you don't make the first move. It's kind of an unwritten rule. They'll let you sit here all night."

Ann looked up at her, a bit startled. "No, I just..." But then she thought for a moment. "What do I say?"

The girl quickly sat down across from Ann, leaned forward, and in a conspiratorial, insider's tone whispered, "I'll see what I can do. What do you think?"

"You'd do that?"

She smiled knowingly and winked at Ann as she clopped back toward the bar on her giant boots. Out of the corner of her eye, not wanting to appear too eager, Ann watched the girl tap a guy at the bar on the shoulder, talk into his ear, and point at Ann. The guy turned his head, a look of mild annoyance on his face, and then nodded. Ann got the sense he wasn't interested, but after a few moments he stood up and casually made his way toward her corner.

He plopped down on the chair across from her and shot her a wide sardonic grin. Ann's heart was beating fast.

"So, tell me, Mom. How old is he?"

"How old..." Ann was taken aback by his bluntness. "How'd you...?"

"Fifty-fifty chance," he said. "I assume you're not here for the wine."

"Fifteen."

"One of the late models, huh? All the bells and whistles," he said. "Happy with your purchase? Everything you hoped for?"

He was maybe twenty-one years old, good-looking but

too thin. His jeans were threadbare and full of holes, the soles of his hiking boots nearly worn through, and his sweatshirt was stained down the front, fraying around the collar. Ann suddenly felt absurdly clean.

"My purchase?" Ann said. "He's my son."

"Of course he is, how rude of me."

Then he crossed his arms, abruptly going silent, and looked straight into Ann's eyes, waiting for her to speak. Ann felt the pressure of his stare and struggled for several moments to form a thought.

"I was hoping you could help me," she finally stammered.

A scrawny young girl, not more than sixteen, appeared out of the gloom and sat down beside him, put her arm around his neck and twirled his greasy hair with her finger. Her Salvation Army ensemble included a vintage, mid-80s wool pant suit, gray, badly worn and rumpled, accented with dingy white tennis shoes, a black tee shirt, and an old Washington Redskins baseball cap. It wasn't the calculated second-hand chic cultivated by normal disaffected teens, but rather the consequence of genuine poverty.

"Who's your friend?" she asked.

"Just another satisfied customer."

"Yeah?" the girl said, looking at Ann. "No complaints?"

Ann was speechless.

The girl continued, "My name is Imelda and this is Stuart. I'm sure he forgot to introduce himself. He's terrible about that. Do you have a name?"

"Ann Franklin."

"See, Stu," Imelda said, hitting him playfully on the shoulder. "They have names too."

Again they went silent and looked at Ann, anticipation on their faces. It struck Ann as a calculated move to put the onus on her and knock her off balance. If so, it was working.

"I guess I'm not the first parent you've seen," Ann said, trying to crack a smile.

"Three or four a month," Stuart said. "A bit tedious, if you want the truth."

"Am I wasting my time?" Ann asked.

"Depends what you think your time is worth," he answered. "In my estimation your whole life is a waste of time."

"Now what way is that to talk to our new friend?" Imelda scolded.

"Whatever was I thinking?" he said, blandly.

"Can you help me or not?" Ann said, impatience creeping into her voice.

"Hard to say, Ann," Imelda said. "What sort of help do you think you need?"

"I would've thought you'd know better than anyone."

"Oh, right," she said, sarcastically. "Our genetic defect."

"Well..." Ann hesitated.

"She thinks we're broken, diseased," Stuart added, "Isn't that what you're saying, Ann?"

"No... no! That's not what I meant at all," Ann said, frantically backpedaling. "You're putting words in my mouth."

"Oh?" he challenged. "So you don't think we're diseased?"

"I've never thought that way about my son," Ann said. "Never! That's your word. Not mine."

"And what's your word?"

"I don't know. Call it a syndrome... or... maybe a disorder," Ann said, scratching around in her brain for a euphemism. "What difference does it make? It is what it is. Who cares what you call it?"

"Then why not just call it a disease?" he said. "Because that's exactly what it is."

Ann screwed up her face. "But I thought..."

"You thought we cared what you think," Imelda said. "But now that you've had a moment to reflect on it, doesn't that seem wildly implausible?"

"What?" Ann said, incensed. "You were just messing with me?"

"Relax, Ann," Stuart said. "You came all the way out here. You deserve the whole show."

Ann put her hands to her face, kneading her temples, trying to piece together in her mind what had happened. No doubt they were screwing with her, having a big laugh at her expense. But on the other hand, they were still there. And what was a little humiliation compared to the nightmare in Jeremy's immediate future? *Deal with it, Ann! It's research. Leave your pride out of it!*

"I suppose I deserved that," Ann said.

"Why?" Imelda asked. "Have you done something wrong?"

"Playing God. Messing with Mother Nature," Ann said. "Isn't that what they say?"

"That's what Meredith said. Is it also what you say?"

Ann looked at Imelda curiously, certain she was walking into another trap.

"What else would you call it?" Ann said.

"The polio vaccine. Penicillin. Stem cells," Stuart said. "Playing God? Or do you only haul out that label when it blows up in your face?"

"Is that important?" Ann asked.

"Makes all the difference in the world," Imelda said. "Can't you see that?"

"Maybe..." Ann said, tentatively. She sat there for several moments, looking at them, trying to decide if it was her move.

The clock continued to tick. "Unbelievable," Stuart muttered under his breath. He looked at Ann with disdain and, after a few more moments when she failed to reply, "Well??? Can you see the difference or not?"

Ann's instinct was to storm out of the bar in a huff, and it took everything she could muster to resist that urge. *Remember Jeremy. That's why you're here.* Unfortunately, the effort left her shaking with anger and worse, still in need of an answer to Stuart's demeaning question. She closed her eyes and tried to focus, struggling just to formulate the problem. What's the difference between the Xen and the polio vaccine? Isn't that what he said? Playing God? Wasn't it all pretty much the same thing? *What the hell does he want from me???*

Stuart and Imelda waited patiently. Ann tried not to look at them, but still got the feeling they were thoroughly enjoying themselves. *Snotty little brats!* By then the pause she'd introduced into the conversation was in the late stages of pregnancy. *Too bad!* It was obviously a test and Ann decided it was more important to say something insightful than fret over which principles of etiquette she might be violating. A full five minutes elapsed before she spoke.

"You're right," Ann said, slowly, trying almost too hard to get it right. "We only feel bad about playing God... we only call it 'playing God' when it ends in disaster. Otherwise, it's just progress."

Stuart and Imelda looked at one another in mock amazement and exchanged admiring grins.

"Give the little lady her prize!" Stuart said.

She felt a bit silly about it, but Ann was suddenly beaming with pride. And why not? Sure, the Xen were an unmitigated catastrophe but, for all that, no one had ever argued that they weren't geniuses. Behind all the sarcasm, they had just paid her a genuine compliment, and Kudos from the Xen were a rare and precious commodity.

"I'm hungry," Imelda said.

"I'm thirsty," Stuart added.

They both looked at Ann and then glanced suggestively toward the bar.

"Right," Ann said, getting the message.

She squinted into the gloom in search of their waitress but when that proved fruitless, decided to walk over and order directly from the bartender. She arranged to keep the drinks flowing and also ordered three BLTs. He disappeared with her credit card to place the order and start up a tab.

There was a girl sitting next to her at the bar, nearly as

young as Imelda and terribly thin. From the vacant look on her face and her bloodshot eyes, Ann figured she'd either been crying or was severely intoxicated. She pictured her son there beside her, drunk, withdrawn, wasting away. She looked away as a shiver ran up her spine.

Technically, the Xen were not exempt from underage drinking laws and had Leesburg's finest chosen to make an issue of it, all of the teenagers in Fester's could have been ejected and the bar's liquor license revoked. But as was common during those times, eyes were averted and exceptions were made. Only by comparison to Germany's perpetual self-laceration over the atrocities of World War II can one grasp the depths of shame to which the country sank in the aftermath of the Labbitt Halsey fiasco. To criticize or, God forbid, blame them for their lot in life, would have represented the zenith of political incorrectness. That they accepted so little in the form of compensation served only to aggravate the open wound. So long as they didn't hurt anyone, the Xen were allowed to do pretty much whatever they wanted. With all hope exhausted, the entire country had become their hospice.

Nearly every one of the estimated nine million Xen in America lived off of the Xen Relief Act, a monthly stipend paid by the government to all Xen, no questions asked. In return for their XRA checks the Xen adopted something akin to the code of vampires, keeping low profiles and generally flying under the radar. They were certainly cognizant of the unease their existence caused, and their shadowy lives may have been a gift of some kind. In any case, they clearly grasped the terms of their charity and took great pains not to bite the hand that fed them.

The bartender returned with the first round, which she gathered up and took back to her table. As she approached, she caught a glimpse of Stuart and Imelda sitting in silence, expressionless, as if immobilized by her absence. When they saw her they immediately perked up and eagerly accepted the drinks. But their sudden transformation struck Ann as disturbingly unnatural and prompted her to examine the rest of the patrons more closely.

Though they were grouped more or less as one would expect in a pub, two or three to a table, they appeared, almost without exception, to be oblivious to their companions. Perhaps they derived comfort from nothing more than their proximity to other humans. She hadn't noticed before; the music masked the lack of commotion. But Ann got the impression they wouldn't care at all if someone yanked them up from their seats and rearranged them at random. Although a few words were exchanged here and there, no one seemed to be engrossed in a conversation. Instead, they were focused on nothing but their drinks and, judging by the abundance of blank stares, some distant locale that must have been infinitely preferable to planet Earth.

Stuart watched as Ann surveyed the room. "As good a place to wait as any. Wouldn't you say?"

"Wait for what?"

"A key to a vault with no lock. A path through a maze with no exit."

"Oh shit," Imelda said. "Run for your life, Ann. Once he starts waxing lyrical, it's all downhill from there."

"One innocent line," Stuart said with mock derision, "and you're on me like the plague. Really, I don't know why I keep you around."

Stuart paused to shake his head woefully while Imelda took a sip of her beer. Ann seized the opportunity to steer them back on course.

"I know this may be asking a lot," she began, "but could we possibly have a normal conversation?"

"Why would you come all the way out here for a normal conversation?" Imelda asked. "Can't you do that at home?"

"What I meant to say... I'm running out of time. My son is running out of time. If you're going to spin me in circles all night, I'd appreciate it if you'd respect my sense of urgency and say good night."

"Fair enough. And let me be similarly forthright," Stuart said. "You're being vetted."

"Vetted?" Ann said.

"We have an associate who's looking for a certain someone, maybe you," Imelda said. "He's conducting… what would
you call it… I guess it's an experiment."

"Sounds fascinating," Ann said, sarcastically, "but I
don't have time to be your friend's guinea pig."

Stuart gave Ann a hard unsympathetic stare, but then
let his face slacken.

"Your call," he said blithely, and they both clammed up
again.

Their well-timed silences were exasperating, but Ann
couldn't help being impressed. It was a cut-throat tactic she
herself often employed to great effect.

Years ago, on her first gig out of college, she'd learned
the hard way that there was nothing to be gained by debating
a point if her opponent was out of options and she held all the
aces. And that was certainly her dilemma right then. Ann knew
if these two were to argue with her, try to convince her of anything, they would, in effect, be taking partial ownership of her
problem and though they probably didn't care, would share the
blame if their recommendation didn't pan out. Ann had always
been leery of colleagues who innocently tried to get her "input"
on remedial courses of action that were only necessary because
of their own incompetence. It was a cynical attempt to spread
the blame around, reduce their own exposure, and because of
Ann's seniority, possibly pass the buck altogether. It demanded tremendous self-control. The naïve knee-jerk instinct was
to point out their idiocy and give them their marching orders,
but Ann was always careful to thwart such ambushes by sitting
back in her chair, thoughtfully stroking her chin, and letting
the poor schmuck stew in his juices until he drew the obvious
conclusion: *You dug this hole yourself, and it'll be a cold day in hell
before I get caught with a shovel in my hand, admitting my complicity
by helping you dig your way out.*

Still, though she may have been wise to it, sitting on the
other side of the desk stung just the same. It was disorienting

being beaten at her own game, and it was some time before she finally admitted defeat and spoke.

"What sort of experiment?" she asked.

"Let's not get ahead of ourselves, Ann," he said. "Like I said, you're being vetted. Just think of yourself as an expert witness and me as the wily assistant DA."

"This sounds like fun!" Imelda gushed.

Ann felt her blood pressure rising and wanted to scream, but knew it wouldn't accomplish anything.

"Fine," she growled. "Play your game."

"Great," Imelda said, slipping into her role as the judge. "Councilor, your first witness, please."

"Ms. Franklin," Stuart began in a dignified, courtroom tone, "you've known of your son's condition for more than a decade. What does it say about your commitment to his welfare that you've only now launched your campaign?"

His words cut like a laser straight to the core of Ann's guilt and her anger instantly evaporated, making way for her familiar crushing mountain of shame. She'd asked herself the same question many times over. So many, in fact, that it had long ago lost its character as a question, becoming reincarnated instead as a stone-faced sentry, posted at the door to her future, leaving her stranded on the threshold of the life she might otherwise have had. No answer would ever satisfy him because there was no answer. His presence was more a reminder than a challenge. *I'm here because you screwed up. Simple as that.*

The waitress returned while Ann was deep in the mud, puzzling over her response. Stuart and Imelda pounced on their sandwiches as if they hadn't eaten in days. Quite possibly they hadn't. Ann wasn't hungry, and when they finished, Ann pushed her plate across the table, providing something other than her perplexed expression to keep them entertained. At one point, she stole a peek at Imelda, hoping she might be let off the hook. But instead she got the feeling they were prepared to let her sit there all night. Or at least until she closed out her tab.

More time passed and the patent leather boots again

came clopping back across the floor. Ann heard mumbling as the waitress cleared the table, but she couldn't make out the words. The burden of her deliberations had dragged her into a trance-like state, her surroundings adopting the murky indeterminacy of peripheral vision. She assumed they were ordering more drinks. Maybe another round of BLTs. *I have to answer this infernal question!*

Ann was becoming aware of how much time had gone by since Stuart asked his question—at least twenty minutes— and she flirted with the prospect of admitting that she didn't know the answer. But she strongly suspected they wouldn't accept that, and might even declare an end to the proceedings and send her packing. In truth, it had been ages since she'd faced the question head-on. *Maybe I should have done this years ago.* She started to wonder if her intervening life experience might provide a novel perspective, a connection she'd never considered. Could she have helped Jeremy years ago? It was a perfectly legitimate question. *Think, Ann!* Why had she waited so long? What was she so afraid of? No sooner had she phrased it thus, than the answer came to her in a flash. She looked up at her tormenters, face pale.

"I've... been living in denial," Ann whispered, visibly startled by the revelation that had just passed between her own lips.

The two of them swapped another pair of astonished grins.

"Not bad," Stuart said. "But in denial of what?"

"That should be obvious," Ann said.

"Maybe it should. But I think you'll soon see that it's not."

Ann sat several moments, stunned once again, no longer certain she knew what had seemed so perfectly crystal clear only seconds before.

"I've been in denial of my crime against Jeremy, my son," Ann said. "What else could it be?"

"Come now," Imelda said. "You don't really believe

you've committed a crime, do you?"

Ann had never been forced to think so hard about anything in her entire life and her head was beginning to rebel,
pounding with every beat of her heart. In her experience,
these sorts of conversations were supposed to be hypothetical,
whimsical arcana to discuss over drinks during happy hour.
Proof that she'd really attended college and belonged in the
club. There weren't any right answers. It was all a matter of
opinion. And yet these two treated these esoteric matters as if
it were etched in marble, no less certain than the Pythagorean
Theorem. *No wonder they stay drunk all the time.* She gave them a
plaintive look, but got back nothing but confirmation that they
were not in the business of granting reprieves. *Fine! We'll do it
the hard way!*

"Yes!" she said, bitterly. "I have committed a crime
against him. The worst crime a mother can commit."

"Let me remind you, Ms. Franklin," Imelda said, "you're
still under oath."

"Oh, for crying out loud!"

"Did you or did you not admit earlier," Stuart said, now
playing a belligerent prosecutor, "that your crime was that of
'playing God?'"

"Call it whatever you want," Ann growled.

"And did you not also testify that playing God is an epi-
thet that can only be applied retroactively, inasmuch as it refers
to consequences, not intentions?"

Ann's head was spinning wildly. "Why are you doing
this to me?"

"Objection, your Honor!"

"Sustained!" Imelda chimed in. "The witness will answer the question."

Ann's jaw hung open as Stuart and Imelda once again
presented a united front of insolent silence. It was intolerable!
Somehow, inadvertently, Ann had granted them permission to
step outside the limits of common decency and from that vantage point hammer her with impunity. Every single word out

of their mouths was a direct assault on her character, but all she could think to do was sit there and take it. Jeremy's life was still as much at stake as it had been when she walked through the door. What choice did she have? Plan B was nothing more brilliant than to come back tomorrow night and start from scratch. Worse, aside from pulling a gun on them, there was no way to fight back. Never in her most degrading nightmares had she felt so unfathomably clueless. After another few minutes of groping through the dark in search of an escape hatch, she performed a few of her Yoga breaths and resigned herself to addressing their latest challenge.

"Yes," she said, recalling her original response and praying it was still the right answer. "'Playing God' only applies after the fact."

"Therefore," Stuart said, "you couldn't ascribe criminal intent to someone accused of playing God, could you?"

"I guess not," Ann said, miserably.

"Then would you agree that the only remaining means of establishing guilt is to prove negligence?"

"I have no idea what you're talking about," Ann said. Her brain by then was aggressively resisting any new information out of sheer self-defense.

"Your Honor?"

"Negligence," Imelda started, "is the failure to exercise reasonable care when such failure results in injury or damage to another. It implies knowledge of or power over at least one proximate cause of said injury."

"Stop!" Ann begged. "Please! I just... I can't keep up. I'm sorry."

"Ten minute recess?" Imelda offered. And once again Ann found herself under the oppressive weight of their silence.

She hadn't looked at her watch recently but suspected, considering her state of exhaustion, that it was well after midnight. She tried to count the number of drinks she'd had. Six? Maybe seven? The drive home was going to be an adventure. She picked up her glass and polished off the last of her chardonnay, then leaned back in her chair and let her eyes pan across the fuzzy walls. The display was obviously a creation of the patrons themselves, patched together piecemeal over the years—a new, impromptu genre of historical narrative. Closest to her was a page from a book, across the top of which read, "Human, All Too Human." An ironic smile crossed her lips. *Ain't that the truth!*

If there was any good news it was that Ann had wholly abandoned any effort to appear clever, making it marginally easier to focus on whatever it was they were trying to get her to see. When she first walked through the door she'd hoped to come across as…well, at least competent. Though looking back on it, she had to admit she hadn't the vaguest idea what that might have entailed. But as luck would have it, none of it even mattered; the customary rubric of social intercourse was strangely absent from that place. During the interminable lulls that followed each and every one of their damnable questions, Stuart and Imelda lapsed into a state of suspended animation. And though Ann was painfully aware of the silence, they didn't twist the knife by drumming their fingers on the table, sighing out loud, or tapping their feet on the floor. They just sat there and waited, exercising a quiet patience that, in polite society, would have qualified as superhuman. Over the course of the evening, Ann had gradually embraced these bizarre new rules and by then was learning to let them ease her pain. Another quarter-hour drifted by before she was ready to resume the fight.

"Can I ask a question?"

At the sound of Ann's voice they snapped out of their hibernation and looked her in the eye.

"What is this meant to accomplish?" she asked.

"Our associate," Imelda began, "gave us fairly strict guidelines. Among other things, the right candidate must demonstrate at least some proclivity for self-reflection."

"What do you two get out of it?"

"Finder's fee," Imelda said.

"It also provides a temporary rationale for doing more than staring at the wall," Stuart added.

"If that sort of thing is important," Ann said, "why don't you just get a job?"

Stuart and Imelda looked at one another.

"Of course you couldn't know it," Stuart said, "but that tangent would take us right to the heart of what it is to be Xen. Fascinating, sure, but just a wee bit over your head."

"Sorry I asked."

Imelda gave Ann an uncharacteristically sympathetic look. "I feel bound to tell you that even if you get through this, our friend probably can't help your son. He didn't tell us exactly what he's up to, but I can't imagine it has anything to do with circumventing the buzz."

"Is there any point in going through with this?" Ann asked.

Imelda raised her eyebrows. "Begging your pardon, Ann, but I gather that your plan, such as it is, amounts to little more than jumping in the river and trying to avoid the rocks while the current sweeps you downstream."

Ann's head drooped toward the table and she nodded grimly.

"I'll grant you that demonstrates an admirable degree of open-mindedness. But, other than keeping your head above water, what's the *point* of any of it?"

"I have no idea," she mumbled.

Ann swirled around in the current for awhile, struggling to free herself from the eddies until she became aware of yet another lengthening silence. She lifted her head and gave them an expectant look, but they gave it right back.

"I'm lost," Ann said.

"Councilor?"

"To this point," Stuart began, "we've found you not guilty of playing God on the grounds that it is an *ex post facto* charge. However, it remains to be determined if you exhibited criminal negligence, which is defined as an inexcusable failure to prevent harm to another. How do you plead?"

As with everything else they'd been saying that night, it took Ann an inordinately long time to make sense of what she'd just heard. She understood all the words. That wasn't the problem. What she found so bewildering was the sheer speed with which these convoluted ideas rolled off their tongues. A janitor, wandering into one of her software interface development meetings at SST, there to empty the trash can, would probably feel roughly the same thing if he ever bothered to listen.

"Guilty?" she asked as much as declared.

"Indeed," Stuart said. "Then please tell the court what exactly you could have and should have done to prevent your son's current predicament."

"I should have listened to my heart," Ann said.

"Your heart?"

"Yes," she said. "That's right."

"Does your heart possess any knowledge of genetic engineering?"

"No."

"Any tidbits of wisdom on analogical intelligence?"

"No."

"Then what precisely was your heart trying to tell you?"

"That going to Labbitt Halsey was wrong," Ann said with conviction.

"Your Honor," Stuart said. "Permission to treat Ms. Franklin as a hostile witness."

"Proceed," Imelda said.

"What???" Ann said, becoming alarmed.

"Isn't it more likely that your heart was merely giving voice to a general sense of trepidation?"

"No."

"... a rational fear over bringing a child into the world?"

"That's not all it was!"

"... of embarking down a new and uncertain path?"

"It was real!" she screamed. "You miserable, fucking bastard!"

Stuart paused briefly but was unmoved by her explosion, a malevolent smile on his lips. Ann was shocked by her own outburst and looked around nervously. Some of the patrons were talking quietly. Others were drinking. No one seemed to notice.

"Ms. Franklin," he started again, keeping the pressure on, "with absolutely nothing in the way of specifics, how can you sit there, sixteen years removed from the incident, and claim the slightest inkling of foreknowledge, the tiniest shred of clairvoyance, when even today you have no idea what would have been needed to prevent this calamity?"

Silence.

It wasn't fair. He was stripping her of her most cherished grievance; but for her weakness and Darryl's intransigence, Ann would have strode in on her white horse and saved the day. That version of events had always been beyond debate. It was simultaneously the source of her greatest pride and deepest shame, a heartfelt conviction that had sustained her through all the tribulations, all the self-doubts and setbacks that were part and parcel of raising a Xen child. However bad things got, she could always take comfort in one, immutable truth. *I'm the good guy.* But now it was beginning to look as if her divine insight—the font of her self-righteous indignation toward Darryl *and* proof of her own beneficence—had been no more significant than a mild case of indigestion, an anomalous hormonal spike that she'd mistaken for woman's intuition. Ann felt herself slowly go numb. Somewhere in the distance, out in the fog, she thought she heard the waitress come and go at least twice more before she spoke again. By then, it was well after two in the morning.

Ann looked up at them and tried to speak, but in lieu of words she gave them a bleary-eyed stare. It was just enough to restart their engines.

"Congratulations, Ms. Franklin," Imelda said. "This court finds you not guilty of either playing God or of negligence."

"I'm sick," Ann said.

Stuart reached down to the floor and picked up a rough canvas bag that doubled as Imelda's purse. He fumbled through it, eventually producing a ball-point pen. He used it to scribble something on a cocktail napkin.

"You still interested?" he asked, holding it just out of Ann's reach.

Ann had all but forgotten that that was where this road had begun. Ann stuck out an unsteady hand, swallowing hard, just in time to suppress a sudden eruption of stomach acid.

He handed her the napkin. Ann glanced at it indifferently and then clumsily stuffed it in her purse. There was something else she wanted to ask, but was struggling mightily just to focus her eyes on their faces. Only the very tip of her mind was still visible above the surface, bobbing up and down on the sea of alcohol she'd consumed during the previous six hours. After several deep breaths, Ann managed to string together some sounds that were eerily reminiscent of actual language.

"Then why am I in denial?"

"Trust me," Imelda said, "it'll be the strangest thing. You've opened a gaping hole in your psyche tonight. Tomorrow, maybe the next day, assuming you don't pack it full of nonsense in the mean time, the answer will come to you all by..."

Ann was unconscious before Imelda could finish her thought.

Chapter
6

The world filtered back into Ann's brain slowly, in fits and starts, no hurry. There were clanking dishes somewhere in the distance, unfamiliar voices, and the pungent smell of stale beer. Ann's head rose painfully from the table where it had landed with a thud just three hours earlier. She found a partially soiled napkin on the seat next to hers and wiped up the pool of saliva she'd deposited on the table. She squinted at her watch, but her eyes stubbornly refused to focus on the miniature numbers, and the effort only served to aggravate her splitting headache. She slumped in the chair and closed her eyes, breathing heavily and nearly falling back to sleep.

"Coffee?"

Ann peered up and drew the fuzzy outlines of a waitress, not the same one as the previous night.

"Please," she said, her voice grainy. The girl turned to leave, but Ann stopped her. "What time?"

She gave Ann a snooty once-over. "Quarter to six."

Ann's dizziness and nausea kept her riveted to the chair and quashed her fleeting desire to run out to her car. Instead, she spent the next thirty minutes sipping her coffee, fighting back the bile bubbling up from her liver, and attempting to reconstruct the events of the past several hours. She briefly toyed with the idea of racing home, jumping in the shower, and going to work. But the severity of her condition quickly sank in and argued convincingly for more modest goals. Her breath was still highly flammable and her sickening intoxicated aura would be evident to everyone at the office. She'd work from home, or at least create that illusion by exchanging e-mails between naps and mad dashes for the bathroom.

"Here you go, Ms. Franklin," the waitress said, reading Ann's name off of her AMEX card. "They added a twenty percent gratuity. If you want to gripe about it you can talk to Barry." The waitress indicated a tree stump with overalls behind the bar.

Ann shook her head. "No, that's fine."

It was an impressive tab for only three people. Twenty-four beers, eight chardonnays, and five BLTs. *Eight glasses!!!* With tax and tip it came to $172.62. She folded the receipt and put it in her wallet.

"Don't worry about the coffee," the waitress said. "You earned it."

"Doesn't this place ever close?" Ann asked, suddenly aware of the weirdness of waking up in a bar on a Wednesday morning.

"Yeah, right," she said, and walked away with no further explanation.

Ann downed the last sip of cold coffee, arduously hoisted herself up from the seat, and headed for the door. Her neck and back were both begging to be put out of their misery and she was unsteady on her feet, but she desperately needed to get home before the morning rush began in earnest. Fighting traffic out on the Dulles Toll Road in her condition would be a death defying feat.

The next day, sitting behind her desk at the SST Tower, Ann was still chastising herself for getting so drunk at Fester's. In the wreckage of her brain, little remained of her bold experiment but a smattering of bloody odds and ends strewn all over the laboratory floor. Only that morning, more than twenty-four hours afterward, had she found the cocktail napkin in her purse. She assumed one of them must have stuck it in there when she wasn't looking, but couldn't be sure. *What else did I miss?* On it, in purple ink, was written a name, Leon Sharpe, and a phone number with a Leesburg prefix. She'd been staring at it for more than half an hour, combing through the miscellany of her pickled memories for some clue to its meaning. Part of her wanted to drive back out to Fester's after work that very night, resume the courtroom drama, and ask the stenographer to read back the transcript. But she suspected that plan was nothing but stupid self-indulgence, and she ground her teeth in frustration.

Worse, the previous night while lying in bed, but even more acutely that morning, she had become increasingly aware of a nagging sense that something was missing, something extremely important, as if she'd dropped her wallet in the parking lot or left the garage door open. The more she thought about it, the more tightly it gripped her. But the harder she tried to put a face on it, the more unrecognizable it became. She went through her appointment book twice, retraced her steps over the last several days, and conjured up mental images of everyone she could think of who might be waiting on something she'd forgotten. Nothing. *What the heck is it?* As she checked items off of her list and ruled things out, she expected her apprehension to subside, but instead the uneasy feeling only intensified. By ten that morning, it was all she could think about.

"All better?" Andrea said, appearing in Ann's doorway.

Ann looked up from the napkin in front of her and furrowed her brow as if she didn't recognize her long-time colleague.

Andrea studied her for a moment. "I hope that's your new game face. The barbarians are officially at the gate."

Ann snapped out of her funk and affected a warm smile that Andrea returned.

"You going to Axford's big do?" Andrea asked.

On Monday of that week, Doug Axford, VP of the marketing department and lone champion of Kim McEwen, had announced his retirement, effective at the end of the month. SST's CEO, Harold Gregory, had hastily scheduled Axford's send-off for that afternoon in the Tower's main auditorium. Ann typically welcomed the opportunity such events afforded to rub elbows with the other department heads and keep up with the firm's ever-changing power structure. But on that occasion, she already had enough to worry about.

"I'll stick my head in long enough to demonstrate my concern," Ann said.

"You talk to Kim yet?"

"Let me guess," Ann said, "so sweet and cuddly you just want to give her a big hug."

"Phony as a three-dollar bill."

"That reminds me. Who was that guy from CA you had lunch with last month, Frank O'Something-or-other."

"O'Reilly," Andrea said.

"Right. What's his story? Didn't you say he's less than thrilled with his life over there?"

"Yeah. Really sharp guy, too. We might be able to poach him."

"Give him a call," Ann said. "See if you can get his name in the hat. Last thing we need is another sock puppet for Ms. McEwen."

"If you sign off on him, I'm sure they'll give him a good look."

Ann paused a moment to consider it. "No..." she said. "I can't do that right now. But see if you can talk Jerry out of an endorsement."

Andrea gave her a confounded look.

"I promise," Ann said, shaking her head in disgust, "I'll explain it all soon enough."

"Whatever you say, boss."

"It's not like that, Andrea," Ann said. "Trust me. I'm not shutting you out. If anything, I need your help more than ever right now."

"Can you give me a hint?"

"Let's just say this is not the best time for me to be locking horns with Kim McEwen."

Andrea raised her eyebrows and left them up long enough to let Ann know she'd be held to her promise. But then, like the good soldier she was, she let the subject drop. Ann changed gears too, moving on to the strategy meeting slated for that afternoon. They spent the next half hour going over everything Ann had missed the previous day.

Apparently, Irving Sicherman had made some inroads with the rest of the JOMREV evaluation committee. There was now an official request from the DLA for more conclusive evidence that SST could find the necessary personnel in time for the project start date. Also, Larry Elmore, Ann's lead software developer, was threatening to resign if various and sundry conditions weren't met immediately. Such juvenile tantrums were Larry's standard operating procedure, and meant only that he needed some personal attention from Ann, a little recognition of his brilliance and indispensability. In her experience, computer geeks were notoriously high-maintenance and required a special touch. It wasn't a major inconvenience, but a ridiculous, unprofessional nuisance just the same.

"I think that about covers it," Andrea said, getting up to leave.

"Great," Ann said. "And let me know how it goes with O'Reilly."

Andrea gave Ann another dose of raised eyebrows, renewing her mild irritation at being kept in the dark. *Why did I bring that up again?* Andrea wouldn't have forgotten to call O'Reilly, and there was no need to remind her.

"Will do, boss." She gave Ann a weak salute and disappeared out of the door.

Ann and Andrea were close, but theirs was primarily a working friendship, a military alliance, and drew its strength from the austere doctrine of corporate professionalism. They rarely spent time together outside of the office. They did not babble on and on about their feelings or call one another late at night with tearful domestic crises. Their relationship depended on hierarchy, on the respect owed to superiors, and on the kind of icy leadership that would flash-freeze ordinary camaraderie. To burden Andrea with the sordid details of her affair with Calvin and Kim's blackmail would introduce a truckload of sand into their well-oiled machine. All respect would vaporize in an instant. Just the same, Ann would keep her promise. When it was all behind her, she'd have a plausible story ready for Andrea. No question. But it would be thoroughly shorn of every last, wispy hint of sleaze. In other words, it would be pristinely professional.

For the past week and a half, ever since Kim had dropped her bomb in the elevator lobby, Ann had taken to communicating with her through one of her emissaries, occasionally Andrea but usually Cliff Enright. Ann knew herself well enough to doubt her capacity for restraint if she were compelled to deal with Kim on a daily basis. Thankfully, delegating that responsibility was routine and didn't arouse any suspicions. In her position, Ann was not expected to turn all the knobs and flip all the switches herself. But even so, it gnawed on her, day after day, knowing that Kim McEwen had so much power over her.

With Axford already halfway out of the door, it should have been a golden opportunity to issue Kim her walking papers. One phone call from Ann and she would be out pounding the pavement long before she got the chance to start pouring honey into the ear of Axford's successor. Ann had spent years pining for that day and was all geared up to let loose with the streamers and confetti but instead found herself trying out her new role as Kim's chief advocate. Not only would she be unable to fire her personally, she'd have no choice but to defend her if anyone else tried. How she'd muster up the will to appear credible in such an instance utterly exhausted her powers of imagination. Everyone knew Ann couldn't stand the sight of her. And now, free to bare her knuckles, no one in his right mind would have risked a nickel on Kim's future with SST. It would be the height of farce if, in the face of all that, Ann were seen riding to Kim's rescue.

The most galling part was not knowing exactly what Kim had on her. It could have been anything from highly damning audio or video recordings, to a suggestive e-mail, to something as nebulous as a hunch. There was no way to know, so Ann had to assume the worst. And still tightly in the grip of the persistent feeling that she'd overlooked something, she couldn't help replaying her entire affair with Calvin in minute detail over and over in her mind.

She hated to admit it to herself but, especially in the past month or so, it all having become rather routine, she and Calvin had permitted a certain degree of casual arrogance to seep into their behavior where caution might have been prescribed. That's not to say they didn't observe a protocol, only that they may have gotten a bit too comfortable with it, as if they gradually came to believe that it could, all by itself, substitute for the ongoing exercise of vigilance.

Only work-related topics were discussed over company or government channels, whether e-mail or telephone. Everything private went through personal accounts. They met at restaurants far afield of their offices and, though she could have justified them as business expenses, Ann never charged the meals to her SST card. They always left in separate cars and met up at one of several different hotels, never at either of their homes, and Ann billed the rooms to her personal AMEX as well. Though it was true her credit card bills would have been difficult to explain, Ann never expected to be asked about them. What she spent her own money on was nobody's business.

But even with those safeguards in force, Ann realized, there was ample opportunity to make mistakes. Having been at SST for more than a decade, Kim had contacts in every nook and cranny of the company. If she'd wanted to confirm a hunch it wouldn't have taken much for her to scrounge up some anonymous techie down in the basement willing to scour Ann's electronic traffic. Could Ann plausibly swear beyond any doubt that she and Calvin had never—with four months and hundreds of e-mails to consider—accidentally let their playful banter to spill over into their professional correspondences? Impossible. And with her hunch confirmed, what else might Kim McEwen have found? She could have bugged Ann's office or tailed her after work. Anything was possible. Ann and Calvin had only bothered to devise a scheme to prevent detection, not one to frustrate a committed effort to dig up dirt after they'd been discovered. By that point, it made no difference what had initially tipped their hand. Once uncovered, Ann had to confess, they might as well have phoned the details of their affair into the *Washington Post*.

As promised, Ann made a brief appearance at Doug Axford's farewell. She shook a few hands, ate exactly one shrimp, and bowed her head in dismay over the company's dismal future, absent one of its brightest luminaries. Then she bolted for the pool.

Aside from the obvious health benefits and its power to forestall her body's surrender to the advancing forces of nature, swimming had a cleansing, restorative effect on her. Maybe it was the steady rhythm of her stroke. Possibly it had to do with being completely immersed in the cool, bracing water. She didn't care to analyze it. But the pool was the only place she felt wholly at peace, able to clear her mind, take a step back and allow order to return to her universe. Since the moment she pried her head off the table in Fester's she'd been aching to squeeze in a few laps, and she all but sprinted the last few yards to the locker room.

If more than three other swimmers were in the pool, Ann considered it crowded, and on that day there was only one besides her. Very few people used the pool, and almost no one during lunch. The stark contrast between professional attire and the virtual nudity of swimwear stretched modesty beyond its limits, particularly with intimidating bodies such as Ann's on display. Paunches, saddle-bags, chicken fat, and love handles, wrapped safely in baggy sweat suits, naturally gravitated to the stair climbers, recumbent bikes, and treadmills in the gym. Ann claimed the center lane and dived in with hardly a splash, dolphin-kicking halfway across the pool before coming up for air.

She typically counted her strokes and laps, losing herself in the hypnotic cadence. It was immensely soothing. But not five minutes into her workout she'd completely lost track, her mind unable to let go of the persistent sense that she'd overlooked something critically important. That she couldn't shake it, even in the pool, was iron-clad proof that things were seriously awry. She picked up the pace, hoping to quell her unease with sheer exhaustion. One, two, three, four, breathe, one, two... faster and faster. She felt her arms and legs begin to burn. With one last frenzied burst of energy she yelled into the water. It was no use. *Son of a bitch!* This beast, whatever it was, would have to be fed. Until then, her life would not be her own. *But what does it eat?*

Leon Sharpe was the name on the napkin. Having stared at it all morning, the exact shapes of the letters were etched into her brain. "He's conducting some kind of experiment." "He probably can't help your son." Broken fragments of the conversation echoed through her head. It had been an unbearably degrading experience, and though she chided herself for becoming incapacitated, she was grateful for the excuse it provided for being so inept. Still, it could have been much worse and would likely get that way before it was all said and done. If Leon couldn't help Jeremy, what were his real motives? How much valuable time might she waste if it turned out he was just playing with her? Might Jeremy's ominous warning be prophetic?

For all of her agonizing, all of her premeditation, she knew she was kidding herself. She was out of options. From the instant she realized what it was she'd pulled from her purse, she had no doubt that she'd dial the number, probably as soon as she got home that evening. All of her soul searching was nothing but the veneer of due diligence, a skit she was acting out for herself to make her decision seem less rash. *Ah, to hell with it!*

And with that bleak acknowledgement, she clenched her teeth and went back to counting her strokes.

Chapter
7

"Am I living in denial?" Ann asked as casually as she could.

Dr. Franklin gave her a thoughtful look, setting his fork down on his plate. Ann had hoped to catch him off guard, trick him into answering her question as he would any other off-handed comment. But instead he rested his chin on his interlaced fingers and forced Ann to sit there and wait, his brilliance slowly percolating up to the surface. She bit her tongue.

"I tend to think everyone is living in denial of something," he finally responded. "Did you have something specific in mind?"

They were sitting across from one another in Ann's formal dining room, performing the ritual they had more or less explicitly agreed to soon after Dr. Franklin arrived. Their rationale for coming together in the wake of Gladys Franklin's death was to provide mutual support while, if possible, rekindling any embers of their relationship that might still be smoldering somewhere deep in the ashes. To that end, Dr. Franklin dutifully prepared a sit-down dinner each and every evening and set the enormous ten-person dining table for the two of them. Why he hadn't opted for the intimate breakfast nook off the kitchen, Ann couldn't say.

"I can barely remember the last time I had something specific in mind," she said.

"I hate to say I told you so."

"No you don't."

Dr. Franklin gave her a wry grin. "Maybe you're right."

Other than those daily meals, their paths rarely crossed. Ann's house boasted 6,000 square feet of floor space. The finished basement, where she'd installed her father, was larger by itself than the whole house he'd shared with his wife for more than forty years. It featured a spacious bedroom, full bath, kitchen, an Italian-style wine bar, a library, and an entertainment room complete with a pool table and sixty-inch flat screen. Except to see his daughter, he had no reason to come upstairs, and seemed content to spend his period of mourning reading his books and watching his beloved Orioles on television.

"Ever since that morning," she started, shaking her head, "there's something... I can't put my finger on it. Damn it! I could kill myself for drinking so much!"

"I doubt sobriety would have spared you."

Ann furrowed her brow. "You're going to make me work for this, aren't you?"

"Me?" he said. "Where'd you get the impression I have any power over this?"

"Sobriety wouldn't have spared me?" she repeated. "Come on, Dad! You can't toss out little gems like that and expect me to believe you have nothing to say."

"It doesn't mean as much as you think."

Ann threw her elbows up on the table, cocked her head to one side, and shot him an exasperated look that said, "Okay, so what *does* it mean???"

"Look, Annie," he started, "the Xen are notorious for that sort of thing. It has nothing to do with you personally."

Ann didn't speak, instead fortifying her expression with even more attitude, drumming her fingers on the table and opening her eyes wide.

"Has anyone ever 'put a bug in your ear'?"

Ann furrowed her brow. "I suppose so. Why?"

"Well, the Xen do something similar, though it's more like a bug in your head. They work you over until they find a loose end, some detail you've missed, and then slip it in right under your consciousness. If you bothered to read anything more than that mindless claptrap of Meredith's, you'd know what I'm talking about."

"Why didn't you tell me that before?" Ann asked.

"Why…" he started to answer, but then held up his finger, signaling that he'd be right back, and headed for the library. A few minutes later he returned with four thick volumes in his arms. He dropped them on the table with a heavy thud.

"Now, you tell me, Annie," he said, "which fraction of this mountain would you like to know about?"

She scowled at the pile. The books had exotic, intimidating titles: *Concrete Nihilism, Xen and the Hyper-Ego, Phenomenology of the Naught, Master-Slave Revisited*. It made Ann's head ache just to imagine what might be lurking under those covers.

"You know I can't read this stuff," she said. "Other than you, there might be two dozen people on planet Earth who even know these books exist."

"You'd be surprised," he said. "But even so, I think you see my point."

Ann gave him a hard look and then defiantly picked *Xen and the Hyper-Ego* off the top of the stack and opened it to a page near the end. She cleared her throat as she imagined her father might do, preparing to impart his pearls of wisdom to the class. She then began to read aloud, exaggerating her incredulity:

Though bodys-as function as the penultimate composite facets of the ego, and occupy all of tier n-1, egos-as occupy the analogous tier in the hierarchy of the hyper-ego. Nevertheless, tier n-1 of the hyper-ego (the nth tier of the ego) retains its intrinsic character as unifier, though it is, paradoxically, multiplied indefinitely across the entire tier. This multiplicity of mutually contradictory, but coexistent, unifiers is the essence of the hyper-ego, belying the commonly held belief that it is itself merely another superordinate unifying principle. That belief may be understandable, but it would be more accurate to view the hyper-ego as an enduring moment of discord, an uneasy, but durable détente…

Ann tossed the book back on the table in disgust. "I absolutely refuse to believe that any of this nonsense is useful."

"That's just one theory," Dr. Franklin said. "But I'm not sure why you think you can dismiss it out of hand, particularly without understanding a single word you just read."

"I don't *need* to understand it!" she said. "It's like… like asking me to become a cardiologist to mend a broken heart. I don't want to build a Xen out of spare parts out in the garage. I just want to keep my son, *your* grandson, alive."

"Great! Terrific!" he said. "Then why ask me about it?"

"Because thirty seconds ago you said something that *might* have been useful the other night."

"And I know five thousand other things that might be useful tomorrow," he said, indicating the stack of books, "but unless you already know which ones, I have no idea what to tell you."

Their rancor was intensifying and they both realized as much. Instead of letting it get completely out of hand, they exchanged looks of mild irritation and spent the next several minutes chewing their pork roast, mashed potatoes, and corn in silence, allowing the tension to dissipate.

Ann strongly suspected that her father was not being entirely sincere. He had long taken umbrage with her educational and career choices, once referring to UVA's College of Business as a glorified trade school, only marginally superior to the South Baltimore Cosmetology Institute. Though cut from the same cloth, both passionate and committed to their perspectives, the fact remains that philosophers and MBAs harvest sustenance from different fields.

In the past, his digs had never done more than sharpen the barbed but generally civil dialogue that was commonplace around the Franklin dinner table. But now, with compelling proof of his wisdom staring Ann in the face, he couldn't resist the opportunity to pin her to the mat and gloat for awhile. At first, Ann contemplated using *Xen and the Hyper-Ego* to knock the smug look off of his face. But with a few more minutes to dwell on it, she had to grudgingly admit that he might have a point.

"Have you read these books?" Ann asked.

"Sure," he answered, "but this isn't my forte. To be perfectly honest, my take on the Xen leaves much to be desired."

"Still," Ann persisted, "you said you knew five thousand things that may be useful. Obviously there's no time to explain it all, but you could help me yourself. Would you be willing to do that for me... for Jeremy?"

Dr. Franklin sighed loudly and wagged his head back and forth in resignation. "What do you want me to do, Annie, tag along to see this Leon fellow of yours?"

"Maybe," she said. "I don't know. You're the genius. What do you think?"

"I think the same thing I've thought for the last... I don't know... ten years or more. It can't be done! You'd accomplish as much throwing yourself on the mercy of the Almighty as running around half-cocked in search of some miracle cure. Just because you refuse to listen to me doesn't mean I've changed my opinion."

"So much for your fifty-thousand helpful hints," Ann shot back.

"Five thousand."

"Whatever."

Once again they fell silent and let the pork roast soak up the excess vitriol. Henry ate in his usual deliberate, unruffled manner, serving only to heighten Ann's frustration. She again picked up *Xen and the Hyper-Ego*.

"Chauncy Ellingsworth," she intoned, reading the author's name off the spine. "How posh. Has this guy ever stepped one foot out of the ivory tower?"

"He and his wife raised two Xen children," Dr. Franklin responded. "His son died, but his daughter survived and helped him write that book."

"She helped..." Ann couldn't believe what she was hearing. "Then why hasn't anyone heard of it?"

"Probably for the same reason you haven't. That book

isn't for everyone. Besides, it doesn't have a happy ending."

Ann was suddenly dying of curiosity, but a curiosity tempered by the bleak realization that she couldn't read the cursed thing if her life depended on it. She imagined the first Egyptologist, holding his lantern up to a tomb wall covered in hieroglyphics. No doubt they held the key to the whole Middle Kingdom. But, only an arm's length from the wisdom of the ages, he might as well be blind. Still, she opened the book and read another paragraph to herself. When she was finished she set the book back on the table, almost reverently.

"You're thinking I should have told you about this years ago," Dr. Franklin said.

"It crossed my mind."

"Consider this, Annie," he started. "If it didn't do Chauncy Ellingsworth any good, what good do you think it'd do you?"

"I guess we'll never know."

Dr. Franklin finished the last few bites of his dinner, wiped his mouth, and placed his napkin on the table next to his plate. He looked at his daughter with anticipation on his face, but when she didn't say anything he took the opportunity to clear the table.

Ann was lost in thought, staring at *Xen and the Hyper-Ego*, trying to figure out what, if anything, it meant that such things were entirely outside of her world. Of course, the existence of those books was not a complete surprise to her. She knew there were a few academic works on the Xen. But every time she'd read about them in the mainstream press they'd been dismissed for one reason or another. Too speculative. Too abstract. Too political. She'd always assumed they were merely the idle ruminations of eggheads like her father, no application to reality. Was there any possibility she'd been mistaken?

Something in that question triggered the avalanche. The dam burst, the clouds parted, and the solution to the question that had plagued her for the previous three days came flooding into her mind in successive, powerful waves. It was more emotional than intellectual. In one sense, it was a huge relief. But as the idea took shape, sharpening around the edges, it quickly launched its own raft of issues before her mind. In the clarity of that moment, she recalled with photographic detail the very end of her conversation with Imelda and Stuart. *The answer will come to you all by itself.* Not only that, but she couldn't have stopped it if she'd tried. It seemed to rush into her mind from absolutely nowhere, and didn't vaguely resemble anything to which she would normally have attached the term *thought*. No effort was required; there was no need on her part to engage her brain and actively *think*. And, oddest of all, it didn't feel like her own creation, but rather like a gift from a complete stranger. She had to resist the temptation to say, "Thanks."

Ann looked down to find a bowl of cubed cantaloupe where her pork roast was moments earlier. Dr. Franklin was already half-finished with his bowl. She poked at the melon with her dessert fork.

"You okay? You look like you've seen a ghost."

Words didn't come easily, but she managed with effort to string a few together. "My... I think my problem... I just answered my own question."

"Yeah?" he said. "Refresh my memory. Which question was that?"

"I've spent the last fifteen years convinced I owe Jeremy my life in return for what I did to him," she said, not so much to her father as to the far corner of the dining room.

"Had a change of heart, have you?"

"But they were right... Stuart and Imelda... it doesn't make any sense," she continued. "How could I be guilty of something I couldn't have prevented? Something I didn't even understand?"

"I suppose you can't."

"It was all too easy. Seems impossible, but I've been letting myself off the hook all of these years. I sneaked out the back door when no one was looking. Labbitt Halsey and all the rest never had anything to do with it."

"I'll buy that," Dr. Franklin agreed.

"I've never denied what I did to him," she said. "I'm only too eager to admit it. Hell, let's be honest, I never shut up about it! How could I have ever in a million years believed I was in denial of that?"

"So, what do you think now?"

Ann's mouth had been on autopilot, and she winced at his question, suddenly aware that she was exposing her soft underbelly and confirming everything he'd always preached. Just the same, she felt an overwhelming need to put these strange thoughts into words, afraid they'd vanish back whence they came just as mysteriously as they'd appeared. She took a deep breath and continued.

"I'm so ashamed," she said, her voice cracking. "I can't believe what I've done... how selfish I've been."

"I..." he said, but Ann quickly put up her hand to forestall his commentary.

He obeyed, leaning back in his chair.

"This is unbelievable," she said, shaking her head. "How could something so obvious have escaped me for so long? My guilt never had anything to do with genetic engineering or making Jeremy into the person he is. Not a thing. My heart was in the right place. So was Darryl's, assuming he had a heart. How were we supposed to know? Nobody else did. Fifteen years. Ten million families. Are all of us really condemned to burn in hell for making an honest mistake?"

Dr. Franklin acted as if he were about to add something, but Ann shot him a look to let him know she was just getting warmed up.

"But it was so easy to beat myself up about Labbitt Halsey. It was all in the past. Nothing more could be done about it. How convenient. And, stupid as it sounds, I never shook my conviction that Darryl was more to blame for it than I was. Like that made any difference. Look what I did. Just look at it! I offloaded all of my responsibilities onto a bankrupt company and a dead husband. And, as if that weren't bad enough, I felt *noble* doing it! There I was. The last one standing. The poor harried, single mother, alone in the wilderness, solely responsible for her sick son. What a pathetic martyr I've been!"

Ann had whipped herself into a frenzy and paused a moment to gather her thoughts. Though she sounded as if she'd given it a great deal of consideration, she was talking nearly as fast as she was piecing it together, and was more than a little shocked at what she'd just heard herself say. The silence deepened and Dr. Franklin started fidgeting, not sure if his daughter was done or preparing to launch into another monologue.

"Wow!" he said, unable to remain in limbo any longer. "Maybe I ought to share a few pints with your new friends myself. Who knows what I might learn?"

Ann didn't hear his words, but the sound of his voice was enough to nudge her out of her reverie. She faced him with a grave, unyielding expression, the sort that often presages an act of noble self-sacrifice or follows the stoic acceptance of an unbearable loss. Her next sentence was heavy and portentous, though she couldn't yet draw a face on the monster that awaited her.

"I've forsaken my own son," she began, her voice pinched by the knot in her throat. "Floated through life in complete denial of what he really is. I've done everything a normal mother should, and then some. But I'm *not* a normal mother. I'm a *Xen* mother. I've been living in a fairy tale, utterly useless to him."

She paused a few moments to consider the ramifications of what she'd said, and then continued.

"I may as well have killed him myself."

Chapter
8

Ann was on her way back out to Leesburg to see Leon Sharpe. When she called for directions someone named Liza had answered the phone, and it was with her that Ann scheduled the meeting. Though she suspected the address to which she was driving would most likely have five or six occupants—the paltry XRA stipend all but required they live in groups—she got the odd impression over the phone that Liza and Leon were a typical married couple with jobs, a family, and a dog named Spot. It may have had something to do with Liza's unusually cordial tone, but Ann couldn't put her finger on it and it made her anxious. Lately, everything about the Xen made her anxious.

She tried to focus on her imminent meeting with Leon, but even with a full day separating her from her earth-shaking epiphany, she still felt like a stranger in her own skin. Her only solace was that she had somehow found the strength to admit to herself that she had, in effect, shrouded her son in a veil of normalcy since the day he was born. Everything she'd done for him reflected her now inexplicable hope that he would some-day snap out of it and become a regular kid. Of course she never put it that way to herself; if she had it might have been enough to wake her from her dream world. But looking back on it, not once had she tried to meet him on his turf. *Not once!* Worse, she never even tried to meet him halfway. She'd gone through the motions of being mother of the year, but hadn't bothered to get to know her own son.

And the timing could not have been worse. What if she'd ventured into Fester's five years ago? Ten years ago? That would have given her a realistic opportunity to do something for him. She'd have had time to read her father's inscrutable books, learn how to talk to Jeremy in his own language, and find some common ground on which to forge a genuine relationship. It might have been just enough of a buffer, just enough of a reason to live... *But would I have actually done it?*

She didn't dwell on it but couldn't deny, without the urgency of Jeremy's looming disaster, she wasn't convinced she'd have been willing, way back then, to face her self-deception. She may have been living a lie, but that lie was the source of her strength, her righteousness. Without it, she likely would have hesitated before slitting a throat or two, before stepping over the bodies on her march to the throne. It was painful but true; she thrived in her denial and would not have surrendered it without a fight.

Leon's house was larger than she expected; a two and a half story American Foursquare, circa 1940. But it was suitably dilapidated to convince her she'd found the right address. There were large evergreen bushes against the long front porch that were pruned machete-style, just enough to keep them from taking over and making the house appear unoccupied. Ann walked up the steps, her mind still fumbling with the seemingly infinite array of novel images wrought by her new perspective. Only as she knocked on the door did she become aware of her incongruous mood and what scant thought she'd given to what was about to happen. When no one answered, she knocked again and finally heard someone stirring inside. The door swung open to reveal a girl, no older than Jeremy, whom Ann immediately assumed was Liza. Expressionless, she waited for Ann to speak.

"I'm Ann... Franklin. I think we spoke on the phone. I'm here to see Leon Sharpe."

Liza suddenly lit up, as if Ann were a long lost friend.

"Yes, of course! Ann. Come in. Come in. He's expecting you."

As she entered, her nose was instantly assaulted by the strong, musty smell of old wood and paper, like an ancient library. To the left of the foyer were a man and woman, both in their early twenties, sitting in non-matching recliners, watching television, a half-empty bottle of generic rum on a table between them. They glanced up fuzzily as Ann entered, but didn't introduce themselves or otherwise acknowledge her.

"You'll have to excuse Matt and Sara," Liza started. "They aren't big fans of consciousness anymore, but once you get to know them, they're really wonderful people."

"Nice to meet…" Ann started, but they'd already turned back to their program. She looked at her watch: Saturday, just after eleven in the morning and these two were already drunk. Jeremy's face flashed into her mind, prompting a brief wave of nausea. She followed Liza down a hallway toward the back of the house.

"Did you bring your résumé?"

Ann couldn't imagine why Leon had requested it, but following an understandable period of paranoia she decided there was nothing on it that wasn't already a matter of record with someone. Neither did it reveal anything terribly personal, so what harm could it do? She pulled a folded copy out of her purse and handed it to Liza.

"Perfect. Wait here while I announce you," Liza said, disappearing through a door, closing it behind her, and leaving Ann in the dimly lighted hallway. Ann heard the creak of floorboards overhead, suggesting there were at least five residents. The house was big enough for more than eight. Liza was gone several minutes, long enough for Ann to start fidgeting and doubting the wisdom of being there. After a minute or so, she found the courage to sneak a look at some of the adjacent rooms.

The house was painfully Spartan. There were no rugs to cover the bare wood floors, which were in dire need of refinishing. There were no pictures on the walls, and the light fixtures were nothing more than simple paper shades clipped to bare bulbs. Yet everything was clean and orderly, a tribute to function over fashion. The walls were lined with tightly packed bookshelves. There were heavy, dark curtains, all pulled shut, hanging in front of the windows, and the diffuse light they permitted to pass created the hopeless feel of a nursing home, its residents no longer visited by children or grandchildren, left alone to count the days.

The dining room had a large, heavy wooden table with two long benches in lieu of chairs. Ann envisioned a cloister of monks, vows of silence in force, sitting around the table eating gruel from wooden bowls. The house was a place to wait, bathed in perpetual twilight, where time flowed in no particular direction; a sensory deprivation chamber, at once bleak and soothing. Goosebumps sprang up on Ann's arms and legs and she made her way back down the hall to where Liza had left her.

When the door finally opened, Liza motioned her into the office and directed her to a chair positioned in front of a heavy steel desk—the bland, institutional variety one would expect to find in a police station or IRS processing facility. Liza settled into a couch on the far side of the room and did her best to become invisible. Behind the desk, Leon was poring over Ann's résumé, leaving her to stand there for several moments in limbo. At last, he looked up from the page and rose to his feet.

"Ms. Franklin," he said warmly, extending his hand. "It's a pleasure to meet you. Please, have a seat."

He was a large man, at least six-four, not overweight, but not svelte either, nothing like the emaciated Xen with whom Ann was familiar. He wore a tweed jacket and a shirt buttoned up to the top but with no tie. His handshake was firm and sincere but not calculated to intimidate. His hair was very short, neatly cropped and, overall, his appearance filled Ann with a tremendous swell of vindication. Could Leon Sharpe have passed through the long crushing phase that beset most of the Xen and emerged on the other side with a renewed sense of purpose? She could hardly contain her excitement and was aching to hear what he had to say, but there was a little matter she had to clear up first.

"If you don't mind my asking, how old are you?"

"Not at all," he said. "I'm thirty years old."

Thirty years old! *Incredible!* That made him one of the oldest and rarest Xen in existence, as there had been only a few dozen intrepid customers during Labbitt Halsey Genomics' first year of operation.

"Thank you very much for seeing me," she said, trying to suppress her giddy smile.

"You're more than welcome," he said. "Now, before we get started, there are a few conditions I'd like to go over with you."

"Certainly."

"First, you will tell no one of our meetings. I meet with people on my own terms and according to my own schedule. I don't need you spreading the word and bringing an avalanche of desperate parents to my doorstep. Understood?"

"Absolutely," she said.

"Second, you will pay me the sum of one thousand dollars at the beginning of each week that we continue our arrangement and an additional ten thousand if your son... what's his name?"

"Jeremy."

"Right. And ten thousand more if Jeremy survives the buzz. The first installment is due today before you leave and is not refundable. Moreover, either of us can walk away at any time with no questions asked. Is that acceptable?"

It had never occurred to Ann that money might be involved, and the prospect immediately started her stomach churning. Not that she couldn't afford it; her stock portfolio was performing admirably. She felt queasy because, in her experience, money invariably introduced the antagonistic dynamics of bargaining, horse trading, and potentially, fraud. It tended to undermine the spirit of partnership, sharpen everyone's tongue, and transform a friendly meeting into a belligerent poker game. She had hoped to work *with* Leon, not be his customer.

"Your friends, Stuart and Imelda," Ann started, caution in her voice, "said something about an experiment. You wouldn't be trying to confirm your theory that Xen parents can be squeezed for everything they're worth, would you?"

"I suppose you could call it an experiment," Leon said. "But don't let that put you off. It's experimental only because it's never been tried, not because I have a team of mad scientists, scalpels in hand, ready to dice you up and put you under the microscope."

"You've never done this before?"

"We'll be blazing this trail together, Ms. Franklin," he said.

"Don't misunderstand me," Ann said. "The money isn't terribly important. I'm more concerned about wasting precious time."

Leon looked at her thoughtfully. "Consider this. Every other method ever attempted has failed. That means you have two choices: one, do something that is already known to be useless, or two, try something new that, though unproven, has at least not yet been proven futile. I'm offering option number two with no guarantees."

"You're asking an awful lot for something you admit is unproven and that you can't guarantee," Ann said, immensely proud of herself for coming up with such a quick response.

"Perhaps," he started, "but you have no alternatives. I have no competitors. And for those reasons I'm in the enviable position to charge monopoly prices. Econ 101 cuts both ways."

Leon was right, of course. *He's Xen, for God's sake! Why am I even arguing with him???* Ann had no other options and probably should have felt blessed that he hadn't quoted ten grand a week instead of one.

"What would I be buying?" she asked.

"We'll get into that soon enough. But first, we need to take care of a little paperwork. Routine stuff."

"Paperwork?" Ann puzzled.

"This is a release absolving me of any and all responsibility if things don't turn out as you hope," he said, dropping a stack of stapled papers in front of her and handing her a pen.

"Mind if I read this?"

"By all means. Take your time."

She picked up the contract and began flipping through the pages. It was written in legalese and seemed to repeat the same three or four conditions over and over in slightly different terms. She looked at Leon curiously, trying not to appear suspicious, wondering if something like this would hold up in a real courtroom or if it was a contrivance he'd dreamed up exclusively for her benefit. It gave not a clue about what he was going to do for her, only outlined in generic terms the nature of their business relationship: when payment was due, how the contract could be dissolved, the conditions that constituted breach, and an endless list of clauses to limit his liability. Still, when she was comfortable that it didn't contain any hidden provisions for the immediate transfer of her entire net worth to Leon, she initialed each page in the appropriate spaces, signed the last page on the dotted line, and handed it back to him.

"Now, as I mentioned," he said, "your first payment is due today. A check will suffice."

Ann furrowed her brow. "But I still have no idea what you're selling. This contract, or whatever you call it, reads like an apartment lease."

"I understand your reluctance," he started. "It's a lot of money. And if I were selling you a used car I could easily run down its list of features, the terms of the warranty, its maintenance history, and put your mind at ease. Unfortunately, what I'm offering you is quite different."

"And what *is* that?"

"Think of it this way. When you pick up a novel, do you skip right to the last page?"

"Of course not."

"And don't you try to avoid hearing synopses from people who have already read it?"

"Sure."

"Because the purpose of a novel isn't to find out what happens or get to the end. Its purpose is to take you on a journey."

"I see," she said, a hint of sarcasm. "You're saying I just have to trust you."

"But you don't even have to trust me. I'm not asking for everything up front. You can walk away at any time and you'll only be out the money you've felt comfortable spending to that point. It's really a no-lose proposition."

She sat in silence for several minutes trying to balance her pride and the likelihood of being scammed against the indeterminate value of investing her money and trust in a complete stranger. Her main source of trepidation wasn't the expense, but her inability to judge the merits of his proposal. If only there were other choices, some sort of measuring stick or actuarial table.

"Don't you find it the least bit ghoulish that you charge for this?" Ann said. "I mean, have you ever considered doing it simply because it's the right thing to do?"

"Have you ever suggested that to your doctor?"

"No, but I trust him and I can sue him if he cuts my foot off," she said. "If you screw up I have no recourse. I'll just have to live with it."

"I'll grant you, Ms. Franklin, the law of supply and demand is decidedly not in your favor today. And though I'm happy to debate this with you all afternoon if it makes you feel better, we both already know what you're going to do."

Leon picked up the pen from off of his desk and handed it back to Ann.

"Ugh," she muttered under her breath, exhaling with resignation. "I guess you'll have to answer my questions eventually."

Ann pulled her checkbook out of her purse and began writing. As she did so, she thought she heard Liza giggle softly to herself. But when she looked over she saw her reading a book, and the cause of the laughter, assuming there really was any, suddenly became ambiguous and inconclusive. Uneasily, she finished filling out the check and handed it to Leon. He looked it over and smiled.

"Outstanding! Now that we've got all that unpleasantness behind us, let's talk about you for awhile," he said, putting away Ann's check and picking up her résumé.

"What???" she said, somewhat alarmed. "Don't you want to talk to Jeremy first?"

"Not first. Not ever. I know him better than he knows himself. You're the only variable in this equation."

"But… I thought… I have a job. Are you saying this is going to be all about me?" She squirmed uncomfortably in her chair.

"Don't worry, I'll be gentle," he soothed, but then dived right in. "It says here you worked for International Transit Solutions for only five months. Is that correct?"

"Yes."

"Why so briefly? Were you terminated?"

"No. My supervisor and I didn't see eye to eye."

"In what way?" he probed. "I can't help noticing how attractive you are. Was he making unwanted advances?"

"It was a she. But yes, she was. Are you absolutely sure this is necessary?"

"How interesting," he said, ignoring her question. "Did it ever occur to you to use her attraction as leverage to improve your prospects in the company?"

"No, of course not."

"Not even for a split second?" he challenged. "And you should know, this will be much easier if you're completely honest with me. I thought about writing it into the contract, but I couldn't decide on the wording."

"I don't know. Maybe for a split second, but no more than that. The whole idea makes me sick to my stomach."

"The idea of being with another woman or the idea of

using sex to advance your career?"

"Both," she said haltingly, Calvin popping into her head.

"Hmm," he said, giving her a disapproving look. "I'm going to give you a brief glimpse behind the scenes just this once."

"What scenes? What do you mean?"

"Right now I'm calibrating your sincerity so I'll know how much weight to give your statements in the future," he started. "As it happens, hardly a single person on planet Earth would not, if only subtly, manipulate the sexual attraction of others to his own advantage. That you deny doing so casts serious doubts on either your honesty or your awareness of your own motives. Either way, I can't completely trust you."

"Wait… no…" she said. "That's not true."

"Oh?"

"Fine! You're right! I do it, just like everyone else. I even did it with that dyke at ITS, but not for long. The sight of her made me want to puke. Are you happy now?"

"My happiness isn't the point. You claim to be here on behalf of your son, your own flesh and blood. You've already paid me a thousand dollars, and have committed yourself to paying thousands more. Yet you jeopardize everything just to spare yourself an infinitesimal bit of embarrassment. Does that make any sense to you?"

"I'm sorry," she said. "This is all new to me."

"Don't be sorry. I'm perfectly content to cash your check and send you packing if you insist on lying to me."

"That won't be necessary."

"There's something else you should know," he added.

"What's that?"

"Though I'm sure it's very common, I have no idea exactly how frequently people manipulate one another with sex, and I was prepared to accept your first answer had you insisted on it," he explained. "You can't lie to the Xen, and you should guard against ascribing typical human motives to my questions. The only way to get where you want to go is to answer honestly and leave the rest to me. Is that acceptable?"

"Yes," Ann said, meekly.

He paused a moment as if reading the truth directly off of her forehead, but finally said, "Excellent!" effectively expunging her transgression so they could start afresh.

For the next hour and a half they talked about her employment history or, more to the point, the interpersonal relationships that best summed them up; about her family, culminating with the recent loss of her mother and her father's suffering in its wake; and then about her brief relationship with Darryl and the events leading up to their decision to visit Labbitt Halsey Genomics. At first, some of Leon's questions were awkward if not downright painful. And though her instinct in many cases called for evasiveness or at the very least, modesty, she resisted that urge if for no other reason than to avoid another tongue lashing. But before long, as she warmed up to the inquest, Leon's questions became all but superfluous, and she gladly volunteered all manner of unsolicited biographical detail. It was as if the levee had burst and the immense pressure of her years of practiced circumspection was finally being released.

It was all so natural, she was only dimly aware of the peculiarity of their session, a curious marriage of job interview and psychotherapy. But Leon pulled it off so professionally, as if he'd done it a hundred times over with great success, that she freely let down her guard. There was something comforting in it. Though she couldn't begin to explain where any of it was going, she was at least doing *something*, embarking down a path, undergoing a procedure, moving from A to B. As the conversation deepened, she felt herself surrender to it and put her faith in Leon. At one point, a sensation crept over her that she hadn't felt since she first gave herself to Darryl, and that she had assiduously avoided ever since. She was being swept up, letting herself go. For perhaps only the second time in her adult life, she was relinquishing control. And though a predictable wave of apprehension nearly overtook her, it was quickly replaced by the gentle, soothing hand of fate. By the time she got to her current problems at SST, she didn't think twice about telling him everything.

When she finally stopped talking, Leon looked at her affectionately.

"I think that'll be all for today."

"When do we meet again?" she asked.

"It's your dime. Feel free to come by whenever the spirit moves you."

"Should I call first?"

"If it makes you more comfortable, but don't feel you have to. Liza will show you out." He shook her hand warmly and summoned Liza with a nod.

On their way to the front door, Ann turned to Liza.

"You're so young. It's hard to believe you've already been through the buzz."

"I haven't."

"Really?" Ann said, completely stunned. "Then what are you doing here?"

"I met Leon a year ago and knew this is where I belonged."

"What about your parents?"

"It was obvious I was destroying their marriage. Many times I heard my mother crying behind her bedroom door and my father frantically trying to console her. One day I wrote them a note and disappeared. I think they understood."

"Is Leon helping you too?"

Liza smiled. "You'll understand soon enough." Then she opened the front door and bid Ann good bye.

Chapter
9

… two, three, four, breathe, one…

Against her early concerns that Fester's had permanently put the kibosh on her superhero powers, Ann soon discovered an entirely new font of strength in the truth. And though it was certainly disorienting, even frightening at first, it was easy enough to forgive herself for failing to unravel a mystery that only a Xen, or perhaps a highly trained psychoanalyst could have. Even Queen Ann, Mistress of the Minutia, couldn't beat herself up too badly for overlooking something as arcane as the source of her denial.

A desire, largely unsatisfied, prevailed among certain high-powered types to prove to themselves that the Xen were nothing special, that their alleged genius was more legend than fact. But that had never been Ann's goal. In her admittedly brief experience with these inscrutable people, she had already come to one firm conclusion: it was humanly impossible to match wits with the Xen and in any case, the exercise served no purpose. She was in it for Jeremy and had already stopped taking offense when the Xen argued circles around her. And just as significant, absent the vain compulsion to inflate her own ego, there was something soothing, almost sumptuous, in surrendering herself to Leon Sharpe and letting him take her wherever he might.

It was Wednesday afternoon and Ann was alone in the SST swimming pool, lost in the rhythm of her stroke and smiling inside. On Monday of that week she got official word that

Irving Sicherman would be spending time at the SST Tower to personally assess her ability to properly staff JOMREV. Thankfully, Calvin had tipped her off the previous weekend, told her what was coming and what it really meant. When Sicherman arrived that morning, smoke and mirrors in hand, he tried to create the illusion that his presence reflected concern by the entire committee that SST was falling out of favor, or at least under greater scrutiny, and he was there to right the ship. He was intent on working directly with Ann because, naturally, the gravity of his concerns demanded attention at the highest level. But Calvin told her they had acceded to his demands as much to shut him up as anything else. And his authority, such as it was, extended to nothing beyond the staffing numbers. Ann mirthfully replayed that morning's encounter in her mind.

"Kim McEwen?" Mr. Sicherman said, clearly unimpressed.

"She's our team leader on all human resource matters," Ann explained.

"With all due respect, Ms. Franklin," he said, "I'm not convinced you fully appreciate how important this is to my colleagues. I assumed my presence here would be evidence enough. But let me assure you, if this isn't handled properly, SST is at serious risk of disqualification."

"On the contrary, Mr. Sicherman," Ann said. "I understand perfectly. Ms. McEwen has been with the company for more than ten years and is better acquainted with our recruitment procedures than anyone."

"I had hoped you would handle this personally," he said, "if for no other reason than to demonstrate your commitment to the DLA."

"No, no, no!" Ann said. "I wouldn't dream of wasting your time, or the committee's with mere symbolism. I'm thrilled that you're here! And I want to make certain your knowledge and expertise are used where they can be most valuable."

"I suppose…"

"Besides," she said, "I'm far too busy running between

meetings and what not to be of any use to you. You'd end up spending all of your time waiting for me in the cafeteria."

"This is not exactly..." he said, but Ann had already turned her attention to her computer screen and, though she heard him, acted as if she hadn't.

"My administrative assistant, Mrs. Dumfries, can show you to Kim's cubicle. It's a bit cramped, but I think it'll accommodate another chair." Ann said. "I have a meeting at nine so we're going to have to cut this short."

She ushered him out of her office and left him dumbfounded in the care of her fifty-seven year old, librarianesque secretary.

"Feel free to e-mail me if you have any questions," Ann said, disappearing down the hall, just barely getting around the corner before bursting into laughter.

She imagined the two of them working together: Sicherman, with his haughty arrogance, and Kim, with her hypersensitivity thereto. The gods were smiling on her. Two insufferable, squawking birds, downed with one well-aimed stone. If only the rest of life fell together so perfectly.

Andrea appeared in the locker room, gym bag in hand, as Ann was dressing to return to her office.

"I thought this wasn't a good time for you to be locking horns with Kim," Andrea said.

Ann smiled. "How does she like her new playmate?"

The two exchanged self-satisfied chuckles.

"I had lunch with Frank O'Reilly yesterday."

"And?" Ann asked.

"He's champing at the bit, but I'll be straight with you. I saw his résumé and he's not a slam dunk."

"You talk to Jerry?" Ann asked.

"You know Jerry," Andrea said. "He's old school. Won't give a recommendation unless he knows the guy personally."

"I was afraid of that."

Andrea clearly wanted to say something else, but instead went silent, slipping out of her suit and into her workout gear.

Hers was one of the few bodies at SST that could have stood toe to toe with Ann's out in the pool, but swimming wasn't Andrea's thing. Whereas Ann's hair was naturally well-behaved, Andrea was compelled to spend a good thirty minutes each morning crafting the perfect coif – not a masterpiece she was prepared to sacrifice to the chlorine. Still, she was young and confident and opted for lycra shorts and a matching racer top in place of the ubiquitous sweat suit. There was no sense in letting all of her hard work go to waste. And like any good budding executive, she knew as well as Ann the value of intimidating her colleagues in every possible situation, whether or not it had anything to do with the job. After a minute or two of her silence, Ann had had enough.

"What is it, Andrea?"

"You know what it is," she said. "Even with your help, this guy is not a sure thing. Without your help, you can forget about it. It's as simple as that."

Ann paused a moment, her eyes moving back and forth in their sockets as if she were physically looking at the pros and the cons. Finally she spoke. "To hell with it! Send me his résumé."

The following night Ann was waiting for Calvin at the Capital Grille, sipping her Chardonnay and watching a man, three tables over, frantically eyeing the entrance and checking his watch every thirty seconds. After ten minutes or so, he'd reached a state of such nervous agitation that Ann wouldn't have been surprised to see him spontaneously combust. The tension was so thick, soon Ann was dying to see who it was that could inspire so much consternation.

It had been a long time since Ann bothered herself with her own neurotic punctuality. Much of her life was devoted to customer satisfaction and sales. Arriving on time was a no-brainer, a cheap and easy way to put a smile on the client's face and prime him to dispense another few million of the taxpayers' dollars. That her habit bled over into her personal life couldn't be helped. And besides, during her first semester in college an upperclassman once told her something she'd never forgotten. He said it was impossible for an intelligent beautiful woman to appear awkward or out of place, no matter what, even if she showed up alone to her senior prom or to a couples' retreat. It was a bit of home-spun wisdom she was happy to embrace. And it was also among her primary motivations for keeping her chassis in showroom condition.

Calvin arrived within two minutes of eight o'clock. *How does he do that?* Ann wondered if he waited in the parking lot until the last possible moment before making his entrance. He was in civilian garb and glided over to her table, an irrepressible grin leading the way. His obvious good humor sent a wave of adrenalin through her system and she felt her cheeks flush. Since the day Kim had made her announcement, Ann had been walking on eggshells, tapping her reservoir of lame excuses to keep Calvin at bay. Her plan worked well enough to deflect his suspicions, though two and a half weeks later her hormones were in open revolt and their protest had spilled into the streets.

"Ask me what happened today," he said, hardly able to contain himself.

"Do tell."

Calvin reached into his pocket and slowly produced a small silver leaf.

"Oh wow! Congratulations!" Ann said, affecting a smart salute. "It's about time… *Colonel.*"

"You got that right," he said. "I thought they'd forgotten."

Calvin's promotion to lieutenant colonel was a largely symbolic gesture, akin to a lifetime achievement award. With just over five months until his retirement, there was no military necessity, no time to give him a new command. The real benefit lay in the larger pension checks he would receive each month for the rest of his life. Such twilight promotions were common, though not at all guaranteed, and that Calvin felt honored was perfectly justified. Ann held the insignia in her hand, studying it, trying to share Calvin's excitement at being bumped up a notch on the measly military pay scale. *Might he finally be making eighty-grand a year?* She shuddered at the thought as she handed it back to him.

"That's great, Calvin," she said. "You deserve it."

He carefully positioned his trophy on the table in front of him, not yet willing to stuff it back in his pocket, out of sight.

"So," he finally said, "where on earth have you been? I was beginning to think I'd be a full bird by the time I saw you again."

"Trust me, Calvin," she said, "I've been climbing the walls too. It's just… We're so close. I guess I'm getting paranoid. When this is all over…"

"When it's all over, what? We go back to our lives and reflect on the past few months with great fondness?"

"That's not what I was going to say."

"Then tell me, Ann, what happens when it's all over?"

"I've been dying to see you," she said. "Can't that be enough for now?"

"I suppose it'll have to be, won't it?"

Ann reached across the table and squeezed his hand, looking into his eyes. He returned the pressure of her touch and his face softened.

"I know it's asking a lot," she started, "but I need you to have faith in me. After our last dinner… well, in a way, this is only our second date, Calvin. And I'm glad we're finally talking seriously. I really am. But if you push me too hard…"

"Shhh," he soothed, squeezing her hand even tighter. "You're right, Ann. And I'm sorry. I get carried away sometimes. You're worth the wait."

"Thank you."

They looked up to find the waiter hovering over them.

"Need another minute?" he asked.

They quickly, guiltily, broke their embrace and hastily opened their menus. The waiter gave them a curious look but neither Ann nor Calvin could meet his gaze.

"Yes," Calvin said, flustered, "another minute please."

When the waiter was gone they both breathed a sigh of relief and looked at one another with genuine terror in their eyes.

"Sheesh!" Calvin said, shaking his head. "What a couple of wrecks we are."

"See what I mean? We're so close. Wound so tight. It's dangerous. We can't afford to screw things up now."

"A waiter!" he mused. "A friggin' waiter! And I damn nearly fainted. God, I hate this."

They spent the next several minutes with their noses in their menus, striking somewhat exaggerated poses of nonchalant professionalism. When the waiter returned they gave him their orders and then sat in silence sipping their drinks, Calvin now and then stealing a glance at his shiny new leaf.

"Did you ever go see that Leon character you were telling me about?"

"Last Saturday," she said

"What's the story?" he asked. "Anything useful?"

Ann gathered that Calvin's opinion of her quest wasn't much higher than her father's. He still had a sour taste in his mouth from his brief dealings with the Xen years ago. So she related the highlights of her meeting in a blasé, matter-of-fact tone, playing down her optimism and excitement. She also omitted any mention of the signed contract, surrendering her résumé, and the discussions they'd had about Kim's looming blackmail and her affair with Calvin. Instead, she focused on Leon's argument that she didn't really have any better options and that Jeremy's survival would mark the conclusion of their relationship. Calvin listened intently to every word, and when she was finished he sat for several moments, his brow deeply furrowed in concentration.

"I don't get it," he finally said. "You told him your life story. He won't talk to your son. And you're paying him for that?"

Ann had hoped to avoid the details. The day after she'd

seen Leon, still bubbling over with enthusiasm, she briefly considered regaling her father with the wonderful news. But as she ran the likely conversation over in her head, it immediately registered as the ravings of an Amway zealot trying to convince her family that multilevel marketing was the wave of the future. And as she tried repeatedly to put her exuberance into words, she gradually came to realize that her faith in Leon was just that. Faith. There was no way to communicate her profound sense of confidence and Leon's absolute sincerity, particularly to a skeptic, without sounding like an incorrigible chump. It was enough, she decided, that *she* was a believer. And Leon's point still held. *I don't have any other choice.*

"I don't know how it works," she said. "If I understood a thing about the Xen, I wouldn't need his help in the first place."

"Yeah, maybe. But if he's not dealing directly with *Jeremy*, then the only other possibility is that he intends to mess with *you*."

"Relax, Calvin," she said. "All we did was talk. I'm not going anywhere."

Calvin screwed up his face, his alarm becoming more palpable the longer he thought about it.

"No, Ann. I don't buy it. Remember that Xen kid I told you about? The one I interviewed way back when?"

"I remember."

"It took me years to get over that," he said. "*Years*. And he didn't know me from Adam. I talked to him for maybe forty-five minutes. Now you're throwing yourself into the arms of someone twice his age and giving him your entire biography to work with."

"I'm not a child, Calvin," Ann said, becoming defensive.

"Don't you understand?" he continued, fear in his voice. "These people use words like a sniper uses bullets. You won't even see it coming. Then, bang! And trust me, those wounds take a long time to heal."

"Yeah, you're right," she started, sarcasm dripping from her words. "What could I possibly have been thinking? It'd be much better if I sat back in my easy chair and let Jeremy blow his head off. What a fabulous future I'd have to look forward to then!"

"That's not what I meant," he said. "I'm not suggesting you do nothing, and I appreciate your need to act, rashly if necessary. But, even if it's your last option, jumping in front of a train is still a bad idea."

Ann was shaking with frustration. "A train??? What are you talking about, Calvin? Can you cite one single crime ever committed by the Xen? Just one? What are you so worried about?"

"What do you think I'm worried about," Calvin asked, incredulously, "that Leon Sharpe will club you over the head? I'm sure he'll never lay a finger on you. But if all you care about is physical injuries, when it's all said and done and you're mumbling incoherently in your padded cell, I'll ask the orderly to draw a lipstick smile on your face and you can make believe it's the real thing."

"Ohhh, right," she said, "because naturally I'm far too naïve and weak-minded to protect my poor little self from the big bad Xen."

Calvin just shook his head.

"Has it ever occurred to you," Ann continued, "that *your* experience with the Xen might not apply to *me*?"

The waiter arrived with their salads, stumbling into the middle of the exchange.

"I'm sorry, miss," he said. "The kitchen was out of ranch dressing. The chef thought you might like to try his special bleu cheese recipe."

Ann squinted in disgust. "The chef thought wrong. I hate bleu cheese. Just bring me a plate of sliced tomatoes… and don't put anything on it," she demanded, imperiously shooing him away.

"Yes ma'am," he stammered, scurrying off with his tail between his legs.

Calvin watched the poor schmuck go and then turned

his attention to Ann.

"Geez! Why not just kick him in the nuts?"

Ann groaned loudly and dropped her head into her hands. *This sucks!* Calvin hadn't done enough to shake her faith in Leon, a faith that, like most, was buttressed by equal parts fervor, ignorance, and desperation. But unfortunately, what little remained of her frisky mood was now clutching its rosary beads and receiving the last rites. Even heroic measures would be powerless to resuscitate it. She was still massaging her temples when the waiter returned with her tomatoes, and she didn't acknowledge him as he put the plate in front of her and walked back toward the kitchen. Finally, she lifted her head and gave Calvin a solemn stare.

"I freely admit, I don't know how to juggle all of this," she started in slow, measured tones. "Jeremy, my father, you, me, the DLA. I *want* happy endings all around. Nothing would please me more. But, and you can take this however you want, I only *need* one happy ending. Not that I won't fight like hell for the rest. I will. But I'm prepared to sacrifice everything for my son if it comes to that. How you could respect me otherwise, I have no idea. But if that's too much for you, this is your chance to cut and run."

Calvin's eyes opened wider and wider as he listened. And when she finished he sat in a fog, long enough to make clear he was genuinely mulling it over, not merely pausing for effect. She braced herself for whatever it was he had to say.

"Two things," he began. "First, yes, of course you should do everything you can for your son. And you're right, in spite of my own selfish fears that it'll ruin you, I respect you for it."

"I don't see it as a choice."

"I understand completely," he said. "But, second... how do I say this?" He paused. "You remember our last dinner together, don't you?"

Ann swallowed hard. "Yes."

"At first, all I could think about was what an idiot I was," he said.

"Don't say that," Ann pleaded. "You have no reason to feel…"

"Let me finish," he cut in. "I agonized over it for more than a week. But then I looked at it from a different perspective. We're not twenty-three anymore. We have similar goals, unbelievable sex, and we can talk about anything. I know better than anyone how lousy our timing is, but we're talking about the most important decision of our lives."

He paused to look into Ann's eyes, but she didn't know what to say.

"To make a long story short, the ball is in your court, Ann. I won't wait forever, and there's a limit to how much I can invest in *us* while you're sitting on the fence. I realize this isn't exactly the height of romance, but my offer still stands. Accept it, and I'll happily go down in flames by your side."

"I'm so sorry, Calvin," she said. "I never meant to hurt you."

"I'll get over it," he said. "But I think it's only fair of me to expect some reciprocity before I drink your Kool-Aid."

"Of course," Ann muttered.

The waiter brought their entrees and they ate in silence, trading looks of sorrow one minute, affection the next, then back again. There was so much to absorb, so much compromise, so much sacrifice. But as their meal wore on and their subliminal exchange deepened, it gradually became clear that they would both take the leap and rely on providence to cushion their fall. Ann squeezed Calvin's hand once again with great feeling. *Why can't I say "I love you?"* When they were finished, the waiter returned for their empty plates.

"Can I interest you folks in some dessert this evening?" he said.

Ann gave him a remorseful look. "No, thank you," she said, and then turned to Calvin while still addressing the waiter. "And I'm sorry for being so rotten to you earlier. Tell your chef I appreciated the gesture."

"I'll do that," the waiter said, smiling broadly.

Chapter 10

After the day Ann had just endured, the drive home from the Tower felt like a Papal reprieve. She was so impressed with the slick way in which she'd dealt with Irving Sicherman and Kim McEwen, that it came as a complete shock to learn how well they hit it off. In retrospect, it should have been obvious. Putting her enemies together to work out their battle plan was a stroke of pure idiocy. With only two days behind them and the help of Scott Miller, SST's weasel of an HR director, the two of them had built a powerful case against, not only Ann's personnel strategy, but against JOMREV's entire projected budget. And in an unprecedented demonstration of his membership in the vertebrate subphylum, Jerry delivered the news.

"I hope this isn't as bad as it looks," he said.

"I used the GSA's own numbers, Jerry," Ann responded. "Of course they're crap, but that's what the government expects."

Ann's estimated budget relied on the General Service Administration's labor rate schedules for the various experts who would man the JOMREV project. Technically it was a legitimate strategy; those schedules existed for precisely that purpose. But everyone knew they were notoriously slow to reflect the rapidly changing landscape of the actual labor market. As it happened, the DC area was in the midst of a severe labor shortage and everyone wanted twice what he made the previous year. To make their case, Sicherman and McEwen contacted ten of the individuals Ann had used in SST's proposal as "representative samples," and discovered that nine of them were either not interested at all, or would be only if they could expect far more money than the budget permitted. Since labor costs constituted more than eighty percent of the total, Ann's budget was clearly unrealistic.

"Mr. Sicherman has already reported all of this back to the committee," Jerry said. "It's not going to go away by itself, Ann."

"This is garbage, absolute garbage!" she said. "You know how it works. It's always the same. We use the GSA numbers to win the work and then use the contract's hardship provisions to drive up the price after we've signed on the dotted line. That's the way the government wants it! It's easier to squeeze Congress later, after things have fallen apart, than it is to show up with your hat in your hand asking for a boatload of cash up front."

"I'm not sure what you want me to say. I'm telling you the way it is. How it usually works is beside the point."

"Fine," she growled. "I want proof that Lockheed and Grumman are going to be held to the same ludicrous standards. I want it in writing and I want it reflected in an RFP amendment. Let's see what the Pentagon brass thinks when JOMREV suddenly becomes a half-billion dollar monster before a single line of code has been written."

"Maybe. But you might also want to consider a backup plan," he said. "Even if you get everything you want, Lockheed and Grumman can still low ball it with their own people."

"Yeah, yeah," Ann said, shaking her head. "Damn it!"

"I guess you know what you're doing this weekend."

Ann grumbled something under her breath, waved Jerry out of her office, and then got Andrea on the phone.

"Get everyone together in the war room… Good, I don't want Kim there anyway… Just roll up your sleeves. We've got work to do."

***

Coming in from the garage through the kitchen door, Ann expected to be greeted by the usual silence: Jeremy in his room reading and her father in the basement, lost in the newspaper and nursing his fifth brandy. Instead, she distinctly heard a heated conversation coming from the living room—not acrimonious—but impassioned just the same. She strained her ears as she poured herself a glass of chardonnay, but couldn't decipher enough to ascertain the topic. She was, however, able to identify the participants. She worked her way slowly into the other room, pretending to leaf through the mail that was in a pile near the front door, not wanting to disturb this unprecedented *tête-à-tête* between her father and son.

Dr. Franklin's bottle of brandy was on the coffee table between them, presumably so he wouldn't have to get up and walk to the bar so frequently. She'd noticed that his daily intake had gradually increased, but she didn't know by exactly how much. It was understandable under the circumstances, and she wouldn't dream of scolding him for it. His great loss, the long, lonely days, the unfamiliar surroundings—of course he'd need something to take the edge off. But though it may have made sense, it also served to highlight the fact that her father was now a permanent resident of something akin to purgatory. His life, at least the segment to which others would refer when recalling his memory, was over. And the lingering caricature of Dr. Henry Franklin, cut loose from its moorings and robbed of its anchor, was adrift in the moment and rapidly succumbing to a thoroughgoing sense of cosmic irrelevance. He looked happy just then, talking to Jeremy with childlike enthusiasm, but Ann saw a broken man.

"...that may be true," Jeremy said, "but only in a sterile academic sense. As lived, the self functions as a primordial source of momentum toward an ultimate unity with the world. Any apparent deviation from that teleology is simply a misunderstanding."

"Again," Dr. Franklin started, "I agree with you in principle. But the alternatives needn't necessarily be characterized as deviations, though you may be right that they represent a compromise."

"Which alternative do you have in mind?"

"I'm thinking of the Buddhists, specifically the state of nirvana. In principle, that moment is the realization of the self's goal."

"Yes, but it's the unity of a self and of a world, both completely divested of their particularity. In essence, it's the unity of a naught with a nothing. I'd call that more than a mere compromise."

"But only if the content of the unity is more important than the unity itself, and that's an argument you've yet to prove."

Ann stood quietly and listened for several minutes, trying desperately to make some sense of their exchange, but to no avail. It should have been wonderful to see the two of them locked in intellectual combat, but instead it made her feel like a total stranger. Here were the two most important people in her life, people with whom she'd struggled for years to develop a rapport. And yet, having never gotten to know one another before today, they had more in common with each other than she would ever have with either of them. They both walked freely through a world that would forever be off-limits to her, and it made her feel completely alone.

"What I think you're missing," Jeremy continued, "is that nirvana depends at least partly on an unconscious or perhaps spiritual decision to recast the true function of the self as an illusion. Peeling away the layers of the onion almost certainly works, but in doing so, the endeavor becomes merely the latest instantiation of a tired old universal phenomenon."

"That's exactly my point!" Dr. Franklin almost shouted. "If you acknowledge both the absurdity of establishing a unity between two incompatible substances, but also the desirability of that unity, then why not strip away that which makes them incompatible and take some solace in that 'tired, old universal phenomenon' as you call it?"

"It's like I've been trying to tell you. The Xen aren't devoted to unity for its own sake, as the Buddhists are. Laudable as their goal might be, it requires its pursuers to deny reality. Moreover, nirvana is not a persistent state, and while I have no doubt it gives a tremendous sense of peace while it's in force, once it fades, the genuine complexity of the world returns and demands attention. In a nutshell, the Xen see nirvana as cheating."

"Cheating whom? Or what? For someone committed to the meaninglessness of everything, you certainly hold yourself to ridiculously high standards. I'm willing to concede that the Buddhists ignore reality, but so what? Once you've established its irrelevance, as the Xen have, what is gained by paying it so much heed?"

"Whoever said we paid it heed?" Jeremy said. "The world doesn't present itself as a choice. When I said it *demands* attention, I meant exactly that."

Ann had no idea why, but Jeremy's last comment plunged Dr. Franklin into silent contemplation. His eyes were focused on a distant land somewhere far beyond the fireplace. Jeremy sat quietly and looked intently at his grandfather, his lips working, as if he knew what was under consideration and could lend assistance telepathically. The sudden lull in the conversation was unsettling and Ann's heart started racing. She had no idea what they were discussing but was dying for some sort of closure. After what seemed like forever, her father spoke.

"I think I understand."

Jeremy responded by leaning back in his chair, the tension of the debate seeping out into the cushions. The anticlimax was more than Ann could bear.

"I see you two have met," she said to no one in particular.

"How was your day?" her father asked without any real interest, still deep in thought. Jeremy looked over his shoulder and saw her for the first time.

"Evening, Ann."

She put her hand tenderly on her son's shoulder. She

hadn't seen him so animated in years and, in her eternal optimism, couldn't help wondering if their extraordinary conversation betokened some dramatic turn of events. Her eyes darted back and forth between them, hoping they'd volunteer an explanation and not force her to form a coherent question. Nothing.

"So, are all of mankind's problems now a thing of the past?"

"Nope," Jeremy started, "but as always, they are a thing of beauty."

Dr. Franklin looked up at his grandson with a sly grin of confederacy that inadvertently cast Ann as a clueless bystander. Her heart sank and she felt sick to her stomach.

For reasons she couldn't make explicit to herself, none of this boded well for the weekend. Since Tuesday, she'd been nurturing a fantasy of taking Jeremy into DC to wander through the marble and limestone district. She'd ask dumb questions and Jeremy would tell her all about the various luminaries there immortalized. Superficially, it would be indistinguishable from their traditional zoo visits, but her true aim on this occasion was to begin forging the authentic relationship that her newfound wisdom suggested was necessary. She'd been ignoring the growing meteorological evidence for rain, but now, in light of all this, her fantasy seemed doubly naïve. Still, she had to give it a try.

"Listen, sweetie, I was thinking maybe we'd go into the District tomorrow, take in some of the sights. How do you like that idea?"

"I don't think so, Ann. Why don't you take Henry? He's in serious need of some culture."

"Hey, don't get me into this," Dr. Franklin said. "The Orioles are playing tomorrow and there's a Barcalounger in front of the TV with my name on it."

"Aw, c'mon," she persisted, "it'll be fun. We haven't done anything in weeks."

She said it affably enough, but Jeremy turned on her

with utter revulsion. "Please! For God's sake, Ann! Tell me, how can I disabuse you of the notion that we will someday be a regular, old-fashioned family?"

"I just..."

"I'm not going down there to skip and jump and eat ice cream and spend all afternoon trying to manufacture one single moment that you can use to fuel your delusions. I'm sure this is awful for you, but I am not what you're pining for."

"Wait a minute, Jeremy," Dr. Franklin said. "That's not necessary."

"Ah, to hell with it!" And Jeremy stood up and headed for his cave.

Ann was speechless. Dr. Franklin got up to console her, but she couldn't face him. As far as she was concerned, he was now part of the problem. She turned away from his outstretched hand and walked quickly toward the sanctuary of her master suite.

Walking down the hallway to her room, she expected to throw herself down on her bed and cry like a baby. The last three days of hope had gone up in smoke, and Jeremy had just ruthlessly clarified something that, though usually avoided out of courtesy, in all honesty, hadn't been terribly opaque to begin with. Instead, she closed the door behind her and stood motionless in an anesthetic stupor.

She undressed mechanically and hung her clothes in the appropriate sections of her massive walk-in closet. It was part of her evening ritual and, though not typically the source of any great comfort, on this occasion she became unusually conscious of its familiarity and gratefully immersed herself in the mundane process. After she'd bought her house, one of her first priorities had been to quash, once and for all, the clothing rebellion that had, for as long as she could remember, beset her domestic rule. There would be no more ambiguous piles of laundry composed of once worn, but potentially re-wearable items. Flimsy hangers from the dry cleaner's were discarded immediately and clothes were hung on a set of sturdy wooden hangers that included the necessary clips and protrusions to properly accommodate everything in her wardrobe. Shoes stood at attention on racks that ran the length of two of the closet's four walls underneath the hanging clothes. And, in an act of heresy before the goddess of footwear, when the rack was full, no new shoes could be purchased until an old pair was tossed.

The first ten minutes or so of this escape into order and efficiency was enormously relaxing, almost cathartic, but soon it intruded into her mind that it was nothing but stupid self-indulgence. And then, with hormonal rapidity, her serenity evaporated and transformed into irritation and just as quickly, into anger.

She returned her suit to the "late spring" section and hastily pulled on a pair of denim shorts, a tank top, and a pair of three-inch sandals. Everything in her manner suggested that she was about to run off on some very important mission and there was no time to lose.

She passed Dr. Franklin on her way out of the house and he lifted his head arduously to mumble something at her. Absent Jeremy's intellectual stimulation, the brandy had rushed to fill the void in his brain and he was teetering on the edge of incoherence. Ann couldn't be bothered to stop and decode his slurring, and she barely paused to acknowledge him before grabbing her keys and purse, firing up the BMW, putting the top down, and revving the engine as if preparing to test its quarter-mile prowess.

Route 7 westbound had an unmistakable Friday evening atmosphere. There were teens in their parents' cars, driving fast and erratically, windows open with arms, legs, and heads sticking out into the warm June air, music blaring. She caught a glimpse of two young girls in a back seat clandestinely drinking something from a paper bag, carefully shielding themselves from the watchful eyes of the police. It was electric, and Ann did her best to fit in, turning up her stereo and contributing a hundred watts of Aerosmith to the mix.

Before she realized it, she was approaching Leesburg

and, if anything, was more determined to get into some kind of trouble than she was when she left her house. She pulled into the driveway of Chez Xen, half thinking she might insinuate herself into their Friday night plans and show these deadbeats how to party properly. As she walked up the steps to the porch, she got the feeling the house was empty, except that the front door wasn't completely closed. It was deadly quiet and she peeked in to see if there was any visible activity. Nothing. But before she could knock, she heard a sound that made her blood freeze. A scream. It was the sound of infinite loss, the sort of cry that might issue from the trembling lips of a mother who had just looked on helplessly as the barbarian horde slaughtered her family and burned her home to the ground.

Though all but paralyzed with fear, Ann instinctively pushed the door open, prepared to render assistance, and braced herself to witness the font of so much anguish.

Chapter
11

From the clarity and volume of the cry, Ann guessed that it issued from the first floor, somewhere near the back of the house. She walked through the door haltingly, nearly blurting out the customary "Anyone home?" before proceeding all the way in. There were no lights on and the setting sun, no match for the heavy curtains, managed only to reveal the gross outlines of walls and furniture. In the dim light, Ann caught sight of the dining room table and benches. As before, it was encircled by monks, huddled over their wooden bowls, gloomily pondering whatever imponderables monks typically ponder. She couldn't imagine what made them so serious.

The hall leading to Leon's office was nearly pitch black, but on the opposite side of the dining room a somewhat brighter light glowed around the perimeter of a door she assumed led to the kitchen. She walked on her toes across the rough wood floor, silencing the clop of her heels, as if sneaking up on one of the monks in preparation for clocking him over the head. As she approached the kitchen, she heard a faint, phlegmatic gurgling sound. She strained to identify it and after several moments concluded that it was most likely made by an animal, if not necessarily a human. She stood outside the door, listening, trying to decide if this was the sort of thing she wanted to wade into. Just then there came another bloodcurdling scream and Ann pushed the door open.

The window faced west and the vinyl blinds were half

open, letting in much more light than the curtains in the rest
of the house. The glaring sun was sitting on the horizon and
it took Ann's eyes a moment to adjust. The kitchen faithfully
upheld the theme of functionality over fashion that typified the
other rooms. There were no pictures on the walls or magnetic
doo-dads stuck to the refrigerator. The counters were clear of
debris and the sink was empty, save a dish draining rack. The
linoleum on the floor was clean but old and the edges curled up
slightly in places along the walls.

In the middle of the floor Liza was lying awkwardly,
stretched out and leaning heavily on her left elbow, her head
drooping over a large puddle of vomit. Her long brown hair
was matted and dangling in the noxious fluid and, judging
from her abdominal spasms, the puddle was in imminent risk
of deepening. She was wearing nothing but an oversized, white
tee shirt, soaked with any number of bodily fluids, featuring a
very faded and unidentifiable portrait of someone who had apparently embarked on a 1997 World Tour. Held limply in her
right hand was a chef's knife, not especially long, but in her tiny
hand it looked like a claymore. She didn't immediately notice
that Ann had joined her.

"Liza!" Ann gasped as she reached into her purse for
her Blackberry and started dialing.

Liza looked up with a pained expression, struggling to
place the interloper.

"NO!" she finally said, waving her knife in the general
direction of the phone. Ann hesitated briefly, but obeyed, returning the phone to her bag.

"Are you..." Ann started.

"What the fuck are you doing here??? Go away! This is
not for you!"

"But..."

"NO! I mean it!" And she hoisted herself with great effort into a sitting position, her legs sprawled out in front of her
into the vomit, her weapon poised menacingly.

Ann was shaking violently but still managed to take a

faltering half-step in Liza's direction.

"NO!" Liza screamed and, while in mid-shriek, gripped the claymore with both hands and plunged it through her left calf.

The tip of the knife penetrated the linoleum beneath her leg with a sickening thud and a bright red arterial stream flowed out onto the floor. Ann felt her knees go weak and the blood rush out of her brain. Her left ankle twisted painfully off of her sandal as she fainted. But before falling, she stumbled half-conscious out of the swinging door and her head landed squarely on the corner of one of the dining room benches, knocking her out cold.

It wasn't like an old Western. Ann didn't regain consciousness all at once, rub her head cavalierly and jump to her feet, primed for the next scene. It was a gradual process, and began with a tangle of random images that were more or less tenuously related to her surroundings. By then it was completely dark and she couldn't tell immediately if the instructions her brain was sending her eyelids were being honored. She blinked several times until the strain convinced her that they were, in fact, open.

Obviously, she had passed out at a fraternity party. The rough wood floor vaguely resembled that of the Delta Chi house at UVA, and though she'd never imbibed enough to find herself face down on it, there was a first time for everything. She wondered why no one had picked her up and dumped her on the nearest couch. In the middle of the floor like that, the other drunken partygoers would certainly trip over her. She listened intently for the sounds of merriment, but there was nothing. No music. No laughing or chatter. If the party had broken up, it was likely four or five in the morning and she'd been lying there for hours. A deep feeling of dread enveloped her.

Very slowly she became aware that her body was severely contorted such that, if she had been there for any length of time, long enough to stiffen up, any sudden movement would be extremely painful. Instead, she lay there for several minutes, trying to locate her extremities without moving them. Her waist seemed to be twisted a hundred and eighty degrees and she wondered idly if her back was broken. Gingerly, she wiggled her fingers and got back from them enough evidence to convince her that they were still attached and responsive. Her toes were similarly accommodating.

The dead silence and total darkness made it exasperatingly difficult to get her bearings, like trying to figure out which way is up after having been spun in circles underwater. She moved her neck slightly and discovered that her head was pressed up against something hard, maybe a door jamb or table leg. The movement also triggered an intense throbbing pain, especially keen in her left temporal lobe, to which she instinctively responded by curling into the fetal position and grabbing her head in both hands. That movement in turn, confirmed that she had, in fact, been there awhile, as the pain of straightening her back briefly rivaled that from her head. Tears welled up in her eyes and she began to sob convulsively; understandable, perhaps, but even as she did so it seemed out of all proportion to her circumstances, as if she'd completely lost control of her emotions.

Her blubbering and crying lasted an absurdly long time, and when they finally abated she remained frozen in the fetal position, thoroughly rattled, uncertain how her scrambled brain might respond to even the most innocuous endeavor. After a very long pause, she laboriously rolled herself onto her hands and knees and pushed herself up from the floor. A huge mistake. Immediately, like a storm, her entire body was consumed by the most acute nausea and dizziness she'd ever experienced, and in one colossal spasm she relieved herself of at least everything she'd eaten in the past twelve hours, if not also the better part of her stomach lining. It was an exhausting expulsion, the force of which dragged her back to the floor like a sack of wet sand. It also confirmed her theory that she'd been drinking heavily and was still at the Delta Chi house. Miserable and in excruciating pain, she stared helplessly into the blackness. Disconnected thoughts ran through her mind of being discovered by whichever fraternity brother woke up and staggered downstairs first; of trying to explain her behavior to Julian, or Eric, or whomever she was dating; of crawling to the phone and summoning an ambulance. Gradually, she lost consciousness again and didn't regain it until after dawn.

When Ann came to for the second time, she did so with a considerably greater sense of urgency than she had the previous night. The feeble light streaming in from around the drapes was sufficient to remind her of her location, and she was instantly gripped by the overwhelming conviction that something terrible had happened, though she had no idea what. With great effort, she struggled to her feet, only to discover that her left ankle was unwilling to hold up its end of the bargain and she fell painfully back to her knees. The intense pounding in her head made her dizzy and blurred her vision, but on the second attempt she managed to stand up on her right foot, using the wall for support, and hobble into the kitchen.

She had no explicit memory of the previous night, but strangely wasn't surprised by what she saw, and so assumed she must have somehow been a party to the gruesome scene. Liza was lying exactly where she had been when she stuck the knife through her leg, only now she was on her back, unconscious, and the bloodied knife was off to one side. The bleeding had stopped, but there was a large pool of blood on the floor. Her lips were blue and her left foot was purple.

Ann got down on her hands and knees and leaned her ear over Liza's mouth. *Thank God! She's still breathing.* She grabbed a dish towel that was hanging from the refrigerator door handle and tied it tightly around Liza's wound, then located her purse and once again started to dial 911. But she got only as far as the second digit before she stopped. Something occurred to her, and she turned off her phone and returned it to her purse with stoic resignation. She couldn't believe it at first, but as the idea ricocheted around in her traumatized brain it soon became perfectly obvious. Liza wasn't drunk or sick. *This is her buzz!*

A thousand times– maybe ten thousand– she'd run it over in her mind what she'd do if she happened to be present during Jeremy's buzz– and she had every intention of being present. She'd read countless magazine articles, Dr. Meredith's book, and thought it through in microscopic detail. There was a procedure for this, and that procedure absolutely did not involve calling the police or the paramedics. By all accounts, that was as good as signing their death certificates. No, this had to be handled delicately, respecting the nature of the beast. But everything was so different. Never in her fantasies was Jeremy seriously injured, and never had she been required to perform her role just after suffering major head trauma. She knew she might not get it right, but she also realized she'd have to go through it soon enough anyway.

She looked down at Liza's crumpled figure. As much blood as she'd lost she might be in a coma and already as good as dead. The buzz was an intensely personal, if not always private affair, and Ann was as aware as anyone of the admonition against meddling in it. But in this case there didn't seem to be anything to lose. Without help, Liza would almost certainly die right where she lay, and the conspicuous absence of her housemates suggested they had no intention of intervening. Therefore, there was no additional risk of driving Liza to suicide; the worst had already happened. Also, it could be argued that Liza had only stabbed herself because of Ann's intrusion. If so, Ann owed it to her to get her back on her feet. And finally, if suicide had been Liza's intent all along, she could finish the job later. However she looked at it, there didn't seem to be a downside to helping her.

Liza's only chance of survival was to regain consciousness so she could get some fluids back into her system. Ann pondered the feasibility of dragging Liza up the stairs and into a bathtub, and gingerly put some weight on her bad ankle to see if it was up to the task. It hurt, but it didn't feel broken, at least not like her other ankle had felt when she broke it during gymnastics practice back in high school. She put a bit more pressure on it and the pain didn't get any worse. An x-ray could wait. For now, she'd assume it was only sprained.

Ann started by peeling Liza's fouled tee-shirt off and wiping her down as well as she could with wet paper towels. It wasn't exactly necessary, but the thought of throwing her over her shoulder, covered in bloody vomit was more than Ann could stomach. Thankfully, Liza didn't weigh more than eighty-five pounds and, were it not for Ann's ankle injury and dizziness she could have had her up the stairs and into the tub inside of a minute. As it happened, though, it took more than ten, and she had to stop several times on the way, sometimes from fatigue and other times to reposition the load. When she finally got to the bathroom, she was exhausted and not certain she'd have the strength to complete the task.

The bathtub was a vintage 1940s cast iron sort that stood well above the floor on four iron feet. White enamel was worn away in places to reveal the gray metal beneath, and there were dark rust stains around the drain. Ann turned on the water, not sure if Liza would benefit most from cold water to jolt her back into the world, or warm water to stimulate circulation. She decided either extreme would be too great a shock and settled on tepid. Then she folded a towel and placed it near the edge of the tub to protect her knees from the hard tile floor, enabling her to hoist Liza up and over the lip without having to stand. It was an awkward procedure and she nearly dropped Liza on her head before allowing her body to flop into the water. Again, Ann sat on the floor in exhaustion, her head pounding with every beat of her racing heart. When she was finally done panting, she hung the towel over the back of the tub and tried to position Liza's head on it as comfortably as possible. Not a chance. Liza's lifeless body repeatedly slipped down into the water, and Ann was forced to hold her by the back of the neck to keep her from drowning.

It was more than ninety minutes before Liza began to stir. Only the faint sound of her breath kept Ann going that long, and even then she nearly dozed off a dozen times. The arm she'd been using to prop up Liza's head had stiffened and was numb with pain. Had Liza not come around when she did, Ann would probably have only waited another thirty minutes or so before risking that 911 call.

It was a risk because the Xen had long ago stopped commanding the same level of attention from emergency personnel, whether police or medical, that was expected by everyone else. Such professionals are no-nonsense problem solvers, hero types, and they had, through the years, gradually lost patience with the Xen. There were the repeated, frantic calls to the same address. Round the clock suicide watches. Tense stand-offs. Abusive treatment and a total lack of gratitude from their patients. And, for all of that, none of it had any discernable effect on the outcome. In brief, they were not rewarding targets of salvation and so, with the blessing of the Xen themselves, had been officially and preemptively designated DNR in nearly all circumstances. Ann wasn't simply rationalizing to spare herself the trouble. Liza was almost certainly better off in her untrained hands than in those of a paramedic or doctor who had both the legal and emotional justification to focus on more tractable cases.

Liza's stirring eventually turned to moaning and her eyes slowly opened to slits. She lay in the tub for several minutes, motionless, squinting uncomprehendingly at the ceiling, a stunned expression on her face. Ann put a glass of water up to her lips and she drank reflexively, not yet sufficiently coherent to refuse treatment on principle. When she started shivering, Ann turned on the hot water. Over the next half-hour, Liza gradually regained her color, and a half-hour after that seemed on the verge of speaking. By then, her skin was thoroughly pruned.

"My leg hurts," she said softly. "Help me out of here."

With some effort, Ann managed to get Liza out of the

tub, dried off, and into her bedroom. There, Ann helped her
into a ratty old bathrobe, likely acquired from the Salvation
Army, and got her situated on her bed. There were two twin
beds in the room and between them a wooden crate, turned
endwise, that served as a bedside table. The walls were free of
posters of the latest teen idols. There wasn't a jewelry box on
the plain white chest of drawers. No shelves full of china dolls.
The only evidence of life was a stack of books, probably the last
ones Liza had read, piled on top of the crate.

"Do you mind?" she said, indicating Liza's wound.

Ann took her silence as consent and gently removed the
soaking wet towel from Liza's leg. It could have been worse.
The knife had penetrated the thickest part of Liza's calf muscle,
but parallel to the tibia. As most of the important tubes and
cables also run parallel, Ann guessed that the blade had probably not severed as much as it would have had it gone in per-
pendicularly. And though it would certainly require medical
attention, the bleeding had stopped and her purple foot seemed
to be returning slowly to its normal hue rather than darkening.

"Don't move. I'll be right back," Ann said, and hobbled
off to find a suitable replacement dressing for the wound.

Wandering around the house, she had to fight the urge
to start throwing back curtains and opening windows. It was
a perpetual funeral in there. Dark and stale. She sympathized
with their plight, though without fully understanding it, and
didn't begrudge them their lifestyle if that was the only way
they could cope. But what could possibly be served by exaggerating a hopelessness that was already so starkly depressing
in its own right? She looked under the bathroom sink, not really
believing there would be a stock of bandages and gauze, and
she wasn't surprised to find nothing useful. Ostensibly, she was
looking for another hand-towel, but given the altruistic flavor
of her mission, she felt immune to charges of trespassing, and
exploited the opportunity to rummage through the other bedrooms.

There were three other bedrooms besides Liza's. Two of

them were configured more or less like hers, though the smaller of the two contained bunk beds. The largest room, which Ann assumed belonged to Leon, was somewhat more lavishly appointed than the others and featured a queen size bed, over which hung a huge reproduction of El Greco's, *View of Toledo*, the only departure from bleak utilitarianism anywhere in the house. The picture was so large, at least four feet by five, it seemed to swallow the occupants of the room into its terrifying world. Ann had never seen it before and was so astonished by its presence there that it veritably riveted her feet to the floor.

It depicted a peaceful, unwary town, frozen forever in the moments before its obliteration by monstrous black storm clouds. Ann stood before the painting for several minutes, mesmerized, her eyes tracing the outlines of the buildings against the yawning abyss that loomed behind them. The tension, pulled tautly between two extremes, captured the very instant when life becomes death, innocence becomes guilt, hope becomes doubt, and love becomes apathy. In the context of that house– that grim reminder of fate's iron grip– it was transformed into an open window, a direct portal to the pit of hell. It filled her with emptiness, but she couldn't take her eyes off of it. Only when she felt completely suffused by its awfulness could she tear her eyes away and resume her search.

With the bedrooms behind her, she opened a door in the hallway that she had assumed from the start was a linen closet, but instead found herself in a tiny room, no bigger than a large shower stall. In it was a strange looking impromptu contraption fashioned out of two-by-fours, resembling a cross between an exercise machine and a medieval torture device. It was built to accommodate one person in a reclined, sitting position and had a foot pedal that was connected by a length of twine to the trigger of a twelve gauge shotgun, mounted to the frame with a bolt through its stock. The back wall of the closet was reinforced with several sheets of three-quarter inch plywood that were peppered with dozens of tiny pellet holes and splattered with darkened blood stains. Ann's mouth fell open in shock and her heart stopped in mid-beat. As the cold truth of this instrument of self-annihilation sank in she again felt her knees go weak. But she forced herself to remain conscious, backing quickly away from the monstrosity, her hand over her mouth to suppress either nausea or a reflexive cry of horror. She slammed the door behind her, and back in the relative safety of the hallway, collapsed to the floor and dissolved into tears, shaking uncontrollably in absolute terror.

She couldn't have said exactly how, devastated as she was, but she knew in her heart that the image of that machine had, in an instant, changed her forever. It was one thing to read about the trial of the Xen and wring one's hands over its abstract dreadfulness, but it was quite another to look directly down the barrel of their alienation in all of its morbid splendor. Not only had she been robbed of that comfortable distance in general, but now, if things turned out badly for Jeremy, she would be forced to endure that ghastly image for the rest of life, but with her son in the driver's seat.

The thought was so intolerable she could feel her mind erecting a prophylactic barrier to shield her from its full significance. There are terrible things that must be faced in the harsh light of truth and kept squarely before the mind. The world is often cruel and ugly, and a sane person will not shrink from that fact. But there are other things, darker still, that however great the need for a remedy, are of a sort that threaten to undermine the very structure that is required to address them. And in those exceptional cases, the mind's instinct for self-preservation knows when strategic retreat is the greater part of valor.

More than twenty minutes passed before Ann regained enough composure to focus again on the task at hand. When she did, she quickly found another towel and some safety pins and headed back to Liza's room. There she found Liza laid out on her bed, eyes open but expressionless, staring blankly into the distance. She dressed the wound without a word and then installed herself on the adjacent bed and for awhile at least, tried to maintain her vigil. But it wasn't long before her throbbing head and exhausted body got the best of her. She laid her head down on the pillow and fell into a deep sleep.

Chapter
12

The pain was so extreme as Ann's eyes opened that it felt as if she'd been awakened by a second, even sharper, blow to the head. She buried her face in the pillow and instantly burst into tears. Very strange. She wasn't a crier, never had been. Of course, she'd been assaulted simultaneously on all fronts, and no one could have begrudged her a good cry. But even so, the tears soaking into the pillow right then did not issue from any identifiable emotion or sensation. Despite her condition, they weren't tears of pain, or sadness or, obviously, joy. They gushed forth spontaneously and unaccountably from nowhere, as if her mind and body were no longer communicating. Neither were they adult tears, but rather the convulsive, full-body sobs of a young child who had completely succumbed to whichever hormone happened to seize hold of her. Many minutes passed before they finally let up just as mysteriously as they'd begun, leaving her drenched in sweat from the grueling spasms, head screaming in abject misery. She remained motionless for several more minutes, terrified that the slightest movement would trigger something even worse.

The sun was setting, and as her eyes slowly adjusted, she wondered if, after being gone without a trace for more than twenty-four hours, her family was concerned for her welfare. Unlikely. Dr. Franklin was probably drunk by then and Jeremy... would he even be aware that she was missing? Lying there, blood pounding in her ears, she understood for the first time the appeal of that awful depressing house. What wretched despair, what crushing loneliness hadn't those walls quietly absorbed? Enough, certainly, to make them wise beyond their status as mere inanimate objects. Like an ancient temple that preserves the story of its long-extinct tribe: worn marble steps gracefully recalling the countless hopes and fears that crossed its threshold; an elaborate mosaic celebrating a valiant struggle against their fearsome enemy. The walls didn't judge, but devotedly recorded the sorrows and passions of those they sheltered. Ann felt eerily at home inside them, and it seemed right to let them add her brief chapter to their saga.

When she felt reasonably certain the storm had passed, she slowly rolled her legs off the side of the bed and eased herself up, clutching the bedclothes with both hands for support. Liza was still in her bed, awake, pressing a wooden box roughly ten inches square, tightly against her chest. Her eyes were red and her cheeks were moist. Ann limped over to Liza's side and stroked her shoulder, soothing her. Her body felt hot and feverish. No doubt her leg had become infected.

"Shhh, it's okay now."

Liza turned to face Ann with glassy eyes, then heaved herself up and leaned back against the headboard. She rubbed her eyes and blinked several times before speaking.

Hoarsely, barely audible, she said, "I never expected it to be this bad."

"Is it over?"

No response.

"Can I get you anything?" Ann asked.

Liza gave her a searching look as if only then she'd become aware Ann had been with her through the whole thing.

"Why are you here?"

"I came by to see Leon and found you," Ann said. "What else could I do?"

"I suppose you think I owe you my life." Her voice was unsteady as her body shivered with fever.

"We really need to get you to the hospital."

Liza looked absentmindedly at the towel Ann had wrapped around her calf. The wound wasn't bleeding but a steady ooze of pinkish plasma had soaked into the towel. She started to remove it and winced as she did so.

"Let me help you," Ann said.

It was an ugly gash and red striations snaked away from it, confirming Ann's hunch that it had become infected. It was also beginning to smell. They both stared at it without speaking.

"I heard you out in the hall earlier," Liza finally said, not looking up from her leg. "I guess you met Dr. Remington."

Ann's heart quickened and her stomach flipped over.

"You know," Lisa continued, "it won't be long before your son…"

"Don't!" Ann said, cutting her off. "Please don't."

Ann felt herself rise out of her body and peer down on the scene from up around the ceiling. Under different circumstances she might have cocked her hand back and slapped Liza across the face for making such a cruel observation out loud, but the harsh truth of her words was hard to deny. And in any case, Liza had already suffered more punishment at her own hand than Ann could ever mete out. She relented and forced a weak smile.

"What's this?" Ann asked, indicating the wooden box.

Liza released her grip and Ann carefully took it from her. It had a glass front and the inside displayed five medals embossed with tiny ballerinas: two gold, one silver, and two bronze. Behind them was a photograph of Liza, much younger, standing on the center podium in her tutu, flanked by the second and third place girls, smiling triumphantly.

"You look so happy," Ann said.

Liza nodded gravely and then gazed dreamily off into the distance as if trying to catch sight of a tiny wisp of smoke in the fog.

"Someone died this weekend," she continued, eyes

downcast. "But no one will come to her funeral to pay their respects. Her mother won't shed a single tear at having lost her baby girl so prematurely. She's already as good as forgotten, and even I can hardly remember her."

Ann lowered her head, not able to endure Liza's tortured expression.

"I remember her from when I was still very young, from the time before I started thinking. She was so alive. So full of wonder. She loved to dance."

Liza paused a moment to linger over the sacred photo, drawing her finger across the glass.

"Sometimes I wonder what she'd be like today," she continued. "I think she would have bleached her hair blonde and been a good old-fashioned bimbo, a real Barbie doll. I'm sure she could've pulled it off. All the boys would pine for her, and she'd tease them and string them along, only to push them away at the last second, leaving them devastated and loving her even more. The other girls would be green with envy. What fun I'd have had!"

Ann sat on the edge of the bed and ran her fingers tenderly through Liza's hair, trying to believe that syrupy sentiment alone could placate the beast.

"I can still hear her faint cry echoing deep inside me somewhere. I can't tell you how many times I've laid alone in this bed and strained to hear her voice. I can feel her in the pit of my stomach, way down, pleading to be let out of her cell. But I can't help her. Sometimes I fall asleep to the sound of her tears."

In that unguarded moment Liza was utterly vulnerable, the very picture of innocence. And everything she said hit so close to home, that Ann too found tears running down her cheeks.

"I'm so sorry, Liza. I had no idea."

"I miss her," Liza said bitterly, lips quivering. "I miss her so much." Then, without the slightest warning, she rose up on her haunches, looked to the heavens, and let forth a horrific shriek, so bitter and gut wrenching that Ann half-expected a shower of blood to accompany it. Immediately afterward, Liza smashed her fist through the front of the display case and began violently ripping the box apart, all the while screaming like a lunatic, oblivious to the broken glass, to say nothing of the bloody mess she was making of her hands.

Stunned, Ann reflexively jerked her head away from the flying debris and in the process, lost her already tenuous balance, landing on the floor in a heap. She tried to get to her feet, but the impact of Liza's scream and her subsequent fall left her head swirling so turbulently that all she could manage was to slither across the wood floor, pulling herself along on her elbows, toward the relative safety of the hallway. Worse, still clad in her shorts and tank-top, nothing separated her from the shards of glass that littered her path. Before she made it six feet, she was bleeding profusely. Just as she reached the doorway she collapsed.

Ann's brain was able to form only a hazy, fragmented history of the rest of the evening. It was long afterwards before she pieced it all together and realized that more than five hours elapsed from the time she passed out until she answered the doctor's first question. She vaguely remembered waking up on the floor, a thousand stinging bees all over her body. Terrible pain. Blood on her clothes and face.

Liza hadn't stopped with her cherished ballerina display. All of her belongings were strewn around the room, many of them smashed and broken, her dresser drawers all pulled out and thrown against the walls. Liza herself was unconscious, covered in blood, wedged awkwardly between the bed and the wall. How she did it she had no idea, but Ann crawled down the stairs and located her cell phone. Her next memory was of the paramedic's face as he wheeled her into the emergency room.

At the hospital, in the intermittent spans during which she was able to form semi-coherent sentences, Ann repeated, *ad infinitum*, to every face that appeared over her bed, that Liza's bills would be paid in full and she was to be treated exactly as if she were not Xen. For good measure, she threw in a few ill-considered threats of legal action if her demands were not honored. But though the echo of her entreaties sounded perfectly rational in her own ears, the incongruous reactions Ann got from nurses and doctors all suggested she was either speaking in tongues or dreaming the whole thing.

To say that she'd slept at all during the previous two days would give far too much restorative credit to her numerous periods of unconsciousness. Coupled with her severe concussion and blood loss, Ann was exploring the outer limits of her body's tolerance for abuse. And the result was a woman alternately agitated, catatonic, paranoid, tearful, and any number of other states that had no straightforward relationship to her circumstances.

The next several hours were a tempest of chattering hospital personnel, noisy electronic gadgets, rides up and down in elevators, a terrifying stint in the maw of the MRI machine, and countless stabbing pains attributable to either the insertion of needles or the removal of broken glass. Long gone were the clothes she'd come in with, replaced by drafty hospital gowns that left her feeling exposed and helpless. It was every bit as awful as anything she'd ever imagined, let alone experienced personally. And as the night wore on she gradually retreated farther and farther away, deep into the recesses of her mind, where she could safely watch the torment unfold as if befalling an unfortunate stranger. On one occasion she even prevailed upon God, to whom she'd never before spoken, to take her away right then and spare her the horror that awaited her with the rising sun.

Chapter 13

"There's my Annie," Dr. Franklin said, a tortured smile on his face. "You gave us quite a scare."

"Dad?" Ann said, squinting into the bright fluorescent lights of her recovery room.

"Shhh, relax. The doctor says you shouldn't get all worked up. Your noggin is still pretty tender."

"What day is it?"

"Tuesday," he said.

"May…"

"June fifteenth."

Ann paused to consider it. "What happened to Monday?" she finally asked.

"Congress took a vote, decided we could live without one this week. No one likes Mondays anyway."

Ann struggled with the concept, furrowing her brow, trying to figure out what Congress might have substituted for the gap in the calendar.

"That was a joke, Annie," he explained. "You were out like a light all day. Your brain needed a break. Monday came and went just like it always does."

"Where's Liza?" Ann asked.

Dr. Franklin leaned back in his chair giving Ann a clear line of sight to the bed next to hers. Liza was asleep, an IV dripping into her arm, both hands wrapped in gauze and immobilized by a pair of matching aluminum frames.

"How is she?"

"She's a mess, quite frankly," he answered. "Did you agree to pay for her treatment?"

"I think so."

"The doctor said you went on and on about it when they brought you in," he continued. "Said you wouldn't sit still until she agreed."

"That sounds about right."

"I don't know how to tell you this, but Liza spent ten hours in surgery having her hands reconstructed. I talked to her doctor. They never would have gone to all that trouble for a Xen if you hadn't insisted on it."

"I'm glad they listened," Ann said.

"Yeah?" he said. "You might not be when you hear the rest of it. Her bill is already more than forty grand, and she's going to need all kinds of physical therapy and follow-up care when she finally gets out of here."

"Forty grand?" Ann said, mildly alarmed.

"And if she doesn't stay on top of her therapy, the doctor says her hands will seize up like a pair of lobster claws and all of that surgery will be for nothing."

Ann could feel her blood pressure rising. "I can't... not now, Dad."

"Sorry. You're right. It can wait."

"Is Jeremy okay? Is he with you?" Ann asked. Her heart started racing as she became aware of how long she'd been gone.

"Yes and no," he responded. "Except to eat, he hasn't come out of his room since the night you left."

Ann puzzled at the news.

"Maybe he feels guilty," Dr. Franklin offered.

"Or maybe..."

"Good morning," said a woman from the doorway. She was dressed in scrubs, a stethoscope around her neck, carrying a clipboard. She had a warm smile and exuded the steady, almost god-like confidence of a veteran medical practitioner. "My name is Dr. Bronson. How are we feeling today?"

"I've been better," Ann grumbled.

"Indeed," Dr. Bronson said with a sympathetic chuckle. "You took quite a tumble. But if you're feeling up to it, there are a few things I need to go over with you."

"Of course."

Dr. Franklin relinquished his seat and stood at the foot of the bed so he could hear.

Dr. Bronson explained Ann's injury to her, what they were doing to treat it, as well as Ann's responsibilities over the next week or so to help it heal completely. Ann did her best to assimilate the barrage of complicated medical jargon, but drifted in and out of the conversation. As often as not the doctor addressed herself to Dr. Franklin, whom she perceived would be Ann's primary caregiver over the course of her recovery.

Ann had suffered a grade three concussion complete with a small, but potentially hazardous, subdural hematoma. It was a borderline case and the doctors briefly considered drilling a hole in her skull to relieve the pressure, but instead opted for close observation and corticosteroid drugs to control the swelling. So far, Ann had responded well to the treatment and was out of immediate danger. However, for the next week to ten days, Dr. Bronson prescribed bed rest, no caffeine or alcohol, absolutely nothing stressful, and a mild diuretic to control her blood pressure. Ann's ankle, as she guessed, was only sprained, but would also benefit from the bed rest.

"Just park yourself on the couch, find a quiet place in your mind, and let your father here do the rest," Dr. Bronson said with a smile. Then she handed him a bottle of pills and pointed at the label while she explained the dosing instructions.

So far, so good. But the rest of the news was less heartening. Dr. Bronson handed Ann a brochure entitled *Coping with Post-Concussive Syndrome*, and pointed to a series of graphs and bulleted lists as she talked. It warned of an indeterminate period of mild to moderate cognitive dysfunction including anything from dizziness and headaches to sporadic amnesia, emotional instability, and difficulty thinking clearly. It also stressed that, without proper care, the ruptured vessels between her brain and skull could begin hemorrhaging again, putting pressure back on her brain and, in a worst case scenario, plunge her into a coma or even kill her.

But Ann didn't need a brochure to tell her what she already knew; she wasn't herself anymore. She tried to attribute it to the overall emotional strain of the last few days and her lack of sleep. But as she listened to the sound of Dr. Bronson's voice it became abundantly clear that her brain was sputtering along at considerably less than its usual clip.

Later that afternoon, her father gone, Ann rolled onto her side and looked at Liza, wondering if she was in any condition to talk. She watched her chest slowly rise and fall with each breath. It was relaxing, listening to the rhythmic sounds of her breathing.

"Are you going to stare at me all day?" Liza suddenly said.

"I'm sorry. I was..."

"Was it your idea to book this honeymoon suite?" she asked coldly. "Is this the scene where we exchange tales of our harrowing journey and cement our mutual bond?"

"I..."

"Because if that's what you're thinking, you're crazy. If anything, we have less in common now than we did before, and we didn't have much in common then. I'm Xen. You're normal. If you had the dimmest understanding of what that means, you'd have gotten back in your car last Friday and gone home."

"You don't mean that," Ann said, but without much conviction.

"My parents were idiots too, but at least they had enough sense not to chase after me."

Liza turned her head and gave Ann a malevolent glare. "Do you know who your son's real mother is?"

"Excuse me?" Ann said.

"Her name is Maria Nechaeva. She lives in Moscow. If

she's still alive, she'd be about eighty-five now."

"What???"

"Labbitt Halsey told you the Xen gene was engineered in a lab and based on their extensive research of hundreds of geniuses from around the world. Isn't that right?"

"Yes, they showed us a video that highlighted some of them, their personal histories, achievements, that sort of thing."

"Well, it was all a lie. They got the gene from one person."

"That's ridiculous!" Ann blurted out. "How on earth could you know that?"

"Leon figured it out himself. He realized the technology for that sort of hyper-specific genetic engineering simply didn't exist – still doesn't. The Xen gene has to be a *regulator gene*, one that governs the expression of hundreds, maybe thousands, of other genes, just like the conductor of an orchestra. You'd have to understand the entire human genome *and* the brain to explain how it works. Leon tracked down one of the Labbitt Halsey lab technicians and grilled him until he confessed and told him what they'd really done."

"I don't believe it."

"Leon even got Mom on the phone once," Liza continued. "Obviously she wasn't thrilled at first– the company promised to keep her name confidential– but you know Leon. Before long she loosened up and told him the whole story."

"It's impossible." Ann mumbled.

She was trying not to believe it, but in her heart she knew Liza was telling the truth. She slumped heavily onto the pillow, stunned into silence and lost in thought. It was too much to absorb all at once, especially in her condition. But the broad implications were clear enough. Hadn't Jeremy always felt like an alien to her? And how many times had she herself commented on how little they had in common? As much as she resisted it, she couldn't help acknowledging how easily it explained the awkward feelings she'd always had toward him.

"Remember my dancer?" Liza asked.

"Yes."

"There's someone inside Jeremy, too. You may even have met him a few times. But the person you gave birth to, the stranger who's been living in your house all of these years… that's not *your* son. That's *my* brother."

Chapter
14

"What's all this?" Jerry said, nervously leafing through a document Ann was distributing to the team.

"This," Ann said, addressing all present, "is the only way we're going to win this thing."

Out of the office for an entire week, Ann returned, if not completely healthy, at least rejuvenated, and was steadfastly committed to reestablishing her authority. The previous Friday morning she'd disobeyed Dr. Bronson's orders and peeked at her e-mail. Her intention was only to get caught up, monitor her team's electronic cross-talk, and learn enough to rejoin the cast in more than a supporting role. But not five minutes into her reconnaissance she discovered that not only was JOMREV unraveling fast, but also a way to get the project back on track while simultaneously reinstalling herself at the controls of the train. She briefly considered running into the office right then, but her father would have none of it. And though Ann let his protest tip the scale, her real concern was that the image of herself, limping in on a crutch, her foot wrapped in an ace bandage and sheathed in a nylon boot, lacked the requisite *gravitas* to inspire the troops.

In Ann's absence, Jerry had taken over the project, though Andrea would have been a better choice. It wasn't so much a power grab as a floundering effort to get a grip. For all of his brave talk and words to the contrary, JOMREV was the largest project for which Jerry had ever been personally responsible, and the waves were beginning to lap at his pilings. By then, he had instructions from SST's board of directors to give daily progress reports. He was in constant contact with legal, HR, and accounting, none of which bothered to mask its disgust with "your fiasco," as one of them called it. Irving "Rasputin" Sicherman was slowly boring into Jerry's brain with a series of shrewd and calculated maneuvers, and had—at least to Jerry—transmogrified into the hallowed voice of the DLA. And now this: Queen Ann, raised from the ashes, barking orders, and promising to send his world spinning even farther off its axis.

As they dug deeper into Ann's document their expressions of dismay quickly intensified. Ann had decided against e-mailing it to them because she wanted to get as much mileage as possible out of its shock value. So far, so good. Larry, Kim, and Scott were soon huddled together, frantically whispering their concerns to one another and clearly thrown for a loop. As Jerry read, he seemed to be collapsing from the inside out.

"Holy shit, Ann!" Larry finally said. "Do you... We only have... I mean... Holy shit, Ann!" And he pressed his nose back into the pages.

Ann let them stew for a few more minutes and then carried on in the most authoritative tone she could muster. "I realize this will entail some fairly significant changes to the project, but in view of the increased labor costs, we have no choice but to cut the fat out of the implementation."

"Cut the fat?" Larry began again. "This is a completely new system. It took my team three months to design the old one. How the hell am I supposed to do this in the next nine days?"

"Not only that," Jerry chimed in, "but we've only made it this far in the process because the DLA liked our original proposal. What makes you think they'll accept all of these changes this late in the game?"

"They'll accept it," Ann started, "because we're going to argue that all of these changes will result in a system that is functionally equivalent to the one we've already presented."

Larry and Jerry looked at each other in disbelief.

"Do you really think they'll buy that?" Larry said. "I mean, they're not complete idiots over there."

The crux of Ann's overhaul involved ignoring the DLA's requirement that as many as 1,200 of its staffers be trained on the new JOMREV system, even though many of them would only use it a few times a week. That requirement mandated a very large roll-out, considerable training costs, and a major cultural change in the agency – all of which greatly increased project risk and cost. Instead, Ann was now proposing that SST train approximately seventy-five DLA experts to operate the system, full-time, on everyone else's behalf. It was an ingenious plan, but Larry had a point. With best and final offers due the following Wednesday, it was probably too late to be making such radical changes.

"You're right, Larry," Ann said. "They aren't complete idiots. And that's why we have to do it this way. Let me direct your attention to lines 650 through 812 of your revised spreadsheet." They dutifully flipped to the indicated lines. When they got there, they all knew exactly what she was talking about and their faces dropped with resignation. "Without putting too fine a point on it, we all know that this will cost a lot more than we're telling them. I assume, when you wrote this, you were hoping they wouldn't notice that we left no time for beta testing or QA, no time for training, and no margin for error. Well, you're dreaming. They'll never go for it."

Larry stared at the offending pages for a full minute before speaking, as if an alternative might miraculously present itself. "Of course, you're right, Ann," Larry said, "but it's six of one, half a dozen of the other. Isn't it just as likely that they'll reject your changes? The only difference is that my changes are easy to make, whereas yours will involve killing ourselves until next Tuesday. I don't know about everyone else, but I burned up most of my midnight oil last weekend."

"Yes, there's an equal chance that my suggestions will

be rejected," Ann admitted. "But there's a critical difference. We can defend my changes when they come back to us and demand clarification. Your plan depends on them being asleep at the switch, and that's an unrealistic expectation."

"I don't believe this," Larry grumbled.

As much as they all hated to admit it, it was becoming clear that Ann was right and they would have no choice but to lace up their boots and start marching. It would be a horrendous task, and they were each scanning Ann's hand-out in search of items that pertained specifically to them, trying to calculate how much sleep they might be able to eke out over the next week. In most cases, the results were grim.

"Then if we're all agreed," Ann started, "let's dig in."

The next five hours were spent mapping the broad outlines of the myriad changes they'd all have to make and issuing the team its instructions. No one was happy about it, and there was audible grumbling and several acrimonious exchanges along the way, but everyone accepted Ann's new strategy and seemed willing to take one last bullet for their fearless leader. In view of Ann's still incomplete recovery, it was a remarkable achievement. Though, by the end of it, she was fighting a fairly aggressive case of the shakes and likely would have buckled if it had gone on much longer.

At three o'clock, back in the safety of her office, Ann was exhausted and on the verge of collapse. For the most part she'd gotten her way, though with a few concessions, and she agreed to make the changes to the documents and e-mail them out to the team by the end of the day. Her headache had gradually intensified since that morning and her increasing dizziness was making it next to impossible to focus on her computer screen. The glare of the display was too intense. Hard as she tried, she could only look at it for thirty seconds at a stretch before being overwhelmed by nausea and forced to stop, breathe deeply, and wait for the storm to pass. After two or three such episodes she finally gave up and resigned herself to working with pen and paper. She'd have to ask Andrea to type up her changes and send the e-mail. The florescent lights weren't helping either, so she turned them off in favor of the incandescent lamp she had on her desk. Until then, she had always considered it exclusively decorative, but now it was a godsend.

As she worked, she felt something nagging at the back of her mind. At first she chalked it up to stress, but there seemed to be more to it than that. After more than an hour of toying with her, it suddenly came to her in a flash. She hadn't noticed it during the meeting because she was so focused on the tasks at hand, but obviously it sank into her subconscious. It was Kim! She'd been staring at Ann with an enigmatic look on her face through the whole thing. Ann closed her eyes and struggled to read Kim's expression from memory.

It was a decisive and judgmental look, as if to say, "Do you really think you're going to get away with this?" As she held the image of Kim's face before her mind she became convinced that her reprieve was about to come to an end. All that remained was to brace herself for whatever her nemesis had in mind. It should have scared her half to death. But almost as soon as she realized what was coming, and after an understandable moment of panic, she found herself strangely liberated by the prospect. It had been hanging over her for so long by then that any resolution, however ignominious, was preferable to another day in limbo. With that thought, she shrugged her shoulders and dived back into her work.

By the time Ann pulled the BMW into her garage at seven that evening, there was no doubt that she had overdone it on her first day back. She was shaking with fatigue and able to walk only with great difficulty. What little remained of her consciousness had been exhausted during the harrowing drive home, focused like a laser on the road three feet in front of her car. Her posture and gait were devoted to nothing more than preventing any unnecessary movements of her head. And her left foot, though it hadn't argued too loudly about being wedged into a three-inch pump that morning, had swollen back up and was now angrily demanding its freedom. It looked as if Ann were sneaking up on someone, tip-toeing across broken glass, gripping hand rails and door jambs to steady herself. She wondered if that was how it would feel to die.

In the kitchen she was already winded, compelled to lean heavily against the counter for support while she caught her breath. Her bed seemed miles away and she felt there was a good chance she wouldn't make it farther than the nearest couch before disintegrating. Lately she'd noticed that her brain was ignoring superfluous stimuli. In its current condition there was only so much it could do, and in a way she was grateful for the defense mechanism, its innate ability to screen her from so much extraneous information. But that adaptation had been why she missed Kim's prolonged stare at the meeting, and now, standing there in her kitchen, she only slowly became aware of a conversation in the next room that she would typically have noticed as soon as she walked in the door. Who was in her house? It was a man's voice. Not her father's. Calvin? Had they made plans for that night? She slowly dragged herself into the living room.

"Oh my God!" Calvin said as soon as he saw her, jumping up from the recliner and escorting her to the couch where Dr. Franklin was sitting. "Quick, Henry, give me a hand."

Dr. Franklin leapt up from the couch and helped Calvin get Ann settled in, pulling her shoes off, covering her in a blanket, and gently positioning pillows under her head. It took all of thirty seconds and when they were done they still had the balance of their urgency to expend, and they did so by frenetically running around the house, making tea, discussing the merits of rushing her back to the hospital, and otherwise wringing their hands over their charge. The commotion was infectious and more than Ann could take.

"Please, you're driving me crazy," she begged. "All I need is rest."

Reluctantly they obeyed, and plopped down in unison on the matching recliners, fidgety, and still unsatisfied that they'd done all that was required by the dire situation.

"How's Jeremy?" she asked.

"How's *Jeremy*?" her father repeated. "How are *you*? I've seen cadavers with more color."

"He's right, Ann," Calvin added. "I'm sure it sounds awful, but maybe we ought to give Dr. Bronson a call. What do you say?"

"No, I'll be fine."

Her body had reached a point of exhaustion well beyond mere sleepiness, and it would be some time before it could purge itself of the adrenalin that had fought gallantly all afternoon to keep her upright. In the meantime she had no choice but to endure the gradual dénouement.

"I came over here to chew you out for ignoring me all weekend," Calvin started, feigning irritation, "but here you go again, just like a woman, turning the tables on me."

It took her twice as long as it should have to figure out what he was talking about, but when she finally did she forced a meager smile. Looking at the two of them, her father in one chair and the man who wanted to be her husband in the other, both of them pale with concern, she felt safe for the first time in weeks. A soothing cascade of security and warmth washed over her body as her mind slowly drifted away.

Chapter 15

As the week dragged on, Ann felt increasingly like a star quarterback, the Super Bowl only hours away, afflicted by a sudden case of the flu. Every drop of her soul ached to perform, grind her foe into the turf, and hoist the trophy overhead. She was well aware, even with tremendous effort and not a little luck, such opportunities came about once in a lifetime. To be relegated to the bench, to let the whole team down, all because of something so insipid was inexcusable. No one would believe her. It was the height of cosmic injustice that a run of the mill medical glitch could cast such a dark shadow over her moment in the sun.

On the Tuesday after her re-ascension to the throne, Ann was forced to work out of her house. She'd been so focused the previous day on coaxing her minions back into formation, that she got behind on her anti-inflammatory drugs and was now paying the price. Her clock radio set the tone, awakening her with the impact of a sledge hammer. Bad as that was things only spiraled downward from there. Within two seconds of the alarm, she was in a full sprint for the bathroom, colliding with her open closet door en route. She spent the next ten minutes with her face in the bowl and the thirty after that curled up in a ball, gasping for air, on the cold tile floor. By the time her convulsions relented, she felt certain the dire predictions in Dr. Bronson's brochure were well on their way to materializing.

"And I thought a good night's sleep was all you needed," Dr. Franklin said, on seeing Ann emerge from the stair-well. "Shows what I know."

"Where are my pills?"

"Sit," he ordered, then got up and headed for the kitch-en.

He returned a minute later with a glass of water, a bag of ice, and a yellow capsule. Ann washed down the pill, then stretched out on the couch and put the ice on her forehead.

"They sent Liza home yesterday," he said.

Ann managed a barely perceptible nod, but didn't respond.

"I'm guessing the bill is already in the mail."

He paused, but still nothing.

"Your colonel seems like a solid citizen," he continued. "I didn't know you were seeing anyone—not that it's any of my business. You can imagine my surprise when he called and told me who he was, that you two have been together for almost six months."

"I wasn't sure how serious we were," Ann whispered.

"He's pretty sure, unless I completely misread him. I hope it's okay that I let him put you to bed last night."

It hadn't occurred to her to wonder how she'd gotten from the couch, up the stairs, undressed, and tucked into her bed. But she let her silence allay his concerns.

"Jeremy's been ordering books by the truckload lately," he went on. "I've nearly thrown my back out the last couple of weeks lugging Amazon boxes up to his bedroom. You better give the UPS driver a good tip next Christmas."

From his incessant prodding, Ann guessed that Dr. Franklin was angling for some sort of confrontation, most likely related to the money she was hemorrhaging on her various Xen causes. But she was in no condition to spar with him and instead grunted impatiently as she turned her head away and nestled deeper into the couch. He must have gotten the message, because he was soon lost again in his *Washington Times*.

For the rest of the week, Ann divided her time fairly

evenly between her home office and the SST Tower. Ever vigilant, Dr. Franklin seized any opportunity to stuff one of her pills into her mouth and, though she didn't adhere to much of a schedule, he gradually exhausted the prescription bottle and breathed a sigh of relief when it was finally over. For her part, Ann was compelled to delegate most of her day-to-day responsibilities to Andrea, and also rely on her for reports from the front. Securely in command, at least for the time being, she reluctantly accepted that her convalescence would serve her better in the long run than would micromanaging the best and final offer. Besides, everyone knew what to do and she could keep them on course with only intermittent contact. Her job wasn't the problem. What plagued her more and more as the week drew out was her growing conviction that it was only a matter of time before Kim McEwen dropped the other shoe.

"Hello?"

"Remember that park in Oakton where we used to play tennis?" Calvin's voice was clipped and panicky and he obviously wanted to get off the phone as fast as possible.

"Yes."

"Be there at seven," he said.

"Why there?" she asked nervously.

"We're screwed. Can you be there or not?"

"I'll be there." And the phone went silent.

The Oakton Municipal Park was a generic city park: brown wooden signs with yellow letters, a grassy, wooded area with picnic tables and barbeque pits, two tennis courts, basketball hoops with their nets missing, and a large open field for Frisbee, sunbathing, or company picnics. Ann parked in the gravel lot and sat at one of the shaded tables.

Per usual, she was fifteen minutes early and passed the time by watching a pair of eleven or twelve year old boys play their own unique brand of tennis. Their faces were blood red, dripping with sweat, and the game was clearly a matter of life or death. The object, apparently, was to whack the ball as hard as possible directly at one's opponent, either hitting him squarely in the face or, if that failed, at least forcing him to dive out of the way. Not surprisingly, every fourth or fifth shot sailed over the fifteen-foot chain link fence surrounding the court, prompting a spirited debate about who was most at fault and therefore responsible for retrieving the ball from the woods or parking lot. Absent the ball, points could also be scored by throwing one's racket at the other's head.

Calvin's immaculately restored, black, 1968 Camaro SS pulled into the parking lot at precisely seven o'clock. Ann listened as its eight monster cylinders rumbled and grumbled by, triggering a familiar twinge of ambivalence. She knew how important it was to him, but her ideal of manliness included suits, ties, and stock portfolios, not socket wrenches and timing belts. And she wasn't convinced that Calvin's reference to Ann as "the other woman" was entirely in jest. Neither could she be certain that his reluctance to abandon such a conspicuous vestige of pubescence was consistent with his transition into the elite world of consulting. He gunned the engine before killing it and then made his way to Ann's table.

In place of his usual smooth manner, was a purposeful, military gait. His face was pale and nervous, as if he'd just been worked over by an expert interrogator. *This can't be good.* He sat down across from Ann and looked around in all directions like he suspected they were under surveillance.

Ann had expected Kim to drop her bomb within the relatively safe confines of SST, but apparently that was a miscalculation. For some reason, Ann hadn't considered the value Kim might see in bringing Calvin into the mix. It represented an interim step, a way of shaking things up without toppling the whole house of cards all at once. It raised the stakes and greatly strengthened Kim's position. Ann had to admit, it was very clever and more than she expected from her.

"Looks like your paranoia was right on the mark," he said grimly.

"What did she say?" Ann asked.

"The jig is..." Calvin started, but then stopped short and gave her a stern curious look. "*She*? Who do you think I talked to?"

"I assumed..." she stammered. "Never mind. You were saying?"

"Oh, no you don't. Who's this mysterious *she*?"

Son of a bitch!!! Who had Calvin talked to? "It's not important."

"Like hell it isn't!" he shot back.

Ann exhaled volubly and closed her eyes. "I figured it'd be Kim McEwen," she confessed. "She's been acting weird lately. But I guess I was wrong."

"How lately?" he asked, skepticism in his voice.

"I don't know," she lied. "Maybe three weeks."

Calvin slapped his hands on the table and rolled his head back, looking skyward. "Three whole weeks! Are you kidding me?"

"Give or take," she said. "But it was subtle, Calvin. Little things. I thought it was just my imagination."

Calvin furrowed his brow and stared intently at the table in concentration. Then he finally said, "This doesn't make any sense. Not one damned bit."

"What are you talking about, Calvin?" Ann said, becoming impatient. "Will you please just tell me what happened?"

"Irving Sicherman happened," he said. "Took me aside this morning, told me he has proof of our affair, and now we're going to do exactly what he says or go straight to prison. Is that clear enough for you?"

Ann dropped her head. "What proof?"

"How should I know? What difference does it make? Don't you have any idea who he is? He's the second highest ranking civilian at Fort Belvoir! He doesn't need any proof now that he knows what's going on. All he has to do is snap his fingers and everything we've ever done since grade school will be under subpoena by the federal government. Our private e-mails, phone records, computer hard drives, credit card accounts. Everything!"

Ann was losing patience with his lecture, and when he was done she said coldly, "Correct me if I'm wrong, *Colonel*, but you're as much to blame for this as I am."

"Three weeks, Ann," he said, sarcastically. "Three damned weeks! I would have raised holy hell before sending that SOB to the Tower if you'd told me about Kim. And what on earth were you thinking, putting the two of them together? It's as if you secretly wanted to get caught."

"Enough!" she screamed, looking him straight in the eye, but then catching sight of the two boys, now staring slack-jawed at the two of them. "Can I help you with something?"

The boys nervously turned away from Ann and tried to get back to their tennis match, but Ann had stolen their thunder. Within five minutes they were on their bikes and headed for the exit. As they rode by, one of them turned to Ann and yelled, "Hey lady! Screw you!" They both laughed hysterically and accelerated out of the park. Calvin picked up a stick and threw it in the general direction of their retreat, but it was more symbolic than retaliatory.

Silent minutes slipped by as the couple averted their eyes from the carnage of their first real fight. Calvin found another stick and was absentmindedly breaking off small segments, practicing his free throw technique with a nearby barbeque pit. Ann was staring blankly at the now empty tennis court, sitting helplessly as the bile of her outburst slowly seeped out of her pores. Predictably, the fury of their exchange almost immediately started her eyes pounding, her head spinning in pain, and it wasn't long before she doubted her ability to drive safely.

"What do you want to do?" Ann finally said.

Calvin brushed off his hands and slowly turned to face her. "I know you don't respect me…" he started, a note of resignation in his voice, "You think I'm a dumb soldier. And maybe you're right."

"That's not true."

"You'd have told me about Kim McEwen," he continued, "asked for my advice, if you really considered me an equal and wanted me in your life."

"It's like I said. I wasn't sure," Ann said. "You're blowing it out of proportion."

"Don't sweat it, Ann. You're entitled to your opinion," he said, "but so am I. And in my opinion, you're lying to me. It kills me to say this, but I don't think I trust you anymore. And that's going to make all of this a lot more difficult."

Ann bowed her head and barely managed to suppress an episode of theatrical, post-concussive blubbering. Though successful, the effort nearly caused her to faint and she was unable to respond to his charge.

"I've been playing it over and over in my head for the past fifteen minutes," he continued. "And it doesn't add up. I saw it in your eyes when you tried to steer me away from Kim. You're hiding something. Tell me I'm wrong."

"You're not wrong," she said, hoarsely, crumbling under the weight of her lie.

Calvin looked her straight in the face and raised his eyebrows in anticipation.

Ann told the brief story of Kim's threat, more than a month earlier, in the elevator lobby. She added that Kim hadn't made any explicit demands or done more than shoot Ann the occasional snotty look ever since.

"I thought all she wanted me to do was protect her stupid job," Ann said. "And I was happy to do it. Small price to pay. I had no idea she'd take it this far."

Calvin took it all in, but once again he pinched his brow in confusion. "This still doesn't make any sense. Are you sure that's it?"

"I think so," Ann confirmed. "Why?"

"Because Irving never said anything about McEwen. I didn't get a name or anything, but I'm sure he said 'he' and 'his' whenever he referred to his confidant. He was definitely talking about a man."

"Who?" Ann asked, but then her heart started racing and she looked nervously away from Calvin.

"Search me."

He resumed scowling at the table, wheels spinning in his head. A good two minutes passed before the color drained from his cheeks and he looked up at Ann, barely able to make eye contact, absolute terror on his face.

"You... didn't mention any of this to your Xen buddy did you?" he asked, his voice cracking. "Please tell me you didn't."

"I..." she said. "Why would he care?"

"Oh my God!" Calvin gasped, clutching his head in his hands. "You did, didn't you? Oh my God! Oh my God!" He repeated it at least ten more times, the last few of which he augmented by banging his head on the table.

Ann reached across to put her hand on his shoulder, but as soon as he felt her touch he angrily moved away. His eyes were wild and Ann could see his jaw muscles pulsing as he ground his teeth.

"Calvin, I..." she started

"Quiet!" he growled. "Why even ask what I think of the Xen if you're going to turn around and do something like this? Why even ask???"

"You have no idea what you're talking about. No proof at all," she shot back. "I didn't give Leon any names, and he has no reason in the world to get involved. You're jumping to conclusions! Think about what you're saying!"

"And you think I'm naïve," he said. "Sicherman is not a recluse. If you told your pal anything about the project, he could easily find his name on the Internet. And as for having 'no reason in the world,' I don't care how smart you think you are, you wouldn't understand a thing about his reasons for anything even if he tried to explain them to you!"

"And you think you would?"

"Not a word!" he yelled. "But that's exactly my point!"

"Stop!" she pleaded. "There's another possibility."

"Like what?"

"I came into this conversation thinking it was Kim," she started. "Now you think it's Leon. But it's just as likely it's someone else entirely. Someone from Lockheed or Grumman or the DLA. Someone who saw us at Sam & Harry's or the Courtyard or who knows where."

Calvin went limp as he listened. "This sucks."

More silence. More wracking of brains. Calvin made a three-pointer into one of the more distant barbeque pits. Now and then Ann slapped at the mosquitoes buzzing in her ears. With the departure of a flabby middle-aged couple on a loud motorcycle, only Ann's BMW and Calvin's Camaro remained in the parking lot.

"I need time to think," he said, abruptly standing to leave. "I'll call you in a few days."

"Calvin?" she said, stopping him. "I… I'm sorry."

He gave her a gloomy smile and continued to his car. When he was gone, Ann was finally free to release the theatrical sob she'd been bottling up. By then, however, she had no trouble identifying the cause.

Chapter
16

Ann had tossed and turned all night, alternately shivering then sweating, and as she drove toward Leesburg she was in a foul mood, cranky and irritable. Over the years, as her mental picture of Jeremy's buzz gradually took form, never once had she thought to cloud the image with the veritable tsunami of extraneous issues that plagued her right then: her mother's death; Kim's, and now Sicherman's, blackmail; the JOMREV mess; Calvin tugging her heart in six different directions; and, on top of it all, chronic, debilitating headaches. She'd always planned to take a week or so off, longer if necessary, and devote herself exclusively to her son. But lately, running hither and yon, putting out fires and performing triage on the survivors, she'd be lucky if she didn't miss the whole thing, one day dragging herself out of her car to find Jeremy hanging from the ceiling or slashed up and down, marinating in his own blood.

Yet another unpleasant fact she'd always chosen to ignore was the suddenly palpable possibility that Jeremy's buzz would be every bit as violent and horrific as Liza's. The literature was rife with such examples, and though the Xen usually committed more or less 'traditional' suicides, there was no shortage of gruesome, gut wrenching accounts that no doubt left any hapless witnesses scarred for life. Until then, Ann had never been able to make them real to herself. Jeremy was so docile, so weak and frail. She let herself believe that his transformation would be more a spiritual, almost touchy-feely event than a grisly, chaotic bloodbath. But faced with her vivid memories of flying glass, cutlery, that tiny mangled body, and the crazed, inhuman look in Liza's eyes, Ann's quaint little narrative took on the farcical naiveté of a children's book. If Jeremy got it into his head to go completely off the rails, she'd never have the strength to prevent him from doing whatever he wanted.

As she walked up the steps to the porch, she half expected Liza to answer the door, but as it opened she realized how silly that was. Her hands still wrapped in plaster casts, Liza couldn't have gripped the knob.

"I'm here..." she started.

"I know why you're here," Steve grumbled. He was thickly built, in his early twenties, and sported an expression of supreme contempt. "Sit over there," he said gruffly, indicating the dining room bench onto which Ann's head had slammed almost exactly two weeks earlier. "I'll tell the professor his lab rat is here."

"Sorry?" she said, but he was already halfway down the hall. *Lab rat?*

Ann took a seat next to one of the monks that materialized as soon as she walked into the room, and that her imagination would apparently resurrect on every visit. Their expressions were indecipherable, not exactly blank, but too blunted to read under the shadows of their hoods. As she watched them eat, she felt more compassion for their solemnity than she had before. Perhaps the monastery was not merely the adult analog of a child hiding under the covers. When the sky turns to lead and the earth begins to boil under one's feet, it may be the only rational choice.

She sat in the gloom and within a minute or so started catching bits and pieces of an increasingly contentious exchange coming from Leon's office. The voices were muffled by the door and she couldn't tell who was saying what.

"... waste of time... I didn't ask... god damned charity... not your house, you bastard... Vera's pissed... some fucking money... get the hell out, Steve..."

The door flew open and heavy steps approached the dining room. Ann was petrified.

Steve stopped in the entrance to the hallway, crossed his arms, and glowered at Ann. He looked her up and down, appraising her as he would a side of beef, wholly incapable of even pretending she was a human being. Her heart was racing and she averted her eyes demurely.

"Nice rack," he finally offered, his eyes still riveted directly on her. "Figure that'll soften up the professor, do you?"

Ann looked nervously at her chest. She was wearing a tight, purple tank-top, her standard uniform in the summer. Nothing unusual. Though it was true, that morning she had considered wearing something looser, less flattering, but...

"Steve!" Leon bellowed from his office.

Steve tilted his head slightly to acknowledge Leon's threat, but then turned back to Ann, squinting, a malevolent grin on his face. She'd never before been in the presence of an overtly antagonistic Xen and couldn't have predicted how frightened, how paralyzed, she'd feel. She desperately wanted to make a stand, let him know that she was not a legitimate target of such undiluted scorn. But she couldn't force a single word through her lips, even as his stare reduced her to a pathetic sniveling animal.

Steve walked right up to her and squatted so he could face her eye to eye. Then he put his hand on her knee. Ann instinctively recoiled from his touch and pushed his hand away. But when he put it right back, she couldn't bring herself to escalate the confrontation, instead sitting frozen, rifling through her mind for a means to extricate herself without setting him off.

"Shhh," he soothed, kneading her skin with his fingers. "I'm not usually into bestiality. But if Leon's little science project works, maybe we'll talk. Once you've had a Xen, you'll..."

"God damn it, Steve!" Leon growled, bursting into the room and knocking Steve off his feet. "Get the hell away from her!"

On the floor, leaning back on his elbows, Steve looked

up at Leon with a playful grin. "Aw, c'mon, professor. You can have her empty head. Can't I have the rest?"

Ann got to her feet and looked down at Steve with revulsion. Leon's appearance had suddenly lent her the strength to retaliate. "Go to hell, mutant!"

At that, both Leon and Steve raised their eyebrows in unison and looked at Ann. Calling the Xen *mutants* was the height of political incorrectness. Ann immediately started backpedaling.

"I..." she stammered. "That's not what I meant. I just... he was insulting me. It just came out. I'm so sorry."

Steve stood up and straightened his clothes, brushing off his jeans. "Maybe you found a contender after all," he said to Leon. He then gave Ann a lascivious wink before disappearing up the stairs.

"Come on," Leon said, motioning Ann in the direction of his office.

In the five minutes she'd known him, Ann already thoroughly despised Steve. Never in her life, even at Fester's, had she felt so low, so despicable. The episode left her shaky and unsettled. Her mixed up emotions were swirling and she had to fight to keep them from bubbling over in some mawkish display. She breathed heavily, audibly, trying to relax. Leon looked back when he heard her.

"You don't have to worry about Steve," he said.

"I will anyway."

"Suit yourself."

Leon's office had been reconfigured since her first visit. Gone were the metal desk and the couch on which Liza sat. Instead, the room was empty except for two chairs, facing one another across a wooden table roughly two feet by three. On it was a manila folder, a digital recorder, and a pen. Ann looked around, half-expecting to find a newly installed one-way mirror.

"What's all this about?" she asked.

"I haven't seen you in three weeks," he started. "I hate

to do this, but if you're only able to devote two days a month to this, we need to accelerate the process."

"You know why I didn't come back sooner."

"Yes," he said, "but the reasons don't really matter, do they? You might have a dozen more next week. Please, have a seat."

Leon sat down across from her and turned on the recorder. "Interview number two. Subject: Ann Franklin. Date: June twenty-six." Then he opened the folder.

"I believe this belongs to you," he said, handing her a sizable stack of papers across the top of which read, *Loudoun County General Hospital*. The pages itemized in great detail every drug, diagnostic test, consultation, procedure, and piece of equipment used in Liza's treatment. To the right of each line was a large number and on the last page was a huge number: *$66,911.20*. Ann felt faint.

"Yes... thank you," she rasped. "How is she?"

"She can't eat, use the toilet, or bathe herself," he said. "Vera is doing the best she can with her, but... Well, to be perfectly honest, it's obvious to all of us that Liza never would have survived without your interference."

"Then I'm glad I was here," Ann said.

"Are you?"

"Of course I am," she said.

"I realize you have a very selective memory. Typical of a normal," he started. "But do you remember reading in Meredith's book what happens to the Xen when they're prevented from doing whatever it is they're hell-bent on doing? Think real hard. I'm sure it'll come to you."

Ann paused a moment, but not because she didn't know the answer. "I remember," she said morosely. "He said they'll go through with it as soon as they get the opportunity."

"Either one of Liza's injuries could have killed her. And both of them together certainly would have. She committed suicide, Ann. Pure and simple. Even if that's not what it looked like to you."

"I couldn't just leave her like that," Ann said.

"Leave her like what? She hadn't done anything to herself before you stumbled in."

"She was holding a knife!"

"And maybe she would have held it all night! During my buzz I sat for fifteen straight hours on the edge of a cliff up in the Blue Ridge Mountains. But for some reason I didn't jump and, thank God, there weren't any humanitarians like you around to push me off."

"Push you off?" Ann said, incensed. "You make it sound like I stabbed her myself."

"Didn't she ask you to leave as soon as you opened the door?"

"That's not fair," Ann said.

"And aren't you well aware of the proscription against interfering?"

"Look, Leon! You told me I could come over here, no appointment, whenever I wanted," Ann said, her face flushed with irritation. "If it was so damned important that no one be here, why didn't you warn me? Give me a call? Send me an e-mail? Hell, you could have posted a sign on the door: *Buzz in Progress. Run for your life!*"

"I also could have nailed the windows shut, built an electric fence around the yard, and posted armed guards at the doors."

"Yes!" Ann said. "You could have!"

"Sure," he agreed. "Maybe next time I will. And now that we've gone over everything *I* could have done, I'd like to get back to what *you* could have done."

"Sorry?"

"Deflecting the blame onto me doesn't change the fact that all you had to do was walk away."

"I already told you," she said. "I couldn't do that."

"But if I'd posted a sign you could have? What if we post one on Jeremy's door? Will you leave him alone too?"

"I..." Ann stammered.

"Let me put it another way," he said. "Why are you here? Why do you drive all the way out here, spend your hard-earned money to hear me talk, if you're not going to listen to a single thing I say?"

"I have to do what I think is right," she said. "What more can you ask of me?"

"If you already think you know what's right, what do you hope to learn from me? Isn't your presence here an admission that you *don't* know what's right?"

Their conversation had been heated right from the start, but now it was becoming more Xen-like and Ann's head was beginning to ache. Of course Leon was right, the only reason she was there was because she had no idea what she was doing. And though he could have made it more difficult for Ann to enter the house, once she'd heard Liza's scream, no mere sign on the door would've stopped her. Tacking one to Jeremy's door would be a complete waste of time.

"Is that all I'm paying you for?" she asked. "To convince me to do absolutely nothing?"

"If we accomplish that much, it'll be money well spent. But to answer your question, no, that's not all you're paying me for. Like I said at our first meeting, I'm trying something new with you."

"But you can't tell me what that is," she said. "Isn't that right?"

"I guess you do listen after all."

Ann smiled gloomily and let her eyes fall on the hospital bill on the table in front of her. Before she realized what she was doing, she found herself juggling accounts in her head, selling her underperforming issues and exercising some of her SST stock options. There would be less money allocated to grave contingencies such as losing her job after a failure to win JOM-REV, hiring a lawyer if it came to that, and caring for Jeremy, should his buzz, like Liza's, land him in the hospital. Ann could afford it, but one more unforeseen catastrophe and things could get tight.

"While we're on the subject of money..." Leon said, pulling another sheet of paper out of the folder and putting it in front of Ann. It was an invoice for two thousand dollars.

"You've got to be kidding me," Ann said.

It had been her understanding that Leon would be paid on something like a per-visit basis, as-needed. But he directed her to the clause in the contract she'd signed that stated, more or less clearly, that payments were to be *continuous until such time as one or both parties opt to terminate the relationship.*

Ann stared at the clause, not really reading it, and then stared off into space, trying once again to apply order to the intrinsically senseless. There was no denying it. Her faith in Leon was based exclusively on his personality and her own desperation. At no point in their relationship had he made the slightest effort to convince her that there was any reason to hope, any reason to believe that he wasn't simply taking her money.

"I need more from you," she finally said.

"And who could blame you? From your perspective, I haven't done a thing for you. Jeremy is still wasting away, I presume. After Liza's buzz, well, I'm surprised you had the courage to come back out here at all. And then there's all this money you owe me. It's terribly frustrating, isn't it? I'd probably be having second thoughts myself."

"That's exactly right," she said. "And since you obviously know everything, why don't you tell me. Where am I wrong?"

"If only you knew!" he began. "I've been working overtime on your case. Really knocking myself out. I wish I could tell you all about it. The suspense is killing me, so I can only imagine what you must be feeling. But rest assured, everything is moving along swimmingly."

Ann's face dropped as he talked. "My case? Swimmingly?" she asked, a hint of sarcasm in her voice. "Look, Leon, as smart as you are I have to assume you're confusing me on purpose. To what end, I have no idea. But would it kill you, just this once, to speak *my* language? Throw me a flimsy little rope to cling to? Is that asking so much?"

Leon gave her a long, earnest look.

"The Xen get to make one important decision in their lives and, for better or worse, it comes right in the middle of our most emotionally unstable moment. We get to decide whether to live or die. That's it. Everything after that is meaningless, but those of us who survive can at least take some small comfort in the fact that we chose to be here. You stole that from Liza. In effect, her buzz is still unresolved."

Ann was dumbfounded. "What... does that mean? Might she have another buzz?"

"No," he said. "The buzz is a genuine metamorphosis. Once it's done, there's no going back. The reason it marks the moment of truth for the Xen isn't because it answers a question one way or the other, it's because of the intensity with which it provides the only possible answer to the only meaningful question. All of us resolve the same question the same way. Suicide is not one of two possible answers. It's a natural instinctive response to the *burden* of the answer itself."

"What question?" Ann asked. "What answer? I still don't understand. What did I steal from her?"

"Liza will never again experience the answer in its pure, unreflective form. Even today, only a week or so removed from the buzz, she's already buried it under a mountain of analysis. Any response now would, by necessity, be derivative and contrived."

"I have no idea what you're talking about," Ann said, "but it sounds like you're saying she's over the hump. If the intensity of the buzz is gone for good and that's why the Xen kill themselves, then what's left to worry about?"

"The burden is left," he said. "But unlike the rest of us who made an unfettered choice to bear it, Liza is now hopelessly separated from her honest sincere reaction. It's always the same with people like her; that knowledge will eat away at her until she drinks or starves herself to death. Trust me, it won't be pretty."

"Oh my God!" Ann said, suddenly panicky and sick to her stomach. "There must... I mean... No, I refuse to accept that."

"Then you better take her home with you, because the rest of us have already accepted it."

"What???" she gasped. "She's your friend, your house-mate! Take her with me? How can you be so cold?"

"Cold?" Leon challenged. "And what would you have us do with her when her casts come off? We don't have the money to take care of her, even if we thought there was any point to it."

"She... I can't take her home," Ann stammered hoarse-ly. "But I'll do what I can."

"According to the paperwork she brought home from the hospital," he said, "her therapy will cost $375 per visit, four times a week for three months and then regular follow up visits after that. That doesn't include her prescription pain killers and muscle relaxers, or the exercise equipment she's supposed to use daily here at the house. She'll also need to be chauffeured to all of those appointments."

Ann's brain flooded with images of Liza in her house, wasting away, drinking herself into a stupor day after day, screaming and crying, puking on the floor, and ignoring her treatment. It was the polar opposite of the example she'd choose for Jeremy, assuming she had a choice. In any case, with so much going on, where would she ever find the time to devote to such a project? It was absolutely out of the question. She felt the blood drain out of her head as her face went chalky white.

"I'll hire someone for her. That's the best I can do."

"You may want to mention to whomever you hire," Leon started, "that they'll be dealing with an uncooperative, withdrawn, and most likely intoxicated, patient."

As the complexity and expense of Liza's care sank in, Ann closed her eyes and let her head drop into her hands. *How on earth did I get myself into this?* Part of her felt a crushing re-sponsibility for everything that had happened, though, less because she was directly to blame than because she had, right from the moment she'd walked into it, volunteered herself as Liza's guardian angel– a position she now doubted the wisdom of accepting. But the rest of her couldn't shake the suspicion that it was all nothing but a royal screw job. Maybe Leon was busy with her "case," whatever that entailed, but the other denizens of Chez Xen– of which, Ann gathered, there were at least four besides Leon and Liza– were free to while away the days drinking themselves stupid and comparing weepy tales of woe. *Why am I putting up with this?* The more she thought about it, the angrier it made her.

Ann finally lifted her head, her eyes narrowed to slits. "You say this is hopeless?"

"Depends what you're hoping for," he said.

"Six months, maybe a year, she'll be dead anyway? Isn't that right?"

"Quite possibly."

Ann drummed her fingers on the table, letting him know that she was on the verge of a decision. She hoped he might back down from his hardened position, but he just sat there and watched her.

"Then forget the whole thing," she said, resolutely. "If none of you care, then neither do I!"

Chapter 17

By the end of June Ann had gradually, grudgingly come to accept that her life was no longer her own. Grudgingly, because not since her brief stint with Darryl, years ago, had she labored under the yoke of someone else's priorities– except her son's– for more than a week at a stretch. To do so was not only humiliating, though it was certainly that, but also quite simply a waste of her time. To the extent that she worked toward someone else's goals her own master plan had to be shelved. And life was too short and precious to be squandered on the random concerns of assorted third parties.

Her tribulations increased with the dreaded best and final offer presentation, an event that ricocheted back and forth from an inevitable failure to a miraculous coup and then back to a grim reality, all in a span of only two days. Ann expected her radical proposal– to cut JOMREV costs by training only a handful of expert users– to be at best politely rejected, and at worst laughed off of the table. With Irving Sicherman in charge and with a firm grip on Calvin's leash, Ann only dared hope he'd be content to grind her into dust, award the contract to Lockheed or Grumman, and show her ignominiously to the door with a smug, got-what-you-deserved, look on his face. But instead, something truly amazing happened.

As Ann made her case, Irving and Calvin sat quietly and listened, faces blank and unreadable, giving no indication that her proposal was the least bit controversial. As Ann carved up their cherished supply system the rest of the committee sat in uneasy silence, apparently waiting to take its cue from Sicherman. Judging by the looks on their faces, each one of them went through all five stages of grief, from denial and anger all the way to depression and acceptance, right there in the presentation room at Fort Belvoir. When Ann finished her spiel and asked for questions, Sicherman quickly huddled his colleagues together, prompting an animated exchange of frantic whispers and arm waving. Ann stood alone at the front of the room and waited a full five minutes, straining to decipher the few words that wafted back to her ears. When they finally broke up, Colonel Oxford thanked Ann and SST for coming and sent her on her way. Not one single question from the lot of them. Ann was crestfallen, though in all honesty it hadn't been a complete surprise by any means.

Later that afternoon, back at the SST Tower, Jerry came bounding down the hall and into Ann's office, his manner all but defying gravity.

"You must have done something right in a previous life," he said, cheeks yanked back into a big goofy grin.

Ann's eyes nearly popped out of her head. "No way!"

"Yup," he said. "They actually swallowed it, hook, line, and sinker."

"I don't believe it," Ann said, and sincerely meant it.

"Believe it. The revised RFP should be posted within the week. You got your way, Ann. Congratulations. I doubted you big time, but you're officially my hero again."

The gods granted Ann fewer than twenty-four hours to revel in her stunning victory. For the very next day she got a call from Irving Sicherman, during which he "suggested" a series of one-on-one meetings with Ann to discuss various and sundry aspects of her novel ideas for JOMREV. He went on to express his enthusiasm for a long and fruitful relationship between the DLA and SST, and specifically all of the magnificent things they could accomplish together over the next several years with Ann as program manager and he as the contracting officer. By the time he hung up the phone, leaving Ann dizzy and nauseated, everything was perfectly crystal clear; he didn't want a pound of flesh, he wanted all of it.

It was Ann's understanding that Sicherman's aim, though abhorrent, was fairly straightforward: he intended to use his leverage to force her into his bed. When he scheduled their first meeting for eight in the evening at Clyde's, a place she and Calvin frequented, her fears were all but confirmed. But as their conversation dragged on, never once did he make even a cloaked, implicit request. It was nothing but JOMREV this and JOMREV that for three solid hours. The evening ended, he bid her a respectful good night, and went on his merry way. Their next dinner was virtually identical. All business. And the one after that was much the same. *Could this little ghoul possibly be so devoted to his work?* After their fourth "date," Ann was beginning, in spite of herself, to wish he'd bring things to a head, make some kind of demand. At least that way she'd know where she stood. Being his concubine was unthinkable, and she had no intention of complying, but being his conversation slave was only marginally less irksome. As he rambled on endlessly about computation cycles, bandwidth, and stovepipes, Ann often caught herself fantasizing about Irving Sicherman's gruesome demise.

When she wasn't out with Sicherman or plagued by the anticipation of his increasingly frequent and lengthy phone calls, Ann found herself consumed by guilt over Liza. Less than a day after her final, emotionally charged meeting with Leon, her self-doubts and second thoughts about forsaking Liza began to set in. It seemed unfair to punish Liza for Leon's icy disregard. They might both be Xen but that conceded, they were as different as two people could be. She tried halfheartedly to resist it, but Ann's fancy soon cleansed Liza of whatever filth she accumulated from Leon, allowing her to glow in the same angelic light as Jeremy. And so, in the lull following her ambiguous best and final offer triumph, Ann dug herself, in increments, deeper and deeper into the minutia of Liza's medical condition.

Ann's first foray was a visit to Liza's doctor, who confirmed the litany of costly and time-consuming things Leon had already laid out for her. She also learned the difference between strong and weak tendon fixation, range of motion, biofeedback, electrical nerve stimulation, scar massage, dynamic splinting, and at least a dozen other complicated-sounding techniques, all of which were covered in great detail by a stack of marketing pamphlets and brochures the doctor was only too happy to peddle. Ann spent half the weekend reading them and the other half feeling like a dupe for doing so. Still, by the time she reached the last page, she knew enough to order Liza's rehab equipment off of the Internet and be reasonably confident she was getting the right items for a fair, if high, price.

Afterwards, Ann stubbornly refused to think any more about it. The equipment was already above and beyond the call. But as the week wore on, the many warnings and instructions outlined in all of those cursed pamphlets slowly wormed their way into her brain and she realized there was no way out of it. Liza was required to exercise on her own at least six times a day. Someone would have to help her out of and back into her splints. She had to make all of her doctor's appointments. There was no way on earth any of that would happen without Ann's constant vigilance. A week later she was on her way out to Leesburg to introduce Liza to her very own part-time nurse.

Vera answered the door.

"This is Miki Lee," Ann said. "She's a nurse. Can I please talk to Liza?"

Vera craned her neck back toward the interior of the house. "You win, Steve!" she yelled.

"What did he win?" Ann asked, the disgust of her first encounter with Steve evident in her voice.

"I said you'd be gone at least a month," Vera started. "He said two weeks tops."

"I'm not back," Ann said. Then repeated, "Would you please get Liza for me?"

It took Liza forever to limp down the stairs, and when she finally got to the bottom Ann had to force back a reflexive gasp. Her skin was cadaver-gray and her hair was stringy and knotted. If she'd been found in that condition in a ditch somewhere, no one would have bothered to call an ambulance before notifying the coroner. On seeing her, Ms. Lee raked a harsh uncompromising glower across the faces of Vera, Steve, and Ann, condemning them in turn for allowing this poor girl to deteriorate so grievously. The judgment stung, but Ann was immediately heartened by the great concern it implied. At five foot nothing, Nurse Lee didn't initially strike Ann as suitably imposing for this particular assignment. Liza would be a handful all by herself, and who could predict what that bastard Steve might pull? But it became clear within thirty seconds of their arrival that she was, in fact, the perfect choice.

Miki Lee was Korean, had arrived in the states only five years before, and spoke the standard, choppy English stereotypical of such transplants. She told Ann she was forty, though except for the wisdom in her eyes, looked no older than twenty-five. Her build was svelte but sturdy, and her quick decisive movements suggested boundless energy. Ann met with her in Leesburg, fearing no one would be willing to endure Chez Xen without a protracted acclimation period fortified by constant assurances. She expected it to take all afternoon and was prepared, if necessary, to chaperone next time as well. But no sooner had Liza made her entrance than the Wanju Dynamo threw open her medical bag and went straight to work. That anyone else remained in the room was a matter of complete indifference to her. It was also clear that her inability to grasp the nuanced jibes endemic to all things Xen would be more of an asset than a liability. Ann breathed a huge sigh of relief, looking on with satisfaction as Liza's injuries fell under Miki's expert eye, confident that Steve, Leon, and even the whole North Korean army were no match for Nurse Lee.

Ann's headaches slowly, agonizingly dissipated, leaving behind only the lingering residue of her cognitive lapses and emotional instability – and that only when she had too much wine or too little sleep. She even managed to get back into the pool now and then, an activity her rickety brain had since resisted. It had been simply too disorienting to float freely, detached from *terra firma*. She started slowly, only a few laps the first day, but within a week was back up to ninety percent of her pre-concussion workout. It should have been a tremendous reprieve, validation that she had put her injuries behind her. But try as she might the peace of mind and clarity of purpose she'd grown to depend on stubbornly refused to return. Instead, she felt herself swimming away from her life rather than toward her next victory, dragged under rather than buoyed by the water. It wasn't long before she caught herself, more and more often, busy in her office, out to lunch with clients, a long list of excuses to avoid the pool altogether. Anything to distract her. It was too depressing to think about.

Two days after depositing Miki Lee at Chez Xen, Ann was again knee-deep in work. Sitting behind the desk in her home office, she watched with an unexpectedly painful twinge as the little Windows clock in the lower right hand corner of her computer screen ticked over to midnight on the fourth of July. It was a day for backyard barbeques, parades, and fireworks for most. But for Ann it would be just another sixteen-hour stretch of e-mail, spreadsheets, and conference calls with exhausted, irate members of her staff. Though she'd gotten her way on JOMREV, her victory meant the DLA had been forced to compress the next round of bids into a ridiculously short span of time to meet its deadline. Had their expressions been poison, Ann would have been killed instantly when she announced to her team what they'd be doing over the holiday weekend. And, unpleasant as they'd been, that day promised to be by far the worst. Even Cliff, who took a certain pride in his corporate asceticism, had completely lost his sense of humor. He'd long since begun omitting the opening salutation and by then had omitted the closing one as well, his e-mails curt and to the point: *Did you get that hardware interface info yet?... Where the hell is Kim on the past performance?*

By half past one Ann was drifting in and out of consciousness, compelled to remain online until she was certain the last of her team had packed it in. A year, even six months ago, such a show of solidarity would not have been necessary. Her sterling leadership more than compensated for any distemper occasioned by her regal bearing. But the good old days seemed so distant, she didn't dare presume that she might still be able to trade on those moldy obsolete credits. She pushed the keyboard forward and laid her head down on the desk, idly listening for any beeps or blips that might demand her attention. Sleep overtook her almost instantly.

For more than an hour she remained completely motionless, dead to the world, save a few wayward strands of hair that were close enough to her nose to testify she was still breathing. It was then, somewhere in the netherworld between waking and sleep, that she caught hold of a few notes of a song she hadn't heard in years. A smile crept across her mouth but her eyes remained closed. She listened blissfully, still asleep, while the beautiful, somber tune commandeered her memories to build a dreamscape of Jeremy's last piano recital. He wore a tuxedo and sat up straight and proud, his face lost in his music and mirroring the solemnity of the piece. The audience listened in rapture as Schumann's *Traumerei* echoed through the nineteenth century Victorian parlor. In the front row of chairs, not six feet from the piano, were several tightly corseted and fine young ladies, any one of whom would have traded her honor to be seen on Jeremy's right arm. Ann surveyed them critically, alert to the tiniest lapse of etiquette, the slightest blemish on their uniformly milky white skin, indulging the age-old maternal conceit that her judgment would weigh heavily on her son's choice. He would have only the best.

Ann awoke to the sound of her own sigh. Ever so briefly, she felt as though something precious and deeply significant, now slipping away, had been granted her, leaving behind only the bittersweet residue. But she immediately afterwards became aware that the notes of her dream were continuing to fill her ears. She blinked with confusion into the darkness, a look of profound disorientation on her face. A moment or two passed and she finally sat up, furrowing her brow, straining to distinguish reality from fantasy. The little computer clock read 2:45. *Could it really be?* A few moments later it couldn't be denied. The music was not in her head, and it was even more beautiful than it had been in her dream.

Ann had purchased her seven-foot-long, black-lac-quered Yamaha exclusively for Jeremy soon after they'd moved into the house. But to her knowledge, this was the first time he'd ever played it. By cruel coincidence, it was around the time of their move, four years ago that summer, that Jeremy began receding. She had it tuned every year, at first because she honestly believed he might one day take to it. But last year she did it, and was aware that she'd done it, for the same reason a widow goes on wearing her wedding ring years after the death of her soul mate – despite the fact that her friends' attitudes have long since devolved from sympathy, to concern, to pity. The piano was scheduled for another tuning later that summer, and Ann had been toying with the idea of declaring an end to the charade. After this night, however, she'd tune it every year like clockwork for the rest of her life. No apologies.

She stood slowly, quietly, terrified that anything she did might bring an abrupt end to the serenade. Despite her best efforts, the door squeaked, the floors creaked, and her knees and ankles cracked and popped. Even so, whether indifferent or oblivious to her intrusion, Jeremy kept right on playing even as she sat down in a chair near the piano. He was still playing *Traumerei*, over and over, slower and slower, with no break between performances, gradually diminishing, as if it were one eternal song that could only end when it died of its own unfulfilled longing. Jeremy's eyes were closed as he played, which somehow made the tears running down his face all the more desperate. Ann bit her lip hard, struggling mightily against the reflex to make her empathy audible, possibly disrupting his catharsis in the process. Instead, she shared his silent tears and sniffled as respectfully and infrequently as she was able.

From a music appreciation course she'd taken as a freshman– one she'd expected to ace but which turned out to be gallingly difficult– Ann still recalled the thumbnail biography of Robert Schumann. She only remembered it because Professor Beinart had gone on and on about it for several class periods, rather as if he himself were no less an example than Schumann of the curious relationship between artistic genius and mental illness. Riding the waves of his relentless manic depression, Schumann had composed *Traumerei* during a particularly unpleasant point in his generally unpleasant life, prevented from being with Clara, his one true love. Wracked by a crushing sense of meaninglessness and lost innocence, plunging helplessly into yet another psychiatric morass, his life was in a perpetual state of unraveling. And in the hands of a lesser composer, such wretchedness might have issued forth in notes of fury and bitterness. Who could fault a man, suffering such a cruel and arbitrary fate, for lashing out at God and cursing the very firmament? But that isn't where Schumann's heart took him. Instead, he withdrew to a time of simplicity and wonder, deep into the safety of his childhood. And it was there, ensconced within the sweet, unclouded optimism of youth, that the chaos of his broken heart and mind at last found asylum.

Jeremy played for another ten or fifteen minutes, during which time Ann came to understand that this was not meant to be a verbal exchange. *Haven't we already said enough?* When he finally stopped, his eyes remained forward but he tilted his head slightly in Ann's direction, not exactly looking at her, but acknowledging her presence. Then he scooted over a few inches to the left side of the piano bench. It wasn't a terribly subtle gesture but Ann still couldn't quite believe it, not until he played the first measure of a song they used to play together– Ann the right hand, Jeremy the left– when he was very young. It was Stephen Sondheim's, *Send in the Clowns*. It wasn't exactly a children's song but, then again, Jeremy had never exactly been a child.

By the time Jeremy was five years old his skills had so outstripped Ann's that he could no longer be bothered to humor her. Indeed, it was upon his golden fourth year on planet Earth– the precious time before he began losing interest in her– that their current reverie drew its breath. Ann had always assumed that he had long ago forgotten all about it. She sat down next to him and they began, Ann singing along silently to herself. Not surprisingly, the lyrics came alive with all manner of hidden meaning and depth, perhaps even beyond the composer's intentions.

> *What a surprise! Who could foresee*
> *I'd come to feel about you what you felt about me?*
> *Why only now when I see that you've drifted away?*
> *What a surprise... What a cliché'...*

Before they got to the end, Ann had no doubt he'd picked that tune for a reason, though she wasn't as sure to whom the sentiments were meant to refer. Oddly, they seemed to make equally as much sense either way, rather as if both of them were finally staggering out into the light, but just as the sun was setting.

When the song was over they sat in silence, not looking at one another, bathed in the affectionate but tragic glow of their belated reunion. Ann wanted the moment to last forever but hadn't a clue how to make that happen. Thankfully, she didn't have to figure it out. Just then, without warning, Jeremy wrapped his arms tightly around Ann, buried his face in her chest, and began weeping like a baby. The sound of his sobs, so sincere, and so hopeless, instantly broke Ann's heart to pieces. She couldn't have guessed until it burst the enormous volume of pent up emotion that had been accumulating behind the dam. The flood was so intense she felt dizzy, almost drunk, as she squeezed him tightly against herself, aware somehow that

that moment was not only the first, but quite likely the last of its kind. Jeremy seemed in no hurry for it to end either, and they remained in one another's arms until their tears ran dry.

"I miss you," Ann said, her voice breaking.

"I miss me too," he whispered.

Chapter 18

After work the next day, Ann paid Leon's cursed invoice in person, not in the least ashamed at returning with her hat in her hand. From then on, she never looked back. It was the first in what quickly became a very intensive series of consultations with Leon.

From the very beginning, from the moment she'd enlisted his services, Ann understood that Leon's purpose was to help Jeremy through the buzz. In that regard, she expected at some point to be given a more or less clear and unambiguous game plan. The project manager in her craved a syllabus. But by their third meeting it was already becoming obvious that nothing like that was in the offing. He answered her questions. They talked for hours. But for all that, none of it seemed to go anywhere. Leon had an extraordinary talent for oblique tangential responses. Interesting certainly, but the same question kept forming on Ann's lips.

"Why am I here?"

"The eternal question..." Leon mused, a sly grin on his face.

"I meant, here in your *house*," she said.

"If it were any other house, it might make a difference. But since it's *this* house, it comes to roughly the same thing."

"Of course it does," she said with mock sarcasm. "I'm sure I should know that by now."

"Isn't that why you're here?" he asked. "To find out

why you're here?"

"Heaven forbid it might have something to do with my son."

Leon sighed and shook his head. "Is that really all you want to do, save your son?"

"Maybe that's not *all* I want, but I'd settle for that much."

"Save him from what?" Leon asked. "For what?"

"Death. Life. In that order. If there's more to it than that, he can come out here after his buzz and you can tell him all about it."

Leon inserted a long pause in the conversation, drumming his fingers on the table and moving his lips as if talking something over with himself. Ann waited patiently.

"I didn't want to do this," he started, "but you're the most hard-headed person I've ever met. I'm afraid we'll never get to step two if I don't give you another brief peek behind the curtain."

"About time!" she said.

"I still can't give you all of the details, but I can tell you generally what I'm trying to do."

"Blah, blah, blah," she said. "Out with it."

"It occurred to me some time ago that Xen parents might be in the unique position to exert a kind of subliminal influence over their children. I'm sure it can't be more than subconscious, entirely primordial. It certainly won't be intellectual. But done right it might— just might—tip the scale."

Ann's eyes opened wide. She couldn't quite believe it. It was exactly what she wanted to hear.

"I've always felt that way myself," she said, her voice full of significance. "What do I need to do?"

"That's just it," he said. "It'll only work if he sincerely believes you understand what he's going through. You can't fake it. He needs to know that you are right there with him."

"Right *where* with him?" she asked.

Leon smiled. "Which brings us back to your original question: Why are you here? Clearly we need to start by determining exactly where *here* is."

And so it went, session after session, for more than two weeks. On each occasion, Ann left Leon's house with a great sense of accomplishment and relief. Huge questions were raised and then dispatched in excruciating detail. But soon afterward, no later than the next morning in her office, even more questions arose, impenetrable ones, clouding whatever it was that seemed so clear just the day before. By the following evening, she was hopelessly beset by a new swarm of questions, and had no other choice but to run back out to Leon, lest she spend all night tossing and turning and otherwise driving herself completely to distraction.

On one such night, just as she was getting in her car, struggling to put her chaotic thoughts into words, Irving Sicherman called and "requested" a meeting. Ann slumped in her seat, utterly deflated, but as always, agreed to see him.

It was their sixth meeting, and Ann was coming to grips with a horrible, indisputable fact: the JOMREV project was sufficiently complex to provide an inexhaustible reservoir of discussion points, any one of which could be dressed up and made to appear vitally important. All it took was a rigid anal compulsive adherence to every nit-picky principle of project management and, *voila*, even the auxiliary staff training schedule, thirteen months hence, could become a burning issue at that very moment. After all, without meticulous planning, who knows what might go awry? Irving droned on while Ann tried on a series of phony smiles, searching her face for a tolerable compromise between sincerity and muscle fatigue.

There was no telling what made her do what she did on that particular night. It was most likely a combination of all the troublesome questions she was being prevented from asking Leon, along with the fact that five more minutes of JOMREV might prompt her to bludgeon Sicherman to death with her soup spoon. She had no real desire to hear about his personal life, but at that point anything at all would be an improvement.

She leaned back in her seat, disengaging from the conversation. "You certainly know how to show a girl a good time."

He looked at her nervously, giving the impression she'd jolted him out of his comfort zone. She waited for him to respond, hoping he'd be able to switch gears.

"I guess I'm not much fun, am I?" he finally said.

"Oh, I don't know," she said, relieved. "I think you just need to relax a little. Get your mind off of work. What do you and your wife do for fun?"

"My wife?" he mumbled, as if confused by the question. "We don't do anything. She hates me."

Ann's eyes opened wide and she laughed lightheartedly, trying not to offend him. He smiled sheepishly but after a bit more prodding, launched into a long rambling story of his life. He started slowly but once he got rolling, it was as if the flood gates had been thrown open. Clearly it was something he desperately needed to get off of his chest.

His wife, Geraldine, was the daughter of family friends, and she and Irving had been clumsily maneuvered together through the incessant machinations of their mothers. At the time, Irving was thirty-five. Geraldine was one year younger. Neither of them had been on a real date in years, and it was painfully obvious, at least to Irving, throughout their forced courtship, that pity was the overriding motive. Moms to the rescue! Unfortunately, they were so caught up in their altruistic fervor, no one bothered to consult the couple about their feelings on the matter.

Geraldine had been diagnosed with multiple sclerosis when she was only twenty-two. The disease progressed at a leisurely pace, but by the time of her marriage to Irving she had developed, among other things, balance problems that caused her to fall frequently, zero sex drive, and she was nearly blind in her left eye, making it impossible for her to get a driver's license. In view of the terrible injustice of the cruel disease, she might have garnered a great deal of sympathy. Instead, she became bitter and spiteful, blaming everyone and everything for her condition. Her parents attributed her wild mood swings and vitriolic tantrums to the MS and indeed, that may have been part of it. But, compelling as that explanation may have been, no reason on earth for her behavior could offset the unpleasantness of being in her presence. It wasn't long before her friends stopped coming by, and eventually she was left alone at home with her mother.

For his part, Irving was not a complete monster. He'd known Geraldine since they were both in grade school. They'd attended different schools and were not exactly childhood friends, but saw each other frequently when their families got together. He still vaguely recalled several pleasant occasions on which they ran and played like regular happy little kids. Perhaps it was those memories, possibly the endless entreaties of his mother, or it could have been the fact that he was, truth be told, painfully lonely himself. But at long last, noble sentiments coursing through his blood about saving Geraldine from a lifetime of misery, he agreed to see her.

Amazingly, Geraldine managed to retract her fangs long enough to convince Irving she wasn't the ogre everyone accused her of being. She didn't especially like him, but anything was better than living in that purgatory with her mother. And what choice did she have? Men weren't exactly beating down her door. Irving was better than nothing. Wasn't he? She played those notes of humility just long enough to get him to the altar – and no longer. Even before they got back from their honeymoon in the Bahamas, she had reverted back to her same old caustic hateful self.

On the oceanfront in Nassau, the newlyweds were standing on a wooden platform around a tiki bar. Geraldine lost her balance and fell harmlessly, maybe eighteen inches, onto the beach, spilling her Mai Tai all over her new dress. They'd been drinking for quite awhile and enjoying themselves thoroughly, so when Irving looked down at her, he did what seemed like the perfectly natural thing. It turned out to be one of the biggest mistakes of his life, a crushing burden he'd be forced to bear throughout his entire marriage, even to that very day.

He laughed at her.

To anyone familiar with the dynamics of a bad marriage– the corrosive one-downsmanship that spirals sickeningly into contempt and disgust– the scene that followed Geraldine's misstep would've been no great surprise. The fight itself, or at least the part that could be referred to as "open hostilities," lasted a whopping ten straight hours. Hotel décor was smashed. Clothing was ripped up and thrown out of windows. Security was summoned twice by the hapless residents of adjacent rooms. And, worst of all, words were exchanged that could never be taken back. It finally ended when Irving agreed to rent a different room for the remainder of their honeymoon and take a separate flight back. When they got home to Virginia, they decided more or less independently and never openly, to remain married to placate their parents, and because they felt they had no other options. Those were the reasons they would've been willing to admit. Though it was just as likely their marriage endured because each knew the other experienced it as a nine by five cell, and neither was prepared to grant the other's parole. In the sixteen years since, they had "made love" exactly eleven times.

Ann listened to Irving's story, not quite believing his candor about such revolting personal details. It wasn't impossible to imagine his plight eliciting sympathy from some quarters, but to Ann it had the rotten putrid stench of pure evil. Sure, it was the story of two ruined lives, but lives ruined by cravenness and vengeance. Ann could find no room even for pity. The whole thing made her sick.

Still, she now realized that Irving Sicherman was a very dangerous man. What wasn't he capable of? Biding his time for decades in a loveless marriage, presumably so he could stand over his wife's deathbed and laugh in her face as her eyes darkened and she drifted away to the corner of hell they'd carved out for themselves. He'd been well-schooled in the cold art of retribution. Nothing he did or said could be taken at face value. Ann imagined Irving and his wife slowly luring one another into various traps over the course of weeks or months, surreptitiously floating the prospect of reconciliation or companionship, only to pounce when the other let down his guard. It sent a shiver up her spine and she decided JOMREV needed more discussion than she realized.

Ann managed to pry herself free of Irving's clutches before eleven, the hour she'd arbitrarily selected as the cut-off point for a trip out to Leesburg. It was arbitrary because she'd since come to understand that the residents of Chez Xen slept from roughly five or six in the morning until mid-afternoon. Had she allowed herself to dwell on it, their schedule might have given her cause for concern. In her world, responsible adults paid at least perfunctory homage to the diurnal cycle. But firmly in his thrall, she dismissed all of Leon's potentially disquieting behaviors as harmless eccentricities. And on the up side, it meant she could drop by whenever she needed to.

Ann almost always left Leon's office in one heightened state or another. Sometimes contemplative, completely lost in thought. Other times stirred into an emotional frenzy. Still others with an exasperating sense that one critical piece of some particular puzzle was missing. Early on, it began wreaking havoc with her sleep, keeping her up all night thinking, or infecting her dreams with disturbing phantasmagoria. It gradually deteriorated into a full-blown case of chronic insomnia, fraying her nerves even further and otherwise disposing her to manic flights of fancy one minute, and then with bipolar rapidity, sudden plunges into melancholy the next. It was following this most recent visit to Leon's that she decided Jeremy needed to know exactly what she was up to. And though it was three in the morning when she got the itch, it couldn't wait.

"Sweetie?" she said into the gloom of Jeremy's bedroom. It'd been a long time since she'd last seen him asleep. "Are you awake?"

In decidedly un-Xenlike fashion, Jeremy shot bolt upright in his bed, his eyes darting fuzzily around the room. "What? What is it?" But then he saw Ann and his body went slack. "What on earth are you doing?"

"We need to talk," she said, eyes ablaze. "I have something very important to discuss with you."

Jeremy sighed and let his head fall back on his pillow. Ann sat down on a stack of books at his bedside.

"I guess you probably know," she started, "I've been talking to a Xen man for the last month or so."

Nothing.

"He's got my brain going places I never thought it could go, places I never knew existed."

"I'm happy for you, Ann," he said, blandly. "Any chance your brain could find a place that isn't in my bedroom?"

Ann chuckled at his response and then said warmly, "My comedian."

She squeezed his arm and gazed deeply into his eyes. Jeremy squinted back at her with a wary, doubtful expression.

"Well?" he finally said. "Are you going to tell me about your big breakthrough or sit there and stare at me all night?"

The substance of Ann's "breakthrough" issued from a fitful dream starring Dr. Remington. She awoke with an unusually clear, if not altogether rational, appreciation for the gruesome device. A gun, she reasoned, would give Jeremy the option to commit an unambiguous suicide if, God forbid, that's what he felt compelled to do. Awful, to be sure, but preferable to the chaotic debacle of Liza's buzz, the results of which were impossible to interpret. Ann figured if Jeremy were given a tool to kill himself outright, cleanly, he might not inflict a rash of lesser injuries on himself, ending up dead even if suicide was not his real aim. Maybe she couldn't save him if it wasn't meant to be, but she could at least minimize the probability of losing him to the frenzied emotional mayhem leading up to the decisive moment. It wasn't a solution, but it was a start. She also hoped that telling him about it would demonstrate some understanding of his situation and facilitate the "primordial" link Leon spoke of. Jeremy listened as she explained, his face gradually softening.

"That's quite a theory," he said glumly. "Maybe I underestimated you."

"No," she said, "you didn't. I've been a terrible mother and I know it's too late to apologize. But I'm going to be here for you in whatever way I can. I won't interfere."

Jeremy's eyes drifted into the darkness. For a moment he seemed lost but then spoke. "You probably think the Xen are never amazed, never awestruck or captivated by the world. We come across so blasé and jaded, as if we knew everything there is to know right from birth. That's not how it is."

"You're getting close, aren't you?" she asked. "That's why you stopped reading."

"How can all of this," he said, waving his hand over the mountain of books, "amount to so little? It's ironic that the same spectrum that lends color to life, when combined, turns into ugly brown muck. In the end, that's all the world can be. Meaningless pretty colors or ugly brown muck."

"What color is the world now?"

Jeremy looked her in the eye. "I appreciate what you're trying to do. It's heartwarming in a way. But every step you take in this direction is a step closer to your own undoing."

"I don't see it that way," she said. "For better or worse, you're still my responsibility."

"Taking responsibility for something over which you have only the illusion of control is a reliable method for separating yourself from your sanity. It's your choice, but you're playing with fire, Ann. Don't ever say I didn't warn you."

"Of course not," she said.

"Then buy that gun if it makes you feel better," he said. "But do me a favor."

"Anything."

"Don't put it in here," he said. "Make me ask you for it."

Ann swallowed hard.

"And close the door on your way out."

Jeremy turned on his side, showing Ann his back, and the conversation was over.

Chapter
19

After her talk with Jeremy, Ann went back to bed but didn't sleep. Her son's buzz had for so long been an abstraction, looming way out there in the future, that it genuinely startled her as the awareness dawned that the future was now. There was no more time for preparation or agonizing. No more time to pore over the minutia of contingency plans J through Z. It was show time. And with that, Ann notified Jerry and Andrea that she would be out of the office indefinitely, offering by way of explanation nothing but a vague mention of a family emergency. She agreed to work from home and do whatever she could to help the team, but refused to promise even that she'd be available to deliver the JOMREV re-bid presentation herself. Neither of them received the news with great equanimity.

It wasn't long before Ann discovered that one unintended consequence of her self-imposed house arrest was the front row seat she suddenly had of the ongoing dissolution of her father. Coming home from work to find him slouched in his chair, glassy eyes unable to focus on the TV that nonetheless, flickered and droned on incessantly in front of him, was bad enough. But to watch the dismal scene unfold beginning to end, day after day, was truly unbearable. He awoke later and later each morning and rarely came up from the basement anymore. Ann couldn't be sure he ate more than one meal a day and his clothes had begun to dangle off of him as if they were still on the rack. If she wanted a conversation she had to time it to coincide with his brief period of lucidity, roughly noon to two, the time after which he'd shaken off the previous night's cobwebs but before he'd drifted away into his next anesthetic stupor. It was terribly sad and depressing, enough to make Ann doubt the wisdom of marriage altogether. There seemed to be only two choices: either marry someone you wouldn't miss or risk spending your twilight years as a living corpse, yearning for eternity.

As a rule, she avoided him and respected his decision to remain out of sight, assuming he viewed it as a matter of pride. And in any case, with her thoughts busily plumbing the depths of her own tolerance for suffering, girding her against the less palatable possibilities for Jeremy's buzz, Ann had little left of herself to devote to the niceties of her father's desolation. But on one occasion, after watching him stumble around the kitchen for fifteen minutes in search of a light bulb, her alarm got the best of her and she couldn't hold her tongue.

"You're not even trying anymore, are you?"

It was early afternoon but Dr. Franklin was already swirling around the bottom of the bowl. "What would you like me to try?"

"You know," Ann said, arms crossed, "I bought a gun the other day. You can borrow it. It'd be a lot cheaper than drinking yourself to death."

"You bought… Why do you need a gun?"

"You wouldn't understand," she said, turning her back on him, wishing she'd kept her mouth shut. Dr. Franklin despised guns. She'd heard all about it through the years. He understood the Second Amendment to be an obsolete, eighteenth century recipe for raising a militia, not an invitation to turn the streets into a shooting gallery.

He puzzled for a moment or two and then spoke. "You got it for Jeremy, didn't you?"

Ann swung around and gave him a hard look, as much as confirming his hunch.

"What on earth were you thinking?"

"Forget it, Dad."

"And what if he uses it? Did you give any thought to what would happen to you?" he asked. "Regret wouldn't even begin to cover it. You'd be ruined for life."

"It's not about me."

"Not now it isn't. But it sure as hell will be," he said. "That's a mighty big chance you're taking, betting your whole future on the flip of a coin."

"I don't need your advice on this one," she said coldly, and stormed off in a huff.

By the time Ann had been out for a week, the discontent among her minions at the office had quickly grown from a rumble to a dull roar. The re-bid presentation, the one Ann's own actions had precipitated, was only three days away. Her absence during the final push, her stubborn refusal to take part in the rehearsals, and her sporadic interest in even reviewing the proposal strategy, tested the limits of her team's commitment. Rumors began to circulate about the exact nature of Ann's so-called family emergency. Had she been diagnosed with cancer? Did she have some sort of legal trouble? Might she be hiding a sordid illicit affair? Kim McEwen gleefully stirred the pot, though never giving away anything specific. She didn't have to. Everyone's imaginations were more than equal to the task, at least as juicy and salacious as anything reality had to offer.

Finally, Andrea could no longer remain silent and paid Ann a personal visit one evening. After a few awkward pleasantries, she got to the point.

"You know me, Ann," she started. "Normally, I'd just assume you know what you're doing and run with it. But some of this stuff... I don't know."

"Like what?"

"For starters, what's up with this hard copy documentation library?" Andrea asked, indicating a page in her notebook. "Your original proposal had all of that online. One person could manage the whole thing. Now we've got personnel and equipment costs all over the place. Printing, distribution, shipping, annual updates, and reprinting, storage—the whole nine yards. It's almost as inefficient as the mess they've got now."

"There's a good reason for that."

"Care to share it with me?"

"I wish I could."

Andrea shook her head. "And then there's this old fashioned, classroom training program you suddenly insisted on," she said, flipping to another page. "Teachers, laptops, LCD projectors, travel expenses, books, and pedagogical aids. On and on. What happened to our distance learning solution? It took us three months to get Graham Johannsen over at Learning Curve all ramped up. And then, out of nowhere, 'thanks, but no thanks?' He nearly cried when I broke the news to him."

"He'll get over it," Ann said.

"Let me guess. You wish you could explain that one too."

"Look, Andrea, I have my reasons. That's all you need to know."

"No, Ann," Andrea said. "It's not. You seem to forget. Since you started popping in and out of the office whenever the spirit moves you, and especially this last week when you've been completely MIA, I've been the one painting a happy face on all of these bizarre decisions. I make things up. I tell everyone it's your call and to stop whining. But I'll be honest with you. I'm running out of lipstick for this pig."

"When it's all said and done and SST wins, no one will even remember."

"Assuming that ever happens," Andrea said. "There's one more thing. This new CMS vendor you want us to use, Haruspex, LLC."

"What about them?"

"It's not official yet, but the Michigan Department of Transportation is expected to announce a $30 million dollar lawsuit against them later this month."

Ann looked as if she'd just been slapped in the face.

"Didn't know about that, did you?"

"Does MDOT have a case?" Ann asked.

"What difference does it make? Where on earth did you dig these jokers up? We had Oracle fully priced out and ready to roll. Who's ever heard of Haruspex?"

"Relax!" Ann said, getting testy. "If they go under, we'll bring in Oracle. Bait and switch. Happens all the time."

"Yeah, but the bait is supposed to be the appetizing option, not the cold spinach you feed them instead. My point is, two months ago this lawsuit never would've slipped past you."

"The presentation is only three days away, Andrea. What difference does any of this make now?"

Andrea paused and shook her head slowly, a betrayed expression on her face.

"I don't get it. What's the big secret?" she said. "You wouldn't tell me what was up with Kim McEwen. And now you won't tell me where you're getting all this golden inside information. Technically, that's your prerogative. But it's my prerogative to stop spinning it. Leave people to think whatever they want. And, trust me, the truth couldn't possibly be worse than some of the stuff I've overheard."

"Like what?"

"It's not important," Andrea said, looking Ann dead in the eyes, letting her know two could play that game.

Ann sighed loudly. "Damn it."

Ann met her glare, but there was no way Andrea was going to back down. She'd finally found the end of her rope. Ann may have been her superior, but in the DC consulting world that only meant Ann set the direction and got larger commission checks. It didn't mean she could expect Andrea to jump whenever she cracked the whip. Andrea had an MBA and an MS in information systems from Penn State; a sterling résumé. She looked and dressed like an Anne Klein model. All she'd have to do to find a new job is take the elevator down to the Palm Restaurant in the Tower lobby and drop a subtle hint that she wasn't completely enchanted by her current employer.

She'd be gone the next day.

Ann's face slowly softened, becoming almost contrite. "I respect you more than anyone else I know, Andrea. I know it sounds ridiculous, but that's why I've kept you in the dark."

"What's that supposed to mean?"

"I've been meeting with Irving Sicherman..."

Andrea gave her a dubious look.

"Not like that," Ann clarified. "Just business."

"*He's* been feeding you all this intel?" Andrea asked, flabbergasted. "That's illegal—unless he's also been giving it to Lockheed and Grumman. Besides, I thought he hated the sight of you. This doesn't make any sense."

"He doesn't exactly say it out loud," Ann said. "I read between the lines."

"How, pray tell, do you get *Haruspex* from between the lines?"

"He happened to mention that Colonel Summers worked with them once and had a positive experience."

Lieutenant Colonel Beverly Summers was under Colonel Oxford's command and a member of the JOMREV evaluation committee. According to Sicherman, she had, years earlier, worked with John Harmon, the current president of Haruspex, even before he started the company. Apparently, she was well impressed.

Andrea knitted her brow, obviously trying to assimilate this sleazy, backdoor manner of gathering business intelligence. It wasn't a technique espoused by Penn State's College of Business, and her close proximity to such dealings made her a bit queasy.

"What does he get out of it," Andrea asked. "Is he expecting a kickback or a job or something?"

"He hasn't asked for anything."

Andrea scrunched up her face even tighter. "None of this makes one scintilla of sense. He's been fighting SST right from the start. There's something you're not telling me."

"You're right," Ann admitted. "And I'd rather not."

Andrea squinted at her. "You're sure you're not sleeping with him?"

"Very sure."

"Then how do you know he's not feeding you a great big pile of horse shit?" Andrea asked. "I mean, if it was me and I wanted to sabotage SST, I'd be telling you exactly the same things."

"That's not what he's doing."

"You're going to have to do better than that, Ann," Andrea said. "I have to know for certain that I'm not unwittingly involved in something illegal. Call it self-defense; nothing personal."

"I can't go into detail. But I promise you, even if it all blows up in my face, none of it will land on you."

"Does it have anything to do with this family emergency of yours?"

"Not exactly," Ann said.

"C'mon, Ann!" Andrea said, trying to sound playful. "My imagination is having a field day with this. Fraud, extortion, bribery, espionage—don't force me to make up my own explanation. I'll have no choice but to take it straight to Jerry."

"You'll give the poor schmuck a heart attack."

"He's already halfway there!" Andrea said. "I'm surprised he hasn't come over here himself."

"That would be bad."

"Look, you hired me right out of college," Andrea said, trying a new tack. "I'd like to think we're friends, able to give one another the benefit of the doubt. Whatever it is, we can work it out together. You may find I'm not as naïve as you seem to think."

"I've never thought that," Ann said.

Andrea kept up the pressure of her stare, letting Ann know there were no fire exits or escape hatches. Either tell her what she wants to know, or face the board of directors. It was no use. Andrea wasn't going away.

"Oh, to hell with it! What do I have left to lose?"

Reluctantly, and with as many qualifications, disclaimers, and explanations as possible, she told Andrea the sordid tale: her defunct affair with Calvin, Kim's use of the scandal to protect her job, and Sicherman's veiled blackmail. She omitted anything about her and Calvin's plot to sway the committee. And she also neglected to mention the mysterious someone who allegedly passed the news on to Sicherman. The story was bad enough as it was. Andrea plastered a solemn expression across her face and listened intently, not giving any overt indication that she was titillated, disgusted, or otherwise affected. When Ann was finished talking, Andrea sat in silence for several minutes before responding, long enough for Ann to imagine what it would feel like to have a pair of handcuffs slapped on her wrists.

"Are you sure they have proof?" Andrea finally asked.

"No, but it doesn't really matter at this point. My compliance has been just as good as a confession."

"Maybe," Andrea said, deep in thought. "So, why are you working from home? What's the emergency?"

"My son is Xen."

Andrea's head fell forward and her mouth dropped open. "What???"

Ann couldn't explain why she'd revealed that fact as well. Andrea may have had a right to know about the blackmail, but Jeremy was still a private matter. Still, as Ann considered the impact of her disclosure, it didn't seem to make the slightest bit of difference. Painful as it often was, she wasn't exactly ashamed of having a Xen son. Neither was it an uncommon state of affairs. Millions of parents were in the same boat. *Why do I keep these things secret?*

"That's right," Ann said, morosely.

"How old is he?"

"Fifteen."

"Oh my God, Ann!" Andrea said, genuine sympathy in her voice. "I always thought you were so…well, together. All spit shine and hospital corners. But now, everything at the same time. Your concussion. Sicherman. I am so sorry, Ann. I had no idea."

"I can handle it."

"And didn't your mother pass away recently?"

"Yes."

Andrea was shaking her head in astonishment. "What's holding you up? I don't see any strings."

"I've had a lot longer than you to get used to the idea."

"I guess," she said, head still shaking. "But really. Holy shit, Ann."

"I know."

It took several minutes for Andrea's head to stop shaking and her brain to refocus on the reason she'd come over in the first place. By then, Ann was becoming aware of a major change overtaking their relationship. She was also aware that the next two minutes might well determine her entire future. Ann never imagined, six years ago when she hired her, that Andrea Gates would one day be her judge, jury, and possibly executioner. With that incongruous insight, her eyes became stoic and serene as she waited on the verdict.

"I never had a big sister," Andrea said. "Not until I met you."

"The honor has been all mine, Andrea."

"You and the colonel should go to prison for what you've done. SST should be disqualified immediately and become the target of a federal investigation."

"I can't argue with you," Ann said, realizing that Andrea hadn't yet made up her mind.

"I know it's not fashionable anymore," Andrea continued, as if talking to herself, "but I was raised to tell the truth and play by the rules. My parents are still happily married after thirty years. I never cheated in school, and I'm more successful than anyone I know of who did. Hell, I still get a tear in my eye when I hear the *Star Spangled Banner* at the Olympics. Maybe it's silly, but these things matter to me, Ann."

"I'm sorry to put you in this position, Andrea. It's not

fair. Whatever you need to do, I won't hold a grudge," Ann said. "Besides, anything's better than leaving my fate to Sicherman or McEwen."

Andrea looked randomly around the room, visibly struggling with her conscience. At last, she looked Ann right in the eye.

"You never told me any of this. Understand?" she started. "I never came over here. As far as anyone—including you—is concerned, I don't know a thing about it. Agreed?"

"Absolutely," Ann said.

"Now that I know what's going on, I can act accordingly. But don't even dream about asking me to help you fix this mess. If it all falls apart, you're on your own. If I owed you anything for my career, now we're even."

"I understand."

"One last thing," Andrea went on, "when JOMREV is over, I want you to resign and find somewhere else to work. I'm sorry, but I don't think I can ever look at you the same way again. Frankly, I don't want to try."

"As soon as it's over," Ann repeated gloomily.

"I'll show myself out," Andrea said as she stood up to leave. But before she got to the door, she turned back to Ann. "For what it's worth, I sincerely hope you find your way, Ann. I'll pray for you."

She listened as Andrea's car pulled out of the driveway. When the engine faded away, Ann dropped her head onto her desk and cried for an hour. More than once during that span her thoughts turned to the gun she bought for Jeremy. *How much worse could it be?*

Chapter
20

In the days leading up to the JOMREV re-bid presentation Ann's mood fluctuated wildly between rebellion and abject humility. *I'll pray for you.* The words rang in her ears, one minute crushing her into dust, the next driving her into a rage. Being the object of anyone's pity was, on its face, an empirical absurdity. If Queen Ann deserved pity, to what depths of condescension must one stoop to address the truly wretched? *Preposterous!* It was nothing but a rough patch, a bump in the road. Jeremy's buzz. JOMREV. Sicherman. With those dragons slain, the villagers would emerge from their root cellars, rub their eyes, and spontaneously burst into song for their conquering hero. That Andrea– sweet little doe-eyed, holier-than-thou Andrea– didn't have the stomach for blood, meant only that her corpse would be among those strewn in the monster's path. Ethics are a fine thing indeed, but especially when someone else is wielding the sword.

Then again, how could any mere mortal absorb such a relentless thrashing and come away completely unscathed? Ann loved her mother dearly, but in three months she'd barely given her passing a second thought. And the feelings she had were not what she'd have classified as mournful. Instead, they felt contrived and guilty, focused not so much on her mother per se, as on the elusiveness of even a feigned sense of loss. It sometimes felt as if her mother had never existed. Or perhaps Ann had somehow gotten over her already, simply by having left home so long ago. Doubtful. The more likely possibility, the one she tried not to think about, was that a malignant parasite was, even then, slowly gnawing away on her, gently nudging her right up to the edge of an emotional chasm. Any day now, sitting behind her desk, talking on the phone, she'd get the final little push and off she'd go. If it came in the middle of Jeremy's buzz or during some particularly grim scene with Irving Sicherman, the floor of that chasm could be a long, long way down.

Ann found an e-mail from Andrea in her inbox the following morning.

Ann,

Jerry, Cliff, and I have been back and forth on this oral presentation for the past two weeks. I completely sympathize with your personal situation but we're all agreed, if you want this thing delivered, you're going to have to do it yourself. JOMREV is your project and we've dutifully implemented all of your ideas exactly as you've requested, even when it made us cringe to do so.

I know you appreciate directness, so here's the bottom line. We aren't willing to risk our reputations on something we don't understand or believe in. The rehearsal is this afternoon.

Thanks, Andrea

If anything happened to Jeremy in her absence she'd never forgive herself, but there was no way around it. Ann sighed with resignation, dressed, dragged herself out to the garage, and drove to the office. It was a heavy burdensome feeling to which she was beginning to grow accustomed. Lately, everything in her life was tinted with obligation and duty. Precisely when it slipped away she couldn't say, but she was no longer the one setting the agenda. Bit by bit, she was becoming one of the little people.

Mercifully, only Cliff and Joseph Bollinger, a professional orals coach Ann had almost forgotten she'd hired, were present for the rehearsal. Bollinger claimed to be a former stage actor, though there was no mention of which stage or what he might have done on it anywhere in his résumé. Still, he came highly recommended and exuded the confidence and panache the industry had come to expect from an orals coach. Cliff was there to simulate the DLA committee and ask any questions Ann should be prepared to answer.

Despite Ann's foreboding, it was a surprisingly routine session. Bollinger focused exclusively on Ann's technique, body language, delivery, and wardrobe. Stand up straight. Address the audience, not the slideshow. Avoid extraneous gesticulations. Cliff didn't bother to ask any of the questions that had prompted him, Andrea, and Jerry to opt out of the presentation in the first place. Already in the eleventh hour, he must have decided there wasn't any point. Nothing substantive could be changed anyway. Instead, he restricted himself to marginal, secondary issues, the sorts of things that would only become relevant if the committee somehow managed to choke down the main thesis.

All that prevented it from being completely unexceptional was that it marked the first time Ann had seen her entire proposal meshed into a unified whole. Throughout the preceding month, she'd done little more than feed Andrea tidbits of intelligence from Irving Sicherman, issue general instructions, and trust her team to transform it into a work of art. Of course, she knew the overall strategy. It was virtually identical to the one she'd introduced during the best and final offer, the only reason the DLA had reissued the RFP. But seeing the final product riddled with the oddities Sicherman had given her was a minor revelation, and it gave Ann the sinking feeling that Andrea and company may have had a point. Bolstering that opinion was Cliff who, though polite, exhibited none of his standard polemical behavior that Ann depended on to challenge her in such situations. He seemed to have already given up—or God forbid— was handling her with kid gloves. *What am I missing?*

The JOMREV re-bid presentations were conducted with military precision at the DLA's headquarters facility at Fort Belvoir, Virginia, just south of DC. Grumman had given its pitch between nine and ten-thirty, and SST was scheduled to begin thirty minutes later at eleven. Each presentation was to be no more than sixty minutes long, leaving thirty minutes for questions and answers. If a presentation lasted sixty-one minutes, the final minute would not be evaluated. Such inflexibility was necessary because of the government's need for absolute parity in the acquisition process. If a bidder sensed that even the slightest advantage was given to one of its competitors, it could be grounds for an expensive and protracted legal challenge. Any perception of bias by the evaluators could easily cost them their jobs. Fairness, or at least its appearance, was a religion.

Ann, Jerry, Cliff, Andrea, Scott Miller from HR, and Larry were seated behind a table facing a starkly appointed and bureaucratic-looking briefing room. Facing back at them were five rows of white laminate classroom-style desks, each with a row of gray metal chairs behind it. Seated in the first row were Colonel Monroe, GS-16 Irving Sicherman, Colonel Simon Oxford, Lt. Colonel Beverly Summers, and Vince Collins, a senior systems analyst on loan from Booz Allen Hamilton, there to help assess the arcane technical minutia. The remaining four rows were empty. Ann took great care not to make more than professional eye contact with either Calvin or Sicherman. Behind her was a large video monitor displaying the introductory slide of her PowerPoint presentation. Ann stood up, smiled warmly, and began speaking.

"Welcome to SST's JOMREV presentation..."

Fifty-nine and a half minutes later, she was done.

"Thank you."

Colonel Oxford started the questions.

"Yes, Colonel," Ann said.

"I'm confused, Ms. Franklin," he started, sounding genuinely confused. "The purpose of JOMREV is to streamline the DLA's supply system. Is it not?"

Ann's heart nearly stopped and she swallowed hard before she could speak. "Absolutely. And we've..."

"Then maybe you can explain to us why SST's solution requires nearly as many personnel as the current system.

I mean, the whole point of this exercise is to reassign valuable military resources to their primary, war-fighting mission. With your system, all we'd be doing is shuffling desk jockeys from one office to another."

Ann stared at Oxford for what seemed like forever. As the silence deepened, the room became increasingly uncomfortable. Finally, Cliff poked Ann in the thigh to snap her out of it.

"I..." Ann stammered. "We assumed the DLA would be better off... that is, would benefit from a gradual changeover from manual to automated processes."

Then Calvin picked up the ball. "But wouldn't that imply a whole series of interim systems, each with its own training, implementation, and maintenance costs? And if so, why is only the first of those cycles described and priced in SST's proposal?"

Sicherman shot Ann a cryptic grin, apparently content to leave the feeding frenzy to his colleagues. It wasn't long before each and every one of the gems he'd offered Ann over the course of their collaboration was exposed as counterfeit, exactly the opposite of what he'd said it was. In her fifteen years as a professional, it was far and away the most crushing defeat Ann had ever endured. All that saved her from being reduced to bones was the relatively short time the DLA had allocated for follow up questions. When it was finally over, the only member of her team able to look her in the eye was Andrea.

"Just go," Andrea said, stopping Ann from helping them pack up the equipment. "We'll take care of this."

"I can..." Ann started.

"Please, Ann. You've got more important things to worry about."

The grilling had been more than just a bad day at the office. She was in no shape for self-reflection, but knew instinctively that something calamitous had befallen her. A critical neural pathway had short circuited. An indispensable pretense had been exposed as fraud. The specifics weren't important. What mattered was that it felt, for all the world, utterly irreversible.

Ann staggered out of the building into the parking lot, numb, a vacant look in her eyes, and wandered right past her car, nearly to the road, before she remembered what she was doing. Alone in the blazing hot August sun, the world was jarringly alien, hostile, and treacherous. The pavement under her feet was harder than when she'd arrived that morning. Slamming car doors and roaring truck engines assaulted her ears with abnormal harshness. Otherwise innocuous passersby looked threatening and deceitful, potential enemies. The veneer of civilization, stretched thin over the primeval Hobbesian battlefield was beginning to fray around the edges. And for the first time in her life she felt completely impotent, at the mercy of malevolent forces her comfortable existence typically kept at arm's length. The fires of hell could burst forth at any moment and she would be powerless either to prevent or predict it.

Not ten minutes into her drive Ann became aware, all at once, of a paradoxical sense of liberation. It wasn't at all like the familiar reaction she always had to the successful completion of a project– paperwork signed and bills paid in full– that permitted her to breathe a sigh of relief and take a day or two off. It was instead of a thoroughly nihilistic and hopeless variety, the sort of liberation that might be experienced by an astronaut whose tether had just snapped. Without thinking about it, Ann found herself quietly mouthing the old Janis Joplin line: *Freedom's just another word for nothing left to lose.*

When she got home she dumped her suit jacket, heels, purse, and laptop in a heap on the kitchen floor and made straight for the refrigerator. In lieu of her customary glass of chardonnay, Ann popped the cork on a bottle of Dom Perignon. She'd been planning to share it with Calvin on learning of SST's victory in the JOMREV competition, but it was exactly what she needed right then– a morbid, self-mocking celebration of her newfound ignominy. Somewhere near the bottom of the bottle she finally found a measure of peace and retreated from the strife to her master suite.

Chapter
21

Irving Sicherman's enigmatic expression still burned in Ann's mind. There was no denying it; he'd played her for a fool and crushed her. Beat her at her own game. Her job at SST was history and her entire career was in serious jeopardy. The JOM-REV bid was lost. All respect was gone. Her life was now in triage, dead or dying, and her only hope was to stop the bleeding and salvage what remained.

At seven that evening, she finally gave up trying to escape into dreamland. Five hours spent staring at the ceiling, tossing and turning, crying into her pillow, and then staring some more, were enough. Her future wasn't getting any clearer– just the opposite– and basking in self-pity wasn't easing the pain. Whether or not her dilemma had a philosophical component was a purely academic question, something to which she could turn her attention when life afforded her a bit more leisure time. Right then it was the tangible part that demanded action.

It was a sickening realization. Ann had performed damage control countless times, but always within an overarching framework of success and control, never from the prostrate viewpoint of the vanquished. She had no experience being the loser. All she had to work with was the curious sense of liberation that had steadily intensified since it first took hold of her earlier that afternoon. A sweet but decadent feeling, it was gently coaxing her to do something rash, jump without looking. It kept whispering in her ear. *You're already so close to the bottom, how can the fall hurt you now?* That was the essence of her freedom. A cornered animal, beset by predators, succumbing to its instinct for frenzied retaliation; a dissipated gambler, putting the last of his kid's college fund on red and holding his breath. Death throes. Last gasps. There was power there. But by its very nature, Ann knew, she'd only get one shot at it.

As she wandered down the stairs, her synapses crackled with previously unthinkable images. Bloodied, cringing faces. Police sirens. Barking dogs. She wasn't ready for the details, but was vaguely aware that her new gun might play a prominent role. A devious smile twisted her lip.

"Dad?" she said, finding Dr. Franklin sitting in the living room rather than ensconced in her basement. There was a large volume on his lap. "Good book?"

He held up a photo album so Ann could see it. "Your mother was the keeper of the memories. I haven't looked at this thing in..." he paused to study the cover. "To tell the truth, I'm not sure I've ever looked at it."

Instead of his brandy snifter, a can of diet soda was next to him on the table. Ann wanted to believe it was a good sign, but was careful not to jump to conclusions. Nothing, lately, was what it appeared. She took a seat on the couch across from him, knitted her brow, and studied his face with a wary, apprehensive look in her eye.

"I doubt I've taken three dozen pictures in the past fifteen years," she offered. "And I'll bet Jeremy was in every single one."

Dr. Franklin turned the page. "Such strange things, snapshots. I've never given it much thought," he said wistfully. "Little two-dimensional images of three-dimensional beings. I can't remember what I was thinking when any of these were taken. Maybe the aborigines are right; maybe cameras really do rob you of your soul."

"Maybe you've been drinking too much lately."

He closed the album and put it on the table, then took a

deep breath. "I owe you an apology, Annie."

"Forget about it, Dad."

"No," he continued. "It was never my intent to come here and saddle you with my problems. If I'd been able to predict how hard your mother's death would hit me, I'd have stayed home. My behavior has been appalling and I'm sincerely sorry."

"I don't know what to say," Ann said.

"Scream at me. Kick me out of your house. I'm at your disposal."

"You don't owe me anything. I can't claim to know what you're going through. I don't have a clue. Judging by my own behavior lately, I'm sure you handled it better than I would have."

"That's hard to imagine," he said.

She had no idea what had come over him. What mattered was that he seemed to have emerged from the shadow of his wife's death without the need to join her. There was color in his face for the first time in weeks, and he was wearing a clean pair of khakis and a pressed shirt. Ann's face softened as she looked into the eyes of the new and improved Henry Franklin, and she recognized all at once that he was, though far from perfect, her only ally in the entire world. Considering what was lurking in her immediate future, allies were golden.

"I haven't spent five minutes mourning Mom," Ann said, "and here you are wrapping it up already."

"That might be overstating it a bit."

"I've tried," she continued, "but I can't make it real. I need a photograph just to see her face. I guess that's what I get for being a phony for so long."

"We all mourn in our own way," he said, trying to reassure her. "About the time you become convinced you're a cold, rotten daughter, it'll come down on you all at once, like a ton of bricks."

"I can't wait," she mumbled.

"She didn't mean to you what she meant to me. She

was my other half. You've been independent for years. You shouldn't expect her death to affect you the same way."

"I suppose," she said, "but it'd still be nice to feel *something*."

"Jeremy. Work. You've got enough on your mind."

"Please, for God's sake! Stop letting me off the hook," she said, a new edge in her voice. "How can you assume I deserve the benefit of the doubt? You barely know me."

"I know you have a good heart."

Ann shook her head and let out a frustrated sigh. In one respect, it was nice to hear a few kind words. But in another, it felt like he was mocking her, rubbing her face in the stark contrast between her depraved circumstances and his syrupy paternal cooing. To make an ally of him, she'd have to put a stop to his woolgathering, insert her dark cloud into his silver lining, even if that meant turning his stomach or, God forbid, plunging him back into his funk.

"I love you, Dad," she said.

"I love you too, Annie."

Ann gave him a warm but doleful smile. "I wanted to hear you say that one last time before I tell you the truth. I'm afraid those words won't come so easily afterwards."

"Nonsense," he said. "You can tell me anything."

"Earlier you said you were at my disposal."

"And I meant it. I haven't been a father or even a friend to you since I arrived. I let myself forget that she wasn't only my wife, but also your mother. My behavior has been inexcusable."

"There is one thing you can do for me," she said.

"Name it."

"When you hear what I'm about to tell you, you can help me simply because I'm your daughter, for old time's sake if you like," she said, "even if the mere sight of me disgusts you."

"How can you say that?"

"Will you make me that promise?" she asked.

"It's completely unnecessary," he insisted.

"You haven't heard what I have to say."

"It doesn't matter."

"Please, Dad. Promise me."

"Fine. I promise."

Ann took a deep breath and closed her eyes, all but certain he would, in an effort to digest her nauseating fare, instantly switch gears and revert back to his old condescending ethical self. Nevertheless, over the next fifteen minutes, she laid it all out for him, beginning with her illicit affair with Calvin and ending with the catastrophe at Fort Belvoir that morning.

Unlike the version she told Andrea, she not only included every sordid detail of her plan to defraud the DLA, but went out of her way to paint the most unflattering picture of herself possible. It was a full-blown confession with the unwitting Dr. Franklin playing the part of her priest. At various points in her purge he shuffled uneasily in his chair, crossing and uncrossing his legs, wincing, visibly fighting back a sequence of reflexive, visceral spasms. Ann could see on his tortured face that the promise he'd just made, should he decide to keep it, would test the limits of his constitution. When she finally finished, he sat in silence and stared at the coffee table in great consternation.

Ann waited quietly for a response.

"I assume you'll be fired for this," he said.

"Of course," she said, flatly. "My job has depended on this bid since it began."

"But that won't be the end of it, correct?" he asked.

"No."

"Because this fellow, Sic..."

"Irving Sicherman."

"Right," he continued, piecing it together out loud. "If he discloses his knowledge of your affair, you and the colonel could be sued by SST and prosecuted by the federal government."

"That's a near certainty."

Dr. Franklin turned his eyes back to the table, once again deep in thought. Ann sat patiently and watched as he slowly wrapped his brain around the enormity of her dilemma.

"My goodness, Annie," he said gravely. "What on earth were you thinking?"

"You promised," she said.

"You're right. I did. Sorry," he said, but then added, "Still, that's quite a pickle you're in."

"I know," she said, looking down at her lap in disgrace.

"I have no idea what to say," he started. "No idea at all."

"I didn't expect you to have an answer," she said. "I just needed someone to confide in."

"Have you considered turning yourself in?" he asked.

"If it were only me, I'd be thrilled to accept that fate. God knows, I deserve at least that much. But it would entail turning Calvin in as well, and I can't do that without his permission."

"What does he have to say about it?"

"We split up," she said, gloomily. "I haven't talked to him in weeks."

"Are you sure that's a good idea?" he said. "You two are in this together, like it or not."

"I'm aware of that," she said.

Once again Dr. Franklin riveted his eyes to the table and disappeared into his mind. Ann went to the kitchen to brew a pot of coffee and returned to find him in the same condition.

"If you'd come to me with this story a few months ago," he resumed, "you're right. I probably would've written you off completely. How could my own daughter, my own flesh and blood, do what you've done?"

"I wish I had an answer for you."

"But that was then," he said, "before I spent two solid months looking at myself in the mirror, and not being particularly charmed by the reflection."

"My mirror does the same thing."

"That said, I haven't completely lost my perspective. What you did was…well…not good. And you have no one to blame but yourself. If I have more sympathy for you now, it's only because I've discovered how fragile our quaint little illusions can be. Let's just say, being run over by a truckload of humility has made me a bit slower to rush to judgment."

"Is that what's been eating at you?"

"All of my principles, the whole grand intellectual edifice I constructed over a lifetime," he said, raising his hands to illustrate the size of the edifice, "crumbled to dust when your mother died. It was all a mirage, an idiotic conceit that I could hold back the tide with nothing but my mind."

"I guess we both have to learn things the hard way."

"Perhaps," he said, "but in this case you don't have that luxury. If you're arrested, it'll cost you everything."

"What choice do I have? Sicherman is holding all the aces."

Dr. Franklin stroked his chin and put on a face of scholarly deliberation. "I can think of three ways to foil a blackmailer," he started. "You can call his bluff and hope he doesn't have the information he claims to have—a very risky option. You can kill him, which is completely out of the question. Or you can blackmail him right back. Get something on him that will prevent him from using whatever he has on you. As I see it, that's your best option."

"How do I do that?" she asked.

"He's married, isn't he?"

"So what?"

"So, what if his wife caught him with another woman?" he asked.

"He can't stand her. For all I know, he'd revel in her pain."

"Who told you he can't stand her?"

"He did," Ann said. "In great detail."

Dr. Franklin shot her a sagacious look, eyebrows raised.

"Of course!" she exclaimed, suddenly realizing that Sicherman's marital woes were likely fabricated along with everything else he'd told her, possibly for the sole purpose of precluding exactly what her father was now suggesting. "God, I'm an idiot!"

"Give yourself a break," he said. "He's obviously a very

clever fellow. Whatever you do, you'll have to be careful."

Ann paused and squinted into the recesses of her cav-
ernous living room. Something in her father's last observation
made her stop and puzzle. Clever indeed. Even impossibly so.
If Dr. Franklin was right. Irving Sicherman had, from their very
first meeting, somehow anticipated every single move that she,
Calvin, SST, and the DLA committee would make more than
a month in advance. And if his bad marriage was fiction, his
calculations couldn't be credited to years of practice, although
that's exactly what he could have expected Ann to surmise. Particularly in retrospect, it was an extremely impressive performance.

"Annie?"

"It'll never work," she said, coming out of her trance.
"He's been one step… What am I saying? He's been ten steps
ahead of me the whole time."

"Sounds like you underestimated him."

"That doesn't even begin to describe it," she said, tapping her knee with her fingers. "Help me figure this out."

"Shoot."

"Irving learned of our affair at least a month ago," she
started, affecting a Sherlock Holmes tone of voice. "According
to Calvin, it was a man who ratted us out. That means he didn't
hear it from Kim McEwen, which is what I had been expecting."

"Remind me. Who's Kim McEwen?" Dr. Franklin asked.

Ann gave him a brief synopsis of Kim's elevator speech
and subsequent recommendation that Ann protect her job.

"You let those two work together?"

"Yeah, I know. Pretty dumb," she admitted. "Anyway,
when Calvin told me Irving knew about us, I assumed Kim was
the source. But apparently someone else knows."

"Might Ms. McEwen have spread the word?"

"Possibly, but I doubt it. Her leverage depends on keeping it secret. If the affair were public, her threat would be moot."

"Maybe someone else figured it out just like she did," he
offered. "Obviously you two weren't terribly sneaky."

"That was my theory too. But if Mr. X is a hotel manager or waiter or who knows who, he'd have to know Irving Sicherman *and* that I was feuding with him. Only a few people fit that description, and I think I know all of them."

"Hold up a second, Annie," he said. "This is all very interesting, but I'm not sure it matters."

"Of course it matters. What good does it do me to blackmail Sicherman if there's someone else out there who knows?"

"I'll tell you," he started. "It seems clear that whoever told Mr. Sicherman either did it as a favor, or else feels he isn't in a position to blackmail you personally. If the latter is true, you have nothing to worry about once he's out of the picture. If it was a favor, then they're most likely friends and Mr. Sicherman can keep him quiet if that is suddenly in his best interests."

"Unless, of course, this mystery man finds someone else to pick up the ball."

"True," he said, "but it still wouldn't hurt to get Mr. Sicherman off your back. Your mystery man might find it difficult to enlist someone else into his nefarious scheme. Contrary to your newfound paranoia, such unsavory characters are fairly atypical."

Ann sat for a moment and considered her father's arguments. Throughout her adolescence, Dr. Franklin's imperturbable rationality drove her nuts. Like most teens, Ann felt instinctively that her raging hormones could be faithfully expressed only with belligerent displays of ranting and raving. To talk them through in a disinterested tone of academic detachment seemed to violate the sanctity of her hysteria. But in the current situation, his level headedness was a welcome change, even if the subject made her queasy.

"So, what do I do?" she asked.

"I can't quite believe I'm suggesting this," he started. "I am your father, after all. But you're going to have to hire a prostitute, lure him into a compromising situation and get proof. Pictures. Audio. Something his wife would not find amusing."

Ann looked at him incredulously, the sordid details of

her search for such an accomplice taking shape in her head. *Could I really hire a hooker?* Repellent as the concept was, she was nearly on the verge of considering it when something even less appetizing occurred to her.

"It won't work," she said. "He'll see right through it. I have to do it myself."

"You can't be serious!" he said with alarm. "It's out of the question."

"A prostitute would introduce too many random variables. Sicherman would see right through her. He'd pay her an extra hundred bucks, something like that, and she'd tell him everything. End of story."

"Okay, fine," he insisted. "Then pay her a couple hundred up front and promise her ten thousand if she does what you ask. I doubt the SOB has that kind of money to spend on a hooker."

"The money's only part of it," she continued. "You haven't seen this guy. Vain as he is, even he'd never believe a beautiful stranger would fall into his lap out of the clear blue sky."

"I don't know, Annie," Henry said, becoming resigned to the complexities of the situation.

"If it were me," she continued, "I'd lead her on for awhile, see what I could learn, and then walk away without so much as shaking her hand."

"And then you wouldn't know if he was on to you or not."

"Exactly," she said.

Dr. Franklin pondered for a moment. "Then I think we need to start from scratch. I simply can't let you go through with this."

"I disagree," Ann said with resolve. Abhorrent though it was, it was hard to ignore the poetic symmetry between the arrogance she'd employed to dig her hole and the depravity she'd need to climb out. "This is exactly the sort of penance I should have expected all along."

Phrased thus, even Dr. Franklin was forced to acknowledge that his daughter must surely pay a very high price for her transgressions. And though there might have been an alternative to their current scheme, it was not credible to expect anything appreciably less degrading. As the truth gradually sank in, they alternately looked despondently into one another's eyes, then to the floor, and then back again, until Ann finally broke the silence.

"As if this weren't bad enough, Sicherman hasn't shown the slightest interest in any of this. At first I assumed that's what he was after, but he seems to have something else in mind."

"From what you've told me about him," Henry said, "he's very likely intoxicated by the power he has over you. For better or worse, men associate power with sex. Give him a little push and I think you'll be surprised how quickly the idea seizes hold of him."

"Are you sure you're really my father?" Ann asked.

Dr. Franklin forced a pained and guilty smile that his daughter returned. A pair of deep breaths cemented their decision, and they set about fleshing out the details.

It seemed like a reasonable if thoroughly nauseating plan, but Ann couldn't shake her conviction that it had no chance of success. Her mind swept over the previous month, pausing briefly to consider the exact moments during which Irving Sicherman had steered her off course. Never once did he come right out and make an explicit suggestion, tell her to consider Haruspex Inc. or a phased implementation. He communicated all of it with nothing but subtle hints and casual asides. It was stunningly well executed. So well, in fact, that Ann felt certain he'd see her coming a mile away. He may have even set her up to try something like this, may have slipped some innocuous bug in her ear weeks ago that led her inexorably to this point. Who could say? What was clear, though, was that Irving Sicherman had burrowed deep under her skin.

"I've never been so scared in my life," she said.

"I'm scared for you."

They exchanged a pair of pinched uneasy smiles and looked at one another as if for the first time. Dr. Franklin's protracted flirtation with death. Ann's unvarnished confession. The harsh glare of their respective torments was finally bright enough to reveal them to one another as the persons they'd become during their long estrangement. Gone were the condescending parent and obedient child, replaced instead by two equal and independent adults with intersecting fates. As the moment drew out their gaze became thick with meaning, both faces mirroring their mutual transformation, softening in unison, until their expressions gradually embraced the depth and complexity of their new bond. Their eyes left no room for doubt. The Franklins were going to survive as a family or burn together.

Chapter
22

"What do you want?" Ann asked, reading the name on her phone's caller ID.

"Good morning to you too," Irving Sicherman responded.

Ann went silent, feeling no obligation to lubricate the conversation. It took him a moment to figure out what was happening.

"Hello?" he said.

"*You* called *me*, Irving," she said impatiently.

"Now, now, Ms. Franklin, there's no need for all of that. This is a courtesy call. When you hear what I have to say, you'll thank me."

"I can't wait," she said.

"From your tone I gather you blame me for your– what's the word– *eccentric* performance yesterday," he said. "But I assure you, nothing could be further from the truth. In fact, I have good news. Things may not be as bad as you think."

Ann puzzled for several moments. *What is this lunatic talking about?* The mere fact that he was still playing his game meant that things might not yet be completely hopeless. After all, his power depended on there being at least *something* of value left for him to take from her.

"I have no idea what you're talking about, and quite frankly, I'm too tired to figure it out."

"Well," he started, "it turns out SST's proposal wasn't

as unserviceable as it may have appeared. The committee met this morning and, wouldn't you know, we discovered that your unconventional ideas might have more merit than we first thought. Of course, my counterparts think for themselves and aren't by any means convinced. I suspect they'll require a bit more prodding before they see it our way. But it's a start."

"Excuse me?" Ann said, genuinely confused. "*Our* way?"

"Sure," he said. "No one would ever admit it, but these sorts of acquisitions are often much more emotional than technical or financial. Some spackle here, a little cosmetic surgery there and *voila*! You'd be amazed what a huge difference that can make."

Ann stared at the phone in disbelief. "Look, Irving, let's be honest for a second, just to spice things up. I freely admit that I treated you terribly, even reprehensibly, and I apologize for everything I did—any disrespect I showed. I'm deeply sincerely sorry. Trust me. I've never been sorrier for anything in my life. But what more do you want?"

The phone went silent for what seemed like an eternity, more than long enough for Ann to doubt the wisdom of stripping away their façade of professional collaboration.

"I wish you hadn't said that, Ms. Franklin," he said, striking a solemn note. "I'd rather hoped we'd moved beyond that point, become... I don't know... colleagues. I think if you reflect back on the previous month, you'll find that I never asked you for a single thing."

"But..." Ann stammered, suddenly unsure of herself. "You sabotaged my entire proposal."

"I did nothing of the kind," he insisted. "How was I to know you'd incorporate every one of my off-handed remarks into your bid? I thought it was all just friendly conversation. I confess I talk too much about work, especially when I'm nervous, but I never meant for any of this to happen. If you'd trusted me, let me in on your strategy instead of trying to read my mind, I'd have happily set you back on course."

Ann squinted with absolute incredulity, grateful Irving wasn't there to read her face. She didn't believe a word he said but, by the same token, couldn't tell if *he* believed it. His voice had the creepy measured tenor of a sociopath, convinced the nine-year-old girl next door was telepathically transmitting oblique sexual innuendoes. Though transparently ludicrous, Ann hurriedly seized the opportunity.

"In that case," Ann lied, "I'm sorry I doubted you."

"That's the spirit!" he said.

"And you think there's still a chance SST could win this thing?" she asked.

"I'm sure of it, though I must warn you, it won't be easy. We'll have to work very closely, you and me. Casual dinner meetings won't be enough."

"I understand," she said, her stomach doing cartwheels at the thought of it. "And thank you, Irving."

Ann hung up the phone, frazzled and nauseated.

Ann had only been to Calvin's house once, during the initial stages of their romance, back before their passion was outstripped by caution. Since then they'd met only in neutral locations and were never seen together where anyone they knew might be lurking about. His house was a utilitarian two bedroom, one story box, built in the 1950s. It was located in an older section of Falls Church where one could still buy a house, though not much of one, for less than a million dollars. Calvin had lived there for eight years, but had always treated the place as temporary lodgings, a detour en route to his six-figure salary in the consulting world. He never quite apologized for its meagerness, but was visibly ill at ease whenever he entertained people like Ann who had already made their fortunes.

The urgency of Ann's visit and her rationale for disregarding their standard protocol was twofold. Irving Sicherman's call the day before and the unexpected turn it had taken lent credibility to the plan she and Dr. Franklin had hatched for quashing his blackmail. Having destroyed her career, Irving was apparently prepared to move on to phase two. Calvin was the only sensible choice to make the recordings and take the pictures while Ann maneuvered Irving into the trap.

True enough, Ann needed Calvin to help her nail Irving, and that was the explicit reason for her visit. It was as much Calvin's problem as it was hers, and she felt confident no great struggle would be needed to get him on board. But the other source, perhaps even the primary source of Ann's urgency was more emotional than strategic. With the world crashing down around her she found herself ever more often, escaping into her memories of their time together.

It took her an inordinately long time to acknowledge what her heart was telling her, but eventually the news filtered up to her brain and she had to admit that she missed him terribly. Missed everything about him. Well, maybe not the Camaro, but everything else. Those wild blissful nights had, in his absence, emerged in her mind as the precious rarities they truly were. She might never meet another man with whom she fit together so perfectly. But it wasn't only, or even chiefly, their rolls in the hay, but their conversations she missed. Her father could certainly hold his own on nearly any topic, but with Calvin it was different. He opened up her mind, painted the average and the everyday with hues of depth and significance. What she missed, more than anything else, was looking at the world through his eyes.

When Ann arrived she parked on the street and made her way furtively to the front door, looking around nervously for prying eyes. Calvin didn't answer right away, and when he did he didn't open the door all the way, instead peeking out through a four inch crack. Ann could see that he was wearing his bathrobe.

"Ann?" he said. "What on earth are you doing here? This is not a good time."

"I…" Ann started.

"Baby?" said a female voice from somewhere inside the house. "Who is it?"

Calvin closed his eyes and his shoulders slumped. *Busted!* He opened the door the rest of the way.

"Please, Ann," he said, irritably, "come in."

Ann entered the front hall and immediately locked eyes with a bouncy-looking young girl, face heavily made up, clad in nothing but a lace thong, blonde wig, and one of Calvin's camouflage army shirts. Ann experienced a dim glow of recognition and wracked her brains for details, but could not place where or even if she'd seen the girl before. From the look of things, Ann had walked into the middle of a kinky sex game, the girl playing the POW and Calvin her interrogator. She cringed, her heart breaking, and for a split second concurred with Calvin that it was not a good time. But just as she felt herself start to pivot on her heel to leave, she stopped short and looked him in the eye.

"I need to talk to you."

"Are you sure this can't wait?"

"Yes," she insisted. "It's important."

Calvin exhaled with resignation and then turned to his captive. "Sara, this won't take long. Why don't you watch some TV?"

Sara saluted smartly and shot Calvin a suggestive smile. "Yes, sir!" Then she leapt over the back of the sofa and plopped down in front of the TV, grabbing a bottle of beer off of the end table in one hand and the remote control in the other. Calvin directed Ann into the kitchen, where they sat down across from one another at a small two-person breakfast table.

"Kinda young," Ann said, indicating the next room with her eyes. "Is that what you want?"

Calvin squinted at her and then shook his head. "I wanted…" he began, but then let out an irritated huff. "What are you doing here? What's so important that you risked coming here in person?"

"Maybe I made a mistake," she said, getting up to leave.

Calvin grabbed her arm. "Please, Ann! I'm sorry you had to see all of this, but what did you expect me to do, take a vow of celibacy? Now sit down and tell me why you're here."

Ann sat back down and looked at the table, unable to maintain eye contact. "I need your help."

"I don't believe it," he said, sarcastically. "Queen Ann needs help. Hallelujah! Hell has finally frozen over!"

Ann glowered at him. "Let me put it another way, smart ass. *We* need to help each *other*. The noose around your neck is just as tight as the one around mine. Maybe living in denial, playing house with your little tart, works for you. But I have to live in reality."

"Denial? That's a good one! I work right down the hall from that miserable bastard five days a week! Every time I turn around he's in my face, reminding me where I stand. If anyone's in denial it's you. Where have you been for the last month anyway?"

"Trying to pull our asses out of the fire!"

"Is that what you call it?" he said. "That ridiculous proposal you came up with? Oh yeah! Our asses are in great shape now."

"No thanks to you."

"Did it ever occur to you to ask?"

"Why do I have to ask?" she growled. "By what twisted logic have you concluded that *our* problem is *my* responsibility?"

"No calculation, Ann. Just simple observation. You've made it more than abundantly clear that you either don't need my help or, at best, grudgingly accept it only when absolutely necessary. This has been your show since you first decided to keep me in the dark."

Ann wagged her head in frustration. "Is that what you're going to tell yourself when they hand you your orange jumpsuit and slam the prison door shut? Boo hoo? Woe is me? I hate to tell you this, but I doubt the judge will show you any leniency just because big bad Ann Franklin wouldn't let you help cover up your own crime."

"And what would you have me do?" he said, growling right back. "I have no idea what you're up to. No idea if you've got something in the works. So let's say I get all enterprising and set my own plan into motion and lo and behold, turns out it conflicts with whatever you're doing? How would I know? The only option you've left me is to keep quiet, stay out of your way, and pray you don't screw things up even worse."

Ann took a deep breath and looked skyward, drumming her fingers in thought. Their fight wasn't accomplishing anything and the vitriol pooling on the table between them only made it less likely they'd ever be able to work together. She looked him in the eye and forced a thin conciliatory smile.

"You're right," she said. "I haven't handled this well at all and I'm sorry."

Calvin was taken aback by her inexplicable appeasement but to his credit, gratefully walked through the door Ann had opened. "Ah, to hell with it! You're right too. Blaming you for all of this isn't going to make my sentence any shorter."

"Maybe we're both living in denial," she added. "But who could blame us. Reality hasn't had much to offer these days."

They exchanged a pair of deflated smiles and paused a few moments to reflect, allowing the anger to drain out of their quarrel. It became clear almost immediately to both of them that their fight, bitter as it was, had functioned as a comfortable self-indulgent buffer against the far more unpleasant scenario they'd now have to face.

"I don't want to go to prison," Calvin finally said, his head drooping. "I've worked too hard to get where I am."

"Maybe we don't have to."

"You said something about needing my help."

Ann looked distrustfully at the kitchen door and then leaned halfway across the table and whispered. "What about her?"

They both listened for a few seconds, but heard only Wiley E. Coyote's harrowing plunge from a cliff top and subsequent rebound as an accordion. Calvin shook his head. "Don't worry about it. She couldn't care less."

"Who is she?" Ann asked nervously.

"Therapy," he said. "Do we really have to go into that now?"

"No, it's none of my business."

"Listen, I know it's important, but we're going to have to move this along. We've got concert tickets."

"Oh?" Ann said. "What are you seeing?"

"I don't know," he said, a sour note in his voice. "Something Sara picked out."

Ann smiled slyly. "I'm guessing it's not at the Kennedy Center."

"Not exactly," he said, beginning to see the humor in it. "They're called *Public Disgrace*. I'm sure it'll be awful."

"Poor baby," she cooed. "Mid-life crisis not all it's cracked up to be? What's next, Viagra?"

Calvin smiled sheepishly, at which Ann burst out laughing.

"Oh, no!" she cried. "Say it ain't so."

"You try keeping up with a twenty year old," he said, unable to suppress a goofy, guilty smile. "Exhausting as it is, I think I've done a more than commendable job for an old fart like me."

They laughed together, and for the briefest of moments it was as if nothing had ever gone sour between them. Suddenly, it was three months ago. They were gazing into one another's eyes over a candlelit table. But just as they began to lose themselves in the feeling, reality dawned. Things had changed. Sara was right in the next room. Nothing would ever be the same again. Their laughter subsided and their smiles faded, plunging them into an awkward silence. Ann finally broke it.

"I don't blame you for needing therapy," she said. "I've spent the past couple of months alone with myself, and I need some too."

"I didn't…" he started, but Ann cut him off.

"I've only recently started becoming aware of what's really important. I guess I shouldn't complain that that knowledge is costing me everything. In some respects, it's a small price to pay."

"I'll take your word for it," he said, back on his guard. "Now, tell me about this plan of yours."

"Yes, right," she said, pulling herself out of her funk.

Ann laid it all out for him as succinctly as she could. At one point she produced a Web page print out from her purse and handed it to Calvin. It pictured a woman's handbag with a nearly imperceptible hole in one side.

Purse Style Spy Camera with 1/3" Super HAD CCD sensor.

View angle of lens can be adjustable up and down.

Employs Digital Signal Processor (DSP) chip-set for image control.

High sensitivity, low smear, high anti-blooming, and high S/N ratio.

The device Ann had found included a spy camera and a remote receiver that could pick up and record images up to 150 feet away. Calvin was to follow Ann and Irving to some location, preferably a motel room, and ensure the receiver was properly positioned to gather the images being sent by Ann's purse camera. Once he had incontrovertible evidence of Irving's iniquitous intentions, Calvin was to bang on the motel room door, kick it in if necessary, to let Ann know that the deed was done and there was no need to go any further. At that point, it wouldn't make any difference if Irving knew what was going on, because the incriminating pictures would already be safe in Calvin's car.

"I don't get it," he said. "To hear you talk, getting him in bed will be a major challenge. I was under the impression you'd already been there."

"Where the hell did you get that idea?"

"Gee, I wonder," he started.

"What?" she hissed. "What are you implying?"

"Don't give me that puritanical crap," he started. "I thought we had something special, something real. Hell, I was ready to spend the rest of my life with you! But here you go again, with your back against the wall the first thing you come up with is to spread your legs."

Ann's eyes were as big as saucers and she felt the blood rush out of her brain. The sudden awareness of Calvin's opinion of her left her feeling faint and barely able to speak. She wanted to lash out, defend herself, even hurt him physically if she could. But her shock was so severe she found herself reduced to less vigorous options.

"I can't believe you think that of me," she whispered hoarsely.

The crushed look on Ann's face must have made Calvin doubt himself. "Are you telling me you're *not* sleeping with him?"

"Of course I'm not sleeping with him. What the hell's he been feeding you?"

Calvin screwed up his face. "Are you sure?"

Ann just glared at him.

"I've got to be honest with you," he said, "that's very difficult to swallow. Irving's told me just about everything short of how you like your eggs in the morning. He rubs my face in it all of the time."

"And you believed him?"

"Why wouldn't I? He knows things about you I thought only I knew."

"What else has he told you?" she asked, curiosity overpowering her pain.

"Well, let's see. He especially likes that peach outfit of yours, the one with the short skirt."

"I'll burn it as soon as I get home."

"He also said you told him your relationship with me was entirely professional," he went on, "but now he's your sugar daddy. That sort of crap. Out with the old, in with the new."

"That is absolute horse shit!" she said. "I never said anything like that."

"Hmm," he intoned, still unconvinced.

"You know what he told *me*?" she said. "He said his

marriage is a living hell, that his wife has MS, that she can't get a driver's license."

"He told you that?"

"That's bullshit too, isn't it?" she asked.

Calvin gave her a stunned, confused look.

"Isn't it?"

"Yeah…" he stammered. "I've met her a couple of times. She's a corporate lawyer. A bit icy for my taste, but pleasant enough. Why she married Irving I have no idea."

"I knew it!" Ann said.

"Why would he tell you all that?" Calvin mused.

"Don't you get it?" Ann said excitedly. "He's manipulating both of us, driving a wedge between us. Look at us. We're at each other's throats."

"Baby?" Sara said, from the next room. Calvin shuffled uneasily in his chair and a flustered expression crossed his face.

"Look, Ann, this is a lot to digest. I need to give it some thought. But either way, like I said, we have to go."

"Think fast," Ann said, standing to leave. "We're running out of time."

Chapter
23

The blurry outlines of a troubling idea had been slowly sharpening over the past several days, more subconsciously than not, but on the drive home from Calvin's house Ann felt it struggling to take shape. She was so immersed in the daily maelstrom that she hadn't the time to step back and consider the recent events of her life from a safe objective distance. Whether it was the re-bid presentation or her father or the undecided fate of her son, the last thing she had was the luxury of dispassionate reflection. But, perhaps out of sheer self-defense, the wheels in the back of her mind had been steadily spinning away. On Route 7, heading back to Tysons, something made her turn onto the Beltway and head for the Toll Road. For some reason, Leon would have the answers.

Towering thunderclouds in front of her, a tangle of lightning bolts animating their internal structure, promised a heavy purifying downpour. She pulled over on the shoulder and hastily raised the BMW's convertible top, then stood beside her car, looked into the sky, and became oddly captivated by the atmospheric spectacle. A remarkable display of raw energy, it had the flavor of truth without substance, like the first cry of a newborn or the comforting aroma of home, irreducible to its constituents, perfect in itself. The painting in Leon's bedroom briefly flashed through her mind, and in that instant, without warning, cars rushing by at seventy miles per hour, she was granted an ephemeral backstage pass into the incalculable majesty of creation. At once beautiful and shocking, for the first time in her life she beheld the alien landscape of her familiar planet with the wonder and humility it had, up until then, only politely requested. For the first time in her life, Ann was presented an unadulterated sense of greatness.

The rest of her drive was like a lucid dream. All she wanted was to recapture the climax of the sensation she'd just had. Losing it struck her as an unpardonable offense, equal to renouncing one's god or forsaking one's family. Unfortunately, the effort to retain it served only to hasten its passing, and it rapidly decomposed, leaving behind only a shell with which to remember it. A lump formed in her throat as the last of the feeling faded away, just as she was pulling into the driveway.

The rain was coming down hard, and her clothes were soaked by the time she made it onto the porch. Leon himself answered the door.

"You're late," he said, leaving the door ajar and allowing Ann to follow him into the gloom.

Steve and Vera were seated next to one another in a pair of tattered recliners, an open bottle of no-name whiskey on a table between them. Leon took a seat on a couch facing them and indicated the cushion next to his with a wave of his hand. Ann sat down, instantly aware of the heavy oppressive mood among them. Out of the corner of her eye, she thought she saw Steve scowling at her with even more than his customary contempt and revulsion, but she didn't dare look up to confirm it. Vera was lost in a deep trance, her eyes vacant and bloodshot. Something terrible had happened, and Ann couldn't tell if her shivering was the result of coming in out of the rain or because she was scared half out of her mind.

"What happened?" she barely whispered.

Steve, eyes ablaze, opened his mouth to speak, but Leon closed it with a quick turn of his head and a cautionary stare.

"Mourn with us, Ann," Leon said, handing her an iced tumbler of whatever he was drinking. "Liza's dead."

Ann looked at Leon without comprehension.

"You heard him," Steve hissed.

The words hung between them as Steve's glare deepened, penetrating Ann's soul. The moment lingered, an awkward silence between mourners at a funeral. Anticipation, anxiety, emptiness.

"Where...?" Ann finally managed to ask.

Leon looked out of the top of his eye sockets, indicating the second floor. Ann shuddered, violently enough to rattle the ice cubes in her glass. Her eyes closed tight and a wave of vertigo nearly overwhelmed her. She took a careless swallow of her drink and then forced back the ensuing surge of stomach acid as the whiskey burned its way down her throat. After recovering, she took another healthy slug. *So that's it.* Everything had happened exactly as it always did. All of her efforts. Her scars and concussion. The sleepless nights. All that money. A complete waste.

She looked up from the floor and met Leon's eyes, a characteristically indecipherable expression on his face. He tilted his head ever so slightly, or maybe she imagined it, as if to suggest she have a look for herself. The thought filled her with dread and horror, but within a minute or so it took hold of her. And soon enough, it was transformed into a moral imperative. She rose slowly and started toward the stairs. Leon's and Steve's eyes followed her with idle curiosity, but Ann didn't take notice.

As she walked through the dining room, the monks were all in attendance. She couldn't understand why the Abbott allowed them to spend so much time eating, even if it was gruel. She'd always assumed monks spent most of their time chanting, beating themselves with prayer ropes, or at least brewing beer for the local taverns. It seemed an awful waste of their suffering to wile away the hours at the table. Just as she was about to turn away, one of them looked up at her. It was the first time any of them had made eye contact. His face was serene and sympathetic, but he looked worried, as if trying to warn her about something. She still possessed enough of her faculties to know that he was nothing but a figment of her imagination, a product of her overwrought nerves, so she assumed his warning was actually a veiled message from somewhere deep in her own mind. Still, whatever he was, she was glad he was looking out for her. He watched her as she made her way back toward the stairs. Ann smiled to herself and felt marginally safer.

The stairwell was dark and murky, lighted only by the storm. Thunderclaps shook the windows on the landing above her and muffled the chatter, if there was any, between Leon and company, leaving her alone with herself. It was more instinct than desire, Ann's need to lay eyes on the girl onto whom she'd poured out her heart and lavished her hopes for her son. It certainly didn't issue from any deviant voyeuristic need to witness firsthand what her nightmares had relentlessly conveyed in chilling detail, night after sweat-soaked night. As if taking part in a solemn ritual, she was driven by a feeling of primitive reverence to see it all the way through.

Her feet became heavier with each stair, the ascent taxing her resolve. The tiny ballerina, participant in not a single one of life's rites of passage, was only a few feet away, those piercing eyes staring darkly into infinity. As Ann rounded the turn into the hallway, she could feel the weight of that stare bearing down on her. A lifetime of disillusionment compressed into a single moment. Still, she continued, urged on by a voice with which she had no fluency, but which echoed as soothingly as the rain. Her father's ordeal. The mystical thundercloud. The tempest that was undermining her, scouring the ground clean for fresh growth. It swirled around in her mind, freely commingling with her dread, hope, and abandon, all the while whispering a promise of something true, something beautiful, something that could of itself justify the pain even while tightening the screws.

Ann didn't bother to check Liza's bedroom. That's not where she'd find her. Instead she stood in the hallway outside of Dr. Remington's chamber. The door was closed. A pool of blood had formed beneath it. *That's to be expected.* She breathed deeply and pulled it open.

As reported, Liza was dead– emphatically so. Ann stared at the grisly scene, impassive, her emotions too disorganized to select a representative. With such a small pilot at the helm, the miserable contraption looked bigger than before. Until then, Ann had pictured only Jeremy in the cockpit and having imagined it so many times, her attention was immediately drawn to the aspects she'd gotten wrong. She was prepared for the blood, but not for all of the bits and pieces of skull, scalp, brains, and particularly the hair, scattered all over the wall. Nor was the smell expected. Liza had obviously died very recently, and the smell was a combination of the heat still leaving her body and the tangy aroma of ground beef. So recent was the event, it had the tangible feel of arrested motion, as if it weren't quite finished yet. Ann got the sense Liza was still en route, standing wide-eyed in the anteroom to whatever hell the Xen fashioned for themselves, unsure whether to protest or start filling out the paperwork. But more than the forensic details, Ann was struck by the unnatural expression on Liza's face. She'd always assumed it would be a peaceful one, but now, taking it all in, she realized how naïve she'd been.

In the first place, Liza's mouth was wide open, no doubt because that's where she'd put the muzzle, creating the impression she died in mid-scream. Ann always saw Jeremy's mouth closed. Her eyes, lids drooping, were not exactly open or closed and weren't looking in the same direction, giving her a confused, indecisive expression that contradicted the panic one would normally associate with a scream. Taken together, it was terribly disorienting. Liza's face didn't make any sense, communicating neither the tranquility of death nor the horror of suicide. If anything, it reflected nothing more profound than the catastrophic effect of a twelve gauge shotgun on human flesh. Gingerly, Ann closed Liza's eyes and tried to shut her mouth, though it limply fell back open most of the way. Even so, her face looked more realistic for the effort and Ann breathed an uneasy sigh of relief.

When she was done, she looked down to find blood on the hand she'd used to correct Liza's expression. Several small drops and a smear. She absentmindedly fumbled through her purse for a tissue, but then stopped, not able to wipe Liza away. Not yet. Instead, like a pagan priestess bathed in the blood of a sacrificial virgin, Ann was suddenly overtaken by a peculiar, dark sense of intimacy. A strange, sweetish, elemental communion with another's essence. For a moment it promised to bestow a modicum of significance on the tragedy, grant her a reprieve from the exasperating meaninglessness death had embraced ever since her mother's passing. But no sooner did she become aware of that possibility than it evaporated right before her eyes, chased away by her indelicate gaze.

As much as it upset her sense of ethical decorum, in one respect Ann's torment wasn't difficult to explain. The void left in death's wake didn't present itself as the sort of problem with which she was comfortable. It didn't have a definitive beginning, middle, or end. It didn't scream out for a project plan or a methodology. In fact, it left Ann completely cold. Black and empty to its very core, it was an absurdity, stubbornly oblivious to its acolytes, content to let the most profound, crushing loss grieve alongside a maudlin display of balloons and stuffed animals. With all her soul she wanted to collapse into tears and bawl, heart exploding with grief and suffering. But instead she sat in the hall and stared at the corpse, despising herself, watching Liza's blood congeal on the hardwood floor.

Ann listened as the gap between lightning and thunder slowly widened. With the scene bled of its novelty and thoroughly burned into her mind, she drifted back down the stairs. Though she could form no clear sense of its meaning, at least one thing had changed; she now had an image of the event, perfectly accurate in every detail, and couldn't stop her mind from freely transposing Liza's and Jeremy's faces. With that, the last vestige of her fantasy shriveled and died.

Back in the parlor, the furrows in Steve's brow had if anything only deepened in her absence. She looked to Leon for support, but his face had begun to mirror Vera's, both of them surveying the ruins from their lofty Xen perches, far above.

"What's that on your hands?" Steve asked.

Ann looked dumbly at Liza's dried blood.

"Please tell me you're trying to make an ironic gesture," he said. "I'll have so much more respect for you."

"No... It's just... I'm not sure," she stammered.

"Why don't you cut out her heart and eat it? Take a little of her spirit with you? I doubt if she'll mind. It's not the return on investment you hoped for, but by now it's surely time to start cutting your losses."

Ann tried to give him a disgusted look but was too dazed to make it sincere. Instead, she turned to Leon with another feeble plea for help that went unanswered.

"Did she say anything?" she asked, "before she..."

"She told me to tell you how much she appreciated your friendship and affection. No one's ever cared for her like that before."

Ann's heart was breaking. "She did?"

"Of course not," Steve said, a vicious glint in his eyes. "But wouldn't it have been awfully nice if she had?"

"Why do you hate me so much?"

"Hate you? I can't even manufacture enough passion to be indifferent towards you," he went on. "You realize with the money you squandered on that poor wretch upstairs you could have propped up an entire Sudanese village in perpetuity: running water, vaccinations, good schools, all the spears they can chuck. But that's not what you did. It's hardly worth pointing out why you would make such a questionable choice, except that I'm quite sure you have no idea yourself."

"I can't change the whole world," Ann mumbled, no longer confident her words carried any meaning.

"Indeed," he started, "far less than the whole world, I'd argue. But as readily as you accept that limitation you spare no expense to breathe eternal life into your most implausible delusions."

Steve was only twenty-one years old, though the pressure of his Xenhood had long since robbed him of his youthful glow. The habits of his face had left it creased with crooked lines, paths down which only a man three times his age and experience should have already been obliged to travel. It was unnerving to behold so much wisdom in the clumsy grip of a drunk, unbalanced young man, and Ann could manage only a bewildered expression in reply.

"That's right," he continued. "How much was it again? Eighty grand? From a woman without a philanthropic bone in her body? Now you tell me. Does that feel like charity? Or does it smack of desperation? Be honest. I'm dying to hear your thoughts on the matter."

"It was the right thing to do."

"Ha!" he guffawed. "Of course it was 'the right thing to do.' It's always 'the right thing to do' if it helps you sleep or cures your indigestion. How liberating it must be to derive so much sustenance from such an insubstantial vapor. Hell, if you could bottle that shit, I'd buy it by the case."

"I haven't slept at all lately," she said.

"You know," he went on, ignoring her comment, "I used to think you people simply lacked the courage to face your real motives; that somewhere in the backs of your minds you knew what you were up to but preferred not to burden yourselves with the consequences. I wouldn't have respected that either, of course, but it would at least have made sense. I've since come to realize, hard as it is to imagine, that you really truly are utterly clueless."

"I tried to help a little girl," Ann said, becoming defiant. "Maybe I shouldn't have, though I'm still not convinced of that. But whatever else you can say about it, you can't say it was complicated. It was the decent thing to do."

Steve shook his head in disbelief. "Say it with as much conviction as you like, Normal! I have no doubt your redeemer is hard of hearing. But at every moment in your life there's an infinite number of decent things you could be doing, lest we disregard that unfortunate Sudanese village with plumbing issues. Yet right now instead of doing them, you're sitting here with me, chugging whiskey, and feeling sorry for yourself. Have you ever dropped even ten grand on any other decent thing? So my question remains. Why Liza? Why this one particular decent thing?"

"I..." Ann started.

"And that's not even the most perplexing question," he said, cutting her off. "With all you have to be ashamed of it's incomprehensible to me that you should get hung up on your rationale for interfering with Liza. From where I sit, it's no more or less ridiculous than anything else you do. And yet you act as if admitting it to yourself would be tantamount to emotional suicide. Hell, woman, it's written all over your guilty face. Just say it!"

It was exactly like Fester's. Ann's mind was reeling. Everything out of his mouth was a direct challenge to her value as a human being. And as before, she felt the same instinctive need to answer, to push back the boundaries of herself and defend her worth in his estimation.

"From the bottom of my soul, I swear, I'm telling you the truth," she said.

"I don't believe you," he shot back, an unexpected note of sincerity in his voice.

"What don't you believe?"

He squinted at her suspiciously. "Assume, just for the sake of argument that I know precisely what you're thinking. Are you honestly saying you have no idea why you tried to save Liza? And never mind all of your 'right thing to do' bullshit. I'm not buying it."

Ann shook her head, baffled, and Steve's eyes opened wide.

"That's impossible!" he started. "How can your actions reflect your goals so perfectly without your knowing how they're related? How can you not know that you're still clinging to the same old fantasy that inspired you to create the Xen in the first place?"

"Excuse me?"

"You tried to save Liza because you still believe we are the key to your future!" he chided. "And despite everything, all the pain you've endured at the hands of your son, the bloody mess you just witnessed upstairs, you can't let it go. It's a chronic illness. You behave as if the entire world depended on that truth. Are you really going to sit there and tell me you're totally unaware of it?"

"It never crossed my mind," Ann said.

Steve gave her an incredulous look and took a healthy swig of whiskey straight from the bottle, wiping his mouth with his sleeve.

"You can't possibly not know what you're doing and still do it. The laws of probability prohibit you from being completely unaware of your motives. There are too many options. Therefore, when you told me you didn't know why you helped Liza, you must have been lying."

"I didn't tell you I didn't know why I helped her," Ann said. "I told you I did it because it was the right thing to do."

Steve burst out laughing, loud enough to snap Leon and Vera out of their trances.

"What's so damned funny?" Ann asked.

Vera, her face suddenly animated, looked directly at Ann. "Steve can't see the world through your eyes and so assumes your ignorance must be prevarication. Be flattered that he credits you with such an elaborate conspiracy. Most of us have no trouble accepting your simplicity."

Ann looked at Vera in disbelief. She'd obviously heard the entire conversation and yet hadn't stirred or even moved her eyes. It had all sunk in subconsciously or through some other faculty of which Ann knew nothing at all.

"Fuck you." Steve said to Vera, though with no animosity. "I see it just fine. I choose not to believe it." Then to Ann, "You want to hear something ridiculous, even more ridiculous than you? I was supposed to be a dumb jock, a baseball player," he said, standing up, pulling his wallet out of his pocket and throwing a packet of photographs into Ann's lap. Ann flipped to the first two or three. They showed an adolescent boy, Louisville Slugger in hand. "I resisted all of this Xen shit until I was nearly fourteen years old. Fourteen! I used to hit myself in the head with that bat– even gave myself a concussion once. Anything to stop this from happening. But you people did your job well. Now I'm just as useless as the rest of them."

Vera and Leon didn't appear the least bit offended, but the bitterness in Steve's voice gave Ann the impression he might kick her in the face.

"Ah, to hell with it," he said, abruptly storming off. "Somebody needs to take care of Liza before she stinks up the whole damned house."

The three of them listened as he stomped up the stairs and threw open the door to Dr. Remington's chamber. There was a loud scraping noise as he dragged the contraption out into the hall, several grunts of exertion, and then a thud as Liza's body unceremoniously hit the floor.

That thud was the trigger. Not the blood. Not the personal loss. Not the tragedy itself. None of that had been enough. But the sound of a life being discarded so indifferently, so coldly, resonated deep in Ann's heart and she instantly dissolved into tears.

So thoroughly was she lost in her suffering that she didn't notice when Leon and Vera finally took their leave of her, allowing the whiskey and her tears to slowly steal her away into a shallow, fitful sleep.

Chapter 24

It was still early morning — mid-October judging by the spectrum of oranges, yellows, and reds on the foliage. Ann was driving west in her white Toyota Celica, a car she hadn't owned for more than ten years.

The sun was just peaking over the foothills of the Blue Ridge Mountains, burning away the mist and sparkling off of the dew-covered spider webs that dotted the fields. Interstate 66 would have been faster, but Lee Highway was more scenic and on that day Ann was in no hurry. Jeremy, maybe five years old, was in the passenger seat next to her, his nose pressed up against the window, smiling broadly in anticipation of their arrival. He'd never been to Shenandoah National Park, but had read all about it, and was especially keen to snap a photograph or two of a black bear. His left hand clutched a disposable camera Ann had bought him just for that occasion.

"Do you think we'll see a bear, Mom?"

Ann smiled. "If we're lucky."

They drove on through the formerly quaint colonial villages of Gainesville and Haymarket that had, despite being more than forty miles from DC, reluctantly succumbed to the voracious appetite of the exurbs. There were stone farmhouses, some restored, others collapsing gracefully under the weight of centuries. Rows of cannon atop a rise at the Manassas battlefield aimed menacingly at the ghosts of Union troops appeared poised to unload a volley or two at the vinyl-sided townhouses, condos, and McMansions that obscured their view of the advancing army.

As the foothills turned to mountains, vineyards and antique shops gradually gave way to tourist outlets with snow cone machines and public restrooms. For sale was anything from real imitation Indian moccasins, rustic patio furniture woven from willow branches, to frontier-style cedar chests and polished stones and geodes.

Jeremy was nearly beside himself with excitement as they pulled up to the ranger station at the Thornton Gap entrance. Ann paid for a day pass and handed her son the park map given to her by the ranger. He quickly unfolded it and began reading. The centerpiece of Shenandoah National Park is Skyline Drive, an engineering marvel that traces the peaks of the Blue Ridge Mountains for more than a hundred miles, shadowing the Appalachian Trail all the way from Front Royal to Interstate 64.

"Look, Mom," he said. "There's a Franklin Cliffs and Jeremy's Run overlook. We have to go there. We can ask someone to take our picture in front of the signs."

"Sure, sweetie," Ann said, distractedly, but then seemed to remember why they were there. "See if you can find a mountain for me, Bear-something. I think it's south of here."

He scanned the map and then began reading aloud:

"The Bearfence Mountain summit provides a 360-degree view. The round trip from the parking lot is only eight tenths of a mile, but part of it is a rock scramble and can be difficult, especially if wet. Wear sturdy shoes. Pets are NOT allowed on this trail. Park rangers have reported seeing rattlesnakes, particularly in spring and autumn, basking on the greenstone and sheltering among the cracks. Keep your eyes open! This hike is for the sure-footed and those not afraid of heights."

Jeremy looked uncertainly at his sneakers and then at his mother, concern in his eyes. "Sounds kind of scary," he said. "Is that where we're going?"

"I've been there before," Ann said. "We'll be fine. How

far is it?"

He turned back to the map. "Mile marker 56.4, so that's 24.9 miles."

On the winding road, full of hills and hairpins, it would take just under an hour to get there. That meant they could stop for lunch on the way. There was still plenty of time. Jeremy pointed and shouted gleefully as they passed various landmarks described on his map, but Ann kept her eyes on the road.

On that crystal clear day, the vistas along Skyline Drive were breathtaking. The Shenandoah River, thousands of feet below, snaked among hamlets and farms that from so far above, struck the idyllic pose of a train set or medieval fiefdom. One could easily imagine peasants drawing water from wells or dressing in their finery for Sunday services. The road passed by granite peaks, stubbornly vaulted into the sky against a hundred million years of wind and rain. Each was patrolled by a squadron of condors held aloft by thermals rising up their steep faces from the valley below. Whitetail deer grazed along the roadside, chewing contentedly, indifferent to the passing cars. Here and there waterfalls cascaded from high cliffs, nourishing the algae-covered rocks at their feet. And a hundred miles in every direction, ablaze in the shameless colors of autumn, the entire earth was performing one last symphony of abundance before the snow lulled it to sleep for five long months.

On any other occasion, Ann would've parked at the overlooks and gawked in wonder with the rest of the visitors. But instead she had a faraway look in her eyes, and though she couldn't say why, was curiously focused on reaching their destination. They passed the Pinnacles, Stony Man, and skipped right by the highest point on the drive, a transgression Jeremy registered with a crushed expression and short-lived pout. By the time they arrived at Big Meadows for lunch, Bearfence Mountain had gradually metamorphosed from a mild desire to an issue of some importance, and was fast becoming a matter of critical spiritual significance. Even so, Ann was grateful for the opportunity to pause. Whatever awaited them, she felt certain it wasn't only the panoramic view.

Aside from the khaki-clad day tourists, Big Meadows was also a favorite resting area for long distance thru-hikers of the Appalachian Trail. There, one could buy freeze-dried food, bug repellent, and trail maps, take a shower and launder clothes, refill canteens, eat a prepared meal, and call home to inform loved ones that no one in the party had fallen into a crevasse or been mauled by bears. But most importantly it was an opportunity to let the other hikers know who had traveled the farthest, endured the greatest travails with the least reliance on technology, and who was, overall, the toughest and grittiest modern-day reincarnation of Lewis and Clark. Snake and chigger bites, assorted gashes and lacerations, sunburns, scraggly beards, and festering blisters were all on display, offered for comparison, measurement, and authentication.

Ann and Jeremy exited the ranger station, matching subs and sodas in hand, and found a table in the picnic area. Nearby were two groups of hikers lying in the grass, boots off, looking and smelling every bit as natural and organic as the wilderness from which they'd recently emerged. Several hundred pounds of backpacks, tents, sleeping bags, and cooking equipment were strewn all around them. Ann listened idly as they regaled one another with tales of their arduous expedition. One girl, younger than the others, was especially strident.

"Check this out," she said, indicating a huge purple contusion that ran the length of her left calf. She scanned the others' faces expectantly, but got no reaction. "Lucky I didn't break my damned leg," she continued, admiring the wound as she prodded it with her finger. "I hope it doesn't get infected." Still nothing.

She was trying so hard to fit in Ann felt sorry for her. Clearly the girl didn't grasp the nuances involved. Injuries were to be exposed, no doubt, but then cavalierly ignored. Made visible, but suffered silently. Commentary, if there was to be any, had to be supplied by someone else, not the injury's owner. The girl made one last awkward attempt to garner sympathy, but then lowered her eyes and busied herself digging burrs out of her socks. Jeremy watched them intently.

"Maybe someday we'll hike the Appalachian Trail too," he enthused. "Just you and me."

"Maybe."

"Can I go talk to them?" he asked.

"Stay where I can see you."

Fearlessly, Jeremy ambled right up to the group, pointed at the girl's leg and began peppering her with questions. She was taken aback at first but quickly warmed to the inquest, and was soon visibly relieved to finally have some attention paid to her wound, even if it wasn't by her comrades. She invited him to sit down, shook his hand, and introduced him to the others. A couple of them offered cool, imperturbable nods. The rest barely gave him a second look, their extended communion with nature having placed them too far above the washed masses to acknowledge him. Jeremy pulled out his map, undaunted, and began pointing at various locations, to which the girl responded with great interest, as if she hadn't had a decent conversation in months, and even a five-year-old boy was a welcome respite from her friends' arid serenity.

Ann watched with satisfaction as the two of them prattled on, nodding and smiling at one another. At one point he pulled a pen out of his breast pocket to take notes right on the map, eager to capture the essence of the girl's wondrous adventures. It wasn't long before the girl was a thousand miles away, somewhere safe and clean, free of her companions' harsh judgment and far from that endless rocky trail to nowhere. Jeremy had completely won her over.

Her son was everything Ann had ever dreamed of, everything anyone had ever dreamed of: the promise of a better future for all mankind. He and others like him would cure deadly plagues, colonize space, end war, and live in perfect harmony with each other and the fragile world they'd tirelessly strive to improve. They'd make quick work of the natural sciences, transforming their boundless ingenuity into powerful tools of progress, propelling man into…. Of course they'd also supply the destination. The meaning of life itself would be well understood to all, printed on bumper stickers and coffee mugs, and would unite all mankind behind a common vision of the future. Pain and suffering would come to an end or would, at the very least, make sense, redeemed by a higher purpose. They'd look upon Ann and her generation as the Great Benefactors, the intrepid mothers and fathers of posterity who dared to dream. And, and, and…

A tear of joy ran down Ann's cheek as her reverie drifted off indistinctly toward a brilliant shining horizon, and then slowly faded away with its waning star. A hardened resolve quickly replaced her flight of fancy and she wiped the tears from her face, almost ashamed of letting herself go as she had. She motioned to Jeremy to end his conversation and return to the picnic table. Time was getting short.

"That was Lil' Yapper," Jeremy said as they walked back to the Celica. "But that's just her trail name. Everyone gets a new name when they hike the AT. That's what they call the Appalachian Trail. Her real name is Olivia."

"I see."

"Most people start in Georgia, but she started in Maine," he continued. "She doesn't think they'll finish before winter. Gruff– that's the trail name of their leader– wasted a lot of time on side hikes and now they're late. He thinks they can hike through the snow. Lil' Yapper says it's too dangerous, but no one listens to her so she might quit and finish next year. The whole trail is 2,174 miles long and usually takes about six months to hike. Wouldn't it be fun if we…"

"Yes, sweetie," Ann said, cutting him off. "Can we talk about it later?"

Jeremy looked at her strangely, and then in a meek voice said, "I guess so."

Ann could no longer endure his childish excitement. It scorched her conscience and only heightened her crushing disappointment. Back in the car she made a point of focusing exclusively on the road in front of her, not giving her son an opening to restart the barrage of chatter. They remained silent for most of the drive.

"Only two more miles," he offered.

Ann nodded morosely, but didn't respond. Jeremy squirmed uncomfortably in his seat, his face becoming pale as he reread the ominous description of Bearfence Mountain. He was still reading when they pulled into the parking area. She popped the trunk and retrieved a black leather pack that she fastened around her waist. Then she glanced quickly around. There was only one other vehicle in the lot.

"Can I wait in the car?" he asked nervously. "I promise to be good."

"No," she said, flatly.

"Please."

"Don't argue with me."

By the time they started up the trail the sun had disappeared behind an overcast sky. A chilly autumn breeze ruffled the branches and sent waves of fallen leaves skittering across their path. His hand in hers, Ann felt Jeremy shiver as she pulled him along behind her.

"I forgot my camera," he said, trying unsuccessfully to free his hand from his mother's grip.

"That's not important now."

Ann's gait was less a stroll than a trudge or forced march, every step bringing them closer. Jeremy was providing weak but constant resistance, pulling against Ann's grip, and it soon became too laborious to drag him behind her. She stopped to face him.

"Walk ahead of me," she said, pushing him up front and blocking his avenue of escape.

Ann made an impatient gesture with her hands as if pushing him up the trail. At first he just stood there, torn between his escalating fear and his absolute trust in his mother. He nervously surveyed the path in front of them and then turned back to Ann, his eyes begging her to reconsider.

"Go on," she said. "The faster you walk, the sooner we'll be done with this."

After another lengthy pause, he reluctantly obeyed.

It wasn't long before a young couple, no doubt the owners of the only other car in the lot, returning from the summit, galloped past them as fast as they could along the steep incline without ending up face down in the gravel. For a split second, the woman made eye contact with Jeremy.

"Watch your step, little man," she said between heavy breaths.

Jeremy's face turned to chalk and he looked as though he might throw up. Ann watched as the pair disappeared down the hill. *Now we're alone.*

"I'm scared," Jeremy said plaintively. "Why are we doing this?"

"Ten minutes ago you wanted to hike the whole Appalachian Trail. Now this little hill is too much for you? Trust me. You're going to love this."

The relatively smooth dirt trail gradually deteriorated into small, then larger, and finally into fairly substantial, jagged broken rocks and boulders. Jeremy was having a difficult time getting over and between them, sometimes forced to crawl on his hands and knees. He glanced back periodically to see if his mother had had enough, but she refused to let up, prodding him from behind whenever she got the impression he was sandbagging. Just beyond the halfway point the rain started, gently at first, but growing rapidly into a steady shower, transforming the dull gray rocks into shiny black crystals.

"Damn it!" Ann cried as her ankle twisted with a snap off of a slippery rock and she fell to the ground, clutching her injury and rocking back and forth. She knew instantly it was broken. Jeremy looked down into the crazed eyes of his mother, stunned into silence, not sure how or even if he should help her. Ann finally struggled to her feet, cursing under her breath.

"Are you...?"

"I'm fine," she growled through clenched teeth. "Keep

moving."

Jeremy continued onward, Ann limping behind him and grimacing in pain with every step.

The climb got progressively steeper and the rocks slicker and it wasn't long before every inch of progress was bought at the price of staring death directly in the face. One bad foothold would mean a grisly tumble down the craggy escarpment. Unadvisedly, Ann peered down through the rain and mist in search of their most probable landing site. The steep slope resembled the walls of a sacrificial Aztec monument, sharp stones jutting out from the sides, designed to pummel and dismember the unfortunate offers to Huitzilopochtli who were routinely tossed from the altar above. Ann reeled under a powerful wave of vertigo but then quickly turned her attention back to the task at hand, not allowing her fear to deflect her from her destiny.

Jeremy, having become a somewhat more adept climber as they went, arrived near the summit a minute or so before Ann and waited patiently for her on a relatively flat rock platform that marked the end of the hike. It wasn't technically the top of the mountain, but was clearly as far as most people were prepared to go. The peak itself was little more than a spindly column of granite, roughly thirty feet tall that jutted up from a long jagged ridge. There was no question of scaling it, particularly not in the rain and without specialized equipment. On the face opposite their trail, the mountain sloped downward at a somewhat less perilous angle than the one they'd ascended, and dense forest extended all the way to the ridge. By the time she hauled herself up to the platform, Ann was shaking with fatigue, blood oozing from her broken ankle. She collapsed in a soaking wet heap and panted for several minutes before she could speak.

"Look at that," she finally said, extending her finger into the sky. "You can almost touch heaven from here."

Jeremy glanced up doubtfully and then furrowed his brow. "How are you going to get back down?"

"Don't worry," she said, dreamily. "None of that matters now. Sit with me. I have a secret to tell you."

Jeremy squatted down next to her. As soon as he was within reach, Ann seized hold of him and used the remainder of her failing strength to wrestle him flat against the rock, maneuvering her full weight on top of him. With one hand on his neck, pressing his face hard to the ground, she used the other to unzip her leather pack. From it she produced a small black revolver. Jeremy caught sight of the gun out of the corner of his eye.

"Please, Mommy! No!" he cried. "I promise to be good! I promise!"

Ann put the barrel to her son's temple and cocked the hammer, tears and rain streaming down her face. "You're nothing but a dream, a silly fantasy! They lied to me! You'll never be real! Never!"

"I'm sorry!" he pleaded. "I'll try harder! I can do better! I love you, Mommy. Please don't kill me!"

Ann never wanted to believe anything more in her life, and for a moment she relaxed her grip and let her eyes drift into the woods. Incredibly, not ten feet away, stood a fawn, roused from the ferns by the commotion, paralyzed by fear. Ann stared in amazement and for the briefest of instants considered venting her wrath on the stupefied creature, or perhaps even turning the gun on herself. Anything was preferable to the sacrifice she was about to make. But instead she sat motionless and watched the fawn come to its senses and dart into the trees, its puffy white tail zigzagging into the gloom.

With the last option gone, she turned back to her son with a maniacal expression on her face. He was now beyond speech, eyes closed tight, crying softly into the stone. She breathed deeply and pressed the muzzle to his head.

"Forgive me."

Then Ann squeezed the trigger.

Chapter
25

Ann awoke with a start, sitting bolt upright in the dark. The impact of the explosion had nearly catapulted her right off of Leon's couch onto the floor. She was shaking in terror, head pounding, soaked in cold sweat, and several minutes elapsed before she could make herself believe the vivid images racing through her mind weren't real. She could still feel the stinging rain on her face and the throbbing pain in her ankle. The jagged rocks, the fawn's eyes, her gun, Jeremy's petrified expression, were all far more tangible than anything she'd experienced in person lately. And as she roamed in her mind through the nightmare's ethically charged terrain, it wasn't long before she embraced it as an unconditional truth, an encrypted communiqué from the upper echelons that demanded immediate action.

She frantically picked her way through the darkness of Chez Xen, a task made considerably trickier by the sudden onset upon standing of a devastating headache that sent her lurching head first into the coffee table. She barely made it to the porch and down the steps before falling to her knees and vomiting into the shrubs, one excruciating spasm after another, until she collapsed into the wet grass, utterly drained. Typically (not that she'd ever before vomited into someone else's shrubs), she'd have been mortified by such a revolting display, but on that occasion all that mattered was the barrier it had erected between her and her son. Writhing in the muck, the very picture of depravity, was a matter of supreme indifference. Even had the neighbors been standing on the sidewalk, gawking at her in disgust, she couldn't have summoned the will to scurry off or even turn away in shame. Something was different. She could feel it in her bones.

She was in no condition to drive but fortunately it was early, still dark, well before rush hour, and she made it home without incident. Even so, several times on the Greenway she found herself pushing ninety miles per hour. Every second counted. Whatever else her dream might have heralded, she was sure the timing hadn't been gratuitous. In fact, as she pulled into her garage she had become convinced that it represented a psychic link between herself and Jeremy, notifying her of events that had occurred that very night. She threw open the kitchen door and ran through the house toward the stairwell and then down the hall until she was just a few feet from Jeremy's bedroom.

The door to her son's room was open, indisputable evidence that something had happened. Oddly, though she gasped at the sight of it, she realized instantly that the wait was finally over. In ten seconds, for good or ill, the curtain would fall on the last scene of this tragedy. Tomorrow—however unpalatable—would be something new, unknown, and fresh. She leaned against the wall for support, equally strong forces pushing her forward and pulling her back, her heart pounding so hard it hurt. *One foot in front of the other. One step at a time.* She stuck her head into the room, eyes closed, convinced that when she opened them her life—for all intents and purposes— would be over.

The room looked much as it always did: tall stacks of books on the floor, bed unmade, blinds closed. She hastily turned on the light, not believing what her eyes were showing her. She was so certain that it would be a scene of unendurable horror that its absence left her in a state of total confusion. Jeremy was gone. She rushed to the closet. Nothing. Under the bed. Nothing. She ran into the adjoining bedroom, her master suite, then back downstairs. Nothing. He was nowhere to be found.

If the house seemed foreign when she first arrived, it was now an utterly alien world. Jeremy had always been, at least in theory, the justification for everything she did. When she bought the place, she had requested her realtor find a house with a bedroom facing south, unobscured by trees or other houses. That alone greatly complicated the search, but as always, Queen Ann got what she wanted. Now with Jeremy gone, none of it mattered. Not the house, not her career. Not a thing.

It was an uncanny insight, and its consequences came crashing down on her all at once. Suddenly, her primary motive, her *raison d'etre*, had been violently yanked out from under her. For so many years her purpose had not only been perfectly clear, but a point of tremendous personal pride, a genuine calling. Never had she been required to consider the collateral damage her actions might have caused. Jeremy was worth it. The rest of the world would understand, even applaud, such selfless devotion. But now what? How does one suddenly shift gears and fashion a meaning, a reason, from absolute nothingness?

"Dad!!!" she screamed at the top of her lungs. "Daaaaaaaad!!!"

Nearly a minute passed before she heard any evidence of life from the basement, but soon enough Dr. Franklin appeared at the top of the stairs, rubbing his eyes and struggling to focus. Only the dimmest hint of dawn was peeking through the windows into the room. He was clad in a bathrobe, brandishing a mop handle, prepared to bludgeon Ann's attacker. When he found her alone, standing in the middle of the living room, he squinted in bewilderment, certain he must be missing something.

"Annie?"

"He's gone," she said.

The tension drained from Dr. Franklin's stance, his shoulders fell with relief. He leaned the mop handle against the wall, and started toward Ann. But just then a sudden change swept across her face that stopped him cold. Her tears were gone and in their place was an expression, highlighted by a frenzied, malevolent fire in her eyes, of which he'd never have predicted his daughter capable. Rather than tempt fate, he hastened into the kitchen to make some coffee, leaving Ann to adopt a more genial bearing on her own. A few minutes later he returned to find her pacing the room and talking to herself.

"Coffee?" he offered.

Ann swung around wildly and shot her father an uncomprehending stare, as if he'd just arrived from deep space.

"Crushed beans, hot water, cream, sugar," he explained. "You remember."

Her eyes opened wide. "I killed him."

She said it with such conviction, for a moment he appeared to lend credence to the theory, but then he eased into his recliner and calmly sipped his coffee. "Why would you do a thing like that?"

Ann vaguely heard the question, though it seemed to echo down a long subway tunnel before reaching her ears, and by then was too garbled to decipher. Although meaningless, the strange sounds coming out of his mouth had one noteworthy effect; they focused her attention on a ghostly, diaphanous bubble that had, since she first discovered Jeremy missing, been gradually enveloping her, muffling her father's voice and obscuring her vision. As he repeated the question, she stood and stared at his moving lips, her brow deeply furrowed, transfixed by the surreal quality of the tones.

Dr. Franklin soon abandoned his initial line of inquiry and began saying her name over and over with increasing urgency, finally triggering a response.

"Annie!" he said for the fifth time. "Are you in there somewhere?"

He was standing right beside her and she jumped back, startled, somehow having missed seeing him stand and walk over to her. She gave him a desperate, but utterly insane look and then began talking rapidly, mostly to herself, sometimes to her father, but often to no one in particular. Only bits and pieces of the deluge were intelligible

"I sold that car... long time ago... So young! But wasn't he just here?" Mumbling. "When did we go to Shenandoah?... That wasn't my gun..." More mumbling. "But wouldn't I have to be there myself?"

Dr. Franklin rode Ann's heels through the house, keeping watch, though at a safe distance. At first blush, the pattern of her meandering suggested a search for Jeremy, but it soon became clear that she had actually succumbed to whichever demons were currently in charge, wandering between seemingly irrelevant locales that her mental state had, nevertheless, invested with great emotional import.

She opened the pantry and unscrewed the top of Jeremy's peanut butter jar, inhaling deeply as if the smell might reveal a clue to his whereabouts, and then made, with tremendous care, a peanut butter and jelly sandwich that she left uneaten on the counter. Next, in the front hall, she pulled an old set of Jeremy's winter clothes out of the coat closet and meticulously arranged them on the floor, creating the impression he'd lain down fully dressed and then vanished into thin air, leaving behind his parka, snow pants, boots, gloves, and hat in the exact shape of a little boy. Her bizarre escapade slowly ground to a halt when she made her way back to Jeremy's bedroom. There, standing amid the mountain of books, her expression of deep contemplation gave Dr. Franklin the fleeting sense that she was preparing to read Jeremy's entire library and couldn't decide exactly where to begin. But in fact, Ann's translucent bubble was fast becoming an impenetrable shell, so thoroughly separating her from the world that even straightforward perceptions were virtually indiscernible.

Over the course of the next twenty minutes, Ann gradually shrank from the books down into Jeremy's beanbag chair, her posture mirroring her deepening breakdown, collapsing in on itself until she seemed to almost disappear into the corner, her eyes dark and fixed. Dr. Franklin watched as she drifted away and, when he was certain she was effectively immobilized by her condition and unable to do herself any harm, he left her in peace and headed for her home office. Every hour or so he stole upstairs to check on her.

In time, Ann's faculties slowly returned, bringing most of her standard complement of neurons back online. And by late afternoon enough of the fog had lifted for her to separate the unsettling images of her dream from the unsettling images of reality. Still curled up in Jeremy's beanbag chair, she let her eyes pan around the room, soaking up the world from what had been her son's perspective for much of the last four years. Her eyes only twelve inches off the floor, little else was visible but his books. Pile after pile after pile. They didn't appear to be categorized, though the ones closest to his nest looked to be the most recent purchases, less covered in dust. Chemistry books were stacked up with fiction and history. Political science with physics and biology. If there was any rhyme or reason, only Jeremy knew what it was.

She sat up, adopting Jeremy's posture, pulling her knees to her chest, and picked up a spiral notebook– one of at least fifty like it– from a stack next to his seat. She half-expected it to be full of complicated diagrams or mathematical equations, whatever had last captured his mind. But instead she found it to contain a collection of random musings, some written in verse, others in prose. She glanced at a few lines here and there, admiring his style, but then a thought grabbed hold of her and she quickly flipped to the end. There, she found several rough drafts of a poem, the last of which may or may not have been what Jeremy considered the final version. She read it to herself while her lips moved silently with the syllables.

Black

Stealthily the evening creeps,
And blackens out the lighted earth.
It cares not of your fears of dark.
It cares not if it helps you sleep.

The darkness, it is often said,
Belies its tranquil emptiness
With images of loneliness
From souls long since dead.

It issues from the deepest hole,
And finds you when you're most aware,
That someone who was there for you,
Has given up her role.

It matters not that you insist,
"My life is crystal clear!"
For when the blackness calls for you,
It's pointless to resist.

The words made her cold, but she read it over and over, at least a dozen times. Each time she did, her eyes lingered a bit longer over the third stanza. *Given up her role?* Far less than a cryptic message from Jeremy himself would have been needed to start the guilt flowing and the panic mounting. The mere fact she hadn't been home when he disappeared was plenty. And it wasn't long before she imagined him writing that horrible line just the previous night, right around the time he was begging for his life with her gun to his head. *What have I done?*

Ann jumped up from the beanbag chair and made straight for the phone. The police were going do their jobs, Xen or not. By Ann's calculations, the taxes she'd paid to the city of McLean, Virginia over the past several years ought to buy her an entire task force for the next six weeks. She marched into her master suite, not even noticing that her father was in there, and grabbed the phone from her bedside table.

"Who are you calling," her father said, warily.

"I'd like to report a missing person," she said into the phone.

Dr. Franklin quickly reached down and pulled the

phone cord directly out of the wall. "No, Annie."

Ann turned to her father with violence in her eyes.

It took some doing, but Dr. Franklin held his ground and eventually managed to calm her down. He reminded her that the police would have done nothing more than cut her off in mid-tirade and forward her to a Xen crisis hotline. Finding missing Xen was next to impossible and, even when successful, usually counterproductive. The police never looked for the Xen anymore, and the few private investigators still willing to take such cases demanded exorbitant up-front payments and made no promises.

"Damn it!" she said, slamming down the receiver so hard she cracked the cradle.

"You know I'm right."

"What are you doing in here anyway?" Ann asked, suddenly aware that much of her summer wardrobe was in piles all over her bed.

Instead of answering he pointed to a stack of papers on her dresser and continued laying out clothes and fumbling through her closet. Ann watched him for a moment, mystified, but then picked up the papers and began flipping through them. He'd organized them, as much as possible, according to the tale he'd learned about Jeremy's adventures over the past two days. On top was a page of handwritten notes he'd taken during a phone call with VISA's fraud protection division, warning of several anomalous purchases, including bus tickets, meals, and a motel room, stretching across the southeast from Virginia through Nashville and finally New Orleans. On the next page was a computer printout of the purchases themselves, from which it could easily be seen that Jeremy began his journey more than forty-eight hours earlier, traveled by Greyhound, and had apparently settled at or near an establishment in New Orleans called The Velvet Dog, where he'd already spent more than two hundred dollars. The last few pages contained an itinerary and e-ticket from United Airlines, in the name of Ann Franklin, departing Dulles International first thing the following morning.

Ann stared at the packet for a long time and once or twice Dr. Franklin looked as though he might help her connect the dots, but finally she spoke.

"I was under the impression you didn't approve of all of this."

"Approve, disapprove," he started. "You're past the point of no return, Annie. Way past it. What difference does it make what I think? I won't deny it, I'm terrified for you. But let's be honest, as soon as you pulled yourself together, you'd have made those reservations yourself. If you need to classify it, call it a favor."

"Thank you," she mumbled.

"I've never been there myself," he said a bit too loudly, trying to get back to something familiar, "but I'm guessing it'll be hotter than hell in New Orleans this time of year. Help me figure out which of this stuff you want to take."

Perhaps simply to exhaust his nervous energy, Dr. Franklin had laid out nearly everything she owned all over her bed, dresser top, and floor, and was now faced with the impossible task of selecting the appropriate ones. Ann took in the scene and smiled as warmly as she could manage, oddly touched by her father's stilted, but clearly sincere gesture.

"I'll take it from here, Dad," she said. "Why don't you make me a sandwich? I feel like I haven't eaten in days."

On his way out of the room they exchanged a pair of war-weary smiles and wondered to themselves if that would be the last time.

Chapter 26

Ann had the address of the Velvet Dog handy, but to her surprise the cab driver who picked her up at the airport knew exactly where it was. She expected it to be a dismal hole in the wall, somewhere well off the beaten path, not a tourist hang out right in the middle of the French Quarter. So much for expectations.

Instead of going straight there, she grudgingly allowed the driver to recommend a bed and breakfast on Dumaine, a block north of Bourbon Street. She assumed he got kick backs, and as much as that irked her she had neither the patience nor energy to find a vacant room on her own. There was too much to do and very little time.

As she began unpacking in preparation to go in search of Jeremy, she sat down on the edge of the bed and it hit her all at once that she hadn't slept since her brief nap on Leon's couch, more than forty-eight hours ago. She'd spent the previous night packing, putting away the clothes her father had lovingly spread all over her bedroom, and otherwise fretting about the disappearance of her son. Sleep had been totally out of the question. But now her head was fuzzy and she was having difficulty thinking clearly. She desperately wanted to get moving, but her body simply wasn't cooperating. Little as she wanted to admit it, she would be worthless in her current condition. Besides, it was still early and in any case, he'd been down there for two days already. A couple of hours wouldn't make any difference. She flipped off her shoes and laid her head down on the pillow. *Just a couple of hours, then I'll go find him.*

At quarter past eight Ann awoke with a start. The room was bathed in twilight and the sounds of saxophones and trumpets from Bourbon Street echoed in the background. Several moments passed before she remembered where she was and why she felt such a profound sense of urgency. *New Orleans. Jeremy. I have to go.* She took a quick shower and then threw on a pair of denim shorts, flat sandals, and a black tank-top. On her way out of the door she checked her purse for the picture of Jeremy she'd brought with her to show around, and then paused a moment to look at his face. A tear nearly came to her eye, but she shrugged it off resolutely and made her way out onto the street.

The Velvet Dog was barely a five minute walk from her B&B. She turned right on Bourbon and couldn't quite believe what she saw. The entire street was blocked to automotive traffic and was packed with people, at least one from every conceivable category of humanity. There was a woman in a traditional antebellum dress, trying to drum up business for the restaurant behind her. To the woman's left was a stripper in Lycra hot-pants and thigh-high patent leather boots, doing the same for the establishment she represented. A pair of black teenagers was break dancing in unison on a cardboard sheet, spinning on their heads, in the middle of the street. Standing around them in rapt attention was a group of Indians, women in saris, and next to them a Midwestern family, camcorder in hand. On a second floor balcony, a group of college students, undulating to the music blaring from the suite behind them, extremely drunk and in varying states of undress, mooned and flashed the adoring crowd below.

As she knifed her way through the crowd, a huge, muscular man in black leather pants, shirtless but with silver-studded leather suspenders, bumped into her without apology, not acknowledging his transgression. Ann gave him an indignant look and then continued on, shaking her head incredulously.

The conflicting jazz numbers issuing from adjacent clubs mixed together in the air to supplement the turbulent ambiance. Such a dizzying sensory overload, it was impossible to imagine anything– animal, vegetable, or mineral– that would not have blended seamlessly into the milieu. By the time she made it to the Velvet Dog, she felt exhausted and was thankful for the relative calm afforded by the four walls.

With little else to go by, she expected the place to be more or less like Fester's, but that turned out to be dead wrong. Right across St. Peter's was Pat O'Brien's, the self-proclaimed "busiest bar in the world," and judging by the long queue that snaked all the way down the sidewalk to Bourbon Street, there appeared to be few grounds to dispute their boast. The Velvet Dog was not nearly such a draw, but it did see its fair share of overflow from the throngs milling about randomly in the vicinity. Aside from the jazz clubs, restaurants, strip joints, and karaoke bars, there was a smattering of generic pubs, more or less committed to a theme, where one could sit and enjoy a reasonably priced drink without any overt form of entertainment. The Velvet Dog appeared to fall into that category, and at first glance did not appear to be a Xen bar at all.

The patrons were a varied lot, seemingly representative of the kaleidoscopic demography outside, and nothing much could be gleaned from their appearance. But they were drinking and talking and didn't exude the nihilistic detachment Ann had come to associate with the Xen. People were looking one another in the eye and, at the very least, seemed to care about what they were doing. If anything, Ann fit right in, and no one took notice of her. She ordered a soda and claimed a seat at the bar. As her eyes adjusted to the dim, neon glow, she noticed a knot of people, some sitting, most standing, along the wall toward the back of the room. They appeared to be watching something with great interest, and she made her way over to see what was going on.

She had to muscle her way through the first layer of onlookers to see anything, and after she did so it took her several moments to figure out what was so engrossing. Sitting across from one another were two interlocutors, a woman in her mid-twenties and a man, probably in his forties, far-Eastern features, elbows on the table, eyes locked, utterly absorbed in a heated debate. On the table was a large glass pickle jar with a hand-written sign taped to the side that read "Tips," and a slot cut in the lid. It was roughly half-full of cash, mainly ones and fives, but with a few tens and twenties. The young woman was ob-viously in charge of the situation, and at various points in the debate the crowd laughed or let out a collective "Ooooo" in re-sponse to something she said, all of it apparently calculated to rattle the man's confidence. Ann listened intently, trying in vain to discern what it was they were discussing.

It was frighteningly similar to her conversation with Stuart and Imelda, and the pain on the poor guy's face probably resembled her own expression on that miserable night. After only a minute or two she couldn't stand to watch anymore and returned to her seat. There, she summoned the bartender.

"I wonder if you can help me," she said, sliding the pic-ture of Jeremy over to him. "I'm looking for my son."

The bartender looked at her suspiciously. "Is he looking for you?"

"I… What difference does it make?" she said, offended.

"Sorry," he said, flatly. "I can't help you." And he walked away.

As the group of people who'd been watching the debate thinned out, many of them heading for the door, Ann watched the woman as she gathered up the pickle jar and handed it across the bar.

"Hey, Sammy!" she shouted.

"Hey, Heather!" Sammy shouted back playfully.

"Make me a drink while I piss," she said. He smiled warmly at her as she disappeared down a hallway at the back of the room.

At the other end of the bar was a girl whom Ann noticed was looking at her. She got up from her stool, walked over, and took a seat next to her.

"I'm Ann," she said, extending her hand.

"Rachel," the girl responded, shaking Ann's hand.

"Do you know what that was all about?" Ann asked, nodding toward the empty table where the debate had taken place.

"Sure," Rachel said, a twinge of sarcasm in her voice. "That's the Velvet Dog show."

"Sorry?" Ann said.

"I can't believe more people don't know about it," she started. "This is one of the only places on earth—maybe *the* only place— where you can pay your money and let a real live Xen make a complete fool out of you."

"So, Heather is Xen?"

"Obviously," Rachel said.

"What about the other guy?"

"I caught the beginning, before the gawkers showed up. He said he worked in the robotics division of some big Japanese company– Tobijitzu, Korigamo– some damned thing. I guess he wanted to try out his latest pet theory on a Xen before he brought it up with his superiors."

"Doesn't look like he had much luck."

"No one ever does," Rachel said. "But that doesn't stop them from coming."

"What's your story? You seem to know everything about this place."

"I came here with a couple of xenophile friends of mine about six months ago, just to see what the big deal was. I expected it to be a bunch of bullshit, but I got hooked. You can say just about anything you want about the Velvet Dog, but you can't say it's boring."

"Xenophile?"

Rachel explained that the French Quarter chapter of the Xen was uncharacteristically amenable to interaction with normals, and the Xen who chose this locale did so with full knowledge that it would not be the sequestered existence favored by so many others. In fact, the Velvet Dog, as well as the building in which it was located, were owned by xenophiles: normals who in one way or another, fancied themselves to be either naturally occurring Xen or, on some inscrutable level, kindred spirits of a sort. Prime real estate in the heart of the Quarter, it was far too expensive for even a large contingent of Xen to afford on their XRA checks alone. So, in return for their lodgings, the Xen made themselves available—at a price—to the tourists and to their xenophile acolytes. It was a welcome sanctuary for the few, seemingly oxymoronic, extroverted Xen.

"Do you consider yourself a xenophile?" Ann asked.

"Nooo! Just curious," she said, and then leaned close to Ann and continued in a whisper. "If you want my personal opinion, xenophiles are mostly a bunch of presumptuous arrogant assholes. I mean, how big do your cajones have to be to believe you're really that smart? I think the Xen only put up with them because they like living in the Quarter. But if they ever won the lottery, all these butt kissers and hangers on would be out on the street."

"What's your excuse?" Ann asked.

"Me? I go to Tulane, right up the street. Psychology major." Rachel explained. "I can't tell you how much I've learned just sitting here, nursing my Margaritas and keeping my ears open."

"A scientist, huh?"

"I've probably observed at least a hundred debates like the one you just saw," she said, indicating a dog-eared notebook in front of her, "and I'm beginning to see a pattern. I've decided to make it the topic of my master's thesis."

"Really?" Ann said with genuine interest.

"Nearly everyone who sits in the hot seat falls into one of three categories," Rachel said. "The guy who just left is what I call a 'legitimate questioner,' someone who actually wants to know something and can't figure it out on his own. You have to respect someone who is honest enough with himself to endure all that. The second group, and forgive me for saying this, is the 'clueless parent,' people who can't accept the sudden disappearance of their kids."

"Don't worry. I've heard worse," Ann said, glumly, but nevertheless scanning the bar in case Jeremy appeared, not realizing she had arrived.

"Those are the dullest debates. Always the same thing. I think the Xen only see them because, desperate as they are, they pay better than most," Rachel said. "They all think they're here to save their kids, but that's not really it. What actually brings them here is a need to understand, once and for all, what they were living with for all of those years. They need some kind of closure but, quite frankly, there's just no way to explain it to them."

Ann nodded, but didn't say anything.

"See that hole in the wall," Rachel said, pointing to the back of the bar. Ann squinted and nodded her head. "Two weeks ago, some guy came in here looking for his daughter. Of course, the Xen have strict rules about respecting each other's privacy, so it was a complete waste of his time. Anyway, he got so pissed off– I think Zane was the tormenter on duty that day– I thought he was going to kill someone. Instead he just heaved his beer mug against the back wall and started shaking his fist at Zane. He's lucky he didn't hurt anyone. Took Sammy and two of the customers to drag him out of here, kicking and screaming."

"I guess I must look pretty naïve," Ann said. "Especially to someone like you who's seen it a million times."

"Yeah, well, if it's any consolation, I'd probably do the same thing myself," Rachel admitted. "I mean, what else can you do? Kind of a no-win situation, isn't it?"

"You said there were three categories," Ann said.

"Right," she continued. "I refer to the third group as 'jilted intellectuals.' Basically, they're the people who would have been the intelligentsia if the Xen didn't exist, and who come here to prove to themselves that the Xen really aren't as smart as everyone says they are."

"How does that usually go?"

"They all walk in here, brimming over with mental machismo and way too much confidence– though I suppose that's understandable considering what they're up against. About half of them leave with their tails between their legs, and the other half, no matter how silly they look, manage to convince themselves that it was either a draw or that they somehow got the best of it. Either way, those are always the most entertaining debates, probably because they're the only ones who really take it personally, like their self-respect depends on proving the Xen are no big deal. It's kinda sad in a way."

"I can see that," Ann said, her face creased with concentration as she struggled to piece together the complex dynamics of this strange new world into which she'd stumbled.

"The only exception was a guy about five months ago, who actually won," Rachel said. "It was the strangest thing. Heather suddenly stopped talking and got this funny little smile on her face. Then she turned to the bar and yelled out, 'Sammy, buy this man a drink!'"

"Really?" Ann marveled. "Who was he?"

"No idea, but he left here like he was walking on air, grinning from ear to ear."

"Didn't exactly fit into your classification scheme, did he?" Ann asked.

"I would've put him in the jilted intellectual camp, but since he won, I guess it doesn't make much sense to call him jilted. Looking back now, I should have stopped him, found out what he was all about. But at the time I didn't realize how rare he was."

"Only one in all…"

"Hold on a sec. Check this guy out," Rachel said, cutting her off and pointing to a man who'd just walked in off the street. "This could be interesting. Don't usually get two LQs in one night."

Chapter
27

There was an intense but nervous looking man, at least eighty years old, standing in the doorway to the Velvet Dog, squinting through his glasses into the gloom. In defiance of the oppressive heat, he wore long brown trousers and a houndstooth sports jacket that his shoulders might have filled thirty years ago, but which now hung sadly on his bones. Large beads of sweat on his brow and upper lip picked up the neon glow. The stoic lines of a lonely widower creased his face, while his milky white skin suggested a lifetime of fluorescent lights and computer screens, far away from the animating rays of the sun. His posture was proud and erect, but was beginning to lose its battle with the withering emaciation of old age, and appeared on the verge of collapse under the burden he'd carried in with him that night. Possibly a vision of her own father's future, Ann couldn't take her eyes off of him as he made his way to the bar.

"Four nights in a row," Rachel said. "Four straight nights. He comes in here alone, sips his soda water, and then leaves. Never says a word."

"So sad," Ann said, almost to herself.

Rachel looked at her curiously, but only for a second. "He acts like he's not paying attention, like he came in here by mistake. But I've been watching him. He knows exactly what's going on. He's getting ready to unload. I'm sure of it. Maybe tonight."

"Unload what?"

"Could be anything," Rachel started. "Maybe he lost his faith. Maybe he knows he's going to die soon. Who knows?"

"You've seen this before?"

"Not exactly," she admitted, "but look at him. He's dreading every second of this. I'm surprised he hasn't fainted. He doesn't want to be here. He *has* to be here."

So wrapped up were they in the entertainment facet of the Velvet Dog that Ann and Rachel found themselves staring shamelessly at the harried old man, scrutinizing his every gesture. When he glanced up and locked eyes with them, they turned away with awkward and embarrassed expressions, like two silly schoolgirls caught passing notes in homeroom. The episode only heightened the man's apprehension, and he took a long draw from his glass of soda water. From then on, the two of them were more circumspect, catching what they could out of the corners of their eyes.

What they saw was a man doing all he could to stiffen his resolve– breathing deeply, eyes closed, face riddled with ambivalence– almost as if he were summoning the strength for his first parachute jump. Clearly, whatever he had to unload was all he had left. It was painful to watch, and Ann got the sense several times that he was about to walk away again. After ten minutes or so, he got Sammy's attention, ordered a shot of whiskey, and threw it back in one smooth motion. Rachel's eyebrows went up.

"He's never done that before."

"This is awful," Ann said. "I can't imagine…"

"Wait!" Rachel cut in.

Just then the old man stood up and straightened his sports coat, polished off the last of his soda water, and walked slowly but resolutely over to the hot seat and sat down. He was sweating even more than when he'd come in, and he hid his hands in his lap so no one could see them shaking. Ann and Rachel had ringside seats, only three feet away. Rachel opened her notebook to the next empty page and started writing. Ann's heart was in overdrive.

"Heather!" Sammy shouted into the back room. "You've got a customer!"

"Yeah, yeah," came the response. "I'll be out in a sec."

Heather had long, healthy, dark brown hair, and didn't look like any of the other Xen with whom Ann was familiar. She was well-fed, though not quite overweight, and could be charitably described as voluptuous, the sort of woman who was alluring, barely constrained by her clothes, but would be well advised to steer clear of the jambalaya. She wore a red leather skirt, not too short or too tight, but quite flattering, and a pair of strappy four inch heels that she walked on with complete confidence. Her top was a matching red leather vest, fastened with silver buttons, and calculated to maximize the impact of her impressive cleavage. And, in another departure from Xen custom, at least eight of her fingers had rings, all silver, of various designs. Her ears were each pierced three times, and a silver chain connected two of the piercings on her left ear and hung several inches below her earlobe. She carried herself in such a way as to leave no doubt that she was the queen and the Velvet Dog was her realm.

"Hand me that jar, will ya Rach?" she asked as she plopped herself down across from the old man.

Sammy handed the pickle jar across the bar to Rachel who passed it over to Heather.

"Don't get too many old codgers like you in here," Heather began. "Must be quite an angry bee you've got buzzing around in your bonnet."

"I suppose you could say that," he said in a surprisingly gentle voice.

Heather looked into his eyes, sizing him up. He tried to meet her gaze but was soon looking nervously at his hands. Finally she broke the silence.

"So tell me, pops, what's important enough to pry you away from your shuffleboard and crossword puzzles?"

He swallowed hard. "I used to be a professor at..." he started, but was interrupted by Heather tapping her fingernails on the tip jar. For a moment he looked confused. "Oh, of course. I apologize."

The professor reached into his inner jacket pocket and produced a thick white envelope. It was packed with hundred dollar bills.

"This is all I can afford," he said, placing it on the table. "Take whatever you think is fair."

Ann gasped and then covered her mouth. Heather looked up from the envelope into the professor's eyes, and then gave him a warm though somewhat pitying smile.

"Let me give you one freebie first," Heather said. "If the hole in your life is so deep that you believe this can fill it, there's probably nothing I can say to help you. Still, if you do decide to stay, I'll have to assume that this generous offer is proportionate, at least in your mind, to the value of what you might learn here. And for that reason, it'll cost you the entire amount. Maybe you should take a moment to consider it."

"I understand," he said.

"I think you said you were a professor somewhere."

"Caltech," he said. "The California Institute..."

"I know what it is," she said. "What's your specialty?"

"High energy physics," he answered. "I worked in a field called QCD."

"Quantum chromodynamics," she said. "You guys manage to tease God out of your atom smashers yet?"

The professor gave Heather a stunned look. "You're familiar with this subject?"

"Why so surprised? If you didn't think I'd know about it, why would you bother coming here?"

"I was going to ask you something else, something about..." his voice trailed off. "How *much* do you know? I mean, do you... No one knows about this stuff except a few hundred physicists. No one."

"You publish your work, don't you?" she asked.

"Well... yes, of course."

"Didn't you expect anyone to read it?"

"Honestly?" he said. "No, I didn't. At least no one out-side of our little circle."

"You have a larger audience than you realize."

He paused a few moments, his face becoming more ani-mated as he came to grips with his unexpected good fortune. Then he launched into his reason for being there.

"I've been working on the same problem for most of my life," he said, a note of deep reverence in his voice. "I dream about it. I think about it while I'm cooking my dinner, watching TV, driving to work. I couldn't even get it out of my head at my wife's funeral. It's all I am. I came here to see if you could help purge it from my mind, to give me a moment's rest before I die. But…"

"But now you think I might be able to help you find the answer," Heather said.

"Can you?"

Heather eyed the envelope.

The professor took one last look at his money and then pushed it across the table with great significance. Then, in a hoarse voice he said, mostly to himself, "What difference does it make anymore." Ann was flabbergasted.

"Well then," Heather said, cramming the whole enve-lope through the slot in the tip jar, "let's start getting your mon-ey's worth, shall we?"

He nodded dumbly, still a bit dizzy from the price he'd just paid.

"You won't like it," Heather warned. "It's not the gran-diose, all-unifying, principle of everything you got into this business to find."

"How could you possibly know that?" he asked. "QCD is a thoroughly experimental science. We work with mountains and mountains of data. You can't just lock yourself in your bed-room and figure it all out."

"Whoa! Back up a minute, pops," Heather said. "I don't claim to have it all figured out. The Xen are pretty smart, sure, but Mother Nature is a wily old bat herself, as I'm sure you well know. If anything, I may have found a little crack in your theory, a tiny crevice. But I'll leave that for you to decide."

"A crack?" he said, suddenly interested again. "What sort of crack?"

"Let me first summarize what I'm guessing is your main source of pain."

"I'm listening."

Ann turned to Rachel and whispered in her ear. "What on earth are they talking about?"

"Trust me," Rachel whispered back, "it's about to get a whole lot worse. Always does with the scientists. Two minutes of 'Hi, how ya doing' and then two hours of incomprehensible techno babble. My advice, watch the guy's face. His expressions will tell you where things are going."

Heather took a deep breath. "Standard perturbation theory is unreliable in low-energy hadronic interactions with a strong coupling constant. Consequently, you are required to employ lattice approximations based on a Monte Carlo integration of the Euclidean path integral. The validity of such approximations is dependent on the accuracy of your start values and the resolution of the lattice mesh. Unfortunately, linear increases in mesh resolution result in exponential increases in the number of calculations. Currently, even the fastest computers are only able to achieve a margin of error somewhere in the neighborhood of ten percent. And for a physicist accustomed to debating the fifteenth decimal place, ten percent uncertainty is totally unacceptable."

"Yes!" he said, excitedly. "That's exactly it. But I don't know if I'd call that a crack in the theory. It simply means we won't know if it's correct until our computers are a lot faster."

"You may be right," she said. "It might simply be a technological issue. Then again, there may be something more profound going on here. I'm fairly certain there aren't many nihilists among your colleagues out at Caltech. And while you can credit that fact with the success you've had, it's sometimes valuable to pull your theories up by the roots and poke around a little."

"I'm not sure I understand. Every experiment we conduct has the potential, as you put it, of pulling our theories up by the roots. In fact, finding discrepancies is one of the most exciting parts of the business. They signal the possibility of a new advance."

"Then what do you say we start pulling and see what comes up?"

"Sounds good to me," he said.

"QCD is basically an extension of QED, but instead of electrons and photons, it deals with quarks and gluons."

"That's essentially correct, though there are quite a few differences," he said. "You already mentioned the large coupling constant, and there's also the range of colors, flavors, and charges. They seem to obey the same laws, but the calculations are far more involved."

"Granted, but in general you treat gluons as analogs of photons, and quarks as analogs of electrons, at least for the purposes of drawing your Feynman diagrams and applying your Schrödinger equations. Let's ignore the details for now."

"Okay, I'm with you so far."

"So here's my big question. What is the amplitude for a gluon to be emitted, not merely exchanged between adjacent quarks, but emitted from the nucleus altogether?"

"Zero," he said. "Gluons only exist within hadrons. They've never been observed or calculated to exist independently."

"*Exactly* zero?"

"For every purpose we've devised, yes, exactly zero."

"Is that a theoretical requirement or simply a statistical approximation?"

"In quantum theory, those two are hard to separate, but I suppose if you insist on it, there could be some infinitesimal amplitude for a gluon to be emitted into free space. But for every application we've imagined, that contribution would be entirely negligible."

"So far as the strong force is concerned?" Heather asked.

"Yes, of course, that's what we're talking about, isn't it?"

"Up to this point, yes. But I'd like to go back for a minute to this infinitesimal amplitude. Tell me, if a negligible fraction, say, one in a billion billion of gluons were emitted into free space, what would they do?"

"Well, I suppose they'd continue to behave according to the same rules as they normally would."

"Meaning they'd interact with other free gluons, quarks from other hadrons, or possibly electrons or photons. Correct?"

"Sure, any one of those."

Heather smiled strangely. "And if a gluon from one hadron interacted with a distant hadron or with a gluon emitted from a distant hadron, what force would you call that?"

For a split second the professor seemed on the verge of responding, but suddenly stopped short, gave Heather a look of existential shock, and fell into deep concentration. His hands were no longer shaking and his sweat had also abated. The Velvet Dog had disappeared. The months of agonizing about whether or not to visit New Orleans were a distant memory. He was again lost in the problem that had become his identity; nothing else existed. And one could almost see, spinning around his wispy white hair, his calculation of discretization errors for heavy quarks, assorted continuum renormalization schemes, and the consequences of ignoring the fermion contribution to the path integral. His lips were moving in concert with the heated conversation going on in his mind, while his fingers frantically tabulated the various totals.

Ann was spellbound, wondering what on earth could have caused such a profound change in the professor's demeanor. His reverie barely lasted five minutes, but it seemed interminable. Rachel used the lull to catch up, scribbling wildly in her notebook, perhaps hoping to capture enough of the exchange to make it intelligible to a physicist at Tulane and find out what in the world had just happened. After what seemed like forever, the professor finally looked up from his mental calculus and spoke.

"You're talking about gravity," he rasped, an inexplicable veneration in his tone.

"I call it Heather's Conjecture," she responded. "Be sure to mention that to your buddies at Caltech."

"But... I... There is absolutely no evidence for that!" he blurted out, almost defensively. "We've done thousands of experiments and have never detected a free gluon. All they do is exchange energy between quarks within nuclei. Nothing more."

"All because of that large coupling constant?" she challenged.

"What does that have to do with it?"

For the next thirty minutes the two of them went back and forth, sometimes heatedly, faster and faster, until smoke began rising from Rachel's notebook as she broke new ground in the art of shorthand. Heather explained that the coupling constant, whatever that was, could be understood as the "coherence factor" of a given force, describing, for lack of a better word, its "fuzziness." Electromagnetism has a low coupling constant and is therefore relatively fuzzy. It is mostly exhausted in the atomic bonds of matter, but it also "decoheres" and often acts over great distances as electromagnetic waves. By contrast, the strong force's coupling constant is nearly equal to one, making it extremely un-fuzzy, and for that reason very coherent. Still, though highly coherent, it is not infinitely so. If it were, it would not be a force at all but would instead simply collapse in on itself. As a consequence, Heather argued, the unflinching application of QCD principles, assuming computer power could ever rise to the occasion, should result in a very small but nonzero degree of gluonic fuzziness.

The professor did not go down without a fight, bringing to bear an avalanche of published research as well as his own considerable expertise. But finally, grudgingly, he had to admit that at least some fraction, though perhaps not all, of the gravitational force may very well be caused by gluons. And even that fraction would throw the whole standard model into disarray.

"My gosh!" he said, still a bit shaken. "If you're right, this is awful."

"Awful?" Heather said, feigning offense. "To the contrary, it'd be wonderful."

"No," he insisted, "it means that gravity will be forever lost in the margin of error of the best theory we have to describe it. Computers would have to be a billion — maybe a trillion — times faster to predict it. It means there's little hope of ever finding a unified theory of physics. How could you find that wonderful?"

"Not only will you be unable to predict it, you'll also never be able to detect it. Imagine how sensitive your experiments would have to be to tease out the minuscule contribution of a single free gluon on a hadron seething with billions upon billions of local gluons. When this idea first occurred to me, I couldn't decide whether to sit in awe or burst out laughing. Mother Nature has such a flare for the ironic."

"This can't be true," he said, his face becoming even paler than its standard hue.

"I don't think you're looking at this from the right perspective, Professor."

"I don't feel well," he said, and looked it, descending into a meditative silence. He leaned back in the hot seat and stared indistinctly toward the back of the bar. Ann watched him closely as the tension in his frail old body gradually dissipated and his expression of distress slowly gave way to resignation and finally to a curious but profound look of tranquility. It was astonishing to witness. Notwithstanding the scientific revolution that may or may not have just taken place right before her very eyes, Ann had no doubt in her mind that this man was changed forever.

"You still in there, pops?" Heather asked, cocking her head to one side.

"It's funny," he said, thinking out loud, not really responding to Heather. "I hardly dared say it out loud, but I've often feared that something like this might be true, that Mother

Nature would arrange it so we couldn't figure it all out."

"Don't you see the beauty in that?" Heather asked.

"Beauty?" he puzzled. "On the contrary. It's messy and chaotic, an open-ended catastrophe like politics or history. I've always equated beauty with mathematical symmetry and geometrical perfection, not the random, meaningless dissonance of everyday life. Physics was my oasis."

"Was it?" she shot back, a sly grin on her face. "You came here to have it purged from your mind, didn't you? To buy yourself a 'moment's rest?' Imagine how much easier that'll be now that you know there's nothing left to look for."

The professor couldn't suppress an ironic chuckle.

"This is not what I expected when I walked in," he started. "I guess I wasn't prepared to give it up after all. It sounds arrogant, but it never occurred to me that you'd have the answers. Now, in retrospect, I can't honestly say why I came in here. Maybe I just needed someone to talk to."

"Pretty expensive confession, wouldn't you say?" she said, indicating the tip jar.

"Is it enough for one more question?" he asked.

"As long as it has nothing to do with physics. This crap gives me a headache."

"No," he said. "It's more of a personal question."

"Personal, huh? Okay, but I reserve the right to slap you across the face if you stop treating me like a lady."

Several onlookers chuckled slightly, prompting the professor to glance around nervously, as if that was the first time he'd noticed they weren't alone in his living room. He took a moment to recompose himself and then got back to his question.

"Maybe I was naïve to think science could provide a meaning to my life, though I can't imagine any alternative that would've resonated so deeply in my soul. God and I could never get on the same page. And now, after this, I'll go to my grave, without hope, stripped even of the quest that has animated most of my years."

Heather raised her eyebrows in anticipation. "Was there a question in there?"

"How?" he said, a look of sincere desperation in his eyes. "How can you live in a world that you know, beyond the slightest doubt, has no meaning?"

"At least half of my brethren, it pains me to say, decided not to. I hesitate to judge them too harshly, though I can't help thinking they allowed the enormity of the insight, its immediate emotional impact, to obscure the subtle aesthetic of discord and pandemonium that only becomes clear well afterwards."

"You almost sound happy about it."

"Unlike you," she continued, "I don't want to see the cosmos figured out. I take it personally whenever someone suggests that all of creation can be reduced to a simple set of equations. You've spent too much of your life on physics to understand why, but trust me, it's better this way."

"But..." he started.

"Sorry, Professor," she cut in, "time's up. Where you go from here is up to you."

Heather rose abruptly, grabbed the pickle jar off of the table, shouted, "Sammy!" and then tossed it over the bar to him. "I'm taking the rest of the night off."

"Damn, woman!" Sammy said, marveling at the night's take. "You earned it."

On her way to the back of the room Heather slapped Rachel on the back. "Tell your new friend to come back tomorrow, Rach. I'm gonna go drink a bottle of Merlot and get laid." And then she disappeared up a flight of stairs marked "Employees Only."

In an old-fashioned gesture of respect, the professor had stood up with Heather and was still standing, looking rather lost, as the last of her footsteps echoed down the stairwell.

Chapter 28

The creaky, rickety timbers of Ann's B&B transmitted, even amplified, every footstep, voice, and random thud that took place anywhere on its three ancient floors. Ann gradually emerged from a fitful night's sleep, her dreams first incorporating, then overlapping with, and finally succumbing to the ambient hubbub. There was a young couple in an adjacent room debating the merits of forgoing breakfast in favor of a gut-busting Creole feast at lunchtime. A pair of carpenters were milling about on the third floor catwalk, arranging sawhorses and extension cords, in preparation for replacing a section of the eave that had completely rotted away. A young man in a leather jacket holding a motorcycle helmet was standing outside his room, smoking a cigarette, trying to ignore a shrill female voice coming from the other side of his door. Chaotic as it might have seemed, the ruckus coalesced into a strangely soothing tableau of humanity, and Ann listened contentedly as the various storylines unfolded.

She rarely recalled the details of her dreams, but was often struck by the clout of their emotional residue, accepting as an article of faith that they were benign glimpses into her immediate past or future. On that morning, staring at the cracked paint on the ceiling of her quaint little room, she was entertaining a notion that was anathema to all things Ann, a sensation she'd always managed to shrug off even in her most vulnerable moments. She felt herself contemplating surrender. She might have remained in bed all morning had the ring of her cell phone not prompted her to rise. Her home number appeared on the screen.

"Did he call?" she asked immediately, not offering a greeting.

"Of course not," Dr. Franklin responded, "but he did use his credit card again."

"Please tell me he's still in New Orleans."

"Still in New Orleans. Still at the Velvet Dog," he answered. "What kind of a place is that, anyway?"

"What time?"

"Last night, around midnight."

Ann squinted at the phone. "Exactly?"

"Eleven fifty-four," he clarified. "Why?"

"How is that possible? I was there at eleven fifty-four."

"Look, Annie…"

"Dad," she cut in, a reproving tone in her voice. "I need something constructive right now. Do you understand?"

"I was…"

"I mean it, Dad. Con-struc-tive."

The phone went silent for several moments. "Just be careful, Annie. The Xen… This could mean anything. He may not even be down there."

"He's here," she muttered without conviction. "Call me if you hear anything else." And she quickly hung up.

Ann arrived at the Velvet Dog before ten, not sure it would be open, but drawn there just the same. Before reaching the door, she could already hear a heated exchange coming from inside. She hesitated for a moment but then sneaked in quietly, taking a seat near the entrance, not wanting to be noticed. Standing at the bar were a man and woman in their late forties. From the woman's tear-stained cheeks and bloodshot eyes, it was clear the confrontation had already been going on for some time.

Ann instantly pegged them as country folk. The man was slightly overweight and his hands were thick and calloused. The woman was sturdily built, wore a flower-print dress, and her face had the texture of windblown leather. Their bearing was one of defiance but also fear in the face of all the calamity and damnation of the big city, rather as if their mere presence were an affront to everything good and decent, a harrowing odyssey from which they'd emerge only by presenting a united front. The woman did all the talking, or more accurately, screaming, while her husband struggled without much success to console her. Zane, who was standing behind the bar and looking mildly amused, was at the eye of her fury.

"Bring me my baby!" she screamed, nearly loud enough to shatter glass.

Sammy, bleary-eyed and barely dressed, made himself visible in the rear, just inside the employees' entrance. The commotion had obviously jolted him out of bed prematurely and his hair shot up from his head in several different directions. Zane acknowledged him with a cool nod that also effectively communicated to the grieving parents that anything more than shouting would be countered with overwhelming force.

"Darling, please," the man begged, glancing around self-consciously. "I tried to tell you. This ain't the way to go about things. They don't care a bit about you or anybody else but themselves." He directed the last part of his entreaty to Zane, perhaps hoping to shame him into compliance. But it had no effect.

"Let go of me, Tom! If you ain't gonna do nothing, then get out of my way!" the woman shrieked, breaking free of her husband's embrace. Then to Zane, "Collin is all I've got! Don't you understand that? Don't you even care?" She was shaking violently, mucous streaming from her nose and spittle flying out of her mouth. "I'm not leaving until I see him myself or the Lord above strikes me dead right here!"

She said it with so much conviction, Ann thought for a moment the woman might make good on her threat. But no sooner had the last spit-soaked word landed on the bar than she dissolved into tears and collapsed to the floor, wailing in agony, utterly inconsolable. Tom was at a complete loss and obviously had only come to this horrible place at his wife's insistence. He looked back and forth from Zane's icy stare to the blubbering mass on the floor, tears beginning to form in his eyes as well, and then finally, impotent and hopeless, he slumped onto a barstool, buried his face in his hands and stuck his thumbs in his ears.

Ann was spellbound, numb, nearly to the point of forgetting where she was. A shiver raced up her spine and like a reflex sent her recoiling out onto St. Peter's, her rationale for being there in the first place becoming vague and inconclusive. She marched down Royal Street, agitated, eyes straight ahead, all the way to edge of the Quarter at Esplanade Avenue, not seeing anything along the way. Several gaggles of aimless tourists, catching a glimpse of Ann's twisted face as she approached, instinctively surrendered the center of the sidewalk. At the end of the street, standing on the corner and forced to make a decision, she found herself shaking, unable to move in any direction. Part of the sensation was familiar: the pressing need to form a plan, begin step one, and start barking orders. But the other part, the more prevalent part, was alien to her. She strongly believed, even knew for a fact, that whichever way she went and for whatever reason, everything would turn out exactly the same. It made absolutely no difference and yet something had to be done.

Her gait slowly came to embrace her deepening sense of irrelevance and she found herself drifting through the streets, haunting the Spanish architecture like a ghost. Nothing she did could properly be said to have arisen from a bona fide volition or conscious act of will. Instead, her stilted behavior seemed to issue directly from the struggle taking place backstage, one minute prompting her to turn suddenly and pick up the pace, the next minute quashing whatever plan had so prompted her and plunging her back into her daze. She bought a fold-out map from one of the innumerable purveyors of generic French Quarter bric-a-brac, and then spent five full minutes standing outside the shop, staring at it (or perhaps right through it), as if divining for the first time that the lines on the paper represented the city she was in.

She let the map guide her to the local police precinct, housed in one of the most stately old buildings in the Quarter. It was a large gray Romanesque structure with tall Corinthian columns. A steady stream of uniformed officers, lawyers in suits and ties, and a variety of less savory looking characters flowed up and down the granite steps to the entrance. Ann stood across the street and gazed at it sorrowfully, no longer able to muster up any moral outrage at being denied access to its machinery of justice. Briefly, a fanciful idea took hold of her, of offering a thousand dollars to one of the off-duty officers in return for tossing the Velvet Dog and roughing up anyone who stood in his way. What better way to wipe that smug look off of Zane's face!

But just as quickly as it came the idea vanished like a puff of smoke. It was clearly illegal. No one would ever agree to such an outrageous scheme. After almost twenty years, the Xen didn't evoke much emotion at all anymore. It wasn't hatred or even disdain. They were a known quantity– not quite ignored, but already accounted for– rather like the downward pressure on the stock market of high interest rates or reduced oil refining capacity. Long ago, society had simply factored the loss of the Xen into their daily calculations and washed their hands of it. Ann knew it well, but had never before felt so acutely the weight of that indifference. A bitter tear worked its way down her cheek as she turned her back on the police station and slowly wandered off.

By two that afternoon the temperature and humidity were both well into the nineties and she was soaked with sweat. Even so, she nearly fainted before she linked her worsening dehydration with the concept of buying a bottle of water. On Decatur she came upon an Internet café, a rather surprising find; lack of demand had caused most such establishments to shut their doors long ago. Ann puzzled for a few moments, but was once again seized by the seeds of a plan, and she hastened inside, planting herself in front of an unoccupied machine. She typed in the URL of her most trusted support group and then clicked on a link entitled *Xen Blogs*. An enormous list came up– at least two hundred entries– which Ann began scanning for anything related to New Orleans, the French Quarter, the Velvet Dog, or something similar. She struggled uncomprehendingly through a few pages, looking for a familiar name or place, but the strain quickly got the better of her. Her eyes glazed over and she found herself staring blankly out of the front window at the passersby. When a waitress finally came over to take her order, Ann shook her head miserably, barely acknowledging her, and trudged out of the door.

She'd lost track of time but was vaguely aware of the progress of the sun across the sky, noting to herself that it was likely mid-afternoon and that she had somewhere to be later that evening. She roamed in and out of a dozen shops. There was an art gallery devoted to nothing but nude Plexiglas sculptures; a voodoo outlet offering anything the aspiring or accomplished witch doctor might need to bring Grandpa back from the grave or deliver everlasting misfortune to a reviled enemy; a large open-air marketplace, table after table of trinkets and whatnot that appeared to be equal parts tourist trap and fencing operations for pick-pockets; and a very expensive boutique for vintage nineteenth century wedding dresses. In each case, Ann drifted sightless through the wares, ignoring requests to assist her, and leaving without any explicit memory of where she'd just been. After more than two hours, she found herself in a gigantic two-story book and CD superstore, and again went about her methodical search for absolutely nothing.

A caramel-colored teenage girl of indistinct ethnic origin, sporting hip-hop chic complete with a hundred meticulously braided ropes of hair, intercepted Ann before she got lost in the stacks.

"Ma'am?"

Ann didn't hear her, and the girl was forced to tap her

on the shoulder to get her attention.

"You might wanna…" the girl said, indicating an area below her eye while looking at the corresponding spot on Ann's face. "We have a bathroom in the back."

Ann stared at the girl as if she'd just beamed down from Neptune.

"Eyeliner. Bathroom," the girl continued. "Helloooo. Anyone home?"

Ann had no memory of applying makeup that morning, but when she ran her finger across her cheek it came back covered in eyeliner.

"There ya go!" the girl condescended, addressing Ann as she would a lost child.

"Bathroom?" Ann managed to say.

"Right back there, darlin'," she said, pointing. "Knock yourself out."

Ann stood at the sink and looked in the mirror. Her eyeliner had faithfully tracked the course of her prodigious sweat and occasional tear, and had given her the expression of a sad clown. Even in that preposterous carnival of a city it looked ridiculous. And even in her diminished condition she felt a rush of humiliation. *How many hours have I looked like this?* Miserable as she'd been that day, wallowing in her self-abnegation, she was nevertheless dimly aware of a bittersweet element of profundity in it all. No question about it, she was coming apart, and not just at the seams. But in a guilty recess of her heart she hadn't wanted any of it to stop, perhaps captured by a sense of nobility in suffering. This altered state she'd stumbled into had recaptured the essence of that awful, beautiful thundercloud back on the Dulles toll road. There was truth in it, palpable and tangible. Almost overpowering. Not the sort of clinical, intellectual clap-trap favored by her father, a truth denuded of its substance by the clumsy instruments of logic and calculus. Still, no sooner had she caught sight of the clown in the mirror than it turned to vapor and vanished. Her head dropped in resignation. *The Truth wouldn't have a face like this.*

Her makeup thoroughly cleansed and her mind restored to nominal functionality, Ann chided herself for indulging in such an absurd conceit– that she'd stumbled into the divine light– and made her way back to the Velvet Dog. The shadows were beginning to stretch across Jackson Square and the clock on St. Louis Cathedral read five-fifteen. She'd been stalking the Quarter for more than six hours which, among other things, explained her aching feet and the sunburn stinging her shoulders. As she walked down St. Peters her pace slowed, the weight of the world on her burned shoulders. Jeremy wouldn't be waiting for her. Heather wouldn't have any answers or, if she did, they'd be carefully couched in a blizzard of incomprehensible Xen gibberish. The Velvet Dog was just another step on the road to nowhere. She knew it in her bones. But however clearly she saw it, whichever way she turned it around in her head, and no matter what angle she viewed it from, this latest humiliation was inevitable: A to B to C. She exhaled with resignation and walked through the door.

Sammy was behind the bar and noticed Ann as soon as she walked in.

"Heather!" he yelled up the stairs in the back.

Ann made her way uneasily to the bar, not sure why her presence merited so much special attention, but not sure of anything else either. Within a minute of being called Heather bounded down the stairs and through the employee entrance. She was dressed more casually than the previous night. No leather. Less makeup. Modest jewelry. Instead, she had on a pair of denim cut-offs, a tank top, and a pair of flip flops. She and Ann could have been sisters, except that Heather's body, as before, was incensed by any effort to contain it.

"Back in thirty," she said to Sammy as she passed.

"You're the boss," he replied.

"Walk with me, mum," she ordered, not bothering with introductions. "I need some air."

Compliantly, Ann rode her heels back out onto St. Peters. "Where are we going?"

Heather stopped and produced a pack of Marlboros and a lighter from somewhere deep in her cleavage.

"Smoke?" she asked, offering Ann the pack.

"Thank you."

Heather lighted both cigarettes and they walked casually back toward Jackson Square, not speaking. Ann was surprised by how good it felt to smoke and wondered why she hadn't thought of it earlier. She was well beyond the curious elusive point after which defiant self-destructive behavior becomes acceptable. She made a mental note to buy a pack as soon as Heather was finished with her.

The park in the center of Jackson Square featured a heroic statue of Andrew Jackson, victor of the Battle of New Orleans, astride his valiant steed. Flanking the park on three sides were the usual musicians, artists, and vendors. As they passed by, Heather addressed herself to a tarot card reader.

"Hey, Marcia, keeping those evil spirits at bay?" She said it playfully, but with a twinge of sarcasm.

When she saw Heather, Marcia's face turned white and she was barely able to respond.

"I..." she squeaked, and then lowered her eyes, completely flustered.

Ann looked at her sympathetically, trying to imagine the nightmare to which Heather must have subjected her. Perhaps she was drunk, bored, wandering around the Square and happened upon Marcia and her little table. Heather would have reeled her in, given her the sense, as most tourists would have, that Marcia's clairvoyance was truly awe inspiring, a life-altering glimpse into the cloudy nether regions. But then the tone would have changed, subtly at first. Marcia would feel uncomfortable, then queasy. The seeds of doubt would take root. And when it was over, she would forever afterwards question her skills, maybe even her value as a person.

Heather led Ann to a bench in the middle of the park with a good view of the hindquarters of Andrew Jackson's horse. A pair of fossilizing black men in tuxedoes, one on the drums, the other on a trombone, were playing *When the Saints Come Marching In* out in front of the cathedral. A thin group of onlookers stood by and listened, some dropping coins into the trombone case.

"I've got something for you," Heather said, breaking their silence and handing Ann a credit card.

Ann studied it carefully for several moments, trying to understand. It was Jeremy's.

"Is he still here?" Ann asked.

"What do you mean, 'still?' He never was."

No sooner had Heather said it than Ann realized it could not have been otherwise. *Of course he was never here.* She stared dumbly at the card, letting her eyes trace the outline of her son's name. She still remembered the day she'd presented it to him. At the time the gesture had felt like one of the few, but cherished rites of passage they'd been allowed to share. Sporting a goofy conspiratorial grin, she'd surprised him with it one afternoon, acting as if, contrary to some imaginary societal prohibition, she was willing to defy convention, throw caution to the wind, and acknowledge her son's extraordinary needs. In retrospect, however, that stupid card hadn't meant a thing. Sure, he needed some way to buy his books and Ann was savvy enough to trust her seven-year-old with a credit account. But if she'd looked a bit closer at the books he actually bought with it, she'd have realized how painfully insignificant their little secret had been.

Heather sat patiently, lighting herself another Marlboro and stretching her arms out confidently on the back of the bench, as Ann cried softly into her hands. At last she raised her head and sniffled loudly, wiping her eyes.

"Why?" she asked.

"I can't say for certain, but if it were me, I'd want you as far away as I could get you while I went through my buzz."

"But how?" Ann went on. "He stopped in Nashville. He must have been here, if only for awhile."

Heather squinted at her and screwed up her face. "What

on earth are you talking about, mum? That card wasn't tattooed to his ass was it?"

Ann gave her an anguished look, but didn't respond.

"So, obviously, he found someone in your neck of the woods who either wanted, or was at least willing, to come down here and create a little trail of bread crumbs for you to follow."

Ann was still unable to find any words, not so much for her surprise as for her profound disappointment.

"I'm curious," Heather continued. "After as much as you've been through, how have you managed to maintain the illusion that you have any control over this? I have to assume that either you're far more accustomed than most to getting your way, or else you're down to your last marble. Most people in your tax bracket have already read the tea leaves by now."

"I wasn't sure right away," Ann started, an eerie, detached tone in her voice. "I didn't know what he was talking about. How could I? It didn't make any sense."

Heather raised her eyebrows. "You're babbling, Mum."

"He asked if I was willing to risk my life. I didn't answer him, and now it's too late."

"Hmm," Heather intoned. "I wasn't there, but I'd bet there was a bit more to it than that. The streets would be strewn with the corpses of you blubbering parents if all the gods wanted was an even swap."

Ann looked at Heather with bloodshot eyes. "What *do* the gods want?" Her voice was uncharacteristically timid. "I'm willing to pay."

"Ha!" Heather let out. "I'm sure you're willing, but it's your ability to pay that's in doubt. And the gods won't take an IOU."

It was Leon all over again, talking in riddles, leading her in circles. Ann felt her eyes begin to glaze over as she looked fuzzily at Jeremy's credit card.

"You can go now," Ann mumbled. "I'm sorry I wasted your time."

Heather turned to face her with a look of renewed interest, but Ann wasn't paying attention.

"You genuinely loved him, didn't you?"

"I still love him," Ann said morosely.

"No, you misunderstand me. I mean you actually love the person, your son, not simply the dream he represents."

"Is that so hard to believe?"

"Yes," Heather said, "it is. So hard, in fact, that I'd be willing to bet you've never been in love before."

Ann shot her a curious mildly incensed look. "Why the hell would you think that?"

"It's true, isn't it?"

Her face went slack as her eyes fell back to the ground. "Yes," she rasped. "It's true."

"Holy shit!" Heather said, chuckling in amazement. "I've often wondered if someone like you existed."

"Someone like me?"

"Pardon my impertinence, but going to Labbitt Halsey wasn't your idea, was it? You couldn't have been more than nineteen or twenty back then."

"Nineteen," Ann confirmed. "How could you possibly know all of that?"

Heather slapped her thigh heartily. "Unbe-fucking-lievable!"

"What?" Ann asked testily.

"From your perspective this is going to sound ridiculous, so you're just going to have to take my word for it," Heather started. "Typically, though not in your case, a mother's love for her child is a complicated multiplicitous affair, part instinct, but also bound up with a desire to create heirs, continue the bloodline, even the species. A child is a parent's best shot at immortality, and for that reason is a transparently selfish endeavor."

"I've never seen it that way," Ann said.

"I know *you* haven't, but that's why you're so interesting. You've no doubt heard that a mother's love is unconditional. That only makes sense in light of what I just said, that child rearing is largely narcissistic, an eighteen-year-long love affair with oneself. And that narcissism is far more blatant in the case of the Xen."

"And why is that?"

"Because the Xen don't represent just any future, just any blind grope for an afterlife, but a glorious transcendent paradise, a heaven brought down to Earth. We are simultaneously your most cherished dream and most conspicuous conceit."

"Typical Xen cynicism," Ann replied. "In my experience, parents genuinely love their children. And not because they think they're going to live forever."

"Dismiss it if you want to, mum, but loving a child the way you do, particularly a Xen child… you're playing with fire."

Ann leaned back on the bench and gazed into an ancient live oak just beyond Andrew Jackson. Its gnarled branches and massive trunk had witnessed the great New Orleans fire, had watched as the city evolved from Spanish to French to American, survived Katrina, and may have offered shade to Colonel Jackson himself on the morning before his troops laid waste to the bumbling forces of General Pakenham. Ann's entire life could be measured along one of its lesser branches.

"Why aren't you charging me for this?" Ann suddenly asked. "Last night I watched you loot a helpless old man."

"I've been charging drinks on your credit card for the past three days. I figured this was the least I could do."

"I almost fell in love once," Ann offered. "Just recently."

"Let me guess. You martyred yourself on the altar of single motherhood."

"He tried to give me a ring and I panicked. Nearly fainted right there in the restaurant."

"Didn't want to get caught cheating on your son?" Heather asked with a sly grin.

"Why does everything have to be so dark and sleazy with you people?"

"Don't get me wrong. I don't think you're sleeping with

him, or even want to."

"What???"

"But that doesn't make it any less creepy."

"Enough!" Ann growled, though with less emphasis than seemed appropriate. She also didn't make any move to leave. Heather just laughed and then lit herself another Marlboro.

"You better mind your manners, mum," Heather said. "Or I won't tell you how to dig yourself out."

"What the hell difference does it make what you tell me? Everything will still be exactly the same."

"Suit yourself," Heather said, getting up to leave. Ann reached up quickly in spite of herself, and caught her by one of her back pockets. Heather turned and shot Ann an expectant look.

"I'm sorry," Ann said dejectedly. "What do I have to do?"

"That's better!" Heather said. "About time you started showing some respect."

"I have nothing but respect. I'm just... tired."

"I don't doubt it. Flying all over the country. Stalking your son like some kind of psychotic ex-girlfriend. Must be exhausting."

"It's not like that," Ann mumbled, losing her will to object.

"Of course it isn't," Heather mocked. "But whatever it is, there's a very simple way out. Not that you'll have the will to do it."

"How simple?"

"That boyfriend of yours. You think he's still looking for a finger to put that ring on?"

"Not mine," Ann grumbled. "He's seeing someone else."

"Aww, poor baby. Diddums have a fight?" She said it with a silly, pouty face. Ann tried to be angry, but Heather's face was so absurd she couldn't help smiling. "That's more like it! You know, men are a lot more resilient than you seem to think. They prefer a challenge. Reminds them of the hunt."

"Maybe," Ann said doubtfully, "but why now? Why do I need to get engaged right in the middle of all of this?"

"You need to replace your son with a grown-up. And the sooner the better."

"Oh, right. That again."

"Yes," she continued. "And I don't mean you just need a good lay. You need to fall head over heels in love. Anything less won't do the trick."

"This makes no sense. None whatsoever. Besides, like I said, Jeremy needs me right now."

"Sheesh! I had more luck with the physicist!" Heather said. "Let me say this as simply and clearly as I can. True love—that is, *conditional* love occurs when two people adopt one another's goals as their own, embrace one another's hopes and dreams, feel one another's pain and joy."

"Yeah, okay," Ann said. "But so what?"

"You can't do that with your own child. He can't possibly reciprocate. His goals will never be the same as yours. And if you try it with a Xen, you'll end up in a padded cell."

As little as she wanted to believe it and painful as it was to admit, Heather's words had a faint ring of truth. And in that moment of realization, she felt, ever so subtly, the umbilical starting to loosen. It was a disorienting, even nauseating, sensation, watching helplessly as her anchor detached from its hold and she began to drift. Never before had she felt such a thorough sense of groundlessness.

Chapter 29

Ann and Dr. Franklin didn't speak on the drive home from Dulles Airport. Anyone could have seen that she wasn't in the mood for conversation. She'd caught the last flight out of New Orleans and it was just after midnight when she landed. Upon arriving home, Dr. Franklin pulled the BMW into the garage of her house in Tysons Corner, and she had to remind herself that it was hers, at least for the time being.

Five days after his disappearance there was still no word from Jeremy and no reason to hope there ever would be. All the agonizing and expense, the preparations and gut-wrenching countdown– none of it had made the slightest difference. He'd sneaked out in the middle of the night without a sound and by all appearances that was that. No buzz. No catharsis. No nothing. Just *poof*. Gone. To call it an anticlimax hardly did it justice. And after more than fifteen straight years as her guiding light, the gaping hole his absence left in her rationale for nearly everything she did was profoundly disorienting.

Nevertheless, of more immediate concern was the harsh light it cast on all the issues that had recently become matters of benign neglect, but which were arguably just as pressing. Much as she wanted them to, the JOMREV bid and its ancillary problems simply refused to go away. And now, with Jeremy gone, they were thrust to the top of the list by default. A cursory glance at her towering mountain of unread e-mails confirmed as much. Irving Sicherman's name appeared twice, even three times a day. In each e-mail he offered some trivial observation that might be of value, or hinted at a new plan of attack. He always ended with a suggestion they "do lunch" to discuss it further. All of it very innocent and professional. But the sheer volume of text left no doubt—he was losing patience.

Still, as many e-mails as Sicherman had sent, the vast majority came from her team, each a bit more demanding and a bit less sympathetic than the one before. And over the last day or so no one was any longer even attempting to mask his contempt of Ann's lack of urgency. Between the lines Ann could hear the water cooler conversations, whispered out of mock respect, plotting her overthrow. Jerry had installed Andrea as Ann's interim replacement, though everything about the announcement suggested it could easily become permanent, to the effect of: Get your butt back in the office and fix this mess or find yourself a lawyer. Kim McEwen's tone was one of unqualified euphoria, though her scorn was buried in supercilious words of condolence. The last few e-mails were not addressed to Ann at all, but merely copied to her as a courtesy. Apparently, even sniping at her had become boring.

As Ann read, the individual messages slowly congealed into a single, amorphous mass of inertia. And though now and then one of them might have triggered in her a passing impetus to respond, the overall futility of the exercise quickly squelched any such ambitions. Her eyes went glassy and she found them idly tracing the paths of several neighborhood kids, heavily armored in helmets and kneepads, rollerblading up and down the street in front of her house. There were two teams of two, each swatting a tennis ball with hockey sticks. All were loudly and emphatically clarifying the rules of the game to their opponents, sometimes verbally, but usually with a good hard body check, catapulting them into front yards, fire hydrants, and street signs. She tried to fight it, but Jeremy's face, reddened and sweaty, inevitably appeared among theirs. And just as inevitably, the bitter tears again began to flow.

Ann had never taken her son on a summer vacation. By

the time she'd achieved some measure of financial security he was already hopelessly beyond any such frivolous nonsense. When he was ten, she'd suggested spending a month in Greece, thinking Jeremy might like to experience firsthand the cradle of Western philosophy and science. She spent an entire month preparing her presentation, researching every last monument and museum, before she finally mustered up the guts to sit him down and make her pitch. Barely thirty seconds in Jeremy informed her gruffly that Greece hadn't been the cradle of anything more important than olive oil and souvlaki for more than a thousand years. He could get more out of a single book than by moving there permanently. And in any case, seeing the place in its current state of rot and decay would probably just be depressing.

Ann never tried again. And that day marked, at least in her mind, the beginning of the end. Soon thereafter she started becoming acutely aware of how infrequently she saw him. How thin he'd become. How rapidly he was sapping Amazon.com's inventory. Forays into his cave became increasingly painful and rare. In one respect, that was the day she'd lost him.

Later that afternoon, the hockey game having succumbed to the steady stream of homebound commuters, Ann was nestled into her couch in front of the widescreen, picking indifferently at a plastic bowl of microwaveable chicken Alfredo. Rhett Butler was angrily chastising Scarlet for her mediocre parenting skills, announcing that he and Bonnie were headed for London and if Scarlet knew what was good for her she wouldn't raise a fuss. Ann knew the dialogue by heart and watched purely out of nostalgia. It was the first grown-up movie she'd ever genuinely understood, and had the same emotional significance for her that *Snow White* or *The Wizard of Oz* has for most people.

Just as Rhett and Scarlet received the grim news of Melanie's death, Ann heard the doorbell ring. She was so lost in the film it took a second ring before she pushed the pause button and made her way to the front door.

Ann swung the door open and then stared in amazement at the man standing on her stoop.

"I know I shouldn't be here, but…" Calvin stammered. "I… I didn't want to say this over the phone. I hope you can forgive me."

The sound of his voice helped, but she still couldn't quite believe who she was looking at.

"May I come in?" he finally asked.

Ann drifted to the side and made a vague welcoming gesture. Calvin closed the door himself, perhaps sensing that Ann would have stood there in a daze for the next five minutes and permitted all the bugs orbiting her porch light to join them in the foyer.

Ann looked down at herself and realized she was clad only in her emerald green silk robe. It didn't make her self-conscious, but it gave her something to say.

"Please," she said, an odd formality in her voice, "have a seat while I slip into something more appropriate."

He didn't object, but also clearly didn't know what to make of her peculiar manner. "Um… okay… sure. I'll be right in…" he said to Ann's back as she disappeared up the stairs. He sat down awkwardly, then stood up and walked a few nervous circuits around the sofa before returning to his seat.

Ann may not have been entirely lucid, but she still managed to fall back on her feminine instincts. Instead of merely exchanging her garb, she decided to take a shower, apply a light coat of makeup, and otherwise mill around aimlessly in her master suite until she was reasonably confident that Calvin would be on the verge of apoplexy by the time she returned.

Her first sight of him on emerging from the stairwell nearly thirty minutes later confirmed the success of her plan. He was fidgety and agitated, clearly miffed at having his grand announcement, whatever it was, subordinated to Ann's preening. He stood quickly when he saw her, an expectant, almost frantic, look on his face. Ann walked right past him toward the kitchen.

"I need a drink," she announced. "Can I get you anything?"

"No thank...," he started. "A beer, maybe. Whatever you're having."

Calvin collapsed back into the sofa and began massaging his forehead. Ann took her time, clanking glasses and bottles as if to let him know she'd be there whenever she got there.

"Thanks," he said, accepting a glass of Sam Adams and taking a healthy swig.

Ann sat across from him and, borrowing a chapter from Stuart and Imelda's book, remained silent, forcing him to initiate the conversation.

"So, how have you been?"

Ann squinted at him. "My life is coming apart. How about you?"

"I heard about your son," he said. "I'm so sorry, Ann. I... I honestly don't know what to say. I know he meant everything to you."

"Yes, he does."

"I should have been here for you."

"Yes, you should have."

Calvin looked at her sheepishly. "Can you ever forgive me?"

"Is that what this is about? You came all the way over here to atone?"

"No, that's not why I'm here," he murmured.

His vulnerability. His contrition. Ann was beginning to get the sense he might be there, of all things, to reconcile. Perhaps his Viagra-fortified romp with the preschooler had gotten the better of him. Ann smiled inside, coolly raising her eyebrows at his last comment.

"I was hoping..." He cut himself off, summoning a bit of backbone before continuing. "I'm not here with my hat in my hand. I was hoping to talk. See where things stand. But I'm not here to beg."

"Why *are* you here?"

"Last week, when you stopped by my house and saw...
well... It didn't sink in right away. I'm an idiot male. What do
you expect? But your outfit. Your makeup. You were there to
patch things up, weren't you? I didn't even realize it for two
days."

"Things have changed."

"Look, Ann," he said, leaning towards her, imploring, "you don't need to tell me. We couldn't have screwed this
up any worse if we'd set out with that purpose in mind. But I
thought about what you said. The way Irving's been messing
with our heads. I think you're right. Do we really want to let
him win?"

"How romantic," Ann grumbled.

"Romantic?" he puzzled. "As much as I would've loved
to ride in here on my white horse and sweep you off your feet,
we're still staring down a couple of long unpleasant stints in
federal prison. If you're willing to take a rain check on the romance, I'll promise to shower you with rose petals when this is
all behind us."

Ann's face hardened. "So which is it? Do you want to
beat Sicherman at his own game? Sweep me off my feet? Save
our butts? Or what? And why the sudden change of heart? Did
your wind-up doll finally get bored with you? Our predicament isn't exactly front page news anymore. Why now? Why
tonight?"

No sooner had Ann finished her diatribe than she started second guessing herself. It had come out harsher than she'd
expected, sharpened by her recent loss. As disappointed as she
was in Calvin, he hadn't been responsible for Jeremy's disappearance. Ann watched with dismay as Calvin threw his hands
in the air with an expression of resignation.

"Yup," he started, "you're right. I'm nothing but lies
and ulterior motives. What could have possessed me to sully
your purity and grace with such ugliness? I may never forgive
myself." Then he looked back and forth, mouthing words to
himself, as if trying to decide something. "To hell with it! I tried.

Best of luck to you, Ann." And he got up to leave.

"Wait!" Ann said, jumping up to stop him. "I'm sorry, Calvin. Please, sit down. Let's try this again."

Calvin sat down warily, eying Ann. Then he spoke. "Can we get something straight? Just in case you've lost your memory, I don't owe you an apology. I made a perfectly honorable proposal and you sent me down in flames. My little 'wind-up doll,' as you call her, was the only thing that kept me from taking a header off the Wilson Bridge."

"Remind me to send her a bouquet."

"And to answer your question: Yes, all of the above. I want to grind Irving into the dirt, sweep you off your feet, and stay out of the pokey. Call me greedy."

Ann was softening rapidly, a warm smile on her lips. With Calvin by her side, things were not entirely hopeless. The abyss was beginning to recede. The loss of her son was almost bearable. Heather's words on love echoed in her ears as an unexpected rush of adrenalin tingled in her body. "I'd like those things too."

Calvin returned her smile and they sat in silence for several moments, the ice in their hearts slowly melting by the glow of their shared memories. Ann knew, absolutely knew, it was nothing but a mirage. But she wasn't about to turn her back on it. The world owed it to her. Even if it would never last.

"I can't take anymore pain, Calvin," Ann said. "I'm sure of it."

"Then let's get it right this time."

Chapter
30

Discouraging and depressing as the circumstances at SST had become, none of it really mattered. Ann's job had ended the day she promised Andrea she'd resign as soon as the JOMREV bid was over. Salvaging her reputation at the office—even if it were feasible— would be an exercise in pride alone, serving no legitimate purpose. No, the only way out now was to nail Irving Sicherman and scurry out of the back door before anyone came to his senses. To that end, she and Calvin had begun the loathsome task of setting their trap with Ann as the bait.

It was far from the most romantic theme that could have dominated their nascent attempt to reconcile. Ann was still struggling with Calvin's revolting little tryst with Sara, and Calvin was having his own problems shaking the graphic though fictional accounts Sicherman had fed him of his alleged affair with Ann. There were also the frequent and inexplicably timed emotional breakdowns that left Ann inconsolable and Calvin feeling helpless, though less than completely sympathetic, owing to his own Xen baggage. They wanted nothing more than to dissolve into one another's arms, block out the world, and explore their love. But the treacherous road before them demanded a level of caution that was all but inimical to true passion.

"Where is it?" Calvin asked as Ann sat down at the picnic table. Their paranoia had become so intense and uncomfortable that Oakton Park was the only place they were willing to be seen together.

"In the car," Ann replied, looking a bit pale.

"We need to try it out, make sure we know what we're doing."

"Of course," Ann agreed. "But not here."

"No, not here."

Earlier that afternoon, UPS had arrived with a package from MDD Electronics, Inc. In it was a nondescript black "pleather" purse, fitted with a nearly imperceptible camera and transmitter, as well as a receiver/recorder, advertised to be effective up to a hundred and fifty feet away. Ann's hands were still shaking.

"We can do this," Calvin said, moving closer and squeezing her hands. "Then we'll be free."

Ann looked to be on the verge of tears, but instead took a deep breath and faced him. "I know it's not fair, but I have to know." Her tone was sincere, but with an unintended twinge of neediness. "Are you still willing to marry me?"

Calvin kissed her tenderly on the cheek. "As soon as this is over."

"I love you, Calvin."

He looked at her curiously, trying to understand why she'd picked that moment to confess her devotion. He may have detected a duplicitous tone, her employment of the bombshell for less than entirely sincere purposes. And he was just unsure enough of her motives to insert a brief pause before his response. "I... love you too."

His hesitation wasn't terribly subtle and Ann looked him in the eye, alert to any other signs of indecision. All he could manage in response was a plaintive, embarrassed smile. Her face hardened slightly and she instinctively opened her mouth to demand clarification, a dollop of zeal, something to prove he hadn't simply mimicked her out of pity. But no sooner had the challenge formed on her lips than she decided his fumble hadn't been nearly as blatant as it first seemed. She'd caught him off-guard, hadn't she? All but ambushed him. They were in the middle of a completely different conversation. Come to think of it, that pause might have been nothing more than a product of her overwrought imagination. Her face softened again and she returned his smile. Calvin looked confused.

"... Er... In any case," he stammered, "I was thinking. Maybe this weekend we'd take this stuff to a hotel out in West Virginia. A Comfort Inn, Ramada, whatever. Give it a field test."

"Yes, this weekend," Ann said dreamily, still with the same peculiar smile on her face, though by then Calvin was looking at her nervously.

Calvin had selected a hotel off of Interstate 81, sight unseen, on the assumption they'd have no advance knowledge of their ultimate theater of operation. They'd have to adapt quickly to different floor plans, parking lot layouts, and any number of other architectural or landscaping anomalies, to say nothing of the unpredictable responses from hotel management their suspicious behavior might elicit. Ann checked into her room while Calvin fumbled with wires and switches out in his car. Ten minutes passed. Then fifteen. Twenty. Then Calvin's cell phone rang.

"Well?" Ann said

"Did you turn it on?"

"Son of a bitch!" Ann growled.

On further examination of the fine print, a hundred and fifty feet proved to be the maximum range of the device under ideal, line of sight, conditions. With intervening walls or trees, fifty feet was all they could hope for. The parking lot was out. Calvin would have to be in an adjacent room to get a clear signal. Depending on the layout of the hotel, as many as ten different rooms might satisfy that requirement, though they agreed a room directly above or below Ann's would minimize the likelihood of Calvin being seen out in the hall. But, failing that, anything close would suffice. Calvin rented the room above and to the right of Ann's and he set up the receiver. Within ten minutes Ann's cell phone rang.

"Can you turn up the lights?" Calvin asked.

Ann flicked on both bedside lamps. "Better?"

"Yeah. Now sit on the bed and look at your purse."

"Like this?"

"All I can see is the top of your head," he said. "Angle the camera down a bit?"

Ann propped the back of her purse up on the TV remote and then returned to the bed. "How's that?"

"Not bad. But from that vantage point, I'll probably end up filming his back. Can you put the purse on the bedside table?"

"Not enough room."

"What about the other bed?"

"Just a minute," she said, doing as Calvin asked. "Well?"

"No good," he said. "The light from the bathroom washes everything else out."

Light, angle, and distance were all maddeningly difficult to adjust on the clumsy device. And within thirty minutes it was obvious the odds were no better than even that Ann would be able to position the camera without giving herself away, such that Sicherman's mug would be clearly identifiable.

"For crying out loud!" Ann finally said.

"I'll be right down."

In view of these unforeseen challenges, they quickly recognized the need for an abort signal. If for whatever reason the stars didn't properly align for them, Calvin would send a text message to Ann's cell phone telling her to start wheedling her way out of it. Absent that, she'd assume everything was working and wait for him to burst through the door, announce to Sicherman what they'd done, and start the ball rolling in the exact opposite direction. Punching Irving in the mouth was optional and left to Calvin's discretion.

"You damned well better exercise that option," Ann said, trying desperately to believe it would reach that point.

Calvin made a fist and kissed his knuckles with relish. Then he looked into Ann's eyes. "Come with me. I have something to show you."

"Here?"

"Trust me," he said, smiling.

He led Ann up to the other room they'd rented, the one where he'd set up the receiver. At the door he made Ann close her eyes.

"What on earth did you do?" she asked, sensing that something wonderful was about to happen.

"Okay," he said.

Ann opened her eyes. Calvin had obviously squeezed in a phone call or two to someone at the hotel office. There was a table and two chairs set up for dinner, a white tablecloth, a centerpiece of irises, a bowl of strawberries, and a bottle of champagne in a stand next to the table. Ann never would have imagined that the Red Roof Inn, all of fifty-nine dollars a night, would have been willing or able to pull out all the stops, and so quickly. It was the most beautiful thing she'd ever seen.

"How the…" Ann said, beaming, tears of joy in her eyes.

"My lady," Calvin said theatrically, pulling out Ann's chair.

Ann sat. Calvin knelt on the floor beside her, pulled a piece of paper out of his pocket and began unfolding it. "Sorry about the cheat sheet, but I wanted to get this right," he said, smiling.

"It's okay," she said, wiping her face, nearly hyperventilating.

Calvin cleared his throat. "Over the past year I've experienced the best and worst life has to offer. Both extremes I credit to you. Best, when you're eyes are smiling, looking into mine, and you're in my arms. Worst, when you're unhappy and distant from me. We've made more mistakes than the gods are obliged to forgive. And were it anyone but you, I would grudgingly accept their verdict and learn, in time, to thank them for removing the scales from my eyes."

Ann let out an adoring gasp and covered her mouth so as not to interrupt him.

He cleared his throat again and turned back to his cheat

sheet, glancing at her playfully out of the corner of his eye. Ann was struggling to remain earthbound. "But as it happens, I'm not prepared to sacrifice that much for even a divine lesson in humility. You mean far more to me than any bounty such knowledge might one day enable me to reap. My darling Ann," he said, reaching for that ominous pocket once again; though this time Ann made no attempt to stop him. "I promise to love you, cherish you, kiss your royal butt, mow the lawn, shovel the driveway, change the oil in your snooty BMW, kill the spiders in your bathtub, and generally focus my whole existence on nothing but your health and happiness." And with that he opened the lid of the tiny velvet box. "Will you have me?"

Ann was speechless, but managed to extend a shaky finger in his direction. He slipped the ring on. It fit perfectly. Every nerve ending in her body was buzzing with ecstasy. She wrapped her arms around his neck, letting loose a geyser of tears representing the whole assortment of emotions she'd bottled up over the last week and a half.

And, for a few moments at least, it was completely sincere, unmuddied at all by extraneous considerations. She squeezed him tight, forcing herself to believe. But even before Calvin could wipe them from her face, her tears had become contaminated by the poisonous doubts, the fatalistic flavor of her new, unwelcome, but billowing cloud of nihilism. Why couldn't it be real? How would it end? Ann couldn't say, but she'd lately come to appreciate that hopes are most spectacularly dashed when they fall from the same heights of rapture that provide a glimpse of happy endings. All she had for certain was that very moment. And she intended to make the most of it.

After strawberries and champagne, after succumbing to several bouts of cooing and burbling over the sparkle of Ann's ring, they retired to the bed and made love for the first time. At least that was how it felt. Of course it was vaguely familiar, not completely unlike the sweaty torrid rolls in the hay that had brought them to the eve of their uncertain future. But there was no sense of urgency. No sense they were stealing a moment from the powers that be. It felt responsible, grown up, even obligatory. Which is not to say it wasn't at all enjoyable. Still...

It was only four in the afternoon. Absent their customary scramble to dress, gather their belongings, and sprint for the exit, Calvin excused himself, a bit awkwardly, to go to the shower. Ann lay on the bed and looked out of the window, idly watching as cars and semis flew by on Interstate 81, an endless stream of commerce and industry fervently committed to ensuring that tomorrow will be indistinguishable from today. But instead of recoiling from the monotony, Ann longed for it, pined for its predictability and order. Nothing would have brought her more joy than to arrive at SST on Monday morning, hang her jacket over the back of her ergonomic desk chair, make small talk with a passing office flunky, and launch her skiff once again into that endless stream of industry.

"Why don't you give him a call?" Calvin said, emerging from the bathroom, still drying himself.

"Now?"

"It has to be done," he replied. "There won't be a good time."

Gravely, Ann dug her cell phone out of her spy purse and dialed Irving Sicherman's number.

"She lives!" Irving exclaimed upon answering.

"I got your messages."

"I was beginning to wonder if you still loved me."

"Family emergency," Ann explained.

"All fixed?"

"As fixed as it's going to get. What do you say we make a date? I'm afraid this project might be getting away from me."

"For you, anything." His tone was too effusive and it triggered a familiar, sickening sensation.

"Clyde's," Ann suggested. "Tuesday at eight?"

"I'll be counting the hours."

"Right..." Ann said. "Then I'll see you there. Bye Irving."

"Adieu."

Ann looked warily at the phone and then at Calvin.

"Lunatic," she muttered.

Calvin gave her a quick sympathetic smile, but then snapped back into military mode. "It's still early yet. Get dressed. Let's go through the whole thing again."

And that was that. It took exactly fifty-seven minutes to get engaged, celebrate, make love, shower, and get back to business. Ann nodded gloomily and began putting on her clothes.

"And let's try not to screw it up this time," Calvin yelled from the bathroom.

Chapter
31

Irving Sicherman was nervous and jittery and his agitation was contagious, prompting Ann to squirm in her seat in an effort to relieve his tension. She already felt like a ten-dollar whore, like the whole restaurant was staring at her, judging her. Irving had no right to act as though he were the one under the gun. She wore a short skirt with a sheer top, black lace bra, and just a bit too much makeup. It wasn't exactly inappropriate, though it flirted with the line of propriety at a place like Clyde's. And on Ann, sauntering in on her four-inch heels, it definitely meant business. For every appreciative male ogler there was a female counterpart who wished looks could kill. Ann could feel their eyes on the back of her neck.

"Relax," Ann said, reaching across the table to take his hand.

Irving pulled away reflexively, made even more nervous by her incongruous, intimate gesture.

"I'm okay," he said. "Really. It's just been a long... I'll be okay."

Ann looked at him suspiciously. Something was different. He appeared on the verge of collapse, pale, maybe even thinner than the last time she'd seen him. His vulnerability was not altogether unwelcome, but it was hard to imagine such a nervous wreck suddenly changing gears and entertaining the ideas Ann had in mind.

"Are you sure?" Ann asked. "Because you look like you

narrowly escaped death five minutes before you walked in here."

He responded with a pinched smile and totally unconvincing chuckle. Then he looked warily out of the corners of his eyes as if his lousy acting were giving him away to someone off in the shadows. Ann started to turn her head around to see who he was looking at. But before she could, an expression of terror swept across his face. "No!" he whispered frantically, grabbing her arm and, in the process, spilling her water glass right into her lap.

The panic on his face was all that prevented Ann from leaping out of her seat and making a scene. But even so, it took every ounce of self-control she had to sit there and calmly allow the icy cold water to soak in.

"Son of a…" she started, teeth clenched.

"Oh, crap!" he said. "I'm so sorry, Ann! God! I'm such an…"

"Irving," she cut in. Then in a clipped and measured tone. "Could I please borrow your napkin?"

He quickly complied. "I have no idea what's come over me. Pressure from work. The last two weeks. I'm lousy at this sort…"

"Irving!" she commanded. "If you don't calm down right this second, I'm going to start throwing things at you. Understand?"

He breathed deeply and nodded his assent.

"Thank you," she said, trying to calm him with her voice. "Now, would you be so kind as to get me some more napkins?"

"Yes… yes, of course," he said, stumbling to his feet and heading for the bar.

Ann fumbled through her brain for a remedy. The bathrooms at Clyde's were outfitted with posh linen hand towels embroidered with the restaurant's logo, not the bus station air blowers she'd need to dry her skirt. And even that plan assumed she was willing to stand there in her thong and smile politely as the women filed by and smirked. Neither could she stand up, silk clinging to her backside, and beg everyone's forgiveness while she dabbed and patted herself. The only solution was to sit there until she was dry enough to walk out without making a scene. By the time Irving returned, the air conditioner vent directly above her head had chilled her wet skin and left her covered in goose bumps.

"Thank you," she said. Instead of napkins, Irving had brought her a stack of monogrammed hand towels from the men's room. Ann arranged them up and around her skirt, concealing herself as best she could under the tablecloth. The commotion, along with his social ineptitude, conspired to render Irving a complete basket case, and in Ann's wildest imagination she could not envision a means of salvaging the evening.

"Why are you dressed like that?" he suddenly asked. "Are you going somewhere later? Not that it's any of my business."

"I don't always dress for the boardroom," Ann said, lamely.

"It's just that I've never seen you..." he stammered. "You look different... nice, I mean. That's all I'm trying to say."

"Thank you... I guess."

Irving shot her another pinched smile, trying to be suave. But before Ann could even fake a genial response, he abandoned that tack, groaned in despair, and buried his face in his hands. For several moments he kneaded his temples with his thumbs and mumbled under his breath as if debating something with himself. Ann looked on in dismay, but also curious to see where all of this was going. When he finally raised his head and made eye contact again, she gave him a mocking peek-a-boo grin, as a parent would a child. She'd hoped it would lighten his mood, but he didn't seem to understand.

"I can't do this," he mumbled. "I just can't."

"Excuse me? What was that?"

"I thought I could, but I can't. It's as simple as that."

Ann raised her eyebrows by way of demanding clarification.

"You want to hear something ridiculous?" he asked, shaking his head in amazement. "You're never going to believe this. I sure as hell didn't."

Ann renewed her anticipatory expression, but otherwise left him to his babbling.

"They told me *you* were coming here tonight to seduce *me*. Imagine that. *You* seduce *me!*"

Ann's face dropped and she felt her entire body go limp. For the briefest of moments she wasn't convinced she'd heard him correctly. Oddly, what struck her the hardest was not that he knew what she was up to, but that *they* had told him. Besides herself, only Calvin and her father knew what was going on that night. Her mind was racing wildly. There was only one possibility. One of them must have talked. But who? And why? It was inconceivable that her father had sold her out. That left only Calvin. Might he and Irving have conspired to throw her under the bus? Ann recalled Calvin's face from earlier that day, nervous and panicky. There was no hint of duplicity. He was no less terrified than she was. It couldn't have been him.

"Who told you that?" Ann asked, hesitantly, not sure she wanted to know.

"It's true, isn't it? I wouldn't have mentioned it, but, well... that outfit. Those shoes. I still can't quite believe it myself."

"Who?" Ann persisted.

"You know what else they told me?" he went on. "They told me I'd take you up on your offer if I knew what was good for me."

"Did they now," Ann said guardedly, content to let Irving give up as much as possible before making a move of her own.

"That may be a bit of an understatement. It was more like 'do it, or else.' I don't remember his exact words, but I didn't get the feeling it was optional."

"Sounds like you've got quite a situation on your hands,"

Ann said, gambling that "he" or "they" or whoever it was had tightened the screws on Irving enough to inadvertently give her some leverage to negotiate.

"I'd say that's a fair assessment," he admitted despondently, staring at the table and idly rotating the pepper shaker, a quarter turn at a time, between his thumb and index finger. Ann didn't immediately respond, plunging the two of them into silent contemplation of their respective rocks and hard places. And sitting there, pondering the depths to which they were willing to stoop, a faint wisp of fox-hole camaraderie passed between them. Each of them, at different moments, stole a glance at the other, searching for a sign of commiseration. Even so, more than a minute passed before Irving spoke again. "Quite a situation, indeed," he mumbled.

"Maybe they miscalculated," Ann started, giving voice to an incomplete but burgeoning brainstorm.

"Yeah?"

"They're clearly banking on our continuing acrimony to pull this off. Keeping us at each other's throats."

"I'll buy that," he said. "But so what?"

Ann was lost in thought, brow knitted, working her fingers as if her ideas were taking shape on the table in front of her. Finally, she looked up and answered his question.

"So, what if we did something unpredictable?"

Irving looked at her skeptically, but without dismissing her altogether. Then he softened his expression and spoke. "Are we being honest with each other now?"

Ann swallowed hard. "I suppose we are."

"How can I trust you?" he asked. "They also told me you were planning to blackmail me. Is that true too?"

Ann's eyes widened in astonishment, but she quickly shook it off and refocused herself on their nascent alliance. "Listen, I'll tell you everything, but only after you've told me who these mysterious people are. It's only fair."

Irving wagged his head back and forth, a tormented expression on his face. "I can't believe I'm doing this. If they find out…" He shuddered visibly.

"Please."

"We're probably… almost certainly, being watched, so do us both a favor and try to act like we're doing what they expect us to be doing."

Ann started to turn her head again.

"No!" he begged. "Don't do that. Please! They're not nice people."

"Who???" Ann demanded.

"I'm not proud of this," he started, sweat beginning to form on his brow and upper lip. "As you know, about a month and a half ago, I was approached by a man who gave me some fascinating information about you and Major—er, *Colonel* Monroe."

"What did he look like?" Ann asked.

Irving eyed her curiously. "Maybe five-ten, balding, beatnik-style goatee. Why, ring any bells?"

"No," she said, puzzling.

"Anyhow," he continued, "what you don't know is that he and I met regularly after that first time. He wouldn't tell me how he got it, but he always had the latest intel on you and Monroe. All he asked in return was that I follow his advice on how to use it."

"Who on earth is this guy?"

"I'm getting there. I promise. So, maybe a week after our first meeting, he asks me to meet him at a weird theme bar in Adams Morgan. I'd never heard of it. Not my kind of thing. But I agreed. To make a long story short, I woke up the next morning in a hotel across the street. I have no memory of most of the night and no idea how I got to the hotel."

"What happened?"

"I remember arriving. I remember ordering a beer. Then nothing. When I woke up, I assumed, though I'd never been that drunk in my life, that I just overdid it. But now I'm convinced that John drugged me."

"John?" Ann asked.

"He won't tell me his real name."

"How do you know he drugged you?"

"Remember the rebids at Belvoir?" he asked.

"I'm trying to forget."

"That afternoon John calls me and says he has to see me immediately. Life and death. That sort of thing. So I show up at our usual spot, expecting some bit of news about you. After all, your presentation was a total catastrophe."

"Was that John's doing?"

"Every bit," he said. "And I'm sorry. You treated me very badly, but... Well, you didn't deserve that."

"You destroyed my life," Ann said.

"Maybe not. Let me finish."

Ann waved her hand.

"John looked different that evening, like the jig was up, like we weren't friends anymore. I sit down at the table and he slides a manila folder over to me. Doesn't say a word. Inside were a dozen or so photos. I didn't recognize the location, but there I was in living color, naked as the day I was born, one girl on top of me and two others tangled up together right next to us."

"Adams Morgan?" Ann asked.

"Obviously," he said. "John gives me a minute or two to digest it, and then announces that you and SST are going to *win* the JOMREV bid or else those pictures would be addressed to my wife."

"What???" Ann said incredulously.

"That's what I said. But as it turns out, my good pal John actually works, off the books of course, for Haruspex, Inc."

"I don't believe this."

"So I ask him, 'Why did you set Ann up to fall on her face if you wanted her to win all along?'"

"What did he say to that?" Ann had all but forgotten about Calvin, sitting out in Clyde's parking lot, preparing to spring their trap.

"He told me that wasn't my concern. All I had to worry

about was making sure Steady State Technologies won. And that's why I've been assaulting your inbox for the past two weeks."

Though Ann had come to expect her entire world to flip on its axis every day or so, Sicherman's bombshell was beyond the pale. Clearly her plan was now thoroughly defunct; it would have been hard enough to pull it off if Irving *hadn't* known about it. And with him being blackmailed himself, reaching out to Ann for help, the new enemy was suddenly this mysterious character, John. Ann had so many questions, she was struggling to queue them up in a coherent order for her mouth.

"Did I hear you correctly? This John guy, whoever he is, wants you to take me up on my offer?"

"That's what the man said."

Ann pinched her brow in concentration. "But why? What does he get out of that?"

"He said he wants us 'joined at the hip' so to speak."

"But we already are," Ann protested. "What difference does it make if you and I sleep together? It doesn't make any sense. Unless..."

"Yes?" he asked. "Unless what?"

"Unless he doesn't have as much on Calvin and me as he's letting on."

"Hmm," he intoned skeptically. "That's not the impression I got."

"Think about it. Maybe he hears about us from that little bitch, Kim McEwen. No real evidence, but he believes her anyway. Then he tests the waters, rattles our cages. And like the idiots we are, we confirm her allegations. But now he needs real proof of wrongdoing. Something tangible. That has to be it!"

Irving was kneading his temples again, clearly disenchanted with the direction Ann was going. "That's a fascinating theory. But I'm not sure it makes any difference."

"No difference?" Ann blurted out. "It makes all the difference. If the SOB has nothing, Calvin and I are off the hook." As soon as she said it she realized that Irving was now dangling from that hook by himself and their brief alliance might suddenly be coming to an end.

"I'm afraid you may be oversimplifying it just a bit, Ms. Franklin."

"How so?" she asked, feeling much more in charge of the situation.

"John gave me quite a few details about your affair– details that turned out to be true. To assume he has nothing just because now he wants more is a pretty big leap."

It wasn't fair, but Ann felt an overwhelming desire to shoot the messenger. All she could focus on was that tiny crack in the wall, the one that led to freedom and happiness with Calvin. Irving's transparently self-serving objections did nothing but distract her from splitting that wall wide open.

"Listen," Ann started, "I'm sorry you're in this mess. I really am. But I'm not going to give this bastard a smoking gun just to make his and your lives easier."

"I see," Irving said, his face hardening. "Then let me give you a brief glimpse of your immediate future."

Ann waved her hand indifferently, though she was already beginning to doubt the security of her position.

"I will sway the committee and SST will win JOMREV with or without your help. Soon after the contract is awarded, fraud charges will be filed jointly by Lockheed and Grumman against you and Steady State Technologies. The U.S. Attorney General and the FBI will be called in. Everything you and Monroe have ever done or said will be examined with a fine-toothed comb. Starting to get the picture? Now, Ms. Franklin, can you honestly sit there with a straight face and tell me that they won't find a thing? That you and the colonel, though you were outed by your own coworker, have the slightest chance in the world of eluding the entire federal government?"

As Ann listened, her confidence tumbled sickeningly into the same quagmire that had lately consumed every other morsel of optimism to which she'd tried to cling. The pasty little bureaucrat was right. Worse, his portrait of her future also inadvertently explained why John wanted more. Even if he already had enough filth to bury each of them individually, he needed sufficient leverage to guarantee the contract would never be questioned. Only with her and Irving "in bed together" permanently could he be assured that no rifts would develop.

"Damn it!" Ann said, deflated.

"Exactly," he agreed, a satisfied grin on his face.

"So what are we supposed to do?"

"I don't see that we have much choice," he said. "But try to look on the bright side. If we go through with this, SST wins, you're a hero, no one goes to prison, and I get to keep my family. Isn't that why you're here in the first place?"

"I feel sick," Ann muttered.

"Then we're agreed?" he asked.

Ann felt herself nod.

"Good," he said, getting to his feet. "I'll be right back."

"Where are you going?"

"I have to make a call," he explained. "They need time to set up the room. Go ahead and order for me. By the way, what's Monroe driving?"

She couldn't bring herself to answer right away, but Irving's impatience eventually prompted her to respond. "A gray Chrysler," she rasped, the reality of what she was doing beginning to set in.

"Fine. Give me five minutes."

Ann felt a flame, somewhere deep inside her, flicker and then go out, leaving her heart cold and hard. Self-defense, she assumed. Somehow she'd get it burning again. Somehow…

Chapter 32

It was still early, barely eleven, when Ann staggered out of the front door of the Courtyard Marriott. She hadn't bothered to repair her makeup and several guests in the lobby couldn't let her pass without registering their contempt with a round of judgmental leers. Ann refused to take notice. Ironically, had Calvin known where she was, he could've gotten there on foot, the hotel being located only three or four hundred yards up the street from Clyde's. Mindful of that possibility, Irving had circled around the block to get there, just in case. Ann hobbled on her high heels through the parking lot and then along the rough gravel shoulder of the service road that connects Leesburg Pike to Chain Bridge Road.

From a safe distance, Ann scanned the restaurant parking lot for Calvin's rented Chrysler. Mercifully, there was no sign of him anywhere; apparently he'd given up on her. She hung back for a moment while a middle-aged couple, smiling, laughing, and whispering in one another's ears, made their way to their car. Ann remained in the shadows, watching them pass, nonplussed by the purity of their happiness.

As she approached her BMW she noticed a piece of paper pinned under the windshield wiper. *I am so, so sorry, my love. Some guy hemmed me in just as I was trying to pull out. By the time I got him to move his car, you were already gone. I can't believe this is happening. Can you ever forgive me? I'll be waiting for you at your house. Please call me as soon as you can. Love forever, C.*

Sitting in the driver's seat, engine idling, she could still feel Irving Sicherman inside her, his hands groping and pawing, his flaccid sweaty skin against hers. She understood the need to put on a convincing show for their blackmailers, but he seemed to enjoy it more than he should have, huffing and puffing as if his puny lungs might explode, his face twisted grotesquely in ecstasy.

In the time leading up to the appalling scene in room 448– while finishing their dinner and laughing casually as they left the restaurant– she'd become so immersed in the tactical details of their conspiracy that she'd overlooked, or at least gravely underestimated, the emotional impact her actions would have on her. Somehow, sleeping with Irving Sicherman had become nothing more than one of the many steps in their multistep plan, no more or less significant than strolling nonchalantly through the hotel lobby or agreeing to fire Andrea in direct violation of their pact. But now, with that familiar clown-face, lipstick and mascara smeared together on her cheeks, staring back at her out of the rearview mirror, there was no denying it; she had passed through a door that was now nailed shut behind her. Images of room 448 would forever afterwards haunt her sleep, and Ann herself would be complicit in the nightmare.

If ever an event in life demanded a response, this was one of them. She could feel the pressure building, fiercely instinctive and primordial, demanding an avenue of escape. There was every justification for an emotional display, even an outburst of epic proportions, complete with tears, weeping, and all the trimmings. But instead Ann's mind vacillated idiotically between the limitless spectrum of possibilities, helpless to select one, leaving her in a totally unsatisfying state of paralysis. It gradually intruded into her traumatized brain that her incapacity to respond, to lash out at fate, to even permit herself a cathartic cry, was rooted in a deeper and far more intractable question. *What on earth just happened?*

***

That question was still plaguing her as she sat in her kitchen, only half conscious of the barrage of recriminations cascading from the lips of her fiancé. Where had she been? Why hadn't she sent the abort signal? Was nothing sacred to her? There was pain in his voice, an unmistakable edge borne of deep betrayal. He stood over her, hands on his hips, waiting for some validation of his profound feelings of injustice, but to no avail.

Several minutes passed before Ann became vaguely aware, though she hadn't noticed him get up and walk out, that Calvin had left her alone and adjourned to the patio. She took the opportunity to retrieve her engagement ring from its honored spot in the jewelry box in her master suite. Calvin didn't turn to face her as she walked towards him in the dark.

"Here," she whispered, handing him the ring.

He turned slowly and Ann saw that his face had softened, changed from anger to resignation. He took the ring from her without protest and examined it thoughtfully. "I really do love you, Ann."

Ann bowed her head and looked at the ground.

"But I don't know whether to forgive you, beg for *your* forgiveness, or slash my wrists."

"I don't know either."

He managed a painful smile. "I may never understand what happened tonight. It feels like God Himself has it in for us."

"I wish I believed He even cares enough to punish me."

Calvin wagged his head in resignation. "Where did I lose you?"

Ann didn't answer, instead drifting to the opposite corner of the patio and gazing indifferently into the starry sky. Calvin resumed his own celestial review and they stood like that, not speaking, until their hearts gradually caught up with their brains and they accepted the harsh verdict.

"I'd like to be alone now," Ann finally announced.

Calvin glanced over at her, paused a moment, then nodded in agreement. "You're right." He turned toward the door. "Good-bye, Ann."

"Good-bye, Calvin." Ann turned back to the stars, unable to watch him leave.

Ann remained on the patio for at least an hour, though the vortex of contradictory emotions devouring her mind soon rendered her powerless to accurately gauge the passage of time. Fragmented images and ideas arose, one after the other, faster and faster, only to be swallowed whole by the maelstrom, long before achieving any measure of coherence. In response, her mood and manner fluctuated wildly, one moment causing her to burst into tears, the next finding her teeth and fists clenched in preparation for battle. She felt sick to her stomach, energized, exhausted, helpless, enraged, contrite, guilty, the incongruity of her emotions growing with each inexplicable wave. Faster and faster. Wave after wave. All of it, swirling violently in a hurricane of doubt and impotence.

As Ann's disintegration reached its crescendo, her mood gradually defaulted to an all-consuming and utterly irrational rage. Her face flushed blood red. Her eyes narrowed to slits. Every muscle rippled in concert with her blind frenzy. With no apparent impetus, she abruptly stormed into the house and made straight for Jeremy's bedroom. There, in neat orderly stacks, were the hundreds of books that had, in some inscrutable way, brought her to this point. She picked up the nearest volume and tried to rip it in half. The unsuccessful attempt only fueled her rage. She threw herself upon the pile and began tearing out handfuls of pages, an inhuman mixture of wrath and sorrow in her grunts and cries. Blood from deep paper cuts began splattering the walls and carpet. But if she experienced the pain it only served to focus her hatred even more clearly on those godforsaken books.

It wasn't long before she grew frustrated with her progress. There were too many books to tear apart individually and they were simply not yielding to her judgment quickly enough. Riding this new wave of enmity, she grabbed hold of the heaviest book within arm's reach, held it tightly in both of her bloodied hands, and heaved it through the window with an explosion of broken glass and a primal malevolent scream. The force of her throw sent her spinning awkwardly into the pile. An intense pain shot up through her spine, temporarily blurring her vision, but also ratcheting up her already uncontrollable fury. As her sight returned she saw Dr. Franklin standing in the doorway, frozen in horror by the icy cold fire burning in her eyes. Until then, he had maintained a respectful distance, no doubt struggling with his complicity in the events of the evening. Beyond words, flailing and floundering in the books, grinding her teeth, Ann's hand found Jeremy's Beechcraft. She launched it in her father's direction, barely missing his head, and smashing the toy into a hundred pieces against the hallway wall opposite Jeremy's door.

Dr. Franklin staggered backwards in self-defense, nearly stumbling over the plane wreckage, and dashed away toward the stairs. By then, Ann was already well into phase two of her relentless campaign against Jeremy's library. Volume after volume, five or six at a time, were sent cascading out of the window onto the patio, often with an earsplitting crack as they landed flat against the bricks. Lights from neighboring houses came on. People in sweat suits and pajamas, some with flashlights, came streaming out into their yards and driveways, struggling to identify the source of the commotion, and then gawking wide-eyed at the insane spectacle.

In less than ten minutes Ann had completed phase two and was staring idiotically out of the window at her handiwork. It was already bad enough, but Ann wasn't finished. The outlines of phase three swirled into her consciousness and sent her running out the door, down the stairs, and into the garage. Dr. Franklin almost fainted when he saw her charging toward him in the kitchen, unsure until she passed that he was not next in line to share the fate of Jeremy's books.

Ten seconds later Ann emerged from the garage with a

can of lighter fluid.

"Annie!" Henry gasped. "No!"

She ignored him completely, stomping through the house and out to the patio. There, she began dousing the scattered heap of books. One of Ann's neighbors had ventured closer than the rest. Every gaggle of slack-jawed onlookers, it seems, has at least one member who is not content to stand by and watch the train wreck happen without at least attempting to intervene. Mankind may owe its greatest triumphs to such intrepid characters, but they are also often among the youngest souls to discover the hereafter. Having drained the jug of lighter fluid, Ann began searching her pockets for some means of ignition. Nothing. Then something even more terrible occurred to her. She ran back into the house and reappeared in less than a minute, a thirty-eight caliber pistol, the one she'd bought Jeremy, in her right hand.

Without the slightest hesitation Ann fired a shot, point blank range, directly into the pile. The ensuing flames instantly engulfed it, illuminating the faces of the horrified onlookers, all of whom were now in a dead sprint for cover. The prospective benefactor of mankind backpedaled so frantically that he slammed, spine first, into a green sheet metal utility box en route to the safety of his house.

Fewer than five minutes passed between the sound of the gunshot and the scream of approaching sirens. Dr. Franklin had phoned 911 as soon as he'd survived the plane crash. During that brief interlude, Ann stood facing the conflagration, allowing the heat to fall upon her face. The random tongues of fire, some of which were dangerously close to her vinyl siding, resonated well with the cacophony in her mind. And, for that fleeting moment, she found a small measure of peace—enough at least, to put a word to the only coherent sentiment she had left. Ann looked to the heavens, craned her neck back as far as it could stretch, and carved a single anguished syllable into the smoke.

"Mom!!!!!!!!!!!!!!"

When the police arrived, Dr. Franklin was extinguishing the last of the flames with a garden hose. The charred mass was still hissing and popping, smoke billowing throughout the back yard. Ann was crumpled up on the patio in the fetal position, panting violently, soaking wet, immobilized by a massive seizure. The first officer on the scene burst through the door with his gun drawn, his eyes darting around wildly. Dr. Franklin looked at him morosely and the officer quickly realized that the danger had passed. The tension drained from his posture. He holstered his pistol and nonchalantly kicked Ann's weapon safely out of reach. Then he muttered something about an ambulance into his police radio.

Chapter 33

"Thank you all for coming," said a beaming Harold Gregory, standing behind the podium in the Steady State Tower's main auditorium. "Let me begin by simply saying what I'm certain is on everyone's mind. Whew!!!"

Mr. Gregory wiped his brow exaggeratedly. The hundred or so in attendance laughed out loud, some demurely, others with genuine gusto.

"As you've all no doubt heard by now, Steady State Technologies has been awarded the Defense Logistic Agency's $300 million dollar Joint Materiel Requisition and Engineering Validation System." Clapping and cheers arose from the audience. "This great win represents the culmination of more than a full year of painstaking effort by you," he said, gesturing to his minions, "the dozens of tenacious professionals who, despite hardships and setbacks, kept the faith and saw this beast through all the way to the end. Congratulations! Give yourselves a hand!"

The cheers and clapping were louder this time, augmented by a number of pumping fists and several deafening whistles. The JOMREV bid had been a miserable experience and an equally tremendous victory, and there was some authentic enthusiasm among those who had suffered the worst of it. Still, despite all they'd endured, it was a thoroughly corporate frenzy, and quickly subsided as Mr. Gregory put up his hands, indicating that he was ready to continue.

"But there's one remarkable woman without whom we would not be celebrating here today," he went on. "Late last summer when she first approached me with this crazy idea, I told her exactly what I should have. I told her I admired her ambition. I told her we were lucky to have someone at SST who could think so far outside the box. Then I explained to her, in a perfectly reasonable and rational voice, that Steady State wasn't ready to tackle a project as large as JOMREV. We didn't have the expertise to win it. And we wouldn't have the resources to run it even if we won.

"She acknowledged—grudgingly, I might add—" more laughter, "that I was the boss and my decision was law. But I could see in her eyes that she didn't really accept it, that she wasn't willing to let it go that easily. Later that evening, at home, reading my newspaper, I remembered the fire in her eyes. I also recalled a time, years ago, when that same fire burned just as brightly in the eyes of another young executive. Maybe that's what this company needs, I thought. Maybe we shouldn't always look before we leap. I can't say exactly why, but I decided right then to make an exception, take a chance. To heck with it! And though it hasn't been easy, to put it mildly, and I don't know if my heart can take it again, here we are, all of us, basking in the glow of that flame.

"Ladies and gentlemen, let's have a big round of applause for SST's newest vice president and program manager of JOMREV, Ann Franklin!" The audience erupted in hoots and hollers, clapping and cheering as excitedly as decorum permitted. Ann appeared out of the crowd and made her way to the stage. "Come on up here, Ann!" the CEO said, also clapping. "This is your day!"

Ann was dressed in her best Ann Klein fall skirt suit and cream pumps. That morning, on her way into the office, she'd stopped at her favorite salon and had her hair and face done up professionally. She ascended the steps at the left, effecting a serviceable Miss America wave and smile as she walked to center stage. The fire in her eyes, spoken of so highly by Mr. Gregory, was absent, but otherwise she struck the perfect corporate pose: graceful, immaculate, confident, yet humbled by the accolades of her peers.

Gregory shook her hand graciously and whispered something incomprehensible in her ear– nothing meaningful– just a conspicuously secret exchange between superiors designed to separate themselves from the little people. Then he produced a wood and brass plaque from beneath the podium. The two of them held it between them, smiling broadly for the company photographers, drawing out their handshake as the cameras flashed and the audience clapped.

"Steady State's very own," Gregory said, ceding the floor. "Ann Franklin!"

Ann stood alone behind the podium, accepting the last smattering of applause, admiring her new wall hanging. With the last clap she put the plaque aside, produced a short stack of three-by-five cards from her jacket pocket, looked up and began to speak.

"Thank you," Ann started. "Though I'm the one standing here before you, Mr. Gregory is most certainly correct. This was, from the very beginning, a team effort. Only through the dedication of all the talented and hard-working people here today was this moment possible."

Ann hadn't seen her until that moment and thought maybe she'd decided not to attend, but just then she caught a glimpse of Andrea Gates standing in the back of the auditorium, glaring, arms crossed, face hard as stone. Ann quickly broke their eyes' embrace and returned to her note cards.

"It is a great tribute to the vision of SST's executive committee that we are here today in celebration of the largest and most prestigious contract this company has ever been awarded." Ann paused a moment to create a contemplative mood. "I also remember the day I walked into Mr. Gregory's office with my 'crazy idea.' But I remember it a bit differently," Ann shot Gregory a sly grin, confirming that they'd staged this little verbal fencing match. "I could see right away that he was intrigued, that he knew in his gut that this was the direction in which SST should be going. Don't be fooled for a second. The fire burning in the belly of our fearless leader is in no imminent risk of being extinguished."

The words rolled off of Ann's tongue with silky rhythm and pitch. Her expressions perfectly mirrored the emotional content of her speech. The performance was flawless, right out of a seminar on public speaking. She ended with a list of heart-felt thanks for everyone on her team, as well as anyone else she could think of who'd expended more than five minutes of effort on the project. When she finished, Mr. Gregory joined the applause and clapped his way back out to center stage where he whispered more gibberish into Ann's ear, posed with her for another round of photographs, and then resumed his clapping as she made her way back down the stairs.

"Ann Franklin, everyone!" Gregory gushed. "Now, do me a favor and let's see if we can't make a dent in all of this food."

Ann spent the next forty-five minutes gnawing on her finger food, accepting congratulations from and hob-knobbing with the other Steady State big shots, slipping effortlessly into her rightful place among the elites. She was also approached by a number of lesser mortals inquiring about positions on the JOMREV project. She graciously conducted impromptu interviews with several of them, directing those whose skills matched her requirements to an intranet page with the application procedures. Then, before the crowd got too thin to support such a weighty presence, she begged everyone's forgiveness and politely excused herself.

Back in her office, Ann was responding to her e-mail. With the contract signed, Scott Miller was furiously ramping up his recruiting operations to accommodate the deluge of candidates he'd be responsible for screening, interviewing, and running through the SST orientation. He needed to know whether and how much—if any—of the orientation Ann wanted to tailor specifically to JOMREV and how much of it she wanted to present herself. There were requests from the DLA for the project kick-off schedule and venue requirements. Included was a long list of security procedures that would have to be followed by caterers and other vendors Ann might commission for the event. Kim McEwen, of all people, sent Ann a note of congratulations, striking an oddly conciliatory tone, and ending with, "Look forward to working with you again!" Very strange. Either Kim had no real inkling of her role in Ann's travails, or she'd come to understand that her ambush was a flop, and ought now to pucker up if she wanted to keep her job. Ann responded with a polite but bloodless "thank you."

After a half-hour or so Ann looked up from her laptop to find Andrea standing in her doorway. Her posture suggested she'd been standing there for quite awhile, studying Ann in silence.

"Bravo!" Andrea said sarcastically. "I guess it's true what they say about a leopard and his spots. Why I thought, even for a second, that you'd follow through on..." she wagged her head back and forth and summoned a wry grin. "You are a true predator, Ann Franklin. A bloody friggin' force of nature."

"Do you have something for me?" It was not posed as a question.

Andrea produced a carelessly folded piece of copier paper from her pocket and tossed it on Ann's desk. Ann unfolded it and read it without any visible reaction. It was hastily written in pencil and said only, "Ann, I quit. Andrea."

"If you need something more formal, you can write it yourself," Andrea sneered.

"No, this will be fine. Thank you." Ann turned back to her screen.

Andrea remained in the doorway, still unsatisfied with their exchange but without the words to express it.

"Was there anything else?" Ann asked.

"Is that really all you have to say to me? After all of these years?"

"What do you need to hear?" Ann's tone was curiously

sincere, as if she honestly had no idea what Andrea wanted.

"Yes," Andrea started. "That's exactly right. There is something I need to hear. And you can start by wiping that stupid deer-in-the-headlights look off of your face. This is me you're talking to."

"You want an apology? Is that it?"

"What the hell do I care if you're sorry?" Andrea said, becoming hostile. "I want you to look me straight in the face and admit what you did. Admit that you stabbed me in the back. Admit that you're an opportunistic parasite who sold her soul and sold out her friend to save her own ass. That's what I want to hear, you miserable troll!"

Ann stared at her for several seconds, more perplexed than moved. "What difference does it make, Andrea? Everything will still be the same."

"Because I need to know that you're suffering!" Andrea growled. "That you feel *something*! Call me naïve, but I need to believe that people like you sometimes roast over their own fires! So, what do you say, boss? Can you help me out here?"

Jerry appeared in the hall behind Andrea just as she finished her tirade. He gave Ann a thumbs up and sidled into the doorway, as much as telling Andrea that his business with Ann took precedence.

"Thank you, Andrea," Ann said, flatly. "That'll be all for now."

Andrea exhaled with great irritation and dismissed Ann with an exasperated, contemptuous wave of her hand. "Yeah, whatever. Have a terrific life, Ann." Then she stormed out of the office.

"What was all that about?" Jerry asked.

"Wrong time of the month," Ann replied, as she discarded Andrea's resignation in her wastebasket. She had no intention of accepting it, but there was no point in explaining it to Andrea right then.

Jerry raised his eyebrows. "I didn't think women used that expression."

"If the shoe fits…"

He chuckled uneasily. "Anyhow, I don't know if you've seen the new org chart, but just like that—" he snapped his fingers, "—now I work for you. How's that for cognitive dissonance?"

"I heard," she said.

"So, Cap'n," he said, saluting, trying unsuccessfully to mask his discomfort, "what are your orders?" He threw in a pirate's "argh!" for good measure.

"I need a senior developer for JOMREV."

"Senior developer?" he asked, befuddled. "But your budget… You can't afford to use a vice president for that?"

"I know. But the thing is, Jerry," she said, "I don't need a vice president. I need a senior developer."

Jerry stood in stunned silence, his face frozen in rejection. "I thought… I mean… Have you already selected your executive committee?"

"I have some names in mind."

"But…" he stammered. "I don't understand. What are you saying?"

"I'm saying I need a senior developer, not a vice president."

As the truth sank in, Jerry's face gradually shifted from appeasement to indignation. He inhaled deeply to buttress his resolve. "No, Ann, that's not what you're saying at all. What you're saying is that I can drop my pants and bend over or else pack up my office and hit the bricks. Or did I miss something?"

"I'm sorry, Jerry," Ann said without emotion. "You're not an effective leader. I can't risk putting you in an executive role on this project."

Queen Ann had been frightening enough when he was her superior, and he knew better than anyone that his authority over her was no more substantial than the paper on which it was written. Had he ever tried to exercise any real power, he'd have found himself under her boot almost as quickly as would any of her subordinates. Their relationship had been little more than an uneasy truce. But now she was firmly in charge and under no obligation to overlook his shortcomings. Though he'd given voice to a certain degree of "cognitive dissonance," he couldn't possibly have predicted how coldly he'd be judged or how thin had become the thread from which his fortunes hung. Jerry closed the door behind him and took a seat across the desk from his tormentor.

"You've been pining for this day, haven't you?" he said bitterly. "Probably ever since the day I hired you. What the hell was I thinking?"

"That's got nothing to do with it, Jerry."

"I know you've been through a lot lately—your mother, your son. I don't blame you for feeling selfish right now. Completely natural. But you're not the only one with problems."

"This is strictly a business decision," Ann insisted.

"My parents both died years ago. And, yes, it tore me up inside too, thank you very much. But parents die. It's a fact of life. My youngest daughter has Tourette Syndrome and can't hold a job for more than three months. She's still living at home." He looked Ann in the eye. "Didn't know that did you? You know why? Because I don't bring my personal problems to the office. I'm not so damned self-absorbed to believe that I'm the only one at the table who isn't thrilled to high heaven with all the cards he's been dealt."

"Again, you're missing the point."

"Am I?" he challenged. "Then answer me this, Little Miss Strictly-Business. Where were your holier-than-thou ethics while you were out winning JOMREV? Maybe you think you were a lot sneakier than you were, but trust me, no one believes you won this thing on its merits. I don't claim to know exactly what you *did* do, and I don't want to know. But that fancy plaque was a pink slip right up until the DLA's announcement. If the truth ever comes out—if we ever get a glimpse behind the scenes—I'd bet my last dollar that you and this glorious company of ours would end up in court in a New York minute. Tell me I'm wrong?"

"You're not wrong."

Jerry's head lurched forward. He was so stunned by her admission that he couldn't immediately find the right tone for the rest of his argument. "I... well... shit, Ann! Then what on earth are you doing? I'm up for retirement in less than three years! I may not be Winston Churchill, but JOMREV isn't exactly Normandy either. I'm not too proud to accept your leadership advice. Truth be told, I could probably use it. Hell, I'll deliver coffee and a Danish right to your office every morning if that's what it takes!"

As Jerry's grovel deepened Ann found it increasingly difficult to renew whatever conviction had originally prompted her to reassign him. Her eyes became foggy as she listened to him. Her thoughts escaped his grip and disengaged altogether from JOMREV and SST, flailing around randomly in her mind in search of something solid and eternal. Jerry stopped in mid-pucker and gave her a suspicious squint.

"Are you even listening to me?" he asked.

"You're right, Jerry," she said. "I acted hastily. On Monday we'll find a suitable position for you. Thank you." She turned mechanically back to her screen, as if they'd done nothing more important than exchange potato salad recipes.

Jerry was flabbergasted. But just as he geared up to force her to account for herself, he gave her a cautious once-over and decided not to press his luck. "Monday," he mumbled. "I'll talk to you then." Ann didn't pay any attention to him as he slunk out of her office. Within five minutes she'd all but forgotten he'd even been there.

Ann spent the balance of the afternoon responding to every last one of her e-mails, even the trivial "Hi, how ya doin'" ones she'd typically have postponed or ignored altogether. The ritual, though transparently pointless, was immensely soothing. Every one of the e-mails in her inbox was bathed in the nostalgic glow of purpose and significance. Between the lines, Ann could visualize their authors diligently preparing for the new project, advancing their careers, nurturing their children and supporting their families. With each of her responses, she breathed in the lingering aroma of her own cherished goals, even as she felt them forever slipping beyond her ken and evaporating into her mind's insatiable new black hole of irrelevance.

She consciously surrendered to the bittersweet notion that she was still selflessly sacrificing herself for Jeremy, that everything she did was justified by that noble end. The hint of a smile found the corner of her mouth and a sharp twinge in her sinuses harkened the tears welling in her eyes. She allowed them to cascade down her cheeks unmolested. Each one carried away with it a piece of her familiar old surroundings– the safety of Dr. Franklin's words of wisdom, the smell of her mother's lasagna– leaving behind a barren and unforgiving landscape where every pretension to value and decency was punished with a searing blast of icy cold logic.

She remained at her desk until well after seven, answering e-mails, clinging defiantly to the last vestiges of that mysterious entity to which both she and the rest of the world had effortlessly referred to as "Ann Franklin." She held it tightly against her chest until the very last of it slipped from her grasp. Then she turned off her computer, neatened her desk, and stood up, pulling on her suit jacket. As she turned off the light she paused a moment in the doorway, struck by the odd repose of her chair, empty and inert, but waiting expectantly for her return. She smiled at it, head cocked to one side in bemusement, and then closed the door behind her and walked away down the empty hall toward the elevator.

Having missed the worst of rush hour, Ann made it to Leesburg in only forty-five minutes. As she walked up the steps to the front door of Chez Xen, her mind could have equally well been described as crammed full to the point of bursting or completely empty. Either way, she was no longer able to entertain anything that could even charitably be referred to as a thought. The world in front of her was reduced to a colorless, two-dimensional panel located roughly ten feet from her face. The door opened before she knocked. Someone must have heard the BMW's distinctive hum as she pulled it into the driveway.

"Ann," Leon said, inviting her in with a wave. "I'm on my way out. The house is yours. Make yourself at home."

Ann's eyes reflexively oriented themselves to Leon's face, but they betrayed no hint of recognition. He returned her gaze, looking into her darkened eyes with great empathy and feeling. Then he bent over and kissed her forehead sweetly before glancing suggestively toward the stairwell.

"Everything is ready," he assured her. A moment later he was gone and Ann was alone.

She made her way up the stairs, mechanically, but without any obvious signs of dread or hesitation. At the top of the stairs she turned and continued down the hall. The door to Dr. Remington's office was open and the light inside was turned on. Just as Leon had said, everything was ready. Though the contraption was clearly hammered together by amateur carpenters out in the garage or down in the basement, it was surprisingly well-designed and easy to negotiate. Even in her diminished condition, Ann had no trouble getting herself comfortably situated in the driver's seat and locating the triggering pedal. The seat was adjustable, but had apparently already been set for someone of Ann's height. The muzzle of the shotgun rested perfectly on her lower jaw. They had even affixed a strip of rubber to the underside of the barrel allowing it to sit comfortably on the occupant's bottom front teeth.

A fly on the wall would have been thoroughly rattled by what happened next. One might have expected Ann to sit a moment, reflect on... *something*. Take stock of her life. Say some good-byes. But that's not what she did. The decision was made. The wait was over. No sooner had she oriented herself properly in the machine than she grabbed the muzzle in both hands and pushed her right foot down on the pedal. The rope tightened and the hammer fell.

Chapter 34

Perhaps the oddest aspect of suicide by shotgun is that the sound and fury of the blast are not experienced in the least by its victim. The trigger is pulled and then… nothing. The brain is annihilated before it registers any part of the violence its last act initiated. And so, paradoxically, the loudest and bloodiest suicide, the sort likely to elicit the greatest horror from the unlucky soul who first discovers its aftermath, is also the most peaceful. No great wonder the Xen preferred it to say, poisoning or wrist slashing, neither of which is guaranteed to succeed and, even when successful, involve some indeterminate period of great discomfort and existential angst while they run their course. How many suicides have had a change of heart immediately following the point of no return? How many of those have subsequently died in a state of abject panic? Much better to answer the final question once and for all and be done with it.

When Ann opened her eyes the sun was beginning to peak through the storm clouds above the summit of Bearfence Mountain. The rain had ended, replaced by a warm spring breeze. She no longer felt any pain in her ankle. Jeremy was no longer pinned under her knee, begging for his life. He was seated cross-legged on the granite slab, wiping the mud from his face, watching his mother with interest as she stared at the black revolver hanging limply in her right hand. At long last Ann looked up into his face. It was the fifteen-year-old Jeremy looking back at her. Not the five-year-old with whom she'd made the harrowing ascent.

"I took the liberty of unloading it before we left the house," he said, indicating her gun. "No good could have come of it."

"No good at all," she agreed, placing the gun down on the rock with great care, as if it might take offense at being cavalierly flung over the edge of the cliff.

"I'm glad you agree," he went on. "I doubt you have the strength to toss me off of this mountain with your bare hands. And just imagine how awkward it'd be, on our hike back to the car, if you tried and failed!"

Ann sat down and leaned back against a rock she hadn't noticed before but which was perfectly positioned for her. "I guess I owe you an apology. I haven't been quite myself lately."

"And you won't be yourself again anytime soon, either. Putting a gun to your dreams the way you did... Let's just say, you won't forgive yourself as readily as I have. No telling how long you'll be gone."

"I remember seeing a picture of this place once, maybe in a brochure," Ann said. "But we've never been here. I'm sure of it."

"Quite so," he replied. "Though I commend you on your choice. The view from here is striking. Exactly as it should be."

Ann's eyes panned across the horizon, taking in the timeless expanse of peaks and valleys, carpeted in dense forest, rolling gently beyond the limits of sight. The immensity of the scene, the infinite depth of the sky, filled Ann with a warm sensuous glow. "So beautiful," she muttered. For a time she lost contact with the granite beneath her and her mind's eye hitched a ride on the sultry breeze, soaring in among the clouds and condors, now and then looking down, unperturbed, on the rocky summit where her body still lay.

"Beautiful indeed," Jeremy said, his voice bringing Ann's perspective softly back to earth. "Though there is a small item of business we need to conduct before it gets too late. This place may go on forever, but you are only allowed to stay long enough to answer the question you came here to face."

"You're ruining it," Ann said with dismay. "I'm tired of questions. This is where I want to be. This is home."

"Be careful of talk like that, Ann. Soon the sun here will set and the darkness will close in. The rocky cliffs that now seem so distant will creep in and surround you. It won't be long before this glorious panorama is transformed into a tiny claustrophobic prison cell. Be grateful you've been given a glimpse, but don't be fooled. That's all it is. A glimpse."

"A glimpse?" Ann mused. "A glimpse of what?"

"When you pulled that trigger," again indicating her gun, "you made a choice. Now you have to decide if you're prepared to live with the consequences."

Ann stared into her son's eyes with great consternation. "Consequences? But I pulled the trigger, just like you said. It's done. How can there still be consequences? What kind of place is this, anyway?"

The sun was lower in the western sky and the horizon could be seen shrinking with the fading light. Ann sat bolt upright, a wave of panic sweeping over her.

"See what I mean," Jeremy said.

"It's not fair! I don't belong here."

"A moment ago you wanted nothing more than to lie there on your rock for all eternity. Why should it matter if you have the sun on your face? You still have your rock."

"You haven't changed a bit!" Ann growled. "Still Xen through and through!" She looked helplessly at her pistol. "I should have brought a knife!"

Jeremy couldn't help laughing, though it was not at all malicious. "I wonder, Ann, why you don't put the sun back where you want it. You know this place isn't real. What's stopping you?"

Ann looked back and forth between her son's face and the wayward star, struggling to make sense of his curious suggestion. Finally, defiantly, she knit her brow and looked directly into the sun, desperately trying to will it back to its zenith where it could bathe her once again in its light. Several moments passed before her body went slack with exhaustion and she succumbed to the futility of her attempt. "Why are you tormenting me?"

Jeremy looked at her with deep affection, his clear eyes sparkling with sincerity. Her mood instantly softened. "It hardly needs pointing out that you had no hope of moving the sun. Aren't you here precisely because you already know that only too well? Now do me another favor. Look at it again, but don't trouble yourself with its destination."

Ann did as she was told. Only a few degrees above the horizon the colossal fireball glowed deep orange, painting the high clouds in every color of creation. She let the anxiety of its imminent disappearance bleed out of her soul, humbly allowing its inscrutable grandeur to pour into the void. As she watched, awestruck, the last tiny whisper of unease that customarily accompanied her impotence faded into nothing. In its place she was left with only the pure apprehension of beauty itself, unsullied by any concern for its value or aim. "You're right," she said dreamily. "It's better this way."

The two of them, mother and son, watched together in silence until the last brilliant glimmer disappeared behind the earth. When Ann's eyes were suitably adjusted to the dim light, they found Jeremy seated on the wood floor outside of Dr. Remington's office, his smiling face still aglow with the scene they'd shared. Her brain was slow to grasp the change of venue and her disorientation was palpable.

"Blanks," he offered.

Ann looked idiotically at the muzzle, still two centimeters from her mouth.

"Let me help you," he said, standing and offering her his arm. "Easy now." Her entire body was sore, as stiff as the boards on which she'd been sitting. Still, she managed to clamber out of the wooden contraption, careful not to bump the trigger, though she now understood Jeremy had already seen to it that the gun wasn't loaded.

"How long?" she muttered, staggering through the door on her wobbly legs.

"Five hours, give or take," he responded.

"Have you been here the whole time?"

"Nearly," he confirmed. "Just out of curiosity, which mountain were we on? You never mentioned the name."

"But you were there," she said, not yet able to grasp that she'd spent the past five hours sitting in a closet with a shotgun aimed at her head. "It was called Bearfence Mountain."

Jeremy had already positioned a chair, right outside the door, into which Ann collapsed, just as a violent swarm of pins and needles began stinging her legs and back. He sat back down on the floor across the hall from her.

"Was it worth it?" he said enigmatically. "I'd hate to think Leon and company did all of this work for nothing more than the money."

"Worth it?" she repeated.

"You remember," he started. "Last May. The zoo. You said you wanted to understand. I'll be honest with you, I wrestled with the idea for three solid days. That's the equivalent of about three months for a normal. I knew it would be hard on you. Maybe too hard. But in the end I decided to take you at your word."

The last few months, ever since the zoo, filtered back through Ann's mind– every grim episode, every piece of herself that had slipped away, all the loss and misery– a nightmare she had financed herself. That the Xen were behind it was a possibility she'd explicitly denied, but which now seemed more inevitable than surprising. Strangely, she wasn't the least bit angry or even annoyed. Jeremy had taken her at her word.

"What am I supposed to do now?" Ann asked.

"Does it make any difference? Go to work. Don't go to work. Everything is the same. I can't say it's all sunshine and lollipops, but look closer. There's a deep and satisfying freedom in the shadow of futility. Don't you feel it?"

"Freedom?" she puzzled. "I feel lost. Hopelessly adrift,

like nothing will ever matter again. Not for the rest of my life."

"Liberating, isn't it? No more pain. No more doubt. No more paradoxes or unanswerable questions. Nothing but a long soothing stroll toward oblivion. In the absence of truth, what more could you possibly ask of the world?"

Ann paused for several moments, her face lost in concentration. He'd warned her that the knowledge she sought might cost her her life. What grounds did she have to complain that it had been every bit as terrifying as he'd said it would be? And who was she to whine about her own misfortune when it had been her choice to bring a Xen, her own son, into such an uncompromising world?

"The Xen are dead," she said, an eerily detached tone in her voice. "but somehow they're still here. And now I'm dead too."

Jeremy smiled. "Take me home, Mom."

Acknowledgements

I've learned over the course of this process that a novel, particularly a first novel, is a team effort. I received encouragement from many quarters, but a few deserve special mention.

Jill Ryan. A novel is a labor of love, of the author for his work, but also of the author's support group for him. Without my wonderful wife this book, like much else in my life, would never have made it past the planning phase. She was invaluable throughout, helping with everything from character development to book design to publishing.

Kelly Kagamas Tomkies, our editor. Kelly was a tremendous asset, not only with her copy editing skills, but with her creative input and objective perspective. Like most good ideas, her suggestions often took awhile to sink in, but she was almost always, though sometimes grudgingly, correct.

Amanda Cawby, our cover artist and designer. Amanda is a joy to work with, able to transform an abstract idea into a brilliant visual image.

First Draft Reviewers. Several people took the time and effort to read and provide feedback to the first draft of this novel. That assistance and feedback, drawn from a variety of backgrounds and sensibilities, made this a much better story.

This book was set in Palatino Linotype font, a 1999 adaptation from the Palatino typeface family originally released in 1948 by the Linotype foundry and designed by Hermann Zapf. It is believed to be named after the sixteenth century Italian master of calligraphy, Giambattista Palatino. It was based on the humanist fonts of the Italian Renaissance mirroring the letters formed by a broad nib pen, giving it a calligraphic grace.

Cover Design by Amanda Cawby

Interior Design by Jill Ryan, Gadfly
Leesburg, Virginia

Edited by Kelly Kagamas Tomkies

Author Photo by Neil Steinberg, Photoworks
Leesburg, Virginia

Printed by Lightning Source, Inc.
La Vergne, Tennessee

Photo by Neil Steinberg

About the Author

With an insatiable passion for the truth, Andrew M. Ryan naturally gravitated to an education in philosophy, earning his bachelor's degree from Louisiana State University. Beyond his desire to understand the mind, he continues to explore many topics, including cosmology and cognitive science. Ryan is the author of *The Law of Physics*. He has a daughter and lives with his wife in Northern Virginia.

CPSIA information can be obtained at www.ICGtesting.com
Printed in the USA
265825BV00001B/124/P